Readers love the Bra
series by X.

Frat House Troopers

"Yes, this is a highly erotic novel (which I loved) but it's about human sexuality, not sexual exploitation."

—The Book Vixen

Wrestling Demons

"This book is so much more than an MM romance novel…"

—Prism Book Alliance

A Wedding to Die For

"This full length novel is going in my permanent library and I will be reading it again."

—Love Bytes

Spring Break at the Villa Hermes

"This story was sweet, funny, and hot, while still bringing up and addressing serious issues such as being honest and true to yourself, and the struggle for equal rights."

—The Novel Approach

By XAVIER MAYNE

The Accidental Cupid
Husband Material

BRANDT AND DONNELLY CAPERS
Frat House Troopers
Wrestling Demons
A Wedding to Die For
Spring Break at the Villa Hermes
Bachelors Party

Published by DREAMSPINNER PRESS
http://www.dreamspinnerpress.com

BACHELORS PARTY

XAVIER MAYNE

DREAMSPINNER PRESS

Published by
DREAMSPINNER PRESS

5032 Capital Circle SW, Suite 2, PMB# 279, Tallahassee, FL 32305-7886 USA
http://www.dreamspinnerpress.com/

This is a work of fiction. Names, characters, places, and incidents either are the product of author imagination or are used fictitiously, and any resemblance to actual persons, living or dead, business establishments, events, or locales is entirely coincidental.

Bachelors Party
© 2015 Xavier Mayne.

Cover Art
© 2015 L.C. Chase.
http://www.lcchase.com
Cover content is for illustrative purposes only and any person depicted on the cover is a model.

ISBN: 978-1-62380-653-8
Digital ISBN: 978-1-62380-654-5
Library of Congress Control Number: 2015902236
First Edition June 2015

Printed in the United States of America
∞
This paper meets the requirements of
ANSI/NISO Z39.48-1992 (Permanence of Paper).

For J, who probably had no idea that the vows we took would take us on such an adventure.

CHAPTER ONE
PLANS

"YOU REALLY don't have to do that," Brandt said into the phone. It was a Saturday afternoon, and he was supposed to be vacuuming while Donnelly was out shopping for dinner.

"What kind of best man doesn't throw a bachelor party?" Brandt's brother Liam replied. "Look, the best man has three essential duties: ensure you get to the church on time and relatively sober, make a toast at the reception that will be both touching and embarrassing, and throw a bachelor party you won't remember but the strippers will never forget."

"I'm not really into the whole 'get drunk and throw up on a stripper' kind of party, Liam. I'm sure you enjoyed it at the bachelor party Noah threw for you, but—"

"That's all I'm trying to do. Pay it forward. Noah did it for me, I did it for him, and now it's our turn to do it for our little brother."

"Wait, Noah's in on this too?"

"Hell yeah. And since he's basically been in baby jail for the last six months, he's wound up pretty tight. He's looking forward to this like Grandpa looks forward to martini hour."

Brandt sighed. "It's not as simple as that," he said as diplomatically as he could. "It's kind of complicated because of—"

"I know, I know," Liam interrupted. "I'll be honest with you, Ethan. I've never even been to a gay wedding, much less a gay bachelor party. But how much different could it be? It's still a bunch of guys hanging out, having a little drink, getting into a little trouble. I don't see why that's so complicated."

Brandt paced back and forth across the carpet he was supposed to be cleaning. "If you don't see why it's complicated, well, start with the whole stripper thing. How would that work, exactly?"

"What do you mean how would that work? There are guy strippers, aren't there?"

"Yes, there are. But while I appreciate how accepting you and Noah and everyone have been, I don't think you'd really enjoy watching guys take their clothes off."

"But, isn't that what gay people do at bachelor parties?"

"Honestly, I don't know. Gay marriage has only been legal for a couple of years, and I've only been to one wedding."

"The one where everyone got poisoned and one of the grooms died? I'm thinking yours is going to be much better than that."

Time for a new tack. "Look, here's the thing," Brandt said. "This party, if you insist on throwing it, isn't going to be a gay bachelor party. Yes, the two people getting married are bachelors, and some of our groomsmen are gay, but you and Noah will be there, and a couple of our friends from college, and you all are straight, last time I checked."

"Marianne will be relieved to hear that," Liam replied with a laugh.

"And then there are people like Will, who doesn't really count as straight because he's married to Lucas, but he wasn't gay before they met. And the same is kind of true for me and Gabriel. So it's pretty complicated."

Silence on the other end of the line. Then, "Can I ask you something?"

"Of course."

"Why are you getting married?"

Brandt paused, not sure what his brother was getting at. "Because Gabriel and I love each other, and we want to be together, and we'd like to make it official."

"You could do that at the courthouse. Why have the big wedding?"

"Well, first, it's not a big wedding. It's just family and some friends."

"It's a wedding, Ethan. It's more than just having some people over, and you know it. So why are you doing it?"

"Because it's what people have always done to have their relationship recognized by everyone."

"Exactly. You're doing it because it's what has been traditionally done. You may as well admit the tradition is important to you. And part of that tradition is the bachelor party."

Brandt closed his eyes. "I get that, but the tradition depends on everyone being straight and everyone thinking the bachelor needs some kind of last hurrah before chaining himself to the same woman for the rest of his life, with strippers to show him what he's going to be missing out on. That's not really the case here, is it?"

Liam laughed. "You mean you aren't giving up women forever? I'll have to let Gabriel know about that."

"Stop it, asshole. You know what I mean. Gabriel and I aren't the traditional straight bachelors—we aren't even the traditional gay bachelors. What we have is kind of unique, and that's why the bachelor party idea just won't work."

"It will work, and I will make it work, and that's the end of it," Liam said in his stern firstborn tone.

Brandt slumped onto the sofa. "Fine. But I want you to remember when we're picking ourselves out of the glitter-covered wreckage of this party that I warned you it wasn't a good idea."

"You worry too much, little bro. Now go make the citizens safe while I make plans."

BRANDT AND Donnelly sat on their back patio eating dinner with their friend Malcolm.

"How's the cafe doing?" Donnelly asked as he passed Malcolm a platter of grilled corn.

"I think it's catching on. People who have been coming for years keep telling me how nice it is to have someone sprucing it up a bit. I convinced Casey to come in for a couple of weeks to help me get the bakery up and running, and I really couldn't have done it without him. He can't work for me because he's on a wrestling scholarship, but he helped me hire and train a baker. Now I can work on getting the lunch menu going."

"We'll have to stop by soon and see for ourselves," Brandt said.

"It's not like I've spent every day hoping to see you there or anything," Malcolm said with a pout.

"All right, all right, we'll come by soon," cried Donnelly, laughing.

"How's the wedding planning going?" Malcolm asked, cutting into the steak Brandt had expertly grilled.

"The wedding is in great shape," Brandt answered. "It's the bachelor party that has got me worried."

"Why?" Malcolm asked. "I thought the bachelor party was supposed to be the best man's deal?"

"It is," Brandt said with a slow shake of his head. "My big brother Liam is taking care of it, but it's kind of tricky territory."

"Why is that? Booze, strippers...." Malcolm shook his head. "And that's about it, right?"

Brandt sighed. "When was the last time you went to a bachelor party, buddy?"

"Last year. Buddy of mine from college." Malcolm chuckled and shook his head. "Man, that was a night."

"Was this buddy marrying a man or a woman?" Donnelly asked.

"A woman."

"And the strippers were...?"

"Women." Malcolm answered, grinning at the memory. "There was this one who did this thing with a Ping-Pong ball and a kazoo that was just amazing. See, she—"

"Probably better left to the imagination," Brandt blurted. He closed his eyes for a moment before continuing. "Anyway, did the person throwing the bachelor party know you're gay?"

"Yeah, I think so. It didn't really come up."

"Not with strippers like that," Donnelly said. "I don't think it would come up for me either."

Malcolm cackled with glee, and the two men fist-bumped over the table.

"I'm trying to be serious here," Brandt griped, "and I'm surrounded by teenage boys making boner jokes."

"Sorry, Ethan," Malcolm said, sounding almost contrite. "Seriously, it wasn't a problem for me. I was just along for the ride, and I think all of the other guys at the party were straight. Honestly, it was kind of hot to see them get all worked up over the strippers. A dozen straight bros tugging at their crotches while trying not to notice everyone else doing the same thing? You could cut the tension with a knife."

"But we have a much more mixed group," Brandt said, doggedly pursuing the topic. "There's my brothers, who are throwing the party, and Gabriel and I are both having a friend from college in the wedding party, and they're all straight. Then there's Will, who's married to

Lucas, but before that he was straight. And then Bryce and Nestor, who are probably a ten on the Kinsey scale."

"I know Bryce and Nestor are somewhat flamboyant, but I thought the Kinsey scale only went up to six—and that's completely gay," Malcolm replied.

"Yep. They would be a ten," Donnelly said, laughing.

"So they wouldn't go along with a standard-issue bachelor party?"

"Bryce and Nestor are somewhat excitable," Donnelly explained.

"Excitable?" Brandt snorted. "Remember what happened when we made them sit down and watch *Brokeback Mountain* all the way through?"

Donnelly turned to Malcolm. "They had only seen the part in the tent and the two and a half seconds where Heath Ledger is naked. They could describe every frame of those scenes but hadn't bothered with the rest of the movie. We thought it was important for them to have the full context."

"You have never heard such wailing and carrying on," Brandt continued, shaking his head at the memory. "Nestor just collapsed into a catatonic state, and it took fifteen minutes to coax Bryce out of the bathroom, where his keening was enough to wake the neighbors."

"Well, you have to admit the end of that movie is kind of hard to take. I cried when I first saw it, and I'd read the original story in the *New Yorker*, so I knew it was coming."

"But they weren't crying about the ending," Donnelly said. "We hadn't even gotten that far."

"What did it, then?" Malcolm asked.

"Anne Hathaway taking her shirt off," Brandt deadpanned.

Malcolm's mouth dropped open. "The sight of boobs had that effect on them?"

Brandt and Donnelly nodded.

Malcolm shook his head. "I'm as gay as the next guy, but Anne Hathaway? Om-nom."

"Bryce and Nestor didn't see it that way, I'm afraid," Donnelly said, chuckling. "They screamed like Death himself had come for them. Wearing a polyester robe."

"Okay," Malcolm said, once he'd stopped laughing. "So no strippers for Bryce and Nestor."

"Oh, they're connoisseurs of strippers, but the male variety," Brandt replied. "But I don't think my brothers and our college buddies are going to go for that."

"Why not?" Malcolm asked. "Gay guys have to put up with boobies being shaken at them all the time, and not just at bachelor parties. Movies, TV, advertisements—sex sells, and it's almost always women who are the sex doing the selling. Having straight guys go to a bachelor party and look at male strippers would be progress. I think it would be good for them."

"I'm not sure they'd see it that way," Donnelly remarked.

"I'm sure they're very nice people, but I have to ask. Why shouldn't they 'put up' with something we would find sexy? Why do we always have to accommodate the straight folks?"

Brandt and Donnelly exchanged a look.

"That's an excellent question, Malcolm." Brandt took a bite of steak and turned back to Donnelly. "We have some stuff to figure out."

Donnelly nodded but with a look that showed him to be less than confident. "Lucky us."

DINNER HAD been cleaned up, and Brandt and Donnelly were preparing for bed. Donnelly flossed while Brandt washed his face. Then Brandt stood upright and looked at Donnelly in the mirror as he dried his face.

"Should I just tell Liam to forget the bachelor party?" he asked.

Donnelly pulled the floss out of his mouth and tipped his head thoughtfully. "Don't you think that would be kind of disappointing for him? I haven't known him my entire life, like you have, but what I do know is he takes being your big brother really seriously."

"Why do you say that?" Brandt asked, leaning back against the counter.

"Do you remember last Thanksgiving, when your uncle's new wife made that joke after dinner?"

"Yeah, that was pretty awkward. I would have thought Uncle Phil would have given her the heads-up that telling gay jokes wasn't going to endear her to the family."

"And remember later that evening when Liam's car wouldn't start and he asked Uncle Phil for help?"

"Uh-huh," Brandt replied, suspicious of where this was going.

"Well, when they didn't come back after a few minutes—and you were helping with the dishes—I went out to see if they needed more help. Now, Liam made me promise not to tell you about this, but I think you should know. Before I even got to the driveway I could hear voices—angry voices—so I stopped before rounding the corner of the house. Turns out Liam's car was fine; he just wanted to get your uncle alone for a little talk. He asked your uncle to let her know she had offended everyone with that joke, and your uncle told him to mind his own business. I have never seen Liam get angry—he's normally so even-keeled. But as I peeked around the corner, he lunged at your uncle, grabbed him by the collar of his jacket, and got right in his face. Told him unless he and his wife were prepared to stay the hell away from the gay jokes, he should just leave right then. Your uncle gave it right back to him. Said he'd never accepted that you were gay. It was just a phase, and once you came to your senses, you'd be normal again."

"He really said that?"

"Yep. And then your brother got really quiet. He said he loved you, and he was proud of you, and he wouldn't stand for anyone being in the house who didn't feel the same way. It got really tense there for a minute—looked like they were going to come to blows. But your uncle backed down, and that's why he and his wife seemed really quiet after that." Donnelly put his hand on Brandt's arm. "He loves you, Ethan. And I think throwing this bachelor party is his way of saying he's happy for us. He wants everyone to know he accepts us and our marriage just like anyone else's in the family."

Brandt looked into the reflection of Donnelly's eyes in the mirror, and when he spoke again, his voice was soft. "You know, when I told my family about us, I was worried about Liam's reaction most of all. He'd always kind of been my idol growing up. He's always said he supported me, but I didn't know how much of that he was saying because he thought it was what I wanted to hear. It's kind of amazing to know he would take on Uncle Phil. That guy's always scared me a little."

"I don't want to pile on, but I think you need to consider how he would feel if you said he couldn't throw you a party. It would be like you were rejecting his love and support. I know it's going to be awkward, but sometimes things are awkward in the service of a larger goal."

Brandt nodded and hung up his towel. "I guess you're right."

"You forgot the last part," Donnelly said.

"What last part?"

"As usual. I'm right *as usual*. I'd have thought you'd have had that down by now."

"Brush your damn teeth and come to bed, will ya?"

"Well, if you're going to get all romantic…," Donnelly said with a saucy wink.

"THANKS FOR taking the time to have lunch with me," Brandt said as he sat at the table, opposite Will in his sleek sport wheelchair.

"I think you'll discover I can always find time for a lunch invitation," Will replied with a smile. "Delilah's at such a clingy age right now, I think it does us some good to spend a little time apart once in a while."

"How are she and Dylan doing?"

"They're great, thanks. Dylan's got a big part in the school play, so he's turning into quite the prima donna. Lucas says he was the same at that age, so I guess there's hope he'll come out of it." He looked around the cafe. "They serve lunch here now?"

"As of this week they do. A friend of ours moved here from Woodley and bought the place. He started the bakery up last month, and now he's adding lunch. The guy works like crazy, but he's really good at what he does."

"Ethan! So glad you could make it," Malcolm said as he strode up to the table bearing plates. "And this must be Will, whom I've heard so much about."

"Will, this is Malcolm, the mastermind behind the new café."

"Pleased to meet you, Malcolm," Will said, extending his hand, which Malcolm shook energetically.

As always, Brandt was struck by the massive muscles in Will's arm. His training for the biathlon in the Paralympic Games kept him to a rigorous workout regimen.

"Let me know if I can get you guys anything else," Malcolm said as he hurried back to the kitchen.

"Seems like a nice guy," Will said as he picked up his sandwich.

"He is. It's really great he got the hell out of Woodley. That's no place for anyone gay. Or sane."

"He makes a fine sandwich," Will remarked. "And are these homemade potato chips? I could be in real trouble now that I know this place exists."

Brandt laughed and tucked into his own meal.

"So, I have a question for you," Brandt said after they were several bites in.

"Aha! I knew there was an ulterior motive," Will cried, then laughed. "Fire away, and I'll do what I can."

"Did you have a bachelor party?"

Will sat back in his chair, clearly surprised by the question, but then he knitted his brow thoughtfully. "Um, at the risk of sounding like a slut, which time are you asking about?"

"Either, or both, I guess. That's kind of why I wanted to talk with you. You're the only person I know who's been married to both a woman and a man. I wanted to get your thoughts about having a bachelor party."

Will nodded. "I see. I guess my checkered marital history is pretty rare, but I hope it will eventually seem less freakish as marriage equality evens things out."

"We may have a long way to go on that front," Brandt replied. "So, did you have a bachelor party?"

"For marriage number one, Juliet and I were just out of college and the first of our social group to get married. I had a lot of buddies who were really excited about finally getting to have a bachelor party, and they did it up big. Well, as big as our entry-level salaries could handle. Most of the money was spent on cheap, high-proof alcohol and a couple of pretty skanky strippers from a club out by a truck stop down the interstate. I guess I should call them erotic performers, because taking their clothes off was just the beginning." He shook his head at the memory. "At one point they both had their fingers completely—"

"Feel free not to offer any details," Brandt interrupted, holding his hand up.

Will frowned at him in exaggerated judgment. "Can't stand to even hear about women now that you're with Gabriel?" he wondered sarcastically.

Brandt thought about this for a moment. "Actually, I don't know. I thought maybe it was all of the training I've had about sex trafficking and ugly things like that, but I guess it really comes down to not wanting to be reminded of who I used to be."

"Wow, that turned serious," Will said compassionately. He looked at Brandt for a long moment, studying his face. "Can I ask you a question?"

"Sure," Brandt replied a little warily.

"Imagine you're in a strip club, and the woman performing is the most gorgeous vision you've ever seen. She moves like a goddess, and she tosses her top at you, and then she rides that pole like she's trying out for the Olympics as a sex gymnast. As a finale she lays herself in front of you and slides her thong down. Her ass is round and smooth, and she twerks it right at you. Then—"

"Stop," Brandt said, his voice rough. "Just stop." He turned away and took a couple of deep breaths before looking back at Will. "Why would you do that?"

"Because we're the same, Ethan." Will's voice was low and serious.

"What does that mean?"

"It means what I just described gives me the same feeling it gives you. That old tug in the privates that defined our sexuality from the time we first discovered sex. When we fell in love with men, we had to rewire our idea of sex to accommodate the emotional connection we had made." Will cast a quick glance around the room, then lowered his voice further. "I know it's not politically correct, but I honestly believe the original wiring cannot be completely disconnected. You will always feel that twinge for a beautiful woman. I know because I feel it too. It doesn't mean you are being unfaithful to Gabriel or that you aren't fully committed to him. There are people who grew up gay, and even if they fell in love with a woman, they would still feel that pull when they see a hot guy; that's how they're wired. And that's how it is for us; we have straight wiring and gay emotions, and that duality is the price we pay for the love in our lives."

Brandt was stunned. "I had no idea—"

"That I felt it too? It took me a long time to get it figured out. Spent a lot of nights wondering what it meant that I still had dreams about women, and why I don't have the same reaction to Ryan Gosling that Lucas does. At first I thought it was just going to take more time. But a couple of years passed, and nothing changed. Then, when Dylan was a baby, I got us into a group for new parents. It was essentially a mom's group, because I was the only stay-at-home dad. And let me tell you, I quickly gained a deeper understanding of the term 'MILF.' Not that I was tempted to actually do anything about it, but it was a weekly reminder that the sexual identity I had thought was part of my past was still there. God, that year was rough."

"What did you do about it?" Brandt asked.

Will chuckled. "Nothing. Not a damn thing. I wish I had a magic bullet for you, one that would give you boner immunity from women and make Mr. Gosling the man of your dreams, but there isn't one. I've come to the conclusion that even though I love Lucas more than I ever thought it was possible to love someone, and sex with him is amazing, I will always respond to women on a physical level. And if you think about it, that's not any different from any married man. Just because you're committed doesn't mean you're all dead inside. If people stopped being dazzled by beauty when they got married, no one would ever get a divorce or have an affair. A happier world, maybe, but a less beautiful one. And certainly a less human one."

"Ugh," Brandt sighed. "This is a mess."

"Why do you say that?"

"Because you and I are apparently unique in the entire experience of mankind. We hear all the time that sexual orientation is biologically determined and cannot be changed, and that sexuality is not a choice. But you and I grew up straight and had relationships with women, and then we each met a man who we were willing to set that all aside for. A lot of people would say that couldn't happen."

"I've had people say that very thing to me," Will said. "Rude people, even if they may have been simply trying to understand it."

"Here's the thing, though. You and I are the conservative's wet dream. We chose. We are living proof that sexual orientation can be chosen. And that's a huge problem in the struggle for equal rights because if people can choose to change their sexual orientation, then there's no essential sexual identity, and thus no basis for a claim of equal rights. They'll say we made a lifestyle choice."

Will looked at him for a moment. "That's pure horseshit, and you know it."

Brandt smiled. "You're a straight shooter, Will. I've always respected that about you."

"You're right that we represent a problem for the way most people think about sexual orientation, but they're the ones with the problem, not us. We're not the ones judging people based on who they sleep with. If everyone could just stop caring about the kind of sex people have, then it wouldn't matter whether it was biology or choice. It would just be sex, and who cares?"

Brandt shrugged grimly. "That's not going to happen anytime soon. People love to put others in boxes and then assign value to the boxes. And the fact that we seem to have chosen to jump from one box to another makes us… dangerous? The problem is that we are most dangerous to a cause I hold dear. So if I want to help the cause of equality, I can never tell anyone I chose Gabriel over every woman on earth because I love him, not because I am biologically determined to love men."

"Does he know how you feel? Does he know you chose him?" Will's voice was suddenly low and intense.

"He does. It was a hard thing to tell him, but I had to try to find a way to make him understand."

"And does he?"

Brandt nodded. Their understanding was beyond the words he had at his command.

"Then that's all that matters. No one else needs to know, so it doesn't matter whether they would understand it or not. He knows, and that's enough."

Brandt was silent for a moment, absorbing this. "Does Lucas know?"

Will nodded. "He was there for me right after Juliet left, and he actually tried to talk me out of falling in love with him. He had had a bad experience with a straight guy once and swore he would never let that happen again. I think he was expecting me to leave at any moment for the first year we were together. It finally sunk in when we decided to have kids and got married."

"I feel silly asking this now," Brandt said sheepishly, "but did you have a bachelor party that time?"

Will shook his head. "Because gay marriage wasn't legal yet here, we had to go away to get married. Our marriage license was meaningless here until legalization, but at least we had it. It was important for us to do it before we had kids, to give them a proper legal framework. Romantic, right? It wasn't until we got to the courthouse that I realized we were actually getting married. So the idea of a bachelor party didn't really come up."

"But if you did have a party, would there have been strippers? And of what gender?"

Will smiled slyly. "I am really glad I never had to make that decision."

"Crap. Thanks a lot, buddy." But Brandt put his hand on Will's. "Seriously, thanks for talking today. You helped me a lot."

"We have to stick together, Ethan. There aren't many like us."

"Aren't we the lucky ones," Brandt said with a sigh.

CHAPTER TWO
CAREER DEVELOPMENT

"TELL ME again why you want to get another job as a bartender?" the manager asked, looking at the résumé in front of him. "Looks to me like you'd be more qualified to be a paramedic or something."

Oliver laughed modestly. "I know it seems strange, but I'm working my way through med school, and I need all of my daytime hours free for classes. I'm looking for something flexible, with hours mostly at night. Honestly, I like having a job where the most mentally taxing thing I need to do is add up a tab."

The manager shrugged, then glanced back down at the résumé. "You're currently working at... the Tornado Room? Why are you leaving that job?"

Oliver took a deep breath, trying to find the most diplomatic way to explain. "It's a good crowd at the Tornado, but it's mostly hipsters nursing one bourbon and soda until their table is ready. Then they roll the tab over to the table, and I don't end up with much in the way of tips."

The manager looked Oliver up and down. "And you think you'd do better on tips here?"

He'd been practicing for this moment with his best buddy, Millie, who had a wide acquaintance in the gay community. She had helped him craft a smile she said would "bring guys to their knees." He had explained that, being straight, he wasn't terribly interested in having guys on their knees, but he appreciated the advice. She had also helped him choose the tight khaki pants and powder blue, stretchy V-neck shirt he was wearing. He unleashed the sly half grin he'd perfected. "Do you think I might do better on tips here?" Eyebrows up, blink of the blue eyes, and done.

"Ahem." The bar manager cleared his throat and shifted in his chair as if making adjustments beneath the table. "Yes, I think you'd do fine on tips here." He looked at Oliver with a gimlet eye, appraising. "Can I be perfectly frank, Mr. Mitchell?"

"I wish you would, sir," Oliver answered, recalling Millie's recommendation to throw in the occasional sign of submissive respect she said would be the "icing on the Twinkie," whatever that meant.

"Please, call me Gavin. Now, I assume this is obvious, but I need to be sure: this is a gay bar. And unless my gaydar is badly malfunctioning, you, Oliver, are a straight man. Am I right?"

Oliver, surprised, managed not to show it. "You are correct. Would that be a problem?"

"Have you ever set foot in a gay bar before this afternoon?"

"No, sir, I have not."

Gavin nodded. "Are you going to be comfortable with the patrons... appreciating you, physically?"

"Appreciating me by giving me bigger tips because I work out, or appreciating me by grabbing my ass as I serve them drinks?"

"It's a bar, not a brothel, so any ass-grabbing will be dealt with firmly by the staff," Gavin assured him. "But you need to understand your tips here would be directly proportional to your... friendliness with the patrons. A straight guy behind the bar who's just here to look pretty and make drinks will soon lose the interest of the room. But if you are friendly and open and—"

"Flirt a little?" Oliver asked.

"Yes, flirt a little," Gavin agreed. "If you are comfortable with that, then we might be able to work something out. You are clearly qualified in the realm of cocktails." He gestured to the neat row of five different drinks Oliver had made at the beginning of the interview. "How about this. Come by one night this week and see what it's like when the bar is in full swing. If you're comfortable here, then I'd love to have you start on Friday. If it turns out this isn't a place you can see yourself working, then just drop me a text and no harm done. Sound good?"

"Sounds terrific. Thank you for the chance." He shook Gavin's hand and stood to go. As he walked toward the door, he turned quickly to look over his shoulder and, as Millie had predicted, the manager's eyes were locked on his ass. He gave his special grin as he opened the door and made his exit.

This was a job he could do.

"YOU CAN stop jumping up and down now," Oliver said, his voice flat.

Millie paid him no heed but kept bouncing in a manic demented-cheerleader way. "Oh, oh, oh, this is gonna be so much fun!" she chanted, clapping her hands. "I've been wanting to get you into a gay bar for years, and we're finally gonna go!"

"Can I inquire as to why this excites you so much?" Oliver stood with his arms folded and his jaw set, his eyes bobbing up and down in time with Millie's frenetic rhythm.

Millie finally planted her feet on the ground right in front of Oliver and dropped her hands on his shoulders. "Because this is going to be awesome! You have no idea." She again dissolved into giggles.

"I know what bars are like, Millie. I work in one. People go there to drink."

She grinned. "That's like saying people watch the Tony awards to see who wins."

"Don't they?"

"No, stupid," she said with a smack to his forehead. "People watch the Tonys to see what everyone's wearing, and who's going to get outed, and to take a drink every time someone pronounces it 'Broad*way*.' The awards are just an excuse for a party."

Oliver rolled his eyes. "And I'm sure you're just about to bring this back around to our actual topic?"

"People go to a gay bar like Burn to see the hardest bodies grind to the best music, and the bartenders are legendary. It's sweaty and hot and amazing."

He wrinkled up his nose. "It sounds awful."

Millie fixed him with a critical glare. "Did they offer you the job?"

"Yes, I told you they did."

"Then that means you have found. Your. People." She emphasized these last words with a tap on his chest as she bit off each.

"What?"

"They wouldn't have offered you the job if you would look out of place there. This is a huge compliment, Ollie! It means the guys who know what guys should look like think you're a guy that guys would like to look at. That's awesome."

He shook his head, momentarily ensnared by her Gordian sentence. "So what you're saying is that I've successfully attracted the attention of the people whose attention I'm not interested in attracting."

"Yes! I'm glad you're starting to understand. The attention of those people will be what gets you the big tips, mister."

Oliver bit his lip, which was what he always did when he was uncertain about something. "Are we sure this is a good idea?"

"Why are you wondering that now? You already have the job."

"It just seems kind of... I don't know, slutty? I'm basically going to be using my body to make money."

"Okay, so first, on behalf of the slightly more than half the population of the planet who lack the magic Y chromosome, I'd like to say, welcome. When men have the money and power, women do what's necessary to get what we need. And mostly that involves being attractive, no matter what else you've got going for you. You can be a lady rocket scientist, but a lady rocket scientist with a nice rack will be more successful."

Oliver opened his mouth to object as what Millie was describing certainly didn't accord with his experience in the world.

"Bup, bup, bup!" she interrupted, holding up a hand. "You own a penis and are therefore not qualified to comment on the condition of women in the modern world. So hush." Her righteous glare brooked no challenge. "Now, you are in the somewhat privileged position of both being a guy and being able to conjure up a boner that will make another guy's wallet pop out of his pocket. Not because he's buying your favors or because he expects you to put out if he slips you a twenty. But simply because you are nice to look at, and by tipping you, he can bask in a little of your reflected glory. It's the way women have secured the necessities of life for millennia: food, shelter, cashmere scarves."

"Can the penis owner speak now?"

"The floor is yours," she replied, bowing grandly.

"What you describe is cynical and horrifying, but I will grant I am in no position to argue, given that I apparently possess some kind of magic scepter in my pants."

"Now you're catching on."

"But I know absolutely nothing about how to do what you say I should do at this job."

"What do you mean? You serve drinks, you smile, you laugh at their jokes and flirt a little. What's hard about that?"

"But I've never done anything like that."

She crossed her arms and looked at him impatiently. "Seriously? What do you do at your current job?"

"I make drinks."

"Do you smile at a new patron when he or she approaches the bar? Do you laugh when they tell jokes, even if they're not funny?"

"Of course I do."

"Why?"

"Because that's my job."

"I thought your job was making drinks. Couldn't you do that job without being chummy with the patrons?"

He gave a half shrug. "Sure, I guess. I wouldn't get much in the way of tips, though."

She smiled. "Score one for the phallus-bearer. You get that you will earn more in tips if you engage the patrons. That's all you need to do in this new job. It's just that the engagement will look a little different because the patrons are looking for... different things."

"That's what worries me. I have no idea how to... engage... a room full of gay men."

Her shoulders sagged and her smile evaporated. She sighed grandly. "Back to square one. It was going so well."

Oliver held his arms wide in confusion. "I have no idea what you're talking about."

"Come, sit your pretty self down here, and let's talk," she said, settling onto the couch and patting the cushion next to her.

He did as he was told.

"Good. Now, Ollie dear, we need to establish a few things. First, you are a beautiful man."

"Shut up."

"I'm not flattering you, hon, I'm stating a fact. Golden blond hair that would fall perfectly into place after a bomb blast, sparkling blue eyes, cheekbones to make Thor himself curl up and die from envy. But those things, along with your majestic height and your thermonuclear metabolism, are just genetic. It's what you've done yourself that really matters."

Oliver looked down at his body, then back at Millie. "What?"

She rolled her eyes in exasperation. "Are you being intentionally stupid right now?"

"I have no idea what you're talking about."

"How often do you go to the gym, buddy? In the average week."

"Well, I'm really lucky this semester that my classes don't start until nine, so I can work out during the week."

"So, every day?"

"No, not every day." Then he tracked back in his mind over the last few weeks. "Well, I have been getting a run in on Sundays before study group. And then there's a spin class on Saturdays I started going to because the instructor is really hot."

"So, every day."

Oliver nodded a little sheepishly.

"All I'm saying is that it's paying off. Now, I spend a fair bit of my day on Tumblr looking at guys who on their best day are almost as hot as you are on your worst. These pics are getting reblogged hundreds of times. And most of the reblogs come from the kind of guys you would be serving at Burn. When they see you in the flesh, they will be throwing money. Boners and money."

Oliver strained to hold on to some shred of dignity. "That's not why I work out."

"Ugh. Get over it," she scolded. "You work out for the same reason every guy works out. To look good naked."

"That's not why—"

"Bup, bup, bup!" she interrupted, hand up again. "I will not listen to your objections unless you can swear to me that you have never looked into your bathroom mirror and snapped a selfie."

Oliver froze.

"Yeah, thought so." Her expression turned from one of triumph to one of mischievous intrigue. "Full frontal?"

"Of course not," he blurted. "I only take them to track my progress. It's not because I like looking at pictures of myself."

"Then you won't mind if I take your phone and browse," she said, reaching for the coffee table where he'd set it when he came in.

"No!" he shouted, snapping up the phone before she could get to it.

"Mmm-hmm." She sat back on the couch. "Thanks for proving my point." She looked at him pityingly. "I just have one more question, darling. Then I'll let you off the hook."

"What?" he asked tersely.

"Have you ever sent one of these pics to anyone? Perhaps to a fair maiden whose virtue you wished to assail?"

He looked away, knowing she would see the blush of mortification on his face.

"Yep, thought so. Now, let me tell you what's up. The fact that you have taken naked selfies means you're aware you work out to look good. The fact that you have sent a naked selfie to someone means you're aware that person may be attracted to you because of the way you look. Not because you're brilliant, not because you're acing med school, not because you save kittens from burning buildings—"

"That was one time, and that part of the building wasn't even on fire yet."

Her hand shot up again, denying his objection. "The fact remains you have already used your body to get something you want. That's all you'd be doing in this new job—using what you have to get something you want."

"This is a job, Millie. You're turning it into a whole psych profile."

"You started it. You were worried the job would turn you into a slut. I just proved you're already a slut." She smiled at him brightly. "You're welcome."

Oliver slumped, defeated. "You free Wednesday night?"

"To squire you to a gay bar I would skip my mother's funeral. Hell, I'd skip my own funeral."

"You're a good friend. A creepy friend, but a good one."

THE THUDDING bass began pounding in their chests as they approached the club. What had been a nondescript facade during the middle of the day was transformed into an imposing monolith lit dramatically in tones of blue. Two-story stone columns were lit from below with blue lights, and affixed to each was an angular sconce from which flickered a blue flame a foot high. Oliver hesitated, overwhelmed by the theatricality of it all. Millie, with a firm grip on his arm, guided him through the door.

The nighttime look of the establishment was as different on the inside as it had been on the outside. It was dark, for one thing, as the only illumination in the bar area was provided by tiny blue lights in the ceiling, under the bar, and shining up the stone columns that ringed the room. The dance floor, however, was a brilliant oasis of strobing light, and its residents bounced and writhed and glistened in time to a driving beat.

Oliver knew in that moment he had no business being here, and working here was entirely out of the question.

"Come on," Millie said, steering him to a table near the bar.

They sat, and Oliver simply tried to take in the blue sparkly spectacle, to make sense of it. Millie, meanwhile, picked up the drink menu, goggled at it, then handed it over to him. He tried to focus on it to block out the bizarre surroundings, but it didn't help much. The menu contained nothing he could even recognize, much less make.

"Fun, right?" Millie asked.

"I figured it would all be cosmos and fruity drinks with parasols and stuff. I don't know how to make any of these," he said, handing the drink list back.

Millie took it and read down the page. "Ooh, the Chattanooga Cocksucker looks good," she said thoughtfully. "Though I am awfully tempted by the Rear Admiral." She looked up and seemed to notice his doubtful expression. "I'm sure these are just tarted-up versions of the stuff you already know how to make."

"Hey-ay," called a voice from behind them, belonging, apparently, to the server who subsequently appeared at Oliver's elbow. "Welcome to Burn. I'm Xander. What can I get for you this evening?" He placed a drink napkin in front of each of them and switched on the blue electronic flame in the crackled glass candleholder between them.

Oliver turned to get a look at his soon-to-be colleague. He was half a head shorter, but built powerfully. His upper-body musculature was obvious, as the shirt he wore had no sleeves or collar, and the sides were cut nearly down to the hem at the bottom. It was the kind of shirt worn by thousands of college athletes every day in the gym because it was cool and wouldn't get in the way of the weight equipment; here it served to emphasize Xander's bulging and rippling muscles.

Millie was still focused on the drink menu. "Xander, can you tell me what's in a Dirty Altar Boy?"

"Me, by the end of the night," he quipped with a wink.

Millie laughed, then listened as Xander recounted the ingredients in the drink. Oliver heard none of it, so rapt was his attention on

Xander's appearance and manner. He frowned with studious effort, trying to figure what it was in the way Xander moved, the way he spoke, the way he carried himself that made him successful at this job.

"And what can I offer you?" Xander asked, turning to Oliver. "And feel free to order something off menu," he said with a long glance down Oliver's body.

"Can I get a Glenlivet, splash of water?"

Xander's arms dropped to his sides, and he seemed to be out of breath. "Holy shit, is it butch in here or is it just you? Yum." He cracked a grin. "I'll have it for you in a sec. Thanks!" He strode off to the bar to place their orders.

"Holy moly, look at that ass," Millie said as she watched Xander walk away. "There are bubble butts, and then there's that. He must be a gymnast or something."

Though he told himself not to, Oliver swiveled his head around to take a look. Xander wore basketball shorts that barely contained his nearly hemispherical buttocks; they shifted just slightly side to side as he strode away, always bouncing back up into perky alignment. Oliver turned back around, hoping no one saw him look.

"You act like half the room wasn't already looking," Millie said with a laugh. "When you're here, you're free to look."

"I'm not going to stare at some guy's ass," Oliver said, annoyance slipping into his voice.

"Why not?" Millie asked. If the devil ever needed an advocate, she was ready take the case pro bono.

"Because, as you seem to keep forgetting, I'm straight. I have no idea what makes a guy's ass attractive."

"Does that mean you can't even look?" She tipped her head to the side. "He must squat more than you do."

Oliver's head whipped back around. "No way," he said, studying Xander's buttocks. "I'd be surprised if he could do half of my normal set. And there's just nothing going on there in terms of quads."

"Mm-hmm."

He turned slowly back to her. "I see what you did there."

"You mean I proved to you that in a room full of gay men, you are likely the leading expert when it comes to the shape and capabilities of Xander's ass?"

His response was a snarl.

"Look, you don't have to want to have sex with it to know it's a nice ass," she said. "That's all I'm saying."

"I don't get why his ass is so important to you."

"It's important to me because you're acting like a typical straight guy about it. You spend time every single day working out so you have an ass that is quite simply one of the wonders of the modern world, but you claim you don't know what makes a guy's ass attractive. If that's true, then how do you know when you're doing it right yourself? Or are you not aware that your own ass is a work of art? And before you answer, let me remind you that if you tell me you don't think your own ass is amazing, I will ask you to prove you have no selfies with a rear view on that phone of yours." She held out her hand to take his phone.

He didn't hand it over.

"All right," Xander said, appearing with a tray. "A Dirty Altar Boy for the lady, and a tumbler of I'd Like to See You in a Kilt for the gent. Look good?"

Millie laughed gaily and shook her head.

"Thank you," Oliver said, lifting his glass.

"I'll stop back by in a few to make sure you're still happy," Xander said, and took his leave.

They took a drink.

"How's your Altar Boy?" he asked.

"Dirrrrty," she replied with a giggle. "How's your grandpa drink?"

"Dignified, unlike present company," he grumbled and took another sip.

She looked around the room. "I could totally see you working here," she said. "Look at the guys behind the bar. Xander's hot, but that guy with the suspenders? Yowie."

Oliver sighed and turned around to look at the bar. The bartender Millie had referred to was pouring a line of brightly colored cocktails out of a stack of nested shakers he held over them in an arc of precision pouring—to the applause and adoration of his patrons. He bowed graciously and stacks of bills appeared on the bar in recognition of his technical skills. And, of course, in recognition of the way his suspenders clung to the muscles of his chest in the absence of a shirt. Oliver turned back around and silently sipped his Scotch.

"Why so sulky?" Millie asked, able to immediately read his mood, as always. It was both her best and worst quality.

"I figured you were going to ask me to list out the finer points of his chest and arms, and then crow about how you'd proved I'm already madly in love with him because his obliques are perfectly symmetrical."

Millie smiled. "As long as we're on the same page."

As they were finishing their drinks, Xander came back to inquire about a second round.

"In a bit," Millie told him. "Oliver here was just about to ask me to dance."

Xander looked at him as if he would very much like to see him bouncing up and down.

"I was?"

"Oh, yes, you were," she said, rising and taking his hand.

With a reluctant sigh, he allowed himself to be led to the dance floor. They joined a roiling sea of humanity, 98 percent male. They had danced together at a number of house parties and even Millie's sister's wedding last summer, to which Millie had invited him primarily because she enjoyed dancing with him. "You don't dance like a straight guy," she'd said, which at the time he took as a jokey non sequitur but now realized in it something more substantive—and sinister.

The music was so loud and relentless, and the crowd so tightly packed, that as one beat morphed into the next and a surge of new dancers flooded the floor, they lost sight of each other. Suddenly Oliver was dancing alone. Or, rather, dancing with at least a dozen men who surrounded him in a bacchanal of high-energy disco. He craned over and around his new dance partners, looking for Millie, but he could see no further than the writhing, glossy muscle that closed in on all sides.

Oliver, his chest tightening, spun around, trying to find a way out. There was none. He was about to drop his shoulder and smash his way through like a linebacker when he realized the fun Millie would have with that. She would lambaste him for being so threatened by a horde of party boys that he had to go full Hulk and crash himself to safety. She would laugh herself silly over his panic.

"Fuck," he grunted.

He would prove to her he could do this. And if he was going to do this, he was going to fucking do this. He let the beat take over and gave himself to it completely. Soon his entire section of the dance floor was moving along with him, following his every step and twist, mirroring the sinuous shapes traced by his hands. All eyes were on him, and for once in his life, he didn't mind that they were all male eyes. He stopped thinking and danced.

It was almost an hour later when Oliver made his way back to the table. Millie had obviously entertained a number of progressively dirtier altar boys in his absence, for her face was a bit flushed, and she was already giggling as he approached, sweating and breathing hard.

"There he is, the darling of the dance floor!" she called.

He glared at her and was about to unleash a stream of the vilest invective he could dredge up, but at that moment, Xander appeared with a drink for him.

"They tell me you're joining the team as a bartender," he said, smiling broadly. "This one's a special from the man behind the bar. Sort of a 'welcome aboard' drink."

Oliver took the glass and held it up. "And what would this be?"

Xander winked at Millie. "He made it just for you. I think he called it the Dancing Queen," he said slyly.

Oliver stared at the drink for a moment, then gave up his dignity for lost. "Please extend my thanks to the good man behind the bar. I appreciate his effort."

"And he appreciated yours," Xander said as he retreated from the table.

Oliver looked at the glass of bright pink liquid. "Shit," he exhaled.

"I think you'd have to admit," Millie remarked, slurring a little, "that you have made quite a first impression."

"Great," he said, feeling more miserable by the minute as the frenzy of the dance floor faded. "What kind of impression did I make, you think?" He sipped. "Holy shit, that's amazing." He looked anew at the colorful drink, then slumped again. "Shit."

"Look, straight boy. Get over yourself. You came, you danced, you conquered."

"Thanks for abandoning me out there, by the way."

"Abandoning you? I was shoved out of the way by a wall of muscle. Those guys looked at you the way a zombie looks at a brain buffet. Like nothing in their world was as important as getting close to you. I kinda shuffled around the outer circle of your acolytes for a song or two, then came here to allow Xander to drown my sorrows." She sipped the latest altar boy with obvious relish. "He's a pro, Xander is."

"Is there any way I can convince you of how mortifying this whole thing is for me?"

"You might have been able to sell me that bill of goods after the first five or six songs. But you shook your groove thing out there for nearly an hour. You exhausted at least a half dozen of them, who staggered off the floor talking about 'the new guy.' One guy actually fainted when you lifted your shirt."

"I was sweaty! I needed to blot!"

She fixed him with a withering stare. "That's the excuse of a scoundrel, and you know it. You were enjoying yourself out there, and a big part of that enjoyment was that every eye in the place was boring into you. You may as well admit it now and save us both the trouble."

He glared at her and sipped his drink meditatively. "Damn, that's good," he said, in spite of himself. And strong, he didn't say, but he certainly felt it.

She continued to stare at him, eyebrows up, clearly waiting for him to simply concede the point.

"All right, I give. I had fun dancing out there. Happy now?"

She shook her head slowly, her expression unchanged.

"What?" he asked. He took another drink, which he knew even as he did it was not a good idea, but whatever. Anything was better than talking about this.

"You've danced before. I've seen you. You've never danced like that."

He sighed. He knew what she wanted him to say, and under the influence of the strong drink and the loud music, it seemed easier to just say it than to think any more about whether it was actually true.

"I guess, in some small part of me, somewhere, it may have been exciting because they were looking at me. I've never had anyone look at me that way, like they were... hungry? Like everything I did made them want to see more."

"And that's because they are... say it with me. *Men.*"

Oliver winced, even as he knew what she said was true. But his faculties of rationalization swung into operation immediately and threw him a lifeline. "Of course. Guys know what it takes to build a body like this, and they were telling me I had earned their looks. It was kind of like a bro-compliment."

"I don't think their intentions were brotherly," Millie said, smiling. "Some of them looked ready to throw down right there on the dance floor."

Oliver looked at her skeptically. "Come on. You make it sound like I was some kind of go-go boy or something."

Millie's eyes lit up. "That's exactly it! A go-go boy. That's the perfect description of what you were out there. Maybe you should see if they're hiring for that here. You've never made a drink as good as your moves out there." She lifted the bottom of the final altar boy into the air and then wiped her mouth. "And now, I think I should be getting home. You coming, or are you going home with one of them?" She pointed behind him out to the dance floor, where several of the men were looking his way, clearly hoping for his return to the action.

"Yeah, I think I'm going to call it a night while I still have a scrap of dignity left."

"Sure, if that's what you want to call it," Millie cracked as she picked up her purse and got unsteadily to her feet.

He took her arm as they walked to the door.

"I'll never be able to show my face around here again," she said. "Leaving with the new meat? I'm gonna have my hag card revoked for sure."

"Anyone ever tell you you're a delightful drunk?"

She laughed and shook her head.

"Yeah, there's a reason for that," he grumbled as he opened the door and guided her out to the street.

CHAPTER THREE
BROTHERS

"I CAN'T believe you came all this way to talk about planning a party," Brandt said as he opened the door and let Liam into the house.

"It's a beautiful day, and it was a nice drive."

"It's eight in the morning, and it's a four-hour drive. I doubt you just rolled out of bed and thought, 'Hey, it's not even dawn yet, but I sure feel like driving forever to have breakfast with my stubborn little brother.'"

"Matter of fact I did," Liam replied with a grin. "Can I get a hug from my stubborn little brother?"

The brothers embraced.

"Gabriel up yet?" Liam asked.

"It's Saturday, and it's before noon. You can do the math on that one." Brandt laughed. "Ready to eat?"

"Hell yeah. We goin' to that funky diner? Love that place."

Brandt nodded. "Best blueberry pancakes in town. Hope you brought your appetite."

Liam laughed. "One of the best parts about married life is that you can eat what you want. Don't have to maintain the six-pack once you've landed your mate."

"Lucky you," Brandt replied as they walked down the steps to his car. "There are different rules in the world I live in. For example, a six-pack is mandatory forever. If you lose it, you're not allowed out in public anymore."

Liam winced. "The price of living a life of glamour and excitement. But I guess if I showed up in the news as often as you do, I'd have to watch my figure too."

"You're not serious."

"'Fraid I am, little bro. Our local news covered the stuff in Woodley and the great barfing wedding, all of it. Even got an e-mail from a buddy of mine down South who sent me a clipping of you and

Gabriel bringing down that corrupt sheriff. You're getting to be a pretty big deal."

"Bet Uncle Phil loves that kind of publicity for the family," Brandt said sarcastically as he backed down the driveway.

"Wouldn't know. Haven't seen much of Uncle Phil lately." He turned a suspicious look on Brandt. "He told you, didn't he?"

Brandt chuckled. "Yeah. Kept it secret a long time and only told me last week because I was being an asshole to you about the bachelor party."

"God, I love me some Gabriel. Good thing you found him before I did."

"Can you dial it back a bit? Life's complicated enough without you trying to steal my fiancé."

"Fair enough," Liam said with a laugh. "It's just easy to see how you could go gay for a guy like him."

"I didn't 'go gay' for Gabriel," Brandt said, a little more dismissively than he intended.

Liam turned to look at him in surprise. "Well, that's a little… huh. Cold feet before the wedding?"

Brandt shook his head. "No… it's more complicated than you think, is all."

"You keep saying that, like your wedding is a mission to Mars or something. It seems pretty simple from my end: you love him, you get gay-married, you live happily ever after. Where does the rocket science come in?"

Brandt shook his head but didn't make any effort to explain further. Some things just can't be explained except to someone who already understands them—like Will—and even then it's not much help.

They pulled up at the diner a few silent minutes later, and Brandt led his brother to his usual table. Shirley laid coffee mugs before them and poured them full.

Liam brought the mug to his nose and inhaled deeply. "Damn, that's a fine cup of coffee," he groaned.

Brandt smiled and sipped and then looked out the window for a long moment.

"So, you gonna tell me what this is all about?" Liam asked.

"What all of what is about?" Brandt asked, distracted by his own thoughts.

"This drama about the bachelor party. You getting all prickly when I said you went gay for Gabriel. Your general crankiness about the whole thing."

Brandt sighed. "I'm not cranky."

Liam set his coffee down and looked at Brandt piercingly. "Look, if things aren't working with Gabriel and you need help getting out, I will do whatever it takes. Life's too short to get hitched to the wrong person."

Brandt was stunned. Tears sprang to his eyes in an instant.

"I mean it, Ethan. You can tell me anything. I've got your back."

"Is that what you think?" Brandt's voice shook, betraying his real concern: that Gabriel might be thinking the same thing. Suddenly he realized how his reluctance to have a bachelor party might be seen. "That's not it at all."

Liam squinted as if trying to make sense of his brother's words, but he remained silent.

"I love Gabriel, and I want to spend my life with him," Brandt said, wiping his eyes. "But this whole bachelor party thing has made me a little crazy."

"That's the part I don't get," Liam replied. "Tell me what's going on."

Brandt looked at him, wishing he had the words to make Liam understand. He wasn't sure there were any. "It's…."

"Complicated?" Liam asked. He sat back, shaking his head. "Come on. You gotta do better than that."

Brandt stared hard at the table until Shirley came to take their order. Once she left, he looked at Liam and sighed. "I don't think you'd understand."

"Well, then, start with something small. Tell me why the bachelor party has you so crazy, and we'll go from there."

Brandt took a deep breath and blew it out slowly, trying to sort his thoughts into an order Liam could grasp. "Okay, here's the thing. A bachelor party only works if everyone there is there for the same reason."

"To wish the groom well. Grooms, in this case. I don't see the issue."

"The stuff people traditionally do at bachelor parties… just wouldn't be appropriate."

"Why not?"

"Because some of the guys are straight, and some are gay." And some, he didn't say, are somewhere in the undefined middle.

Liam threw his hands up. "That's like saying you can't have a dinner party if some people eat meat and some are vegetarians. If everyone acts like grown-ups, there's no reason this can't work."

"But what if some of the vegetarians can't stand the very idea of people who eat meat? What if the sight of meat makes them sick?"

Liam squinted at him. "What kind of meat are we talking about here?"

Brandt rolled his eyes. "I'm just saying that the whole point of the bachelor party is a last hurrah because the groom is not going to be a free man anymore. All of that stuff we did at your bachelor party? None of that would be appropriate."

"Well, we could tone it down, of course." Liam tipped his head thoughtfully. "But getting the right kind of stripper isn't the issue here, is it?"

Brandt looked down, knowing Liam possessed an older brother's power to instantly see what he was thinking.

"That's it, isn't it? I get it now."

This, Brandt wasn't expecting. "Get what?"

"You don't want anything to remind you of the way you were… before."

"That's not—"

"Don't." Liam held up his hand. "I know you, Ethan. Known you all your life. You can't bullshit me about this. I see what's going on."

Brand slumped and let out a sigh.

"Why didn't you just say that at the beginning? All this drama, and that's all it was? We'll just tone it down and avoid doing anything related to sex."

"And that's super easy, because bachelor parties are never about sex, not at all." Brandt winced at his angry tone, but it all just came spilling out.

"We'll just go out, get a drink, listen to some music, smoke a cigar or two, stay up too late. Easy."

"Fine. Great idea. Where will we go? Will the straight guys go into a gay bar? Will the gay ones feel comfortable at a sports bar? What kind of music would everyone agree on? What if there's dancing? What if there isn't? How much will the straight guys enjoy a bachelor party with no strippers? Probably only slightly more than they would enjoy male strippers, which is to say, not at all. And a cigar room is not the most open-minded place in the world, especially if there's someone making jokes about how much puffing on a cigar looks like a bad blowjob. We'd get thrown out of any place we went, and half the group would want to go one way and half the group the other. And someone's bound to hit on someone else, and that will probably end in a fistfight. So even if you keep sex out of it, it will be there. It will be there, Liam. It will always be there."

Liam blinked under the onslaught of this rant. He was silent for a moment while Brandt caught his breath.

"Ethan," he said quietly. "I can't pretend to know what the last couple of years have been like for you. I didn't see you going through it because we live so far away. I'm sure it wasn't easy. But that's done now. You shouldn't feel like everyone's judging you for realizing you're gay."

"That's not it," Brandt said weakly.

"Then what is it? Tell me. Share the burden with me, and I promise it will make you feel better."

"I don't know how to say this, but—"

"Here you go, gentlemen," Shirley sang out as she laid their breakfasts in front of them. "Anything else I can get you right away?"

"No, thanks," Liam said for them both. "This looks great."

"Enjoy," she said as she turned and hurried off.

Liam didn't pick up his fork. "Ethan, what were you going to say?"

Brandt took a deep breath. "Gabriel and I aren't together because I realized I was gay."

"Okay," Liam replied slowly. He studied Brandt's face for a moment. "I have no idea what that means."

"It means," Brandt said and then swallowed hard. "It means that I fell in love with him. He's the only man I've ever felt... anything for. It's been really hard to admit this, but...."

Liam nodded, waiting.

"I'm not gay."

Liam's mouth dropped open. He took a confused breath, closed his mouth, then opened it again.

"I know it sounds weird."

"I…," Liam began, then stopped. His brow furrowed, and he started again. "I'm kind of surprised to hear that, Ethan. Especially since you are getting married to Gabriel in less than three months. One imagines being gay would be a prerequisite to marrying someone of the same sex." He fell silent and blinked several times. "I'm really confused."

"Sorry," Brandt said dismally.

"No, don't apologize. Never apologize for feeling the way you feel. You know, I always thought that as the youngest of the three of us, you tried too hard to please everybody. I just kind of assumed, when you told me you and Gabriel were in love, that you had spent your whole life trying to be straight because that's what everyone expected of you. And I was really proud of you for finding the strength to come out to the entire family the way you did." He reached across the table and put his hand on Brandt's. "I will love you and support you no matter how you define yourself. You don't have to worry about that."

"Thank you," Brandt managed.

"So," Liam said, "let's get this figured out, then."

Brandt, in spite of the emotional turmoil he found himself in, had to smile. "Always the lawyer, jumping in to get things sorted."

Liam shrugged. "You know how I am with things not being clear-cut." He finally took a bite of his pancakes and chewed thoughtfully for a moment. "So what are we, then? Bisexual?"

Brandt shook his head. "It's not as easy as that. But let me ask you, since you're the word guy. What's the term for someone who's attracted to women in general, but falls in love with one man, the only one he's ever been attracted to, and doesn't ever want to be with a woman again?"

Liam was taken aback. "I didn't think that happened, but—"

"That's my point." Brand held out his hands in surrender. "There's no way to explain this."

"You didn't let me finish," Liam scolded. "What I was going to say is I didn't think that happened, but if it happened to you, who cares what anyone calls it?"

"What do you mean, who cares?"

"I mean who cares? Are you happy with Gabriel?"

"Yes."

"And is he happy with you?"

"I think so."

"And does he know he's the only man in the world for you?"

Brandt blushed. This was getting rather intimate. "Yes, he does."

"Then what's the problem?"

Brandt rolled his eyes. "In general there's no problem. But this bachelor party is a problem. It's going to be a night of everyone being very aware of their own sexuality except for me, because my sexuality is apparently unique in all the world."

"Again, who cares?"

"Imagine the group of us standing on the sidewalk between two clubs. One attracts a manly, cigar-chomping crowd, and the other has go-go boys in hot pants dancing on tables. Half the group wants door number one, the other half wants door number two. What do I do?"

"Which door do you want?"

"Not door number one, because if someone smoking a cigar makes a gay joke, I'm going to unload on him. Not door number two, because I actually don't want to see guys in gold lamé short shorts shaking their butts at me. Doesn't do a thing for me, and I imagine it would kind of gross you and Noah and the other guys out as well. So where does that leave us?"

"It leaves us with you're kind of a party pooper." Liam stuck his tongue out at his little brother.

It was the first good laugh Brandt had had since this awkward conversation began.

"I get it now," Liam said. "I know I keep saying that, but I think I really do get it now. A bachelor party, whether gay or straight, depends on the groom being one or the other. We just don't know where you ended up."

Brandt shook his head. "I didn't trade one identity for another. I didn't stop being straight and become gay. I fell in love. And maybe a part of me was looking for that, looking for someone like Gabriel, that I wasn't even aware of. I don't know. But I do know the 'straight' switch didn't get turned off when the 'gay' switch got turned on. It's supposed to be a binary, but I don't really belong in either place. That's what's making this so hard."

"Okay," Liam said, chewing thoughtfully. "Let's set the party aside for a minute, and we can circle back to it when we've had some time to mull it over. Now, forgive me if this seems rude, but it's all kind of new to me. When you say you aren't gay, how does that work? I mean, you and Gabriel must... well... right?"

Brandt laughed at the awkwardness of his brother inquiring about his sex life. "Yes, we do. Kind of a lot, actually."

"And would he also describe himself as 'straight with a twist'?"

"Actually, no. He's kind of come around to the view that he was probably gay all along, but the trauma of his older brother coming out and getting tossed from the family kept him from acknowledging it. But since we've been together, he's started to see himself more as a gay man."

"So when you are… together… are you the guy and he's the… whatever you call the other one?"

"This is profoundly weird, Liam," Brandt said. "This would be like me asking about your and Marianne's favorite positions."

"Sorry," Liam said, shaking his head abruptly. "This is all so new to me. I didn't mean to make you uncomfortable. I wasn't looking for specifics as much as trying to understand what it means when you say you're not gay." He looked utterly baffled. "Because unless you have the lights off every time, it would be hard not to notice that Gabriel's not a woman. And even then, the guy is like a hundred and ten percent muscle."

"I get it—you have a boner for my boyfriend." Brandt cracked up, joined by his brother. "Okay, if you really want to know." He took a deep breath. "Gabriel and I do… everything. To each other."

"Oh, wow," Liam said, and then took a steadying gulp of coffee.

"Sorry—too much information?"

"No, I asked for it. It's just kind of… well, all I know about how gay relationships work I learned from seeing you two on holidays and from this paralegal in my firm who is only interested in two things: getting absolutely pounded by the biggest guy he can find in whatever bar he goes to, and telling everyone in the office about it the next day. According to him—not that I listen much, but he says it over and over—every gay guy either gives it or takes it, and no one does both."

"I think he's overstating it, but once again, you're looking at an exception to the rule," Brandt said, raising his hand.

"But I guess my original question is still what I don't understand—if you're not gay, how do you manage to have sex with a guy?"

Brandt shrugged. "He's not just a guy. He's Gabriel, and he's amazing, and I love him."

"I love him too, but that doesn't mean I want to—"

"More coffee?" Shirley interrupted.

"Yes, please," the brothers answered in unison, welcoming the intrusion.

Brandt looked into the inky liquid. "It's just different with him. We were so close for two years, and then we just got… closer. When I'm with him, I don't see us as two guys trying to fit their bodies together. I just see… us. It's like the rules don't apply to us. We learned how to have sex from each other, what we want, what feels good to us. I don't know what other guys do in bed, because all I care about is what we do."

Liam nodded and then smiled. "That's… awesome. Good for you. And you're absolutely right. Labels don't matter. What you have is far beyond whatever name anyone could come up with for it." Liam seemed genuinely happy for Brandt.

"So does this help us at all come up with a plan for the party?"

"Actually, I think I do have something that could work. How about I ask for some help planning the event? I head things up for the straight contingent, and you tell me the gayest person on the guest list, and I'll get him to plan the gay side of things. We'll do a mash-up bachelor party that will delight and offend every single person in attendance, maybe all at the same time if we're lucky."

"So instead of taking my advice to give up in the face of inevitable disaster, you want to double down and make it not one but two of the most outrageously stereotypical bachelor parties ever in the history of bachelor parties?"

"Why not? Sometimes when the going gets tough, the tough just step on the fuckin' gas, man. Blaze o' glory," Liam said grandly and held his coffee cup aloft.

Brandt sighed and shook his head resignedly. He touched his coffee cup to his brother's. "To the most glamorous disaster this city's ever seen."

They tossed back their hot coffee, took a breath, and then Liam pulled out his phone.

"Now, who's the most fabulous of them all?"

"The name you're looking for is Bryce," Brandt said reluctantly. Bryce would be more than up to the task, but was it really fair to unleash him on Liam? Though if it really was a blaze of glory he was looking for….

Liam typed into his phone. "Excellent. Send me contact info, and I'll touch base with him today."

"Just a word of warning about Bryce—"

"What, do you think I've never met a gay person before? Come on now, Ethan. You don't have to treat me like I've led such a sheltered life."

Brandt couldn't hide his smirk. But if that's what Liam wanted....

"You're right," Brandt said. "I'm sure you'll have no problem relating to Bryce. In fact, I think you will find him quite interesting."

"This is all going to work out fine, little brother." Liam beamed.

"I'm sure it will," Brandt said heartily. He didn't believe a word of that, of course.

"THANKS FOR taking the time to talk with me, Bryce."

"Oh, the pleasure is all mine. I can hardly believe I'm talking with the original Brandt boy. You sound even more muscular than Ethan, if that's possible."

"I'm afraid it must be a bad connection. Ethan's the looker in the family."

"We shall see, we shall see. Now, how can I help with this bachelors party? It's the first one I've ever been asked to participate in, and am I correct in understanding that it's to be an all-male affair? Because then I can offer you a wealth of experience, both as a partygoer and as a service professional. In fact, some of the parties I have serviced have asked me to make it a regular thing, which is quite a compliment, given the competition in that area from each new crop of muscly country boys who land on our shores, eager to parlay their corn-fed charm into G-strings packed with fives and tens. My, my...." Bryce took a steadying breath. "Now, where were we?"

"I... actually have no idea." Liam took his own steadying breath. "Well, when I talked with Ethan last weekend about the party, he was very concerned that we come up with a plan all the guests would be comfortable with."

"You have come to the right man. I can be very comforting."

"Here's the issue, Bryce. Not all of the attendees are gay."

"I have never been one to judge people on their shortcomings."

"Ah, yes. That's... commendable. But Ethan's primary concern was that since a large number of the guys are straight, whatever we plan for the party should be something they will enjoy. But we don't want to make the gay ones uncomfortable either."

"Now, when you say straight, do you mean latent, in denial, or simply never tried it?"

"Never tried what?"

"Being gay, honey," Bryce cried.

"Um… I guess what I mean is that they only have relationships with women."

"Everybody has relationships with women. You can't really avoid it—they're everywhere."

"I mean they have intimate relationships with women."

"Mm-hmm, I see," Bryce said thoughtfully. "Well, again, I'm not going to judge people for bad decisions they made in the past."

"But these are guys who are in relationships with women right now. Some of them are married to women."

"So you're saying we need to be sure there are no cameras at the party. Very prudent of you. I'll take care of the frisking myself, unless you prefer to have someone in uniform do it. Oh, I have just the man for you—though he can be alarmingly quick with the handcuffs. We'll just tell him to keep his nightstick to himself."

Liam sighed. "Bryce, I think you're missing the point. About half the guests at this party don't have sex with men. Never have, never will."

Bryce's laughter overwhelmed the phone connection. "And I suppose they'll be coming to the party in pumpkin coaches? Your little brother is a hoot, but you, sir, are hilarious!"

"I don't see what's so funny," Liam said, slowly.

"And you're modest too. What a charmer." Bryce took a breath, wiping the tears of hilarity from his eyes. "We both know that straight guys don't actually exist."

"I'm sorry?"

"Oh, nothing to be sorry about. It's just not what nature intended."

"I don't follow—"

"If men were not intended to have sex with each other, then why do locker rooms exist? And the British Navy? What need would we possibly have for football or the priesthood, except as foreplay? Oh, the very idea!"

"Bryce, I don't know how to break it to you, but straight men actually exist."

"Oh, when you make a joke, you *commit*. That's wonderful. All right, I will play along. Now, these straight men you are talking about, you say they've never had sex with a man, and don't intend to?"

"That's right."

"So they've never touched another man intimately? Not in high school, when the hormones are raging? Or in college, when they're thrown together in dorm rooms and forced to spend every moment with other men, even in the showers? You're telling me that there are men out there who have never touched, kissed, or had a sexual thought about another man, ever, in their entire lives?"

"Well, I'm sure there are men out there who—"

"What about you, Mr. Big Brother Brandt? What about you? Can you tell me in all honesty that you have never laid a finger on your fellow man?"

Liam was silent for a moment.

"I don't mean to pry," Bryce continued, "and though I would guard your privacy with my very life, you are under no obligation to tell me any personal details. But I would simply ask you to reflect on whether your own life has been as straight as you claim the men at this party will be."

Liam's silence continued a little longer. "Well... I don't know why I'm telling you this." There was a sound over the line of a door being closed. "But there was a time in high school when a couple of buddies and I... well, there was some touching. Just the once, though."

"Ah, just as I had predicted. Thank you for trusting me with that information, which I shall hold in strictest confidence—especially tonight when I am in the bath. But let's return to your definition of straightness. For reference, I believe you said it involved men who 'never have, and never will' have sex with another man. Does that fit your situation?"

Again, a pause on Liam's side. "I don't know that I would call that one awkward grope sex."

"Oh, so it wasn't sexual, then. You were, perhaps, involved in an ad hoc study group for an anatomy midterm?"

Liam chuckled softly. "No, you're right. Looking back on it, there was a sexual element to it. But we did it because we had no other outlet. It's not like girls were throwing themselves at us."

"They do that?" Bryce asked in a shocked whisper. "My, my. Heterosexuality is like another country."

"They don't literally do that, no. And certainly not at pimply-faced hormonal teenage boys. But that's my point: in the absence of any willing female, guys will sometimes turn to other guys out of desperation. It's like what happens in prison, or in your beloved British Navy."

"I'm not ashamed to report that I am intimately familiar with what happens in both places, having viewed both the entire run of *Oz* and several tours of *HMS Pinafore*."

"I see. Well, my point is that men will turn to sex with other men in those situations; it doesn't mean they're gay. It's called situational homosexuality."

"Oh, is it? Mm-hmm. So when one of your straight men makes the argument that he could never have sex with another man, what he really means is that he could never have sex with another man unless the conditions were right? Something involving a dimly lit prison shower or some kind of musical production number on a sailing vessel?"

"No, that's not what—"

"Because if a man is capable of having sex with another man under any circumstances, then he is capable of having sex with another man, full stop."

"I beg to differ. If there are no other options, then it doesn't make him gay. It simply means he had no other options."

"You are welcome to beg, dear. I do enjoy that. But what you are asking me to believe is that in those situations, sex is more important than heterosexuality."

Liam was silent for a moment. "Well, in a sense."

"So summing up, your definition of heterosexuality is that quality that makes men want to have sex only with women, unless there are no women around, in which case they will have sex with other men but call themselves heterosexual because they would have chosen to have sex with a woman, save for the unfortunate fact that no women presented themselves. Heterosexuality is, therefore, dependent upon the presence of women. Which means that men who have sex with women are merely situationally heterosexual. Or do I misunderstand your argument?"

"Um, well…." Liam cleared his throat. "I think we have to look at who they would choose to have sex with. If a man in prison would prefer to have sex with women, then we would consider him straight. Even if he… um, has sex with other men."

"Ah, so sexuality is entirely dependent on what one chooses to call oneself, regardless of the actual sex one is having? I would counsel caution along that line of reasoning, my dear, because it leads to the conclusion that heterosexuality is just as much a choice as homosexuality, and it need not have any basis in actual practice. Now, personally, I like the sound of that very much, because it means anyone can have any kind of sex they like and not worry about what to call oneself at Thanksgiving dinner with the family. But I think you'll find that many straight men would prefer to think of their heterosexuality as being a permanent part of their character."

"Indeed."

"And yet that doesn't explain all those prison assignations, does it? Or perhaps you have a different understanding of what constitutes a 'permanent part of their character.'"

"This is all really confusing, Bryce. We're just trying to plan a bachelor party."

"Indeed we are. Look at me, getting all wrapped up in the Socratic particulars when there's a party to plan. All I want to say is that we should perhaps worry less about whether everyone stays within their comfort zone, be that zone straight or fabulous, and more about how to make the evening memorable for our darling boys."

"What do you think about two venues for the party—we could start at one where the straight guests would be more comfortable and then move to the other as the evening progresses?"

"Logistically speaking, I think it's a wonderful plan, because it means by the time everyone's getting tipsy, we'll be in a place where they can all dance together. But are straight boys really so fragile that they need a protected environment in which to have a drink and socialize?"

"Let's think about that. Do you have a place in mind for the second half of the party?"

"Oh, yes. There's a newish club called Burn that I think would be perfect."

"And this Burn, what's it like?"

"Hot hot hot. Their dance floor is the stuff of legend, the music impeccably curated, and the staff—honey, one look at the bartenders and your straight boys are going to wish they were in prison."

"I see your point about getting the straight ones drunk before we get there. I think it'll make it easier for them. Now, is there a suitably straight place nearby? Something cigar- or sports bar-like?"

"Ah, of course," Bryce replied. "A place for the men to suck on cigars and watch other men smash themselves together on television.

Goodness, those straight-boy rituals can be so hot." Bryce paused to fan himself. "It just so happens, darling, that there is such an establishment not two blocks away. When it opened we all said 'there goes the neighborhood' because we feared it would bring in too many straight people and suddenly you can't walk home at night without seeing heterosexuals pawing at each other on the street like animals, but I am happy to say that they seem to be behaving themselves."

"Don't like having heterosexuality shoved down your throat, eh?" Liam asked with a chuckle.

"Oh, quite the contrary," Bryce replied. "I think we know each other well enough by this point for you to understand that my throat is quite accommodating to heterosexuality. It's just when it involves women that I get a little queasy."

Liam dissolved into laughter. "All right, my good man. How about this: since I live some distance from the city, can you pay a visit to the venues, and if they seem suitable, perhaps you can take Ethan and Gabriel there to make sure they're comfortable with them?"

"It would be my great pleasure, sir," Bryce replied.

"Excellent. Bryce, I look forward to meeting you in person."

"As do I. Seeing you in the flesh will be a dream come true for me."

"Uh, thanks? Anyway, it's been great to talk with you, and let me know how it goes, okay?"

"I shall report back on our reconnaissance the very moment everyone sobers up. On that you may rely."

CHAPTER FOUR
THE GRIND

AFTER CLASS on Friday, Oliver took the bus to the downtown block where Burn would soon flicker to life. It was only six o'clock, so the club was still preparing to open, and he had to knock on the door to get someone to let him in.

That someone was Xander.

"Oh my God, you're here. There were some doubters who thought we'd never see you again, but when I saw you out there on the dance floor, I thought, 'we've got him now.' And I was right! Welcome to Burn."

"Um, thanks?" Oliver replied uncertainly.

"Come on in, and I'll show you around."

Oliver followed Xander, who hadn't yet changed into his work clothes; what he was wearing at the moment was not ripped so as to expose any flesh.

"Gavin said you'd be working the bar, so let's go there first." Xander led him over to the large and elaborate bar, with its tiers of blue-lit glass shelves reaching more than a dozen feet high. The bar formed an ellipse near the center of the room, and several bartenders covered each of the two long, curving sides. On Friday and Saturday nights, Oliver learned, there might be two or three on each side of the bar.

"Ulysses, this is Oliver," Xander said as he introduced Oliver to the man with the suspenders he had noticed behind the bar earlier in the week.

"Pleased to meet you, Oliver," Ulysses's deep, strong voice replied. Oliver was fascinated by the corded muscle that stood out as Ulysses shook his hand. The guy was a living anatomy exhibit.

Great, thought Oliver. *Just another thing I can't tell Millie without her starting to plan my wedding to a muscleman named Ulysses.*

"Likewise," Oliver said with a smile, shaking Ulysses's hand firmly. *Such soft hands.*

"Gavin wants you to back me tonight, get a feel for the place," Ulysses said. "Once you get your legs under you, we can split the bar tomorrow. Sound good?"

Oliver nodded. Ulysses smiled and went back to his stocking duties.

"Now, let me show you the rest of the place, and then we'll get you something to wear," Xander said, eyes flicking up and down Oliver's jeans and polo outfit.

"I brought some stuff I thought might work," Oliver said, hefting his backpack. "I just grabbed some workout gear."

"Great. The genuine article is always better than what we can come up with in the back. They can sense when you're wearing clothes you've actually sweated in. It's like a pheromone thing." Xander hustled off toward the middle of the club.

Oliver followed him, not wanting to miss any important details.

"Out here we divide up the tables by server. A lot of the patrons come back every week—or more—to be served by the same guy, so we get to know them well. That's why if a server asks you for something special in a drink order, it's really important you try to give him what he requests. We split the first twenty percent of the tip with the bar, but do a good job for me on my specials, and I'll throw some of the bigger tips your way," Xander said with a wink.

"And do you often get bigger tips?" Oliver asked.

"Some of my regulars are very generous," Xander replied. "Very, very generous."

Oliver filed away this information; he thought it might prove useful.

"Here's the dance floor," Xander said, walking onto the smooth floor that, when not lit dramatically with blue spots, looked rather drab. "But you already knew that," he added with a grin. "When I saw you earlier in the week, I figured you'd been hired on as a dancer. I was kind of surprised when I found out you were going to be a bartender."

"Wait, they hire dancers? People get paid for dancing?"

Xander squinted at him as if trying to determine whether Oliver was putting him on. "Yeah, people get paid for dancing."

Oliver shrugged. "I had no idea."

"There's nothing worse than a dance floor with no energy. So we have two or three dancers who make sure things get moving. They also work as shot boys, depending on the mood of the room."

"I'm going to sound really dumb here, but what's a shot boy?"

Xander eyed him skeptically. "There was a rumor going around that you were straight. I'm starting to think that may be true."

"It is, I'm afraid," Oliver replied. "Is that going to be a problem?"

Xander smiled. "Not as far as I'm concerned. I have a strict nondiscrimination policy: if it's a dick, I'm in, no matter where you usually put it." He laughed at Oliver's shocked reaction. "It's just that seeing you out on the dance floor, I would have put money on your being gay."

"I would have lost you that bet, buddy."

"Hmm." Xander tipped his head thoughtfully. "We'll see. Anyway, a shot boy takes shot glasses around the club on a tray and sells them to the patrons. The shots aren't big money, but they rake it in on tips."

"Wow. I've tended bar for a lot of years, and I had no idea it would be so different here. The Tornado Room is looking pretty tame right now."

Xander wrinkled up his nose. "That's the hipster steakhouse over by the capitol, right?"

Oliver laughed. "Yep, that's the place. I know it seems old-school compared to this, but I grew up working in my parents' supper club upstate. One old-fashioned after another, all night long. Once, when *Sex in the City* was on TV, someone ordered a cosmopolitan. It was the most exciting moment of my entire year."

"Well, we'll try to keep things more interesting for you. Come on, let's get changed. Doors open in a few minutes."

Xander led the way to the back of the house, passing the corridor to the restrooms. "We have our own bathroom in the back so you don't have awkward moments with patrons in the toilet. The management's pretty serious about people not gettin' busy in the loo, but a couple of times we've had to get the Jaws of Life out to rescue a shot boy from the grip of a determined customer."

He pushed on what looked like a section of wall, and it pivoted inward. They stepped into a brightly lit locker room, surrounded on all sides with stacks of cardboard boxes full of booze and bar supplies. A wide mirror hung on the wall in the only space not filled with overstock.

"You can use this one." Xander pointed to the locker at the end. "That one used to be Marcel's, but he got his wings last month."

"What does that mean?" Oliver asked.

"He ascended to sugar-daddy heaven," Xander replied. "He tended bar here for almost a year, and then his best customer got a job in New York and took him along." Xander looked at the locker wistfully. "I hope he's okay."

"Why wouldn't he be?"

Xander shrugged. "It's a risky business. Marcel was gorgeous, but he moved away from all of his friends, not to mention the parts of his family who hadn't cut him off after he came out. He'll probably be fine for a year or two, but when someone with smoother skin and tighter muscles comes along, he could find himself out on the street."

Oliver shivered like he'd seen a ghost. "Scary," he said simply.

Xander nodded. "That's why we need a fallback. Mine is commodities futures."

Oliver laughed but then noticed Xander's serious expression.

"No shit. I have some regular customers who deal on the markets, and under the influence of a lot of alcohol and a little of this—" He lifted his shirt, displaying a rock-hard six-pack of muscle. "—they will let slip some interesting bits of information. Sometimes the things I hear let me make advantageous trades."

"No shit?" Oliver was dumfounded.

Xander shook his head. "Thought because I'm pretty I must be dumb?"

"No. I mean...," Oliver blurted but then realized there wasn't a way to answer that question heterosexually, so he stopped trying. He shrugged.

Xander laughed. "Well, let's get into costume. There's just one rule here: if you're serving on behalf of the establishment, you must wear a shirt and shoes."

"And pants, one imagines?"

"Yeah, pants are sort of assumed."

Oliver recalled his earlier visit to the club. "When I was here before, Ulysses was wearing suspenders, but no shirt."

Xander nodded. "The law was written a long time ago, and apparently it only requires that there be some kind of covering over the shoulders. So suspenders count, and tanks, but a halter top wouldn't. So I hope you didn't bring one of those," he said, laughing.

"Left all my tube tops at home," Oliver rejoined. He opened his backpack and pulled out what he had brought to wear. "Where should I change?"

Xander held his arms out wide. "This is it, my good man. You're in the dressing room."

Oliver shrugged. A longtime athlete in high school, he had continued to play club sports through college; locker rooms didn't bother him. He'd even had some gay teammates along the way, so that wasn't an issue either. It was a bit... intimate, given that this time it was just him and Xander. But Oliver filed that away in the "don't tell Millie" drawer and started taking off his shoes and socks.

He stood and pulled off his shirt and then his jeans. He reached for the shorts he had brought.

"Whoa there, chief," Xander cried. "You're not going out there wearing those, are you?"

Oliver was only wearing his boxer briefs, which he looked down at in confusion. "What's wrong with these?"

"They'd be fine if you were just hanging with friends or something."

"Actually, if I was just hanging with friends, my underwear wouldn't matter at all."

"Good point. But the theme of the whole place here is athletics, and the patrons want to see what they consider to be authentic athletic gear. So I always put on a jock and make sure the waistband sticks up a little out of my shorts."

"But a lot of athletes don't wear jocks—I always wear compression shorts myself."

"But it's not reality they're after, is it? They want what they think athletes wear, and what locker-room porn shows us wearing. Compression shorts are not nearly as sexy as a bare-ass jockstrap, right?"

"I'll, um, take your word for it." Oliver had never liked wearing a jockstrap, but for baseball and other sports where impact injuries were a risk, he had often been required to. "I haven't worn a jock in years."

"No worries. We happen to keep some on hand for just such occasions. Or for when someone's jock gets ripped off of them...."

"That happens?" Oliver froze.

Xander shook his head and waved the question away. "Just the once. And that was not the worst thing that happened that night, let me

tell you." He stood on the bench that ran in front of the lockers and
lifted a box from the shelf above them. "Let's see what we've got." He
set the box down on the floor. It bore a label of what was apparently a
store, though not one Oliver had ever heard of: Sporting Wood.

Xander briskly flipped open the box and starting rooting around
inside. "What size you take?"

"Medium, I guess?"

Xander looked quickly up at the front of Oliver's boxer briefs.
"Looks like more of an XL situation to me, but I guess the waist size is
most important."

Oliver felt the blood rushing to his cheeks.

"Here ya go. This one should do fine." Xander held aloft a white
jockstrap and tossed it to Oliver.

"Whoa, is this clean?" he asked as he let it bounce off him to the
floor.

"Of course," Xander said, hefting the box back up to the shelf
above the lockers. "They're samples we get from a store on the
Avenue. They wash them before they sell them to us. But all the same,
it might be a good idea for you to stop by there sometime and get
something you'll be more comfortable in. This one looks the part, but
the fit might not be perfect. Talk to Andy at Sporting Wood—he'll get
you set up."

Great, another guy scrutinizing my junk.

"Better get moving. The doors will be open in a minute." Xander
threw off his shirt and pants and was instantly naked.

Though Xander's back was to him, Oliver still hesitated changing
into the jock. He glanced at Xander quickly, and as the other man
pulled up his jock and shorts, he was struck by how perfectly developed
Xander's gluteals were. It was like he had customized his exercise
routine to develop a bubble butt that would bring in the tips. Oliver
looked quickly back to the floor as Xander turned around.

"Come on, buddy. Shake a leg," Xander ordered, flicking Oliver
playfully with tonight's ripped T-shirt, which he then pulled on.

Oliver took a deep breath and stuck his thumbs into the waistband
of his boxer briefs. He slid them down, trying to look as though the act
of getting naked in front of Xander wasn't freaking him out, which it
certainly was starting to. He fumbled a bit with the jock, getting one of
the straps wrapped around his leg and then having to hop a couple of

times to straighten it out. Finally, finally, he was able to pull it all the way on and no longer be naked.

"Wow," Xander said, looking frankly at Oliver's body. "You are in some kinda shape, man."

"Um, thanks?"

Xander glanced up and met Oliver's eyes. "You're going to do fine. You just have to get over the straight guy thing about having dudes look at you. With that body, and all the rest of it"—he gestured to Oliver's face and hair—"their eyes are going to be glued to you all night. And that's how it should be. You're going to clean up on tips. Just smile and try to look like you're not freaking out, okay?"

Oliver took a deep breath and tried to exhibit a calmness he certainly didn't feel.

"Now get the rest of the outfit on, and let's go."

Oliver pulled on his shorts and the cutoff T-shirt he thought would be the best for his debut: it still had sleeves but was cut off just below his pecs, leaving his abs completely uncovered.

"Fuck me," Xander whispered. He smiled widely at Oliver. "Just one tweak you need to make. Turn around."

Bewildered, Oliver turned around. Xander pulled the waistband of his shorts open and grabbed the wide white strap of the jock. He pulled it up a couple of inches, and then let the waistband snap back into place.

"There. Perfect," Xander said confidently, as if trying to hearten Oliver with his tone.

Oliver looked in the mirror and was stunned. He was dressed as if he were heading out for football practice, but in the context of what he was about to do, he felt like some kind of jock/slut hybrid. He turned to catch the back view and saw the white band of the jockstrap sticking up. It just looked kind of odd to him, but if Xander thought that was going to work for the patrons, he was willing to try it. He had to admit his ass looked pretty good in those tight shorts, though.

"Right?" Xander asked.

It hit Oliver like a ton of bricks. Millie was right; he and Xander both knew how good a tight male ass could look. Shit. He closed his eyes and tried to find his happy place.

"Time to go," Xander said, putting a gentle hand on Oliver's shoulder.

Oliver let himself be guided out of the back room and into the club, which had transformed back into the thumping, blue-sparkling place he had visited earlier in the week. He and Xander walked over to the bar, and Oliver ducked under to join Ulysses.

"Ready?" Ulysses asked. Then he did a quick up-and-down on Oliver. "Oh hell yeah, you're ready. Let's make some magic." He handed Oliver a laminated sheet. "Here's the house drink card. Specials are on the back. Look it over and ask me any questions before it gets too busy. 'Kay?"

Oliver nodded. The drink card listed all of the strange concoctions he and Millie had perused, plus many more that hadn't even been on the menu. But, as Millie had suggested, most of them were simply standard cocktails under new names, and sometimes with a slightly different top note of some kind.

You can do this, Ollie.

Patrons began to filter into the bar, and Ulysses was soon a blur of muscular motion as he both made drinks and showed Oliver around the bar. Within an hour they had settled into a comfortable rhythm, despite the fact that Ulysses had an awkward habit of touching Oliver on the hip when they passed each other in the narrow space behind the bar. At first Oliver thought it was simply to prevent collisions, but it became such a regular thing that he suspected it was intentional. At one point Oliver dodged out of the way, causing Ulysses's hand to miss his hip. The next time they crossed paths, Ulysses leaned in and murmured into Oliver's ear.

"Let me do the drive-by. It's good for tips." He looked at Oliver with his eyebrows raised. "You should try it too."

Oliver, startled, looked at Ulysses helplessly.

Ulysses smiled and patted him on the ass, then went along his way. The next time they crossed paths, Oliver took a deep breath and put his hand on Ulysses's waist as he reached around him to refill the bin of lemon slices. As he did so, Ulysses turned and said into his ear, "Nice. You're getting this."

Oliver looked around and saw no fewer than three patrons staring at the place where his hand met Ulysses's waist. Suddenly, all was clear. The customers were not allowed to touch the muscle behind the bar, but the bartenders could touch each other, and encouraging that vicarious thrill would bring them greater tips at the end of the day. Oliver had to admire the professional manner in which the staff separated the patrons from their cash, much to the delight of the patrons themselves.

Throughout the evening, Oliver focused so much on learning the routine and where everything was (in addition to washing and drying and restocking), he rarely even noticed the patrons who were drawn to the bar to watch him work. Every once in a while, he would catch a glimpse of an appreciative gaze, but Ulysses dealt with the customers, and Oliver only needed to smile and pretend to be flattered by the attention.

As the last patrons drifted out at closing time, Oliver busied himself with getting the bar reset for the next night. Finally he realized Ulysses was just standing there, watching him, Xander by his side. "What?" he asked them, noticing they hadn't moved for more than five minutes.

"We're just enjoying your work ethic, buddy," Ulysses said cheerfully.

"And the way your abs flex when you reach for a high shelf," Xander added.

Oliver instinctively brought his arms down to his sides. "How'd I do tonight?" he asked Ulysses, more as a way to change the subject than out of his desire to have a performance review. Still, it would be nice to know if he did okay his first time out.

"You're a natural," Ulysses replied. "I am very impressed. You did a great job with the stemmed glasses, and when you slapped my ass, the guys almost lost it—nice improv."

"It seemed like the right thing to do, since you were teasing me about not having a cherry ready for you."

"It was definitely the right thing to do. That one guy handed me a twenty after that, and I had to check and be sure it didn't have cum on it."

Oliver wrinkled his nose. "Does that happen?"

"Hasn't yet, but if you keep it up, I think it might."

"I think I'd let you take that tip, thanks," Oliver said wearily. "What else needs doing?"

Xander raised his hand.

"Yeah, not gonna happen," Oliver replied. "So, same time tomorrow?"

Ulysses nodded. "Come a little early and show me you know how to make the drinks. Then we'll split the bar. You'll take this third and

Xander's station, and I'll take the rest and the other two servers. Once you're up to speed, we'll split down the middle." He reached into his pocket and pulled out a wad of cash. He flipped through it quickly, then dealt out a pile of bills. "Here's your split for tonight," he said, pushing the pile over to Oliver.

Oliver picked up the bills and riffled quickly through them. "There's over two hundred dollars here," he said, amazed.

"Backs usually get ten percent, but I cut you in for a third because you worked it like a pro. Tomorrow, you keep whatever you get."

"Plus I'll slip you some," Xander said with a wink.

"Awesome," Oliver said, a bit queasily. "Well, I've been up since seven, so I'm going to head out. Great working with you guys." He headed toward the door.

"Oliver?" Xander called.

He turned back. "Yeah?"

"You might want to change before you hit the streets."

Oliver looked down and saw he still had his jock/slut outfit on. "Oh, right," he muttered. "Thanks." He headed back through the club to the dressing room.

As he pulled his stuff out of the locker, he once again caught sight of himself in the mirror. This time he saw a tired, sweat-stained football player, who had clearly had a rough practice. But he also held two hundred dollars in one hand. Did that make it all worthwhile? He'd have to think about it.

OLIVER RETURNED to Burn the next evening a little before opening time with another set of workout clothes and a new jockstrap he had acquired on the advice of Andy at Sporting Wood. Just as Xander had suggested, it was far more comfortable than the standard-issue model he had worn the night before; Andy had found one with a larger pouch in front to more capably accommodate Oliver's endowment.

In the locker room, he changed into the jock and his other clothes: a T-shirt with sleeves cut off and open almost all the way down the sides, and a pair of shiny basketball shorts that did absolutely nothing to conceal the full pouch of his jockstrap. He looked at himself in the mirror, then hiked up the wide strap at the back of his jock so it showed over the waistband. He nodded to his slutty reflection, then went out to join Ulysses at the bar.

"Looking hot, man," Ulysses said by way of greeting.

"Thanks," Oliver replied, still getting used to having other guys compliment him on his appearance. "How many pairs of suspenders do you own, anyway?"

Ulysses laughed. "I started out with one pair, given to me by a customer. He was a lawyer who had researched the regs on food and beverage service and discovered that suspenders counted as a shirt under the rules. So he brought me a pair—made a joke about it being pro bono, which to him seemed to mean that seeing my abs gave him a boner. Well, I'm pro-boner too, so I've worn suspenders every day since. Never bought a pair of my own, actually. I keep getting them as gifts, and now I've got like four or five dozen. These"—he stuck his thumbs under the wide, industrial-strength fabric—"were a gift from a couple of the hose handlers at Ladder Company Six. They were first responders when a customer tripped and knocked himself unconscious on something hard—the ass of one of our dancers. A couple days later they stopped by on their own time and brought me these. Nice guys, and they do know how to work a hose."

"Wow." This had quickly become Oliver's standard reply upon hearing something so over-the-top he had no idea what to think. It seemed to serve the purpose, in general.

Ulysses grinned, as if he knew exactly what was going on in the straight mind of his new coworker. "Okay, let's get started. Make me a Born That Way, a Bi-Furious, a Saint's Taint, a Cookie in the Middle, and a Dirty Altar Boy." Ulysses pointed to five spots in a line on the bar in front of him.

Oliver nodded. He'd watched carefully every time Ulysses made a new drink last night, and he had spent the day studying the drink card as intensely as he did any of his schoolwork. He confidently picked up five different shapes of glasses and got to work while Ulysses stocked the condiments bins. When he turned back around, there were six drinks standing in a neat little row, awaiting review.

"Wow, that was fast," Ulysses said, surprise in his voice. He stepped over to the row of drinks and picked up the first one. He held it up to the light, then sniffed it approvingly. He sipped a tiny amount and set it down. He repeated this ritual with the remaining drinks, nodding at each one. Finally he looked at the last drink in the line. "What's this?" he asked, looking at Oliver.

"Dancing Queen," Oliver casually replied.

Ulysses looked at him with hint of a grin and picked up the drink to review it like the others. Having tasted it, he set it down. "I've only made that once. For you. How did you do that?"

"Like I said, I grew up in a supper club. If anyone ever ordered anything unusual, I would work like hell to get it right. I have a pretty good taster when it comes to hooch."

"You almost nailed it. I used—"

"Grand Marnier instead of Cointreau. I know. But Cointreau seems like a more... agile choice, don't you think?"

Ulysses shook his head. "You're good, straight boy. You're good."

"That's a great compliment coming from you, sir," Oliver said with a bow to Ulysses.

"Now get these cleaned up and set your station. Doors open in fifteen." Ulysses winked at Oliver as he turned to set about his final prep.

Oliver knew the layout of the bar well enough from his experience the previous night, so he quickly had his area ready to go. The doors opened, and the first patrons began to filter in. Most of these made a beeline for the bar, and, as if they could sense the new talent in the house, most of them sat in Oliver's section. The patrons were a little older than those he had noticed while working the night before, but that was probably because he hadn't had time to even look up for the first few hours, while he figured out the bar. None of the customers were ancient, topping out at early thirties, and Oliver realized that bigger tips would likely come from slightly older customers.

He had expected the constant scrutinizing of his body to be a distraction while he attempted to make the right drink for the right patron, but he was surprised to find that not only did the appreciative gazes not bother him, he in fact found them to be a steadying force, a confidence-building foundation for his work. He prided himself on his precision and technique as a bartender, but on some level, he was aware he could decant tumblers of llama urine and the men at the bar would still smile, glance at his crotch, and knock the drinks back with a wink. It was sort of like working with a jockstrap safety net.

About two hours into the night, Xander came to him with a special request.

"Can you make me a Snowball, and float a little egg white on top, with a dash of salt?"

Oliver wrinkled his nose. "That sounds awful."

Xander shrugged. "I know, but he really gets off on it."

Already grabbing up the ingredients, Oliver was still puzzled. "Why the extra stuff on top?"

"Because he wants me to wank out some precum on his drink."

"Oh, man, that's… probably illegal? It kind of makes me a little sick too."

"He knows I don't really do it. But he likes to think I do, and I like the tips he gives me when he thinks I do. Win-win!"

Oliver caught a glimpse of himself in the mirror behind the bottles as he drizzled the egg white onto the cocktail—his mouth turned down in disgust, his eyes squinted up—and shook it off. If this is what the big tipper wanted, he would deliver. He handed the drink over with a grin. "Here ya go, one special Snowball." He set the drink on Xander's tray.

Xander was clearly delighted with what he found. "He is going to love this." He whipped his head around for a second and then turned back to Oliver. "Almost as much as he enjoyed watching you make it. He hasn't taken his eyes off you since he got here. I would be jealous, but as long as it gets his wallet lubed, I'm happy to have the help. How about I tell him the next one could have your own special ingredient?"

"I think that's the most disgusting offer anyone's ever made me," Oliver said. "Hell yeah." He grinned at Xander, delighted to be a team player.

Xander winked and hustled off with his tray to the back room as if he were going to add his secret sauce to the glass, and Oliver got back to work mixing and practicing his moves behind the bar. Throughout the night he got more creative on his passes with Ulysses, at one point turning his back to the other man as he slid by, causing their buttocks to rub across each other. Having nearly passed by, Oliver stopped and dodged back for a second, rubbing their asses together again. He heard Ulysses laugh, and a few "whoo-hoos" broke out among the patrons. He was getting this.

At the end of the night, after he had wiped down and reset the bar, Oliver grabbed his tip jar out from under the counter. The sheer number of bills it contained shocked him. He dumped it out onto the bar and sorted it quickly by denomination. There was more than five hundred dollars, and he was only working a third of the bar. He was still reeling from the count when Xander walked up.

"How'd ya do?"

Oliver shook his head slowly and gestured to the stack of bills. "I had no idea."

"That wearing tight clothes and flirting with guys could be so profitable?"

"Yeah, something like that."

"Well, I hate to pile on, but," Xander said and fished a roll of bills out of his pocket. "Everyone was quite pleased with your work and the manner in which you did it." He handed Oliver two bills.

Oliver looked at the money Xander had placed in his hand. Hundred-dollar bills. Two of them. "Seriously?"

Xander nodded. "Nice move, by the way, putting the top-shelf stuff on the actual top shelf. I think half of them ordered the premium vodka because they knew your shirt would ride up when you reached for it. That alone pushed up the tabs by, like, double."

"Just trying to maximize customer satisfaction," Oliver said with a grin. He turned back to call to Ulysses. "All set, chief?"

"Looks great," Ulysses said as he looked the bar up and down. "We can split down the middle tomorrow."

"Thanks," Oliver replied. "So, is Sunday a little slower?"

"Oh hell no," Xander said with a laugh. "Fewer dancing boys and more middle-aged closet cases from the sticks who get all Godded up in the morning and come here to drink themselves into another week of denial. It's not as much fun to look at, but in terms of tips, it's the pot of gold at the end of this great rainbow we live on."

Ulysses rolled his eyes. "He gets poetic when no one takes him home on Saturday."

"Fuck you, my good man. So happens I have a regular customer waiting for me outside. He'd be the one in the big new Beamer, if you must know."

Oliver was stunned. "You're just going to… go with him? Is that safe?"

Xander waved a dismissive hand at Oliver's concern. "He and I go way back. Like a month."

"And you're certain you're not going to end up in little pieces in his freezer?"

"Someone's been bingeing on *Dexter*," Xander said with a dramatic sigh. "This is not my first rodeo, mister. I know the drill: got his full online profile, let a friend know where I was going, went to a public place the first time. You don't have to worry, Mom."

"Sorry. This is just all so new to me."

"Yeah, it's a strange new world now that men have to decide how much to trust the other men they meet for sex. Not like women haven't had to navigate that minefield for, like, ever." He smiled ironically and went to change into his "street" clothes.

Oliver laughed. No wonder Millie and Xander had gotten along so well.

THE FIRST week at Burn was a success for Oliver as he easily shouldered the expanded responsibility of handling half the bar. The tips, as Xander had predicted, were even higher on Sunday than they had been on Saturday. The club was closed on Monday and Tuesday, and Oliver used the time to work ahead in his classes so he could handle the late shifts at the bar without falling behind. The traffic, and the tips, ramped up from Wednesday through Saturday, and Oliver looked forward to Sunday, as much for the crowd as for the tips; the Sunday patrons were a more sedate lot, and even though that was likely the result of existential depression, they were much more like the patrons Oliver had grown up with back at his parents' supper club.

About an hour into his Sunday shift, Oliver noticed a new face breaking through the crowd to get at an open stool. He smiled and laid down a napkin before the new man.

"What'll you have?" Oliver asked. He had developed the habit of soliciting the first insinuation so it didn't hit him by surprise later. The patrons who sat at his bar had seemingly endless reserves of salacious requests, all of which Oliver would respond to the same way: a smile as if he'd never heard such talk before in his life, a shake of the head to let them know that his ass was not, in fact, on the menu, and the drink list with the admonition to limit their appetites to what was printed thereon. It worked, and it worked well. And Oliver never had to be the first one to flirt, which allowed him to retain at least the semblance of straightness.

But this guy was different.

"Glenlivet, splash of water" came the reply, in tones Oliver could only describe as "sober."

Oliver didn't even think before replying. "That's my drink," he said with a grin.

Oh, shit. Did I just flirt first?

The man smiled. "You have good taste in alcohol as well as clothes," he said, looking down Oliver's torso to where his half shirt left his abs bare, then back up to his eyes. "Will you have one with me?"

Oliver shook his head. "A little too early in the shift for that," he said, then turned to grab the bottle.

Shit, shit, shit, you just told him you'd drink with him later. Get it together, Ollie.

He handed over the drink and then watched to be sure it was well received. The man tipped it to Oliver in thanks, then sipped.

"Perfect," the man said.

"Excellent," Oliver said, genuinely happy to have pleased him. He turned to his other patrons and to Xander, all of whom were apparently in the throes of desperate thirst.

Oliver watched his Scotch drinker over the next hour; the man didn't talk to anyone and only seemed to look at Oliver. It was a little disconcerting. Finally his glass was nearing empty, and Oliver stopped by.

"'Nother?" he asked.

The man nodded. "Join me?"

As he poured, Oliver put on the facial expression he called "flattered deflection," which he had been practicing in the mirror all week. It mostly involved smiling and looking down, like a child who's been offered candy his mom won't let him have. "Gotta stay sharp," he said.

"You're worth waiting for," said the man, smiling, as he took the tumbler from Oliver.

This struck Oliver as a far more personal statement than the ones he normally received. If a man complimented him on his abs, or wished his ass were on the menu, Oliver could take that in stride. He did, after all, work hard on his abs and his ass. But this, this estimation of his worth—as a man? as a human being?—was unlike anything else he'd heard on the job so far. He had no idea how to respond to it.

"Thank you," he said and immediately regretted it. He thought he should have gone for something sharp like "you're going to be waiting a long time," but upon immediate reflection, he decided that would have been far too harsh. He simply turned away from the man and tried to get his rhythm back.

"You okay?" Xander asked as Oliver made up an order for him.

"Yeah, why?"

"You just seemed a little… off? Just for a second. Thought maybe you'd remembered it was your mom's birthday or something, and you forgot to send a card."

"There's just this…." There was no way to explain it to Xander. "It was nothing. I'm good." He smiled and passed the drinks over the bar.

Xander smirked as if he didn't believe a word of it and went back out onto the floor with his full tray.

The evening wore on, in its subdued Sunday way, until close to closing time. Oliver's Scotch drinker was still on his stool, still not taking his eyes off Oliver, still not talking to anyone else.

"Last one?" Oliver asked him.

"If you'll let me buy you one," the man replied.

There were no other customers in Oliver's part of the bar, and Xander was closing out his tabs, most of the patrons who had been at his tables having found their way into the back of each other's cars already. If excuses were what Oliver was looking around for, he found none.

He nodded to the man and picked up two clean Old Fashioned glasses. He poured a healthy two fingers of the amber spirit into each, then added a small amount of mineral water. He slid one of the glasses over to the man and lifted one himself. They touched glasses and took a sip.

The man set his drink down. "I'm James," he said, extending his hand.

"Oliver." He took James's hand and shook it warmly. Over the past week, he'd had patrons' hands on his arm, on his abs, and once on his ass, but this was the first time one had extended the usual human courtesy of a handshake. It actually felt nice.

"Come here often?" Oliver said, attempting levity.

James smiled, then broke into a gentle laughter. "My first time," he said shyly. "How about you?"

"Been working here all of two weeks," Oliver said, taking another sip of Scotch and feeling the welcome burn in his chest.

"How do you like it?" James asked.

"The people are pretty great, and the tips are epic," Oliver replied. "Never in a million years thought I'd be working at a place like this."

"Well, I think you're doing a great job. But I have this feeling that being a bartender isn't your ultimate ambition in life."

Oliver smiled. "You're pretty good," he said with a nod. "I'm in med school, and working here is going to help me be the first doctor in history to start his career with no loans."

"That's amazing. Didn't think that was possible."

"I've had some help with it, actually. The people in my hometown—little place in the mountains upstate—really need a family doctor, so they took up a collection to put me through school. So my tuition's paid, though I still have to buy supplies and pay lab fees and stuff, and rent comes out of my pocket, but at least I don't have to worry about paying for the actual classes."

"So once you get your degree…?"

"I'll be heading back to set up a general practice in my hometown. By the time that happens, I figure my mom and dad will need some help, and it'll be nice for me to be close to them. They were a little older when they had me, so they're kinda getting up there."

"Wow," James said quietly. "That's really great. I don't think I've ever met anyone whose goal was to go back home and save the town."

Oliver laughed modestly. "All I'd be doing is delivering babies and scolding people not to eat so much. But someone's got to do it."

"And will the town welcome you back with the man of your dreams on your arm?"

The question caught Oliver by surprise. They'd been having a normal conversation, the kind he would have with someone who wasn't paying him for wearing half a shirt and smiling prettily, and then suddenly things curved a bit. But Oliver smiled as gracefully as he could and got back into character. "No man of my dreams, I'm afraid. With school and working, I just haven't managed to meet anyone." He watched James's face to gauge whether this little dodge had worked.

James smiled, and Oliver knew he was off the hook.

"I find that hard to believe. But perhaps your luck is changing," he said with a wink.

And just like that, he was right back on the hook.

"I should really get home," James said. "Like you, I live in a small town, and people will talk if I'm out all night." He stood and laid three hundred-dollar bills on the bar. "I hope I'll see you again, Oliver."

"I'll be here," Oliver said, cursing himself silently as he did so. He just couldn't stop leading this guy on.

James smiled and nodded, as if they'd decided to meet again. He turned and made his exit.

Oliver stood and watched him go, completely befuddled by what had happened. He was still watching the door long after it closed behind James when Xander came up to the bar.

"Well, that ended abruptly. I kind of thought you were working a thing there, but then he left. Unless," Xander said, pointing an accusing finger at Oliver, "you arranged to meet him later, didn't you? You sly dog."

"What?" Oliver said, completely confused. "No, that's not—"

"Oh, I'm so straight," Xander said in a mocking tone. "What am I going to do if a *man* hits on me?" He dropped his voice and looked conspiratorially at Oliver. "Now I see what you're going to do. You're gonna work him like his dick's an ATM."

Oliver straightened up. "We had a conversation, that's all. He wanted to buy me a drink." He tried to say this with all of the dignity he could remember once having. Then he reached out and swept up the three bills on the bar, and his dignity evaporated once again. *Shit.*

"Mmm-hmmm." Xander handed Oliver some additional money, a portion of his take for the night, and smiled knowingly at him. "Night, Oliver."

CHAPTER FIVE
REFLECTIONS

OLIVER STALKED into his apartment just before three in the morning and threw his backpack on the couch before collapsing next to it. He took a deep breath, then two, and reached into his pack for the wad of tips he had stowed there for the walk home. Over the week his nightly take had been in the two- to four-hundred-dollar range per night. Tonight, he realized with growing dismay as the stack of bills rose higher, he had cleared more than seven hundred. And three of those came from James, who had already settled his tab before laying his tip on the bar. In all, his second week at Burn had netted him nearly two thousand dollars in tips alone. He got up, shaking his head at the wad of money in his hands, and walked over to his desk.

There was a stack of bank deposit envelopes sitting in a tray on the side of the neatly organized desktop, and he opened one that was already grossly distended with the previous days' tips. He added Sunday's take to the pile and tried to get the flap on the envelope to close; it refused. He set it back in the tray, making a note to himself to put a quarter of the deposit into the separate account he maintained for tax payments. Every dollar he earned from tips would be accounted for, and he paid his estimated taxes on time and in full.

Nearly two thousand dollars. He hadn't worked any harder at Burn than he had at the Tornado Room, or at his parents' supper club for that matter, and yet he had "earned" a sum far more than he would have gotten at either of those jobs in an entire month of full-time work. All that was different was that he had done the work wearing tight shorts, a shredded shirt, and a jockstrap that stuck out when he reached over to set a drink before a patron.

Was that really worth all of this money?

He walked into his bedroom and kicked off his shoes and socks. He flipped his shirt over his head and tossed it into the hamper in the corner, where his socks had previously landed. Jeans were next, wadded and shot neatly into the hamper from across the room. Three points. His boxer briefs joined them for another two.

The sliding doors of Oliver's closet consisted of large mirrors, which he had covered as best he could with posters, note cards, and anything else he could make stick to the glass surface. The very idea of a large reflective surface next to his bed seemed awkward to him, and he did his level best to avoid seeing his reflection as he went about his daily business. But tonight—or rather, this morning—with the riches his body could bring him sitting in a deposit envelope on his desk, he had a different reaction to seeing his own reflection. Between a poster advertising a truly awful local band and a sticky note reminding him to get the tires on his car rotated, Oliver caught sight of the deep V-cut of his lower torso as he turned to go into his bathroom. This was a scrap of flesh Oliver was intensely proud of, in that it required not only a strong transversus abdominis, but also a very low percentage of body fat. The V-cut was Oliver's commitment to fitness made visible.

Was that what the patrons of Burn were paying for? His dedication to fitness?

He stepped back from the mirror to get a better view but could only see a sliver of his body between the posters and other bits and scraps stuck to the mirror. Turning side to side, he could get no better vantage point.

Well, fuck this.

Maybe it was the late hour, maybe it was his vague feeling of being willingly exploited, maybe it was something deep inside him that was afraid to admit having men stare at him was fulfilling in some way he'd never imagined. Whatever it was, something made him walk up to the mirrored closet doors and tear down the poster that blocked his view. And the one next to that. And all of the sticky notes from last semester's clinical epidemiology course. And all of the rest of it.

Oliver stood before the large mirror, naked. He saw himself naked all the time, of course, and doing so now wouldn't help him figure out what he needed to know. He walked over to the clothes hamper, pulled out Saturday night's work clothes, and disentangled the jockstrap from the shorts. This jock was a sleek bright red number that Andy had recommended for him; it had proven both comfortable and profitable. He stepped into it and pulled it on.

Walking over to the mirror again, he watched how his body moved, how what was covered by the jockstrap was implied rather than displayed. He turned to look at it from behind, how his pale buttocks were framed by the red straps. Taking a step back, he sat on the bed, then leaned back. The red pouch dominated the view, and it seemed to be growing a bit. Oliver looked down in surprise. The mesh of the jockstrap was distending as his penis inexplicably grew.

What the fuck was that about?

Oliver looked back into the mirror and gasped as the head of his cock protruded from the pouch. Was he really getting turned on by the sight of himself in a jockstrap? The very idea short-circuited any rational faculty he had left, and he couldn't think about it clearly. That's why there was no reason, no reason at all, why reaching down and touching his erection made any sense. But it did feel amazingly good. Oliver watched himself stroke the head of his cock, and the increasing portion of the shaft that was emerging from the pouch. A drop of precum appeared, and he rubbed it around his cockhead with his thumb. The groan that emanated from his own throat surprised him. He looked at his face in the mirror and saw his cheeks were flushed, his eyes half-closed in pleasure.

He put one foot up on the bed and noticed the straps of the jockstrap as they met the pouch down between his legs. The hidden flesh of his ass was obscenely exposed, nestled there between the straps, and as dirty as it seemed, all he could think about was what his customers at Burn would give to have this view. As if their eyes were on him now, he roughly pushed the fabric of the jockstrap pouch aside; the rest of his cock and large balls flopped heavily into view. His penis was fully erect, rock hard, and his balls hot and loose. He grabbed and tugged at his nuts with his left hand while he spat sloppily into his right. His hand glossed with spit and precum, he gripped his cock and began to stroke it vigorously, almost angrily, as if the completion of orgasm would reveal something to him, something important about the strange turn his life had taken. He stared at his cock in the mirror, experiencing it both as a part of his body and as a voyeuristic vision. The motion of his hand, practiced over and over again on a daily basis since the age of twelve, was rendered unfamiliar by the reversal of the mirror. He watched it as if it were someone else's hand on his cock.

Someone else's hand.

How long had it been?

How much he wanted to have someone else's hand on his cock, he could not have anticipated before this moment, before watching it in his own closet mirror. The hand that gripped him was surely his, but it looked unlike any part of his body. It was large, it was strong, it demanded his orgasm as payment for its labors. It was a man's hand, and it was on his cock, milking it, urging it toward the goal Oliver and his reflection shared. He would come. There was no way to avoid it. He would come because the man in the mirror wanted him to, would not stop until he did.

The man in the mirror. It was a man.

Oliver's instinct was to shut it down, to look away, to begin fevered construction of a rationalization that would render the stroker in the mirror female, the entire exercise somehow heterosexual, normal. But he lay transfixed by his reflection, watching its insistent stroking as if it really were someone else who handled him. And that someone else was, and would always be, a man.

A man would make him come. A man.

Oliver cried out as if he'd been stung. But the electric shock surged through his groin, and it brought with it the orgasm he needed, he feared, he both wanted and wanted to forget.

He watched it come. In the mirror, he saw the contraction that the other Oliver, the one on the bed, felt. He felt it and saw it, and which one he was experiencing and which he was watching he had no idea, but he knew it was not him who stroked and wouldn't stop stroking. That was the man in the mirror. He rolled onto his back and watched the arcs of white blast up into the air and then land heavily on his chest, at his throat, on his cheek. Still the man stroked him. He shot more than a dozen times—he lost the ability to count any higher—and still the man stroked. He was empty and starting to twitch, and the man only stopped when Oliver summoned up his courage to look him in the eye. Once their eyes found each other, the man's hand relaxed and released his wet, red, and softening cock. It splatted against his lower belly, exhausted. Oliver was exhausted. The man in the mirror was elated: he had gotten what he wanted, had wanted for a long time. He smiled, and Oliver smiled back.

This is insane.

Oliver sat up with a start and saw in the mirror that he was obscenely glazed with puddles of wet that began to run in white ribbons down his body. The red jockstrap, pushed off to the side, was flecked with white as well. He was a mess—on the outside too.

He walked into the bathroom still wearing the jock. He turned on the shower, waited a moment for the water to warm up. When it was almost unbearably hot, he stepped in and let the water run down his body and the jockstrap as well, rinsing the bitter evidence of his bizarre release off and down the drain. He soaked in the shower for a long time—when he finally felt halfway clean, the light of dawn was starting to make its presence known through the small window above the shower. Halfway clean was as well as he was going to do, he realized, so he rinsed off and then dried off and got ready for bed. Walking tiredly into the bedroom, he grabbed an extra sheet from the drawer under the bed and tacked it to the doorframe of the closet, completely obscuring the mirror and any chance the man who had molested him would return. He was going to be alone tonight, no matter what.

How much longer he could stand to be alone he had no idea.

THE NEXT week was midterms, and Oliver got very little sleep on Monday and Tuesday as he crammed in all of the studying he didn't have time to do while tending bar in tight clothing. The tests went well, though, which Oliver found encouraging. If he could balance out his studies and this job, he would be able to choose one of the internships he had in mind. They didn't pay much, but at this rate, he wouldn't need to bring in any money during the summer.

On Thursday night Oliver overheard a spirited conversation between two patrons on a topic he happened to know something about. One was describing to the other his struggle with an inflamed tendon in his arm and was demonstrating some of the supposedly therapeutic movements that had been recommended to him by a series of YouTube videos. Oliver could see immediately that the contortions the man was demonstrating would only lead to further complications, and he mentioned that fact as casually as he could.

"You should be careful not to overextend when you do that stretch," Oliver said lightly. "That could lead to inflammation of the flexor as well as the pain you're already dealing with."

The man looked at him, then smiled. "Thanks, cutie. Are you a personal trainer as well as a bartender?"

"Actually, I'm—"

"Super hot is what you are," the other said. "Which gym do you work at? I might want to schedule something—you can show me your flexor or whatever."

"Wouldn't that be hot?" agreed the first man. "Maybe we could get a group rate!"

Oliver looked from one to the other, aghast at not being listened to. "No, really," he said, "I'm studying to be a doctor."

"Ooh, that's better than playing personal trainer," the first man said.

"I'd play doctor with you anytime, hon," the second chimed in.

Oliver stood silent. He had never been so completely ignored before. He was used to not only being one of the smartest people in the room, but having everyone else around him acknowledge that fact. But a quick glance down showed him the reason: he was dressed like a jock/slut, and people like that—like him—didn't get listened to. He shook his head and got back to his work.

This dynamic was repeated several times over the week; Oliver noticed every time he was ignored, or dismissed, or told that he was being cute when he mentioned anything more complex than what went into a Dirty Altar Boy. Perhaps it had been this way all along, but he was keenly aware of it now and felt the injustice of it every time it happened. It happened a lot. Oliver did his best to set these feelings aside as he had been hired, after all, to make drinks, not to engage intellectually with the patrons. He sucked it up and coached himself to continue flirting brainlessly. He mostly succeeded.

Sunday saw the return of James the Scotch drinker. Oliver had to admit he was pleased to see him as their conversation was far more comfortable to him than the relentless flirt-and-run act he was having to perform with all the other patrons.

Oliver saw him making his way to the bar and had his drink ready for him as he sat down.

"Why, thank you, sir," James said warmly, taking the drink from Oliver's hand. He seemed genuinely pleased.

"My pleasure, sir," returned Oliver, enjoying the formality of being called something other than "cutie."

"Do you think you might be able to join me for a drink later?" James asked with a smile even Oliver had to admit was kind of sexy.

Oliver, fearing he would say something too flirty, simply smiled and went about his work.

As the night wore down, Oliver returned to James, again his last patron, and made two drinks. They touched glasses and sipped.

"So, Oliver," James said in a hearty voice, "how was your week?"

"Midterms went well, and the job gets easier every day. And how was yours?"

James tipped his head in a so-so motion. "My job is a bit stressful," he said. "It's rather like yours, actually. My success depends on making people happy with every move I make."

"But you probably get to wear actual clothes," Oliver said with a chuckle, looking down at his torn T-shirt and visible jockstrap elastic. He looked at James's shirt, which he had not previously noted was finely tailored indeed. He had collected three hundred dollars from the man a week ago as a tip on a bar tab that totaled less than a hundred, so the fact that he had money should not have been a surprise. But the casual way he wore his wealth was a new thing for Oliver, whose hometown boasted no such dandies among its population.

"That I do," James agreed. "Suits and starch and shiny shoes that make my feet feel like they're being mauled by bears. It's pretty great." He sighed. "But it's what I must do."

Oliver nodded. "No one's going to pay us for sitting around *not* looking pretty," he said with a laugh.

"That's the irony," James replied once the sound of his deep laughter faded. "My father started a company back in the eighties that he pretty much gave his life over to. Sold it for a large sum to an Asian consortium about ten years ago, and then he and my mother retired after working their entire lives to build that company. First day of retirement, their plane hits a mountain outside Jakarta, and they're gone. Left me with more money than I know how to spend and not a damn thing to do. It's not like I inherited the family business or anything, because the family business had already been sold."

"I'm really sorry to hear about your parents," Oliver commiserated. "That must have been rough."

James nodded. "It sounds weird to say, since I was their only child, but we weren't all that close. They had worked so hard on the business that we really didn't spend much time together, and I was still in college when they died, so I never had a hand in the business myself. After I graduated, I sat and looked at the bank balance for a year or two and got really bored."

"So what do you do now?"

"I did what second-generation money has always done. I went into politics. Started out on the city council, to which I'm pretty sure I was only elected because the biggest park in town has my family's name on it—my parents trying to 'give back'—and then became mayor, and now I'm the county executive. Super glamorous, right?"

Oliver nodded, impressed. "Must be a pretty progressive place. I have a feeling the folks in my hometown wouldn't be so willing to elect someone—" Oliver had no idea how he could possibly finish this sentence without causing offense. He did the only thing he could do. "—like… us." He felt the wrongness of that word thickening in his chest, but there it was, and it couldn't be unsaid.

Why exactly it made Oliver so queasy to say "us" he didn't understand right away, but on a moment's reflection, it came to him. It was one thing to dress like a jock/slut and let the patrons project their locker-room fantasies on him. But it was another to actively portray himself and his patrons as an "us," as if they all faced the same kinds of challenges in life. It felt… "deceitful" was the only word he could come up with. Whatever he called it, it wasn't a good feeling.

James rolled his eyes grimly, but to Oliver's relief, he let the sentiment hang in the air and then dissipate. Oliver took another drink, mainly to give him something to do with his mouth other than saying anything else stupid.

"Can you I tell you a secret?" James inquired of the amber liquid in his glass.

Oliver was startled by this confidence. After a week of having people think he was too cute to be worthy of actual conversation, the notion of James trusting him with a secret was deeply gratifying. He seemed to be the only one in the place who could see through the trashy outfit and recognize the person underneath.

"Of course," Oliver said seriously, setting his drink down. "I may dress like a slutty football player, but I'm a pretty stand-up guy in general."

James smiled. "I figured that from the whole med school to small-town-doctor thing." He looked down at his drink again. "It's just that"—he looked up, and gestured vaguely at the club—"this is not who I am."

Now *that* Oliver could relate to. "What do you mean?"

"Back home, I'm a completely different person."

Oliver nodded. This is what Xander had been talking about; closeted guys from outside the city who come in on Sundays for a walk on the gay side.

"Do you ever look at your life and think, how did I get here?" James asked, still staring hard at his dwindling Scotch.

Every fucking minute I'm at this job, Oliver didn't say. "I do."

"The people in my county, the ones who elected me, they would...." He shook his head.

"What would they do?" Oliver asked, leaning on the bar, closer to James so he could speak whatever this uncomfortable thing was more quietly. It was a trick that had always worked on the reticent customers at the supper club.

"They saw me here? They would run me out of town—out of the state." James sighed and rubbed his eyes.

Oliver got it now. "Pretty conservative place, is it?"

James gave a half nod and rolled his eyes. "You could say that."

Rising back up to his full height, Oliver crossed his arms and looked hard at his customer. "If you have all the money you need, why would you stay where people have that kind of power over you? Why not just go and be someplace where you don't have to... hide?"

A sad grin worked its way across James's face. "I wish it were that simple. I really do." He knocked back the last of the Scotch in his glass. "One of the things you learn as you get older is that it's not always possible to just up and leave if things aren't working out. Sometimes you have to stick to it and try to make it work. Even if you can't see how it could possibly work out.... Ever." He set his glass back down on the bar and took a deep breath. "And on that cheerful note...," he said, extending a hand to Oliver.

Oliver took his hand, but he gripped it tight and pulled James in a little closer. "Nothing, no matter what it is, no matter how huge it seems, is worth a life spent being someone other than who you are." He looked into James's eyes with an intensity that startled them both.

"Thank you, Oliver," James whispered. "Thank you." He shook Oliver's hand and turned to leave. Halfway to the door he turned again, paused, and then nodded slowly. "Thank you." He turned back and left the club.

Oliver watched him go, wondering again why that sad, Scotch-drinking man got to him more than any of the other patrons of the club. Perhaps, he reasoned, it was the same thing that made him choose general practice as his area of medicine; he liked talking to people about real things, things that mattered to them.

This viewpoint made him feel better about picking up the three bills James had left on the counter. A little better, anyway.

TUESDAY NIGHT Millie invited Oliver over for dinner. They hadn't seen each other in a couple of weeks as Oliver's schedule was pretty tight, what with his courses and his five-nights-a-week work schedule at Burn.

"So you found the only other guy in the world who goes to a hot gay club and from its ridiculous menu, orders a grandpa drink. Good for you."

They were talking about James, of course. Oliver hadn't meant to, but he started to almost without thinking about it. Millie had been quite entertained by his tales of handsy patrons, but he had been drawn to the topic of James almost gravitationally. He didn't know why.

"Do you want to know what I think?"

"No." Of course he did. That was probably why he had drifted to talking about James. As annoying as Millie could be, she had a sense about people—a sense he had come to trust.

"I think you've got a closeted politician on your hands, the next scandal waiting to happen. We'll see him on the news in a month or two, tearfully apologizing to voters for never having gotten around to mentioning that he likes musicals, dancing at gay clubs, and taking it up the butt."

"How refreshingly cynical of you." Oliver shook his head at Millie, but he had thought the same thing himself.

"Well, let's see who we're dealing with," she said, grabbing her tablet from the kitchen counter.

"What are you doing?" Oliver asked.

"We're going to find your new friend," she said lightly, as she swiped and typed. "There aren't that many counties in the state. How long could it take to find a list of county executives?"

"I figured that's what you were doing. What I don't know is—why?"

She looked at him like she thought he must surely be kidding. "Don't you want to know?"

"Not particularly. If he wants to tell me something, that's fine. But why would I want to go stalking him?"

"We're not stalking him," Millie said innocently, but she continued her feverish searching. "We're just gathering information that might be useful."

"First, *we're* not doing anything. You are. And what you're doing is the same thing you do when you have a crush on some new guy at the deli counter."

"Shut up about the deli counter. Can I help it if they keep hiring the cutest sausage handlers?"

"Well, you go ahead, but I'm not interested." Oliver stood and picked up their dinner dishes. "I'll be in the kitchen."

He was washing the last plate when Millie, still sitting at the table, gasped.

"What?" he asked, having forgotten what she was doing.

"You said James, right?"

He nodded.

"You have got to see this," she said, her voice strangely taut.

He put down the dish and wiped his hands, then walked back to the table and looked over her shoulder. There, on her screen, was James. He was standing next to a woman at a podium of some kind, frozen in the act of making a speech. Millie clicked on the frame and it came to life.

"…that's why I consider it my great honor to dedicate this new public library. All the people of this county will benefit from its resources, as I know my wife Stella and I shall." With that his wife cut the big red ribbon with giant scissors, and the video abruptly ended.

"Did he say…?" Oliver said slowly.

"Wife. Yep, he said wife." Millie looked up at Oliver looming over her. "Looks like your new buddy James—Mr. James Buchanan Whitford, if you please—is leading a more exciting life than you thought."

Oliver stared at the screen for a long moment. "Huh."

"Yeah, huh," Millie agreed.

Then Oliver shrugged. "I guess that's what he meant when he said the people back home would be surprised to find him at Burn."

Millie squinted at the screen. "I think the missus would be surprised indeed. She looks like the type who would expect a certain obedience at home. On the plus side, he's really cute. Doesn't look a day over thirty."

"Poor guy," Oliver said as he turned to take the towel back to Millie's kitchen.

"Why do you say that?" she asked.

"He sounded so sad. Like he was trapped in a life he didn't want to lead."

"I have to think most politicians are trapped in a life they don't want to lead. But that's the choice they make when they go into it."

Oliver shrugged. "So now I know James's secret. I still don't know how that helps anybody."

"What I find about secrets is that there will almost always come a time when you are glad you know them."

"I hope you're wrong. Just this once, I hope you're wrong."

Chapter Six
The Glass Closet

The week, his third at Burn, passed in what he would now consider an uneventful manner. Prior to taking this job, he would have considered running a gantlet of sex-crazed men who tipped better the more he flirted with them to have been anything but uneventful, but this was his new normal, and he was doing fine with it.

Sunday came, and with it came James for the third week in a row. Oliver had his drink waiting for him, next to the stool on which he had placed a "Reserved" sign before the doors opened. James seemed flattered by the attention, and then he sipped his drink and his eyebrows shot up.

"Well, this is a treat," he said delightedly.

"It seemed like you might need a little something special," Oliver said. "It's the twenty-one year. My treat."

James blushed and stammered. "Well, um… thank you, Oliver. This is the nicest thing anyone's done for me in a long time." He lifted the glass in salute and took another slow sip.

Oliver smiled, deeply pleased to have made James happy. He turned back to his other patrons and their silly drinks, remembering to brush up against Ulysses as he passed and tease Xander when he came to the bar to place his order since the patrons seemed to enjoy their playful sparring.

About halfway through the shift, Gavin made a rare appearance at the bar. Normally he circulated around the club at the beginning of the evening and disappeared into the back shortly thereafter. Tonight, however, he called Oliver over.

"The floor is dead, and we don't have any dancers here tonight," he said into Oliver's ear over the din of the music. "Ulysses can take the bar for an hour or so—can you go dance? Get some guys out there? I'll make up your tips."

"You want me to... dance?" Oliver figured he must have misheard.

"You're pretty much a legend when it comes to dancing, and if we don't get something going out there soon, we're going to lose the party boys. If we lose them, then the closet cases have nothing to look at, and they'll go too. We might as well close up now."

Oliver was stunned. Before he could think of some way to object, however, his native work ethic kicked in, and he simply nodded.

"Excellent. Xander will help you get ready." Gavin tipped his head to Xander, who was waiting by the passage to the back room.

"Get ready?" Oliver asked, but Gavin had already hustled away. He walked past Ulysses on his way out from behind the bar. "You gonna be okay for an hour?" he asked in passing.

"Pretty quiet tonight. Make us proud, man."

Oliver shrugged helplessly but kept walking. He stopped at James's place on his way out. "They need me over there for an hour or so," he said, looking at the dance floor. "Ulysses will take care of you until I'm back."

"I don't think he's up to your standard," James said with a wink. "I'll be fine until you come back to me."

James's sentiment was far too intimate, and Oliver only realized that when he was halfway to the back room. Up until then, he had simply been touched by its sweetness. What was wrong with him?

"Come on, let's go," Xander said as he hustled Oliver down the hallway.

"What do we need to do?" Oliver asked as he jogged to keep up. "I don't understand."

They burst through the door into the changing room. "If you're going to be a dancer, you need to dress like one. Take everything off."

Oliver just stared at him. "Wait, what kind of dancing am I doing here?"

Xander laughed. "Don't worry, we'll get you decently covered before you hit the floor. Or at least close to decent." Xander rummaged through a bin and pulled out a piece of sparkly blue fabric that was far too small to cover more than Oliver's kneecap. He held it up and waved it about. "Strip! Let's move!"

Oliver took off his shirt and shorts, and stood before Xander in just his jockstrap.

"It's all gotta go, buddy. These aren't big enough to cover the strap, and the jock look isn't really what we're going for on the dance floor."

How the fuck did I end up doing this? Oliver pulled the jockstrap off and was once again naked. At work. *Fuck.*

Xander handed him the stretchy, sparkly fabric and stepped back to let Oliver wrestle with it while he watched. Rather intently, Oliver thought.

He put his feet through the leg holes, and pulled the shorts up his legs. He struggled a bit to get them over his quads—clearly dancing boys skipped leg day on a regular basis. Once he had them wrestled up to his crotch, he was able to stretch them almost up to his hip bones. But just almost—they rode low on his hips, and the V-shaped muscles of his lower torso were completely exposed.

Oliver turned and looked at his reflection in the mirror. He looked ridiculous with the outline of his cock clearly visible. Then he noticed Xander was looking into the mirror as well.

"Well, this looks obscene," Oliver said, deadpan.

"You should see it from the back," Xander replied, his voice hushed.

Oliver turned around and saw that the sparkly shorts were not quite up to the task of covering the muscles of his ass. A significant portion of his cheeks rose over the waistband of the shorts like two honeydews peeking out the top of a grocery bag. He tried to pull them up a bit, but this decreased his ball room to a painful degree, so he relented on that idea immediately. He shrugged to Xander.

"Okay, so there's nothing we can do in the back," Xander said. "Maybe if you tuck in the front?"

Oliver looked at him, dumbfounded. "You want me to try what?"

"Tuck your dick down over your balls. It might give you a cleaner line?"

He shook his head, still in the throes of disbelief that this was happening to him. But he took a deep breath and reached into the shorts. He grabbed hold of his cock and pointed it down, then looked in the mirror.

Xander shook his head. "It still looks like you're smuggling a Carmen Miranda hat. Two mangoes and a banana, cha-cha-cha."

Oliver looked helplessly at him.

"But we gotta go. You look… amazing. You're going to have them falling at your feet, buddy."

"Great. Just what I want." Oliver took a last look in the mirror and tried to instantly forget what he had seen. It would be better for him to just pretend he was wearing the comparatively dignified attire he wore for tending bar. He followed Xander back out to the club.

As they approached the dance floor, Xander leaned in close.

"Go get 'em," he shouted into Oliver's ear. Then Xander laid a hand on his right buttock and pushed him forward.

There were only a half-dozen guys on the dance floor when Oliver made his appearance, nearly stumbling from Xander's shove. The DJ immediately put on a heavy new beat, and the blue pin spots swiveled to converge on the center of the floor, where Oliver stood. He took a moment to feel the rhythm and then began to move. The other dancers on the floor moved toward him, and he grew bolder as a critical mass gathered. He progressed from embarrassed to awkward to fluid to ecstatic in the space of two minutes and was soon at the eye of a maelstrom of male motion. Shirts flew off as others sought to mimic Oliver's glossy, muscled frenzy.

Luckily Oliver's brain shut down—as it did whenever he danced—because being at the center of a writhing mass of men might have given him pause to reflect on poor choices he'd made. But such thoughts would only surface later.

By the time he noticed Xander waving to him, he had lost all track of time. But as he stepped through the crowded dance floor, it occurred to him that the presence of that many bobbing humans (there were women on the periphery) was his doing. In spite of the bizarre situation he found himself in, he was perversely proud of having a job and doing it well.

He was panting, and sweaty, and elated. He was also standing right next to James.

At some point during the bacchanalia, James had moved from the bar to a table near the dance floor—one with a perfect view of the place Oliver had occupied until a moment ago.

"I'm impressed," James said, lifting his usual glass. There was another, identical drink on the table. "Join me?"

"I should probably get changed," Oliver said, pointing to the back hallway.

"I think you might want to sit for a moment," James said with a hint of a grin. "Hide your light under a bushel... or the table, as it were."

Oliver looked down and saw that the front of his sparkly blue shorts was grossly distended by a semierection for which he had no clear explanation. He looked back up at James, eyes wide with panic. He shuffled over to the open stool at James's table and sat.

"It's okay," James said. "I had the same reaction to your dancing."

Oliver, head swimming, reached for the Scotch and tossed it back in one go. "I don't...," he stumbled, then remembered his manners. "Thank you for the drink."

"It was my pleasure. And it is small recompense for all of the pleasure you provided."

Xander appeared at the table with two more drinks on his tray. "Gentlemen," he said as he set the drinks down. "These are on the house." He turned to Oliver. "Gavin says you can take the rest of the evening. People were actually texting their friends to come see you out there. The door nearly doubled in the last hour." He slipped his hand into Oliver's, placing a wad of cash—Oliver's tips from earlier in the evening—into his palm. Xander then nodded to James. "I leave him in your capable hands." He winked and returned to the bar.

James lifted his glass to a bewildered Oliver. "Is there nothing you cannot do?"

"Actually, some of the things I've never done might surprise you," Oliver replied as he took a sip of his second Scotch. His life was suddenly so far around the bend (dancing queen in a gay club! Inexplicable semi from being a dancing queen in a gay club!), it seemed easier just to stop fighting it and laugh along. "I don't normally dance for money, for example." He picked up a napkin and blotted his chest self-consciously.

"But you are amazing at it," James replied. "I'm no expert, but the guys out there really seemed to like it."

"And did you like it?" Oliver asked, for no reason he could think of. It just seemed suddenly very important to him.

James smiled, and his eyes crinkled a little. "Very much," he said softly and took a suave sip of his Scotch. He looked thoughtfully at Oliver for a moment. "So, does one take lessons to learn how to do... what you do on the dance floor?"

Oliver blushed. He was realizing that doing something well meant more to him than what that something was, and appreciation for doing it well could come from anyone, whether or not that someone was, uncomfortably, a man. "No," he replied, but immediately realized that this sounded like false modesty, so he continued, "It's nothing I can even think about. In fact, if I think about it, I start tripping over my own feet. I just kind of... give up? I just let go." He took another drink, wondering if he was making sense. "It's actually the only time I ever let go. Ever."

James nodded, as if this was making sense to him, which made Oliver feel a little better. A little.

"So your week ended on the dance floor. How was the rest of it?" James asked.

Oliver was so relieved to have something normal to talk about in this fucked-up place that he seized on it and didn't let it go. He told James about his classes and about the intrigue surrounding the sudden departure of one of the faculty at the hospital. He talked about his fellow students and his plans for building a practice. After many minutes of this, he realized he wasn't talking about his week anymore; he was talking about his life.

"I'm sorry to have run on so long," Oliver said. "I don't usually—"

"Shh," James said, putting his hand on Oliver's. "I love hearing you talk."

No one had ever said this to Oliver. If a woman had said it, he probably would have proposed marriage right then and there. But it wasn't a woman; it was a man. A man he knew very little about.

"I've run on and on," Oliver said. "Please, tell me about your week, or your life, or anything at all."

James's expression changed before Oliver even finished his sentence. He sighed and looked down at the table. "The reason I like hearing about your life is that it's so full of promise. You're starting things, even things you obviously aren't sure you should be starting, like this side career as a bartender go-go boy, but even that's exciting because it's new. I, meanwhile, watch over the continued progress of a life from which the joy has long since vanished."

"Wow. That's the most beautiful way I can imagine to say the most depressing thing I've ever heard."

James gave a courtly bow of acknowledgment and then looked into the swirl of his drink. "I live in complication, Oliver. Complication from which I am no longer capable of disentangling."

Oliver, never having experienced a mysterious force exerting control over his life, couldn't comprehend the entirety of James's entanglements. So he did what a doctor would do for a patient overwhelmed with strange symptoms: he focused on one detail and started there. "My great-grandfather collected watches, including some from the places he was stationed in World War Two, and I was always fascinated with them. He would take them out of their glass case and show me the dials with strange markings and the intricate workings. He taught me that when a watchmaker adds something to a watch beyond the movement that tells time—like something that shows the phases of the moon—it's called a complication. Complications can be useful because they give us something beyond the ordinary. They can be beautiful."

James looked up, his eyes red and sad.

"What's the matter?" Oliver asked, terrified something he had said or done had caused James distress.

"That was profound," James said in a low voice. "I just wish my complications were the beautiful kind."

"Not all complications have a visible purpose," Oliver said. "Like one that moves the date dial to the twenty-ninth of February once every four years. If you didn't know its purpose, it would just look like a set of gears that moved slowly and pointlessly. But come leap year, a part of it you hadn't even noticed swings into action, and its design becomes clear. Maybe your complications are like that—you just don't know their purpose yet."

James had stopped tearing up. In fact, he seemed to have stopped breathing. "Where… where did you come from?" he stammered.

"From a little town up north. From simple people. Not simple like stupid, but simple like the way nature works. Evolution doesn't tolerate extraneous complication. What lasts is simplicity. So I try to find the simplest explanation, the simplest reason for why things are the way they are. That's always the right answer, in my experience."

"You're just really astonishingly smart," James said.

"Well, they're not going to send the dumb one to medical school. But thank you." Oliver tossed back the last of his second Scotch and was starting to feel the effects.

Xander showed up at that moment with two more.

"Damn, you're good at this," Oliver told him.

"I get better the drunker you get," Xander said, and with a wink he was gone.

Oliver and James talked and drank and were on their sixth or seventh Scotch by the time the life of the club began to ebb. Neither of them was throwing-up drunk, but they were much further gone than Oliver had planned to allow himself to get.

"I should get going," James said, getting unsteadily to his feet.

"You can't drive," Oliver said, his bartender training breaking through the Scottish fog.

James nodded. "You're right. It would not be a good idea for me to get on the dark country roads back home right now." He gripped the table to steady himself. "Actually, I'm not so sure about my ability to navigate the sidewalk."

"Where are you going to go?" Oliver asked.

"There's a hotel near here I stay at when I have to come to the capitol. I'll just get a room there for the night."

"I'll walk you there," Oliver said, standing. And then he remembered he was wearing sparkly blue shorts. "I'll need to change."

"Should I wait outside?"

"No, come on into the back with me. It'll just take me a minute."

Oliver led James on a somewhat zigzagging path through the club and down the back hallway. He opened the door to the back room and motioned for James to follow him. James did, but hesitatingly slowly, as if he were trespassing on a private retreat.

"Are you sure I should—"

"It's fine," Oliver said as he opened his locker and pulled out his street clothes. Without a moment's hesitation, he whipped off the dancing shorts and pulled on his boxer briefs. He thought he caught sight of James glancing at him in the mirror, but he wasn't certain. It didn't really matter to him at this point because the Scotch had demolished his internal narrative of shame at his career choice, and all he really cared about was getting out of here and trying to live a normal life for a couple of days before coming back and starting the whole thing over again.

After tying his shoes, he stood up, having dressed in under a minute. Lots of practice racing from the gym on campus to his advanced anatomy lab had given him the ability to dress in record time. "Ready?"

James suddenly seemed a lot more sober than he had been a few minutes ago. He stood up straight. "Ready."

Oliver slung his backpack over his shoulder and opened the door, motioning for James to step out into the corridor. They exited the club through the back door, which gave out onto the alley that ran behind the businesses on the block. A quick walk along the narrow passageway that led to the street and they were out on the sidewalk just down the street from the club.

"Ah," James said, "that explains why I've never seen you leaving with anyone. You slip out the back when you have company?"

It took Oliver a moment to figure out what James was saying. "No, I've never left with anyone." He wasn't Xander, and James was certainly not his big-Beamer sugar daddy. No fucking way.

James stopped and turned to look at Oliver, his eyes wide. "You really aren't like the others at all, are you?"

Oliver sensed what he meant instinctively. "No, I'm not. And neither are you."

James staggered back, blinking as if Oliver had smacked him across the face. He recovered quickly and shook off the shock. "No," he said slowly. "You're right. Again." He pointed up the street, away from Burn. "This way."

Oliver fell into step beside him, the realization creeping up on him that they were both sobering quickly and yet not abandoning the plan they had made when feeling tipsy in the club. They were being pulled forward by the force of their previous intention, regardless of whether it fit the current reality. They were committed, as their characters dictated.

Two blocks along James slowed suddenly and turned up a wide marble stairway to the entrance of a hotel Oliver had heard of but never imagined himself walking into. A doorman opened the plate-glass door with a bow, and James and Oliver stepped into the hushed lobby. As they walked toward the front desk, it occurred to Oliver that he had offered to walk James to the hotel to be sure he got there safely. That task was now accomplished, and yet he continued to stand next to James, as if waiting for some additional sign that he could leave.

James and the smiling young woman at the front desk conversed in low tones, and Oliver looked about the lobby for a moment. At this hour of the… morning—it was morning, wasn't it?—the lobby was dead quiet. The only sound was a fountain burbling with subdued, faraway splashes. There was art on the walls. Expensive art.

"Enjoy your stay, Mr. Whitford."

This snapped Oliver back into the moment. James wasn't using a fake name. He was really doing this. They were really doing this.

"Come up for a moment?" James asked him, stepping toward the elevators. "Maybe two?"

No, of course not. We're both... men. "Sure."

They walked into the elevator, and James pressed the button for a very high number. He slid his room key into a slot, and the button lit up. The elevator rose smoothly and quickly, and Oliver felt a little lightheaded. It may have been the alcohol, or it may have been the hour. It may have been this thing they were doing. Why were they doing this?

The elevator slowed and stopped, and its doors slid silently open. James stepped out, and Oliver followed. The room was at the end of the hall, the kind of room that had its own nameplate in addition to a number. "City Lights Suite," it read in an elegant script.

James opened the door, and Oliver immediately saw the reason for the name of the suite. The far wall was fully windowed, floor to ceiling, and through all of them shone the lights of the city. They were high enough above the streets that the view extended out to the edges of the metro area, where the lights dwindled and scattered. It was dazzling.

Oliver walked in and stood before the windows. "It's beautiful," he said, wonder in his voice. He turned back and saw James standing in the middle of the room, looking sadly at him. "What's the matter?" he asked.

"We don't have much time," James replied.

"You're right," Oliver said, shaking off the spell cast by the dramatic view. "I should be going."

"No, you can't go," James said.

There was a knock at the door. He seemed to have been expecting it because instead of going to the door, he simply slumped sideways onto the sofa.

The knock repeated. "Room service" called a voice from the hall.

Oliver walked to the door, intent on finding out what exactly was going on. He peered through the viewer, but what he found on the other side was not a room service waiter bearing a tray but a man with a large camera at the ready. Oliver stared at this strange, fish-eyed sight for a moment, then backed slowly and silently away from the door. He stopped when he reached the sofa where James sat, still looking blankly at the ceiling.

"It's some guy with a camera," Oliver whispered to him.

James nodded vaguely, but otherwise gave no indication he had understood what Oliver was saying.

"Why would there be a photographer in the hallway of a hotel at three in the morning, pretending to be room service?"

James just shook his head.

Another knock on the door. The fake room server was getting impatient. Oliver picked up the phone and called the front desk.

"What are you…?" James began but fell silent without finishing his question.

"Can you send security to the hall, please? There's someone knocking on our door."

"Right away, Mr. Whitford," the clerk at the front desk answered immediately. "Is your door locked?"

Oliver jumped quickly to the door and as silently as possible turned the secondary lock into position. He picked up the phone again. "Yes, it is."

"Good. Stay where you are and don't open the door. Security should already be on the floor."

"Thank you," Oliver said and hung up. He went back to the viewer and watched as the photographer looked suddenly down the hall and bolted from view in the other direction. Then two dark blurs raced through the viewer's range of vision, and Oliver heard footsteps pounding down the hall.

The phone rang, startling them both. Oliver picked it up; it was the front desk. "Mr. Whitford, security has cleared the hall. Thank you for alerting us. I assure you it will not happen again."

Oliver, overwhelmed, nodded as if the person on the other end of the line could see him.

"Is there anything else we can do, sir?" the voice inquired.

"Uh… no, no, we're fine," Oliver stumbled, still looking at James, trying to piece together what was going on.

"Good night, then, sir."

Oliver made a confused grunt into the phone, then replaced the receiver.

James was staring out the window. He hadn't moved since the first knock on the door.

"James, can you tell me what's going on, please?" Oliver asked. He should have left already, he scolded himself. And why was he here in the first place?

"It wasn't supposed to be this way," James said, his voice flat and distracted.

"What wasn't?" Oliver asked, his patience wearing thin.

"Tonight. It was supposed to be simple."

"At the risk of repeating myself, what are you talking about?"

James sat silent, looking out the windows.

Oliver huffed out a breath. "All right, fine. I'll be going now. This evening was really weird, and I'm going to go home now."

"No, you can't leave," James said, appearing to snap out of his trance. "They'll be waiting for you."

"Who will be waiting for me?" Oliver cried, his patience at an end. "What the fuck is going on?"

"I don't know if I can explain" came the reply.

"You'd better try damn hard," Oliver said, sitting on the other end of the sofa.

James deflated, as if the will to live were leaving him. He sat, slumped, for what seemed to Oliver at least five minutes. Then, finally, he took a long, slow breath.

"I'm a politician," he began. And apparently, he ended. There didn't seem to be any more.

"I know that," Oliver said. "You're the county executive."

James shook his head. "No, that's my current position. But that's not what I am. What I am is a politician. There's a difference."

"And what would that difference be?"

"A politician doesn't do the job he was elected to do. A politician uses the job he was elected to do as a platform for getting elected to do the next job."

"Will he do that one?" Oliver asked, impatience creeping into his voice.

"No. He uses that one to get the next one. He won't do that one either."

"Well, this is refreshingly cynical. Thanks for the civics lesson." Oliver stood. "I'll be going now."

"No, wait. What I'm trying to say is that for every politician who gets elected, there are several who don't, and more who didn't even run but think they could do a better job than the guy who did get elected. And all of those people are going to look for a way to make trouble for him."

"Ah, I get it now." Oliver sat back down. "Burn is your trouble."

James shook his head miserably.

"That's why the guy outside the door had a camera. He was trying to get a picture of you so he could prove you go to a gay club on Sundays."

"That's not what he wanted a picture of."

"What was he trying to get a picture of, then?"

"You."

Oliver sat back. "Me?" His heart raced as if the photographer were a hunter and he a twelve-point buck. "Why me?"

"Because you're my problem."

"Look, I barely know you. Who would ever even think to look for me?" His breath was coming more rapidly now. "What you're saying makes no sense."

"There are people who suspect that I come to the city on Sundays to do what I can't do at home. But apparently getting a picture of me going into Burn isn't enough—they could have gotten that already. What they want is a picture of me with a guy from the club. And that's what they're going to get because I was stupid and brought you here."

"I'm not 'some guy from the club,'" Oliver retorted, indignation rising in his chest.

"No, of course you're not. But they don't know that. And they wouldn't care if they did."

Oliver looked hard at James. "You sound like you've been expecting this."

"I guess I have. Part of me must have known my secret would have to come out sometime. But I just couldn't hide anymore, sitting at home ignoring what I really feel."

"Stella's not enough for you?" Oliver asked cuttingly.

James jolted at the mention of his wife's name. "How did you—"

"Five minutes on the Internet and you can know everything about anybody," Oliver said, standing again. "For the last time, I'm leaving."

James looked up. "They'll be waiting for you. They'll have someone at all the doors, and they'll get your picture. How do you think the people at home who paid your tuition are going to like seeing their promising med-school student leaving the hotel room of a closeted politician? It won't be just my scandal, Oliver."

Oliver paled. "What have you done to me?" It was both accusation and plea.

"I didn't mean for this to happen."

"That's fine to say, but what are you going to do about it? How do we get out of this? No one can find out." Oliver plopped back down on the sofa, heart pounding.

"You said I seemed like I was expecting this. What did *you* expect? You work at a gay club. You dance at a gay club. You get tipped very well for dressing in sexy clothes at a gay club. Did it never occur to you that any of this might present a risk for your future career?"

"But I'm a bartender. I make drinks. There's nothing wrong with that."

"But you don't just make drinks. You make drinks with your jockstrap hanging out. Before you came here tonight, you had to change out of glittery boy shorts that barely covered your erection. The erection you got from dancing with men."

Oliver was silent.

"You came here with me," James said, his voice suddenly gentle. "You came with me."

And with that Oliver's brain stopped in its tracks. Just stopped. It refused to think the next thought, whatever that might have been.

"Why did you come here with me?" James asked, his voice soft.

"Because I wanted to make sure you were okay."

James smiled weakly. "You're going to make a great doctor. Already trying to take care of people."

"When I found out… about you," Oliver began, "it suddenly made sense how sad you always seem when you leave the club on Sunday nights. I was worried you might get drunk and do something stupid, so I came with you to be sure you were okay."

"Do something stupid?" James asked, eyebrows up.

"Like throw yourself off the balcony out there," Oliver replied, nodding to the terrace overlooking the city.

James turned and looked out the windows for a long while. "Can't say I haven't thought about it," he said, in a voice that was more matter-of-fact than Oliver might have considered appropriate for such a sentiment.

"You have?" Oliver gaped at James in disbelief. "I'm sorry, that sounded kind of judgmental. I just haven't ever met anyone who said they'd actually considered... that."

"I think I'm too much of a wimp to actually do it," James said, turning back to Oliver. "Guess I'll have to keep trying to live instead."

They sat in strained silence for a moment.

"Can I ask you something kind of rude?"

James smiled, a little more strongly than before. "Sure."

"What the fuck is wrong with you?"

"What?" James's voice was baffled, not offended.

"I don't get this at all. You have all the money you need. You could have chosen any kind of life you wanted, and you end up here, doing this. Why the hell did you get married if you didn't want to, you know, be married? How did you end up sneaking around with someone you met at a club, waiting for a photographer to destroy your life? I just cannot imagine how you ended up this way."

"Things weren't that simple for me, back when I made some of the choices that led me here. You're young—you don't know how much more limited our choices were back then."

"Bullshit. What are you, thirty? I'm twenty-four. Life hasn't changed that much. You have the same options now you had back then."

"You don't seem to realize how much life has changed in the last few years. When I started my career in politics, it wasn't possible to get elected dogcatcher in this state if they even suspected you were gay. And my ambitions rose a bit higher than dogcatcher, so I did what I needed to do. It's not like I intended to end up this way. I thought I was choosing one life over another. I didn't realize it would be impossible to keep the one I didn't choose under control."

"What did Stella choose?" Oliver suspected he would draw blood with this, but he had to make James see.

James gave a mirthless chuckle and shook his head. "Stella got exactly what she wanted. Money, a political future, and a man who would let her have her own bedroom and not bother her about it."

"Sounds like an ideal marriage," Oliver said with an impatient roll of his eyes. "How much longer are you going to keep it up?"

"I'm a politician, Oliver. There's always a next election."

"But will there be, once the pictures get out?"

"It's more complicated than that," James said, his voice low and sad again.

"God I hate that word," Oliver muttered.

James shifted awkwardly on the couch. "I'm really sorry. I should not have brought you here." He stood, walked to the desk, and picked up the phone. "Yes, can you bring a house car around for my guest? He will give you the address. Thank you." He hung up the phone. "The car will be waiting for you, to take you home." James fell silent, still standing at the desk, and looked out the window again.

Oliver stood. "I don't know what to... I'm really sorry," he said. He genuinely felt pity for James, whose face sagged under a weight Oliver had no way to understand.

"You should go," James said. "Please, forgive me."

Oliver nodded and turned to leave the hotel room. James walked with him, out the door and down the hall.

"Are you leaving too?" Oliver asked as they stepped into the elevator.

James shook his head. "They'll be waiting for me to try to make an exit out the back. Just walk straight out and don't stop for anything, okay? You'll be fine."

"I don't—"

"Shh," James raised a quieting hand. "Just go. I am so sorry, Oliver. I had no idea you were so... good. I wish you the best."

"But what—"

Oliver was cut off by the opening of the elevator doors. James bolted out of the elevator and disappeared around the corner. Oliver took a deep breath and walked out through the lobby and into the town car the doorman was holding open for him. The door clicked closed, and the car pulled smoothly away into the night. And what a night it had been.

CHAPTER SEVEN
HOSTAGE NEGOTIATIONS

"THANK YOU," Oliver said as he got out of the town car. It was with some irony that he tipped the driver from his own roll of tips. *Pay it forward.*

He walked up to the front door of the building and pushed the doorbell. Twice.

"Yesh?" Millie's voice was fuzzy and tired. Half of that was the result of cheap intercom wiring; the other half was due to it being four in the morning on a Monday.

"Millie, it's Oliver. Can I come up, please?"

"Are you currently on fire?" she asked, her voice clearing a little.

"No, but—"

"Has the zombie apocalypse begun?"

"No," he sighed.

"Then whatever has driven you to ring my bell at four in the morning fails to qualify as an emergency." Nonetheless, the door buzzed.

Oliver opened it and sprinted up the stairs to Millie's apartment. She was standing at the door wearing a robe—and a frown that looked like it had been left to her in Winston Churchill's will.

"Will whatever story you have to tell me result in my complete loss of faith in humanity?" she asked, barring the door until he answered.

"Yes."

"Then you may pass," she said, dropping her arm and granting him access.

"Thank you," he growled as he entered. He proceeded directly to her kitchen, which he knew as well as he knew his own, and began making coffee.

She plopped down on one of the stools at her counter and watched him work. A few minutes later, he handed her a steaming cup of strong black coffee from the Bialetti and sat down next to her. She sipped and looked hard at him—through him.

"He did it, didn't he?"

Oliver's mouth dropped open. "What?"

"Mr. James Buchanan Whitford made a play for you. He tried to make you his mister." She sipped and nodded as if she took his sputtering reaction as confirmation. "And you...." She squinted hard, looked deeply into his eyes. Then she sat back in surprise. "And you let him."

"Fuck," he grunted. He lowered his forehead to the counter with a *thunk*. He went for a second *thunk* because he deserved it for how stupid he'd been.

She put an arm around him. "Men are assholes," she whispered compassionately.

"You are *not*," he muttered into her kitchen counter, "going to give me some kind of sisterhood pep talk."

"But it's all I've been dreaming of for the last month." She seemed to notice his head hadn't left the counter. "Oh grow up, Ollie, dear. From the moment you took that job, we've both known it was heading here."

"We have not."

"I'm not judging you. I would have done the same thing in your place. Did he happen to let slip that he swam for Dartmouth? I hope he hasn't gone all saggy because, honey, he was sex in a speedo. I'd let him practice his breast stroke on me anytime."

"We are not having this conversation."

"We are going to continue having this conversation until you tell me what happened. The only way I stop talking is if you start. How many times have we been down this road?"

He sat up. "Okay. Just give me a minute to put it into words."

"What's it in now, grunts and moaning?"

"Shut up." He took a big swallow of coffee. "So the club was kind of slow tonight. Not many guys on the dance floor, and that's bad for business. Gavin asked me to dance for an hour, try to get people out there."

"Gavin's a smart man," Millie added.

"So Xander gets me this tiny sparkly blue thing to wear, and I dance for like an hour."

"Oh, hot."

"I'm sorry, I should have told you to shut up. Oh, wait—I did. So start doing that, right now? Please and thank you."

She made the motion of locking her lips and dropping the key down the front of her robe.

"James had moved to a table near the dance floor. When I was done, I walked over to him, and then I sat down."

Her eyebrows lifted, and she made some kind of crazy not-really-sign-language motion that probably meant, "But you were wearing only a sparkly blue thing."

Oliver blushed at the memory of why he sat down. "I sat down because I needed to… rest after dancing. He had a drink waiting for me, and then Xander brought another round. Apparently the dancing idea worked, because they told me to take the rest of the night, and they kept bringing free Scotch, so we talked and got kind of buzzed."

Millie nodded, as if this all had gone according to her vision of events.

"So at closing time, we're both kind of hammered, and he says he's going to check into a hotel. I tell him I'll walk him there because it's late and he's drunk."

She slapped her forehead with her palm, but remained silent.

"Anyway, so we go into the back so I can change my clothes—"

She lifted her hands to heaven as if begging to be released from her vow of silence.

"And then we walk down the street to that new hotel, the one with all of the glass and sharp angles?"

She stared blank-eyed, probably from speech deprivation.

"He gets the top suite, and we go up. It was beautiful—amazing views of the city."

She rolled her eyes, clearly uninterested in the view.

"So, having walked him to the hotel as I'd offered, I'm about to leave."

Millie gave him the international sign for WTF: hands outstretched, shoulders shrugged, eyes wide, head shaking.

"But there's a knock at the door, and this voice says it's room service. But I look through the viewer and it's a guy with a camera. Like a stalking-the-president's-kids kind of lens on there. Serious stuff. So I tell James this, and he doesn't seem surprised at all. I call the front desk and ask them to send security up, and they do. The guy gets run off. So now I have some questions for James."

Millie clasped her hands in front of her, begging for release from her agreement to keep quiet. He nodded, mainly because he wanted to know what she thought.

"Thank you," she exhaled, as if she'd been holding her breath as well as her tongue. "Now, let's rewind a bit. You sat down with him after shaking your moneymaker for two reasons. One, you realized how much he must really like you to follow you around the club like a puppy—a big, collegiate-swimmer puppy. Two, you had danced your way to an awkward boner."

He gasped, wide-eyed with shock.

"Oh, yes, I'm familiar with it. It never occurred to you why I have to drag you off the dance floor at every wedding and house party we've ever gone to? Coupla songs in and little Ollie starts feeling frisky. It's kinky, but I figure you gotta let your freak flag fly sometime. But what about the first reason? How does it make you feel to see how much he's into you?"

"It's not like that. We just talked. And drank too much Scotch. We weren't playing footsie under the table or anything. We just talked."

Millie nodded. It was the nod she used when she didn't agree in the slightest with what someone was saying. "Good for you. Now, tell me again how he seduced you into coming to the hotel with him?"

"He didn't seduce me. The club was closing, and we stood and realized the whole place was kind of spinning. He said he shouldn't drive home and was going to get a hotel room for the night. I said I'd walk with him, make sure he got there safely."

"How noble. But you were still in your go-go boy costume, so…."

"So I changed. Then we left."

"No, you said he came with you to the back room and you changed."

Oliver shrugged, not seeing how that added anything.

"Why did you invite him to see you naked?" Millie tossed this hand grenade of a question and then placidly sipped her coffee.

Oliver closed his eyes and took a deep breath. "I didn't invite him to see me naked. The club was closing down, and he said he would wait for me on the sidewalk. I asked him to come with me so he didn't have to be standing out there all by himself."

"Because he's managed to reach the age of thirty, but standing alone on a sidewalk for five minutes would certainly result in his doom."

"Shut up. I changed, we left, done."

"Not done. I don't suppose you were wearing a dance belt under those sparkly short-shorts?"

"What's a dance belt?"

"It's like a jockstrap, but for ballerinas. Or whatever they call male ballet dancers."

Oliver shook his head. "The stuff I'm learning from this job. Anyway, I wasn't wearing anything under the shorts. So yes, I was naked for like a second and a half. So what?"

"Was he looking at you?"

"I don't know," Oliver said.

Millie nodded. "Your answer, as well as the truth, has been noted. Go on."

"Okay, so back to the hotel. I ask James what's going on, and he tells me about how politicians always have enemies, and that some of his must have gotten the idea to try to catch him with a dancer from Burn. They were waiting for us to come out of the room so they could cause a scandal for him. So I can't leave because someone will take my picture and it'll get back to the folks at home what I'm doing for money, and my career as a doctor will basically be over before it starts. So that sucks. At that point I kind of got mad at him for not thinking this all through, and he suddenly decides he's going to get me out of there. He kept saying he was sorry, and he never meant for it to work out this way, which I don't really get because he also seemed to be expecting the whole thing to happen all along. But whatever. He orders up a town car, and goes with me in the elevator to the lobby. When the doors open, he takes off around the corner, saying that's where the cameras will be waiting, and tells me to walk straight out and get in the car. So I do, and here I am."

Millie shook her head. "You poor boy."

"What? Why would you—"

"Your first date with a guy and it turns all weird. I'm sorry."

Oliver narrowed his eyes. "It was not a date. I hate to break it to you, but I'm still straight."

She gave her special nod again. "You've been up a long time. Why don't you grab the couch, get at least a couple of hours of shut-eye, and we'll reconvene in the morning with sharper minds. If I'm right, we're going to need them."

"Why? Why are we going to need them?"

"Because we haven't seen the last of Mr. Whitford's complications."

"Shit," Oliver expectorated.

"MORNING, SUNSHINE," Millie whispered somewhere over Oliver.

Under the blankets, he couldn't see her, but he could hear her cheerfulness, and that was never a good thing. It usually meant she had something to tell him, and the news wasn't good. He sat up, letting the blankets flop down into his lap.

"It's a loss to women everywhere," she lamented. "Now that you've finally realized you're gay, that amazing torso is forever out of reach." She sighed dramatically.

"It's still well within reach for women," Oliver said, feeling around for his shirt. "But *you* never had a chance."

"Ooh, kitty has claws now," Millie teased, making an Eartha Kitt-style cat's-paw motion. "Remind me again, who was the last woman you shared all of that with?"

Oliver scowled at her. "You know I'm focusing on my schoolwork. I don't have time for dating right now."

"Ah, yes. You are simply too busy to engage in such trivial pursuits as heterosexuality. It must be terrible to have to defer your ardent desire for the fairer sex."

"I don't have to justify my sexuality to you."

"Clearly you can't." She stood. "Breakfast? I don't think I have any sausage for you to eat—is that going to be a problem, love?"

"I would eat a foot-long sausage if it would keep you from making gay jokes ever again," Oliver muttered as he stumbled toward the bathroom.

"Looks like I'll be paying a visit to the deli counter today," Millie said with a laugh. "Of course, now that we're competing for guys, I probably shouldn't take you to my hunting grounds."

"You can only call them hunting grounds if you stand a chance of actually bagging something," Oliver called from the bathroom as he washed his face. "Since you always come home empty-handed, I think you should call them something else. Like maybe 'losing grounds'?"

"You gay guys are always so petty and mean," Millie said, then dissolved into giggles.

A few minutes later, they were at the breakfast table, having reached a détente in their mutual snarking.

"So you're probably wondering why I asked you to breakfast," Millie stated rather grandly.

"Because I was already here and eating in front of me would have been rude, even for you?"

Millie held up a conciliatory hand. "Mock if you must, but you shall soon find little cause for jocularity."

"Oh, shit," Oliver said, setting down his fork. "It must be bad if you're breaking out the vocab. Let's have it. What did you find? What happened?"

She grabbed her tablet and set it on the table in front of Oliver. But she slapped her hand down on it, covering it from his view. "Before you watch this, I want you to know it's not as bad as you think."

"Great. Now I'm thinking it's the second-worst thing in the world. Thanks."

She lifted her hand. "This is from that poor excuse for a morning show the local station puts on. I found it about a half hour ago."

The video was shaky, but Oliver recognized immediately what it was. An unmarked metal door opened, and James appeared. He seemed surprised by the crowd of reporters and photographers milling about in the alley behind the hotel; he heaved a great sigh and stepped out to join them. One of them must have asked a question, because James leaned forward, hand on his ear. Then he seemed to understand, drawing himself upright to make a statement.

"I had a late meeting last night," James began. "A meeting that ended with a drink or two. Knowing I was in no shape to get behind the wheel, I checked into my favorite hotel. I heard there was a disturbance in the alley, and on the chance it was my presence in the hotel that had caused it, I came back here to see if I could help disperse the crowd."

"Are you staying here alone?" someone shouted from off-camera.

"Yes, I am staying here alone. I am certain my wife will be much relieved to hear that." There was laughter around the edges of the picture. "Now, if you'll excuse me, I need to get some sleep. And so should you." He stepped back into the hotel and closed the heavy metal door behind him.

Oliver stared at the frozen James on the screen in the still shot from the video that displayed once it had run to the end. Then he looked up at Millie. "He did that so I could get out," he said softly. "He could have stayed holed up there all night and left me to get ambushed on my way out. But he made sure they were busy with him so I could get away."

Millie nodded slowly. Then she put her hand on his. "Maybe not such a bad guy after all," she said. She took a deep breath. "At least, that's the good news."

Oliver started. "What's the bad news?"

"The bad news is that he's given those reporters just what they were looking for. He's thrown the chum in the water, denying that there's anything going on. There's always something going on. You"— she pointed at him—"are what's going on. He can never return to Burn now. They'll surely be staking it out, talking to people, trying to suss out if anyone's seen him there. If he knows what he's doing, he's heading home right now, and he won't set foot outside for a long time."

"Poor guy," Oliver murmured as he looked back down at the screen.

"You really like him, don't you?" she asked, sounding surprised.

Oliver tried to figure out how to explain what he thought about James. "It's like he's two different people. When you talk to him, he's this nice, normal guy. He's super intelligent, but he's not a dick about it. You know how some smart people can be really annoying, like making other people feel stupid is the only way they feel smart?"

Millie rolled her eyes. "I have no idea what you are talking about, Mr. Valedictorian."

He glared at her. "But then there's this other thing in his life, this whole political thing, that just seems like it's completely out of his control. Like he's caught in the gears of it, and it won't let him go."

"People make all kinds of choices in this great big world, buddy. He made some bad ones, and it looks like he's stuck with them. At least he's not your problem anymore. I don't think you'll be seeing him again."

Oliver nodded. "Yeah, good." He took a bite of scrambled egg and looked out the tiny window of Millie's apartment. "Good."

OLIVER WENT through the motions of his Monday and Tuesday— working out and attending class—but viewed it all as though from a great distance. He wasn't sure what had screwed with his head so badly; breakfast with Millie had helped him shake off some of the weirdness with James, but something still hung over him.

He got to work on Wednesday to find Xander talking animatedly with someone at one of his tables; as it was still an hour to opening, Oliver figured he was bringing a new employee up to speed the way he had with Oliver a month before. A month—so much had happened in a month. He walked over to the table.

"Oliver, good—you're here. I'd like you to meet my good friend Bryce, who would like to book a private event."

"Wouldn't Gavin take care of that?" Oliver asked, but he extended a smile and his hand. "Pleased to meet you, Bryce."

Bryce took his hand and gave it the warmest, limpest of shakes. He beamed and turned to Xander. "He is everything you promised, X. He will do nicely."

"Xander?" Oliver muttered, unused to being evaluated in the third person, like a cut of meat in the butcher's window.

"I was telling Bryce about your bartending skills, and he is very interested in having you work the private function."

"There are actually several private functions I would be interested in," Bryce purred. Then he seemed to notice Xander's glare. "But just the one party."

"Bryce is organizing a bachelor party and would like to hold it here," Xander explained.

"A bachelor party? In a gay club?" Oliver was baffled.

Xander cast Bryce a look. "See? Completely straight."

"Like a ruler," breathed Bryce, sweeping his gaze up and down Oliver's body.

"You should see him in his dancing outfit," whispered Xander.

"Oh, fuck," groaned Oliver, and he turned to go.

"Wait, wait!" called Bryce. "Will you tend to our bar?"

"They're looking to book a section of the club and have a dedicated bartender," Xander explained. "You would lose the tips from the bar, but for this kind of thing, the money is usually pretty good."

Oliver looked at Bryce's expectant expression. "Sure. Put me down for it."

Bryce was propelled into a bouncing spasm of joyous clapping, and Xander smiled broadly.

"We make a great team," Xander told Bryce. "People love to watch us work."

"Indeed," Bryce murmured, his eyes glazing over. "Now, I'd like to bring the bachelors around tomorrow night to see the place and meet the two of you. Would that be fabulous with you both?"

Xander nodded and looked to Oliver, who nodded back.

"Oh, they will be so happy," cried Bryce. "Now, what are the chances I can get my hands on a Dirty Altar Boy?"

"Something tells me that's already crossed off your bucket list," Xander replied with a laugh. "But we'll get you a fresh one as soon as the bar is open."

"Kisses, darling!" cheered Bryce, who then set to typing madly on his phone, no doubt dispatching party-planning updates far and wide.

Xander followed Oliver to the bar, where Oliver began prepping for the night. "Thanks for stepping up on the private party," Xander said. "It really helps to have someone I know I can work with."

Oliver frowned. "You wouldn't want to do it with Ulysses?"

Xander squinched up one side of his face. "Nah. Ulysses is great, but he's not as… flexible? as you are in dealing with patrons. He does more of a strong, silent type thing. Just between you and me, he comes off as kind of… straight."

Oliver's mouth dropped open.

"I mean, I know you're *actually* straight, but you don't make a big deal about it. I hardly even notice. For you it's one of the down-low handicaps. Like being dyslexic—or Mormon."

"Thanks?" Oliver replied slowly. He immediately recognized this conversation as one of those that would only get more confusing the more he thought about it, so he decided not to think about it at all. He just smiled and began stocking the bright red cherries in his condiment bin.

THE WEDNESDAY crowd at Burn showed all the signs of a two-day deprivation of silly drinks, driving bass, and visible jockstraps. Oliver was hopping for several hours, keeping the bar patrons tipsy and making sure Xander got what he needed to make his regulars happy. It was with some shock, then, that at around eleven he turned and caught sight of something in the mirror that made him freeze.

It was James.

He whipped around to see him, but there was no one standing where Oliver thought he would find him. *Fuck. Now I'm imagining things.* He grunted in disgust and shook his head. *No, it's worse than that. I'm imagining* him. He settled back into his work and tried to ignore his hallucination and what it meant about his mental state.

"Oliver, I need a special," Xander called.

Oliver stepped over, and Xander motioned for him to lean in close. Xander's specials were often as detailed as they were bizarre, so hearing every word was crucial.

"He's at one of my tables. He's asking for you."

Oliver stood upright, baffled. "What?"

Xander motioned for him to lean in again.

"He's asking to talk to you."

Oliver had no idea what to do. He turned left and right in confusion and then craned fruitlessly over the heads of the crowd around the bar, trying to see whom Xander was talking about. He knew perfectly well whom Xander was talking about, but he needed to see for himself. Why, he wasn't sure.

"Come on," Xander said impatiently.

"Ulysses, can you cover for a minute?" Oliver asked his bartending partner.

Ulysses nodded, his eyebrows raised in concern. Oliver had never before asked for coverage.

Oliver ducked under the bar and followed Xander across the club. At the far end, in a booth, sat James. Sitting close to the wall, he was all but invisible to the rest of the room.

"Thank you, Xander," James said softly.

Xander turned and walked away.

"What's… going on?" Oliver asked. This all seemed vaguely cloak-and-daggerish, which he was not really up for after Sunday's misadventure.

"I'm sorry to show up so mysteriously. I'm assuming from the codfish-like expression on your face that you didn't expect to see me."

"Something like that."

"Can you sit for a moment? I have something important to talk to you about."

Oliver slid into the booth opposite James.

"Thank you." James took a deep breath. "Things didn't end well on Sunday."

As if this was something Oliver didn't already know quite well. "You could say that."

"Not the part at the hotel. That was ugly, but manageable. Unfortunately, things have gotten a lot worse since then."

"Your impromptu predawn press conference in the alley behind the hotel didn't solve all of your problems?"

James sighed. "You saw that?"

Oliver nodded.

"That was… awkward. But that's not what I meant when I said things had gotten worse."

"There's more?" Oliver asked.

"I'm afraid so." He looked around as if worried they might be overheard. "There are people who would like very much to find out who you are."

Oliver gaped. "Me? Why do they want me?"

"They know I wasn't alone, and it's only a matter of time before they find out who you are."

"Who is this 'they' we're talking about, James? What the fuck is going on?"

"They are some quite influential people who have a lot riding on my political career. If it seems to them that my career is going to deviate from its intended track, they very well may…." He stopped and looked down at his hands. "They wouldn't be happy."

"And you're saying they would take it out on me? What, is some thug going to show up and break my kneecaps or something? Because I pour you Scotch on Sundays?" Oliver laughed at the sheer insanity of it all. "You know this is completely crazy, don't you? Or have you been too focused on your 'politics' to remember what reality looks like?"

James leaned across the table. "Oliver, I am truly sorry I involved you in this. I wish I could make you see how sorry I am. But the time for wishing it hadn't happened is over. We need to move now if we're going to stay ahead of this."

"What does that mean? I feel like I'm watching a rerun of some old crime drama. This is all ridiculous."

"Oliver, you don't understand what we're dealing with. We don't have much time—"

James was interrupted by a commotion at the club's door; several dark-suited men entered, sweeping startled patrons out of their way as they strode purposefully toward the bar. They called Ulysses over and apparently showed him something. He shook his head, as did Xander when whatever it was was shown to him. The men moved on to accost patrons, and Xander hustled over to the booth.

"They're showing your picture, Oliver. Some shit's about to go down. If you need to make a break for it, I'll get them out of your way."

"Make a break—what the fuck, Xander?"

"If you can get us thirty seconds, my car is in the back," James said to Xander.

Oliver turned on James, astonished. "Are you serious? There is no way—"

James took Oliver's hand in his. "Oliver, you need to trust me. We have to go. I'll explain everything on the way."

"On the way where, exactly?"

"I can't tell you. Not yet. But I'll explain everything."

Oliver looked at Xander, who had more experience running off with strange men. "Xander, what should I—"

"Go. I'll text you in an hour. If you don't text me back the name of the drink Ulysses made for you your first time here, I'll call the police." He looked over at the men making their way around the bar. "Most of these guys know to lie to anything in a suit. But eventually someone's bound to let your name slip out." Xander leaned in close, his voice urgent. "Those dudes in the suits are the real deal, Oliver. You should go."

Oliver looked pleadingly at James. "I can trust you?" He felt he had no other choice.

"With my life I will protect you."

Oliver blinked hard and shook his head. "All right. All right. We need to grab my backpack on the way out, okay?"

James nodded.

"Good luck, guys." Xander walked over to the men in suits and pulled them away to talk to a patron in the opposite corner of the club. He pointed at the DJ as he passed, and suddenly the volume of the music doubled and the lights dropped. Spotlights shone brilliantly on the dance floor, deepening the darkness over the rest of the club.

"Let's go," James whispered, and they made their way, hugging the back wall, to the door that opened onto the back corridor.

Oliver stepped into the back room and grabbed his backpack, stuffing his clothes into it. He and James ran down the hallway and out the back door. True to his word, James had left his car—a late-model European sedan in black—in the alley. They ran to it; James stepped into the driver's seat, and Oliver threw his pack into the backseat before settling in on the passenger side. James pulled the car smoothly into traffic and drove away down the boulevard.

"Where are we going?" Oliver asked as he buckled his seat belt.

"We need to get out of the city," James replied, eyes locked on the rearview mirror. "I have a place they don't know about."

"Now's the time to tell me who 'they' are, if you don't mind."

"I guess you're right. I wish there were a way for me to tell you without sounding like a complete asshole, but I can't think of one." He merged onto the freeway that would take them out east of the city. "Remember how I said politicians are always running the next race?"

Oliver nodded.

"Well, my next race is for statewide office. But I don't have much name recognition outside of my own part of the state, which makes it tough to do fundraising and organizing for a statewide election. So it makes sense for me to get an appointment to a statewide executive post—that way I wouldn't have to run until after I was already known at the state level. But those are hard to come by unless you have some kind of high-profile qualification."

"Once again, the civics lesson is fascinating, but can we get to the part about why we're being chased by angry-looking men in dark suits?"

"It was a plan concocted by my political advisors. First we targeted a high-profile post, and then we came up with a strategy to position me for it."

"Okay, so you're going to be like tax commissioner or something?"

"That's important, but not exactly high profile. However, the governor is looking to appoint the first commissioner of human rights, and it's a really big deal. Since the whole gay marriage thing erupted, he's been under a lot of pressure to make a high-visibility appointment—someone who will coordinate the state's efforts on equal rights. So that's the position I'm going for."

"I hate to be tiresome, but I'm still waiting for an explanation as to why you're looking in the rearview as if you expect gunfire from behind."

"Your patience will be rewarded shortly. Now, I come from a really conservative part of the state. No one's going to think to look for a human rights commissioner out in my neck of the woods. So I needed to do something that would get me noticed. And that's why I started spending my Sunday evenings at Burn."

"You lost me there," Oliver said. He really had been trying to follow James's meandering explanation, but it all still added up to nothing.

"It's kind of a cliché these days, the closeted politician who gets caught at the gay bar. But we updated that for the current cultural moment. Politicians get caught fooling around with women all the time, and it's not a career killer. If all sexualities really are equal, then if I get caught fooling around with a guy, all I need to do is the apology tour with my long-suffering wife, and we're good. But as a result, I come out as bisexual—with some commitment issues that will be addressed in counseling. Now, who better to be the face of the state's equal rights effort than a young politico on the move who just happens to be bisexual? The governor would have to be crazy not to appoint me right away."

"Yeah, the governor's the crazy one in all of this." Oliver looked at James, the person he had come to think of as intelligent. "Who the hell thinks this shit up?"

James's shrugged. "It was Stella's idea, really."

"Because being cheated on publicly by one's closeted bisexual husband is every woman's dream."

"I know it sounds strange. But Stella is hugely motivated when it comes to politics. She grew up in that world. Her dad is a judge—he's actually the guy whose ruling on gay marriage was overturned, making it legal for gays and lesbians to get married."

"Sounds like a great guy."

"Yeah, he's kind of awful, to be honest. But he's really smart when it comes to political intrigue like this."

"I don't think any of you clowns come off looking very smart."

James gave a small nod. "After Sunday's debacle, I'm coming around to your way of thinking."

"So what happened on Sunday was... planned, wasn't it? That's why you seemed to know that there would be a photographer at the door."

"Oliver, I—"

"You set me up. You brought me to that hotel room knowing I was going to end up getting pulled into this mess."

James sighed helplessly, then nodded.

"But then… why did you send me home? Wasn't the point to get your picture in the paper with a dancing boy from the club?"

"I… I couldn't do it." James looked out the side window at the diminishing lights as they left downtown. "I just couldn't do that to you."

"I don't understand."

"I was supposed to find a go-go boy. Some brainless body who would look good on the news, but whom no one would take seriously if he tried to tell his side of the story." James looked over at Oliver. "I fucked that one up."

Oliver looked back at him, wondering how in a plan so completely fucked up, James could identify any part of it that seemed more fucked up than any other. "And how did you do that?"

"I picked you." James turned his head back to the road and drove in silence for a minute or two. "All of the go-go boys working their trade in this city, and I choose the med student. The one who is not only one of the smartest people I've ever met, but who turns out to be one of the nicest people I've ever met." He turned and looked at Oliver again. "I couldn't do it. Not to you."

"Am I supposed to be flattered? That you started out to take advantage of me but then realized I was a real person and couldn't do it?"

"I don't know what you're supposed to feel. I never imagined being in this situation, but then again it's my own fault, so I can't exactly rail against the injustice of it all. But I will allow that you have that right, and if you're really pissed at me, I understand."

Oliver looked out the window because he didn't want to be looking at James right then. "It boggles my mind that it occurred to no one in your political brain trust that this was a terrible plan, and you were basically going to destroy someone's life in order to advance your career."

"I know you don't want to hear this right now, and I don't blame you, but I honestly didn't think this would ruin the life of your standard-issue go-go boy. I kind of figured that the occasional run-in with a married man would go with the territory. Sure, there'd be a little scandal, but things would settle down pretty quickly. Again, you're anything but standard-issue. That's another reason I had to keep you from getting involved."

"I guess I'm starting to understand what happened. Doesn't mean I think it was a good idea, because to be perfectly honest, everyone involved in it needs their head examined. But setting that aside for the moment, I still keep coming back to how nothing you've said explains why we're on the run."

"On Monday morning I went home after the crowd dispersed at the hotel. I explained to Stella that you had refused to come into the suite with me. I figured if I told her that, she would give up on the plan, and we'd think of some other strategy. But she just went off on me—just… erupted. I've never seen her so livid. She screamed for an hour about how this plan had to work, and she wasn't going to let me fuck it up. I… I kind of caved." James looked ashamedly at Oliver. "I gave in. I said I'd find another club, and another go-go boy, and we'd make it work this time."

"So out of the wreckage of this spectacularly stupid plan, your take-away is 'try, try again'?"

"Not proud of that. But Stella can be hard to mollify once she's on a tear. It seemed easier to just convince her I was willing to try again and figure out what to do later."

"So you were at least considering not going through with it?"

James nodded.

"First intelligent thing you've said."

"Thanks," James replied grimly. "But Stella wasn't going for it. She said that with the timing we'd worked out, it needed to happen this week, and there wasn't time to lay all the groundwork again—becoming a regular at a club, getting close to one of the staff, convincing him to go to the hotel. She said I had to get you to do it, no matter what."

Oliver looked around, heart suddenly racing. He was in a locked car, speeding down the freeway to a destination he did not know, in the company of a man who had just used the words "no matter what." This was bad.

"I think you need to stop the car and let me out now," Oliver said. He worked to keep the rising panic out of his voice.

"Hear me out," James said. "I told her I wouldn't do it, that you weren't the right person to involve in this. She said I didn't have a choice, and if I wouldn't do it, she would go to plan B."

Oliver swallowed and tried to keep his voice even. "What's plan B?"

"That's what I asked, since she'd never mentioned it. She said since she wasn't sure she could trust me—married six years, and this was the first I'd heard of that little fact—she had made arrangements to keep the plan moving forward even if I wimped out." He looked at Oliver, clearly stung by the memory of what Stella had said. "It's like she expected me to fuck this up."

"You're asking me to sympathize with your marital problems while you kidnap me? It's a bit early for Stockholm syndrome." Oliver shook his head. "Plus, you did fuck this up."

"Right you are. Fuck." He took a deep breath before continuing. "She said one of the photographers had gotten a picture of you as we entered the hotel on Sunday, and she was going to use it to find you. Then her friendly staff members would get you to 'confess' on video."

"What was I going to confess to, exactly?"

"To having an affair with me," James said, with a sidelong glance at Oliver.

"And why would I be willing to do that?" Oliver asked. He liked to think he would have been able to take the moral high ground (should he still be allowed on that ground, given his recent poor life decisions) and refuse to cooperate.

"Because the alternative would have been worse." James looked over at Oliver, his eyebrows peaked in sympathy. "You have to understand, Oliver, that not everyone views Burn as just another bar and you as just another bartender. The threat of exposure wouldn't bother a standard-issue go-go boy—exposure is what they live for. Stella was expecting you to jump at the chance to have your fifteen minutes of fame and probably turn the visibility of a political scandal into a lucrative escort career. But you're not like that, and they would have quickly figured out that the worst thing in the world for you would be the scandal itself. It puts your entire career at risk. And they would have used that to threaten you. They would have offered you a way out that would only have hurt your career plan, not killed it off entirely. But your life would have been torn up by the roots, and it would have taken a lot of work to put it back together—probably in another state far from here, where our local politics don't reach." James huffed angrily. "There's no way it would have ended in anything but complete disaster for you, Oliver. So we had to go."

Oliver pondered this for a moment. "But it wouldn't have been a disaster for you," he said finally. "You would have come through this with your career—not your ethics, of course, since you're going to have to admit a total loss there, but your career—fully intact. That's assuming people are as gullible as you think they are, and the governor would be willing to overlook the scandal all of this would cause. Which I'm not convinced about, just so we're clear."

James shook his head and looked seriously at Oliver. "That doesn't matter. I'm not going to let them do anything to you."

"Wait, so you're calling the whole thing off now?"

James nodded.

"And those guys back there"—Oliver jerked his thumb toward the rear window—"are going to try to make us do it anyway?"

James nodded again. "I'm so sorry."

Oliver sat silent for a moment, reviewing the entire situation. "I have to be honest, James. This is the most fucked-up scenario I can possibly imagine. If I saw this on a TV show, I would change the channel immediately. There's no way I'd watch this if it were someone else's life, and yet here I am." He shook his head, thinking about how he should have stuck to tending bar at a boring hipster steakhouse and been happy with the tips he used to get. The wads of cash he emptied out of his jockstrap at the end of the day were certainly not worth all of this. "So, what's your next brilliant plan? I'm imagining something involving crossing the border to Mexico on donkeys, because that would make as much sense as the rest of the crap you've come up with."

"No donkeys in the offing, I swear," James replied. "It's pretty simple. Stella's plan can't move forward without us, so I'm taking us someplace she doesn't know about. Once she sees we're serious about not playing along, she'll have to call off the dogs and ditch the whole stupid plan. Which, by the way, seems even stupider now I've explained it to you. God, what were we thinking?"

"So where are we heading?"

"My family had a little cabin in the mountains east of the city. It's by a lake, off in the middle of nowhere. We hardly used it once my parents' business took off. I'd go there with some buddies in high school and college, and we'd drink and smoke some weed and fish and stuff. I've hardly been there the last few years, and Stella doesn't even know I have it. I have a buddy who became a lawyer, and he said I should make sure to list it in the prenup as my own property. When I told him Stella was insisting on sharing all real estate I brought to the marriage, he said I should transfer it to a trust and keep it out of the prenup altogether. He knew it was about the only thing I had with positive memories of my parents. So that's what I did."

"So just to review, you're taking me to a remote cabin in the woods no one knows about?"

"Sounds bad, doesn't it? But I swear to you, Oliver, all I'm trying to do is make this whole situation go away. You are completely safe with me."

"Prove it," Oliver said, challenge in his voice.

"How am I supposed to prove it?"

"Take the next exit."

They were well beyond the city now, and even the suburbs were starting to disperse into dark rural openness. If Oliver was going to take control of this situation, it had to be soon.

"What's at the next exit?"

"It's the interchange I go through every time I head home for break, where the highway north comes through. There's a big truck stop. Pull in there."

James nodded, though he still looked confused.

Oliver unbuckled his seat belt, reclined his seat with a soft whir of the motor, and climbed into the backseat. There he opened his backpack and pulled out his street clothes. He changed quickly, though the space was a little tight. He climbed back into the passenger seat and returned his seat back to the full upright position.

James took the next exit, as instructed, and pulled up in front of a large truck-stop complex.

"Now what?" James asked.

"Come inside." Oliver opened the car door and stepped out into the cool night.

James followed him, the car locking itself behind them. Oliver entered the truck stop and looked around for a moment.

"Wait here," he said. He walked to the service counter, leaving James standing next to the vats of trucker-strength coffee. He returned a moment later. "Follow me."

They walked to the opposite end of the complex, where a neon sign on the wall buzzed out the word "Showers." Oliver looked at the key card in his hand, walked over to door number six, swiped the card in the lock, and pulled the door open. He motioned with a jerk of his head for James to enter.

"What are we doing here?" James asked, his voice for the first time revealing tension.

"You wanted me to trust you. I don't have anything to go on, so I need to be sure you're trustworthy." He closed and locked the door behind him. "Now, strip."

"What?" James said with a startled chuckle, as if certain he had misheard.

"Take your clothes off," Oliver enunciated slowly. "I need to be sure you don't have a knife or a gun or anything."

James stared at him.

"Now would be good," Oliver said. "Or would you prefer I text Xander and tell him I've been kidnapped? Or perhaps I could just stick my head out the door and yell rape. That better for you?"

"Why are you doing this?" James asked, his voice smaller than Oliver had ever heard it. He began unbuttoning his shirt.

"Because you leave me no fucking choice, James. Think about it. What would you do in my position?"

James, properly chastised, removed his shirt and started on his pants. He kicked off his shoes and stood in front of Oliver in just his socks and boxers.

Millie was right, Oliver thought before he could stop himself. James was all lean muscle. Oliver knew him to be thirty, but he had a body any man Oliver's age would be proud of. Oliver shook his head to free it of Millie's "I told you so" voice, which he could hear every time something Millie prophesied came true. He heard it a lot.

"Turn around," Oliver ordered.

James shuffled his feet and turned to face away. "What are you going to do now?" His voice was shaky, as if he were genuinely scared.

"I told you, I just want to be sure you aren't carrying a weapon. That's all. You sound like you think I'm going to rape you or something."

James exhaled and turned back around. "Sorry. I just… you're suddenly so forceful, I was kind of scared there for a minute. I mean, we're in a truck-stop shower, and I don't have any clothes on, and you're kind of a big guy."

"I think we're fairly evenly matched," Oliver said, failing to keep from glancing down at James's heavily muscled chest. He snapped back to the task at hand. "Car keys," he demanded, holding out his hand.

James reached for his pants and pulled the fob out of the front pocket. "Are you going to leave me here?" His voice sounded less scared than... disappointed?

"No. I'm just going to search the car, make sure you don't have anything like a gun or a guide you downloaded from the Internet on how to butcher a human being."

"I keep that on my phone," James said.

Out of the tension of this strange situation, both men laughed uneasily, as if sharing a life preserver.

"I'll be back. Wait for me here." Oliver put his hand on the door. "Hang a sock on the knob if you meet someone." He shut the door behind him, hearing James's tentative laughter grow stronger.

Oliver went out to the car, and he genuinely considered simply leaving. It would solve his immediate problem, but the men who had stormed into Burn would certainly be looking for him at home by now, and he would have nowhere to go. He popped the trunk and found inside a suitcase containing clothes and toiletries, but no weapon, and several grocery bags full of food from an exclusive grocery boutique that Oliver had heard of but never set foot in. In the last bag in the corner of the trunk was a bottle of Glenlivet—one of the rare, really old ones that was too top-shelf even for Burn's topmost shelf. Oliver closed the trunk and opened the door of the car. He searched the glove box, under the seats, in all of the pockets and bins he could find. He came up with nothing. He shut and locked the car and went back into the truck stop. He purchased a keychain-sized container of pepper spray, tucked it into the pocket of his jeans, and walked back over to the shower area. He unlocked door number six and stepped in.

James was standing, fully dressed, reading the instructions and warnings on the wall. "Sexual activity in the shower rooms will not be tolerated," he read from the sign, "and yet they provide a coin-operated condom machine. Nice to have one's bases covered."

"Ready to go?" Oliver asked.

"We're standing in a shower room in a truck stop, and you have to ask that?"

They walked back out through the convenience store. James stopped to get a cup of coffee from the enormous tank of the stuff by the door. "Want a cup?"

Oliver plucked one of the quart-sized cups from the stack and decanted his own. James paid, and they got back into the car.

They were back at cruising speed before either said anything.

"Well, that was interesting," James observed.

"You act like you've never been ordered to strip at a truck stop before."

"I must have lived quite a sheltered life," James replied with an archly sorrowful voice.

Oliver looked into the darkness for a moment. "Sorry to have to do that," he said.

"It's okay. I would say I would do the same thing if I were in your shoes, but I don't think I would have had the presence of mind to come up with a plan like that." He looked over at Oliver. "You really are the smartest person I think I've ever met."

"Yep, just smart enough to end up on the run from hired goons who want to get a picture of me having gay sex with a politician. And when this hits the news, the last people to see me alive will say I was wearing tight shorts and a jockstrap and seemed to take pride in my work. My funeral shall be free of encomiums to my intellect."

"We'll get through this," James said, a wishful tone in his voice.

"I hope so," Oliver replied, trying to sound upbeat, mostly for his own benefit.

A buzzing from his pocket startled him. He pulled out his phone.

"It's Xander." He looked at James. "I'm just going to ask you this straight out, and I want an honest answer. Are you planning to kill, maim, exploit, or in any other way, shape, or form, harm me?"

"Oliver, I swear to you, I would never hurt you. Never."

Oliver nodded. *Dancing queen.* He hit send and put his phone back in his pocket. Next to the pepper spray.

"How much farther?" he asked.

"About an hour." James looked into the darkness ahead.

"Wish I'd picked up a magazine or something at the truck stop," Oliver said. "They had the new issue of *Teen Juggs*. Of course, I only read it for the articles."

"That was a great piece last month by the chair of the Federal Reserve. I've never known anyone to make such an incisive economic analysis using boob metaphors."

It felt good to laugh.

CHAPTER EIGHT
OUT OF BOUNDS

IT WAS nearly one in the morning when James pulled off the winding rural highway onto an unmarked gravel road. The car bumped along for about fifteen minutes until finally the headlights illuminated a clearing ahead, in which stood a log-and-stone structure. It was considerably larger than Oliver had expected, and there were lights on inside the imposing edifice.

"I thought you said no one knew this was here?" Oliver asked, his grip tight on the door handle.

"I meant no one from my current life knows it's here. But there's a guy who lives a couple miles up the highway from here who takes care of it for me—has for years, since my parents built it—and I asked him to get it ready."

The car pulled to a stop in front of the stone steps that led to the front porch. Oliver opened the door and stepped into the cool night air. The first thing he noticed was a sky full of stars; he'd forgotten during his years in the city how many stars there were out in the country.

"Beautiful, isn't it?" James said, joining him beside the car, looking up.

As Oliver was silent, James walked to the back of the car and opened the trunk. He pulled out his suitcase and one of the bags of groceries. Oliver's chivalrous instincts drove him to shake off his stupor and pick up the remaining bags before he could scold himself for being an active participant in his own abduction. James closed the trunk with a soft, Germanic *whump*, and they walked up the stone steps. James unlocked the door and stood aside to welcome Oliver in.

Stepping into the "cabin," Oliver was stunned. The main room soared two stories high to the peak of the roof on the far wall—a wall made entirely of windows and craftsman-style timbers. James pressed a switch, and a fire crackled to life in the stone fireplace on one side of the room, its reflection flickering on the smooth woods and leathers of the furniture.

"*This* is a little cabin in the mountains?" Oliver looked over at James, who shrugged. "You put a ton of money into this, didn't you?"

"Not me, my parents. I think if they had lived longer, they would have spent it all just as quickly as they earned it, but they didn't really get the chance."

"This isn't what I pictured when you said you'd come here with your buddies to fish and drink." Oliver took a turn around the room, getting a closer look at the furnishings. "This seems far too posh."

"My parents may not have taken much time away from work to enjoy it, but they always bought the best." James sighed and looked around the room. "Now, in a bold role reversal, may I make you a drink?"

Oliver weighed whether it would be advisable for him to drink while being abducted, but two seconds of reflection were enough for him to realize that he could really use a little alcohol in his system. "That would be nice, thanks. As long as you promise not to make me a Dirty Altar Boy."

"I would never ask you to be something you're not," James said with a wink. He picked up the grocery bags and walked over to the kitchen.

Oliver sat on a leather couch facing the fireplace. There was a soft blanket draped over the back, and he wrapped it around himself.

"Here you go," James said, handing Oliver a glass. He set the bottle, the rare old Scotch, on the table in front of the sofa, and sat down next to Oliver. "To great escapes." He held his glass up to Oliver, who joined him in his toast.

"Wow, that's amazing," Oliver said reverently. "That swallow probably cost more than my car payment."

"It's a bottle I've been saving for a special occasion. Or at least one so fucked-up that one may as well drink the good stuff because who knows what's coming next in life, right?"

"True story," Oliver agreed and took another sip.

They stared at the fire for a while.

"Can I ask you something?" Oliver said, still staring into the flames.

"Of course. I shall have no more secrets from you, my good man."

"Was it all a lie?" Out of the corner of his eye, Oliver could see James turn to him, a confused look on his face.

"Was what a lie?"

"Everything. Everything you've said to me since we met." Oliver turned to look into James's eyes. "I just want to know, for the record."

"Oliver, I don't expect you to believe this given all of the things I kept from you, but everything I've ever told you was the truth. I've told you things about myself that no one else knows. And when I told you I thought you were the smartest person I've ever met, and the nicest, that was the truth too." He paused, looking into the fire. "And the part about getting a boner from watching you dance. That was gospel."

Oliver blushed. "Thank you," he said in a small voice. He didn't know what else to say.

"Can you answer me something, then?" James asked, after taking a fortifying sip of Scotch. "Would you ever... I mean, in a different set of circumstances, do you think you could ever... consider a man like me?"

"Consider what?"

"Consider... being with me."

The hot rush of blood to Oliver's face felt like it would set his cheeks on fire. His chest felt tight, and there seemed to be less air in the room than when he last respired normally. He wasn't breathing, at least not until he gasped in a large, sudden breath.

"Oh, I see," James said quietly. "Never mind."

"No, it's not that," Oliver blurted, though what he meant by "that" he had no idea. "It's just that...." Words abandoned him and he searched the flames for any he might be able to use.

"Let me guess," James said kindly. "You have a boyfriend who is just as amazing as you are, and you're going to set up practice in your little town and deliver beautiful babies and cure cancer on the side, just for fun?"

Oliver chuckled because he had no idea what else to do. He had experienced no mortification lately that wasn't immediately magnified by a misunderstanding. It was getting to be exhausting.

"No," he said firmly. "There's no boyfriend, amazing or otherwise." He took a deep breath. "James, I'm... straight."

James's mouth dropped open, but other than that, there was no movement on his side of the couch.

"Plus, you're married," Oliver added, because even though it didn't matter in the way he answered James's question, he still thought it should matter.

James chuckled darkly. "Oh, that." He held counsel with the ceiling for a moment and then looked back down to the fire. "I think it's pretty clear that once Stella finds out I've disappeared rather than go along with her scheme, the whole marriage thing is probably over. We haven't exactly been close for the last few... well, ever." He sighed sadly. "It's been a complete disaster, as marriages go, but I really didn't know any better. My parents were business partners, not lovers, and that's all I had to go on. I thought that's how people did it. I chose a mate based on my ambitions, my desire to make the world a better place, not on what I felt when we were together."

"That's really sad," Oliver replied. "My parents work together too. The supper club takes their every waking moment, from first light through to closing time. But they seem so happy. Both of them told me how lucky they felt to be able to go to work every day with the person they love most. Plus, me, when I was still at home." He looked at James. "We're kind of gooey that way, actually. Sorry."

"So you're actually straight? You don't just play a straight jock down at the club for money? I mean, I'd understand if you're just saying that to let me know I don't have a chance." He smiled stoically. "Message received on that one."

"No, please don't take it personally. If I were gay, I would completely go for a guy like you." *Oliver, what the fuck are you saying?*

"You would?" James asked, a small smile returning to his face.

Oliver blushed and, though his every instinct rebelled against it, he nodded. Millie would have a field day with this one, but he was committed to making his answer, so he plowed ahead. "You're not like the rest of the people I've met at the club. You seem... like a grown-up. I looked forward to seeing you on Sundays because it was so nice to be able to talk about real things, not about the silly stuff everyone else goes on and on about. It was like you were a real person, when I'd given up on meeting one."

"That's very flattering, coming from a straight guy." There was a subtle teasing note in James's voice.

Oliver took a drink. Millie's many arguments about how he wasn't really a straight guy anymore were echoing in his mind, distracting him from what he was trying to think. The Scotch didn't seem to be helping. "How long has it been since you've slept with your wife?" Oliver asked suddenly, without knowing why.

James didn't seem startled by the question. "I stopped keeping track when it had been two years. Seemed depressing to go much further than that."

"Do you have anyone... else?"

James shook his head. "I know this sounds ridiculous coming from someone who has essentially run away into the mountains with the man of his dreams, but I was trying to protect my career. So no affairs, no flirtations, not even any sexting."

"Man of your dreams?" Oliver asked, alarmed all over again.

"Oliver, if I may be perfectly frank, I never imagined I would meet anyone like you. I imagine this is a difficult thing for a straight guy to hear, but you are so beautiful, inside and out... if we had met before I got married, we wouldn't be in this mess."

"I don't think that's a difficult thing for anyone to hear, actually," Oliver said, blushing again. He hoped the heat in his cheeks would stop flaring every time James said anything about him. It seemed immature. He smiled helplessly at James and took another sip of Scotch.

"So. Abduct unsuspecting straight guy into mountain love nest, check. Make an awkward pass at aforementioned straight guy, check. Now what's next on my kidnapper's to-do list? Let's see. Ah, dinner. Well. It's kind of late," James said, checking his expensive-looking watch, "but I suspect you could do with a bite of something?"

"You suspect correctly. Can I help?"

"No, no. Least I can do, having brought you here against your will. Just relax, and I'll make you something that will bear at least a passing resemblance to food." James stood, placed another few logs on the fire, and left for the kitchen.

Oliver pulled the blanket around him (100% cashmere, the label said) and put his feet on the warm spot vacated by James. He was cozy, a little tipsy, and in danger of coming to like being kidnapped. He closed his eyes for just a moment.

"Oliver, dinner," James whispered.

Oliver had drifted off, though for how long he didn't know. He sat up. "Sorry, must have—"

"No apologies," James said with a hand raised. "Please, you are my guest, and I will tolerate nothing but your ecstatic enjoyment of what meager hospitality I can offer. Come have some dinner."

Oliver stood, rubbed his eyes, and looked over at the dining room. Candles flickered down the length of the heavy oak table, as well as from the chandelier above. A bottle of wine and one of an Italian sparkling water stood over two steaming plates, set close together at one end. James led the way to the table, and pulled out a chair for Oliver.

"Laying it on a bit thick, aren't you, considering I'm still straight?"

"Well see," James said. "You may change your tune once you've tasted my puttanesca."

"I'm going to need a lot more than that bottle of wine before I'm ready to do that."

"Luckily, I have a lot more than that bottle of wine." James sat and poured a glass for Oliver.

Oliver looked at the table and the room that glowed with candlelight and at James, whose kind eyes were lit with a joy Oliver had never seen in them before. He'd always seemed on the edge of sadness in the club. Suddenly Oliver felt very warm inside. "This is beautiful," he said, bringing his glass to his lips. He tasted the deep garnet wine, smelled the rich pasta sauce, felt himself to be in the lap of a luxury he hadn't known existed in the world. "Best abduction ever."

James beamed at him. "You say the sweetest things."

Oliver laughed and wrapped a knot of noodles around his fork. "Oh my God," he said around the mouthful of spicy pasta. "This is so good."

"We'll see if it works," James said with a devilish grin.

Oliver fixed him with a scoldy scowl but was too entranced by the meal to do more than that. He was happy enough to leave his rational faculties aside and just enjoy the meal and, as little as he was willing to admit it, the company. He still found James a stimulating conversationalist, and they talked over the pasta, the wine, and a delightful lemon tart. They were sipping port over the wreckage of the dishes as the clock ticked on toward four in the morning.

"Sun's going to be up soon," James said as he set down his empty glass. "We should probably get some sleep."

Oliver nodded as he rose from the table. "Help you with dishes?"

"Oh fuck no," James said with a laugh. "I'll take care of those in the morning. After two bottles of wine and the port and the Scotch, I'd probably just break them all anyway." He stood. "Come on, I'll show you to your room." He gestured for Oliver to walk with him and led the way down a hall on the other side of the cabin from the kitchen.

He stopped at the first door on the right. "Here you are," he said, opening the door and switching on the light. "Bathroom's through there, and you'll find some pajamas in the top dresser drawer."

"You've thought of everything," Oliver said.

"I'm not the type to abduct someone on the spur of the moment," James said in a dignified voice. "I'll see you in the morning… or later this morning, I guess."

"Good night, then," Oliver said, stepping into the bedroom.

"And, in case I haven't said it enough, I'm sorry for how this all turned out."

"You can stop apologizing now," Oliver said with a smile. "I'll be freaking out tomorrow morning when I miss class for the first time ever, but right now… well, I've spent worse evenings. Thank you." He looked into the surprised joy on James's face and felt an unfamiliar heat in his chest. "Well, good night."

"Good night, Oliver," James said and pulled the door closed.

The exhaustion of the day fell upon Oliver, heavy and urgent, and he brushed his teeth, stripped off his clothes, and slid into the sheets naked, as was his habit. In the thirty seconds of consciousness before sleep claimed him, he had to admit this wasn't a bad way to have spent a day.

IT WAS the smell of bacon that awakened him. There was light streaming in the window, through which he could see what James had called a "little lake." Its deep blue water stretched as far as he could see, ringed by dense forest. Oliver picked up his phone and looked at the time. It was after ten, which meant he had already slept through a class and was now missing his lab. He had anticipated that this would cause him significant distress—he wasn't ready for the complete lack of panic he felt. In fact, lying here, feeling the caress of the expensive sheets on his naked body, looking out at the pristine view, smelling what was probably heirloom bacon being cooked on a stove that surely cost more than the house he grew up in, Oliver felt nothing but free.

Free of responsibilities, free of the constraints that bound him to everyday life. This was an experience unlike any he had ever had, and he kind of liked it that way.

He threw the covers off and strode to the bathroom. He showered quickly and pulled on a pair of sweatpants and a Dartmouth T-shirt he found in the dresser. Then he padded down the hall toward the kitchen.

James was a blur of motion, gliding smoothly from stove to refrigerator to table, preparing breakfast. He wore a pair of sweats just like the ones Oliver had found, but that was all he had on. His powerful chest, with its partial covering of carefully trimmed hair, flexed fluidly as he moved from task to task.

Even straight guys notice good muscle development, Oliver told himself. He repeated this—lips forming the words for good measure—before venturing in the kitchen.

"Good morning," James said in greeting, smiling broadly. "Sleep well?"

"Yeah, just maybe not long enough," Oliver said, returning his smile.

"Well, given that we're hiding out, there won't be much excitement here today. Perhaps we can catch a nap." His eyes bugged out in embarrassment. "I mean we can both take naps. You know, separately." He blushed and shook his head helplessly, trying to recover from his slip.

Oliver smiled at James's fluster. "Relax. You don't have to pretend this isn't a classic porn setup we've got going here. I've seen a few 'cabin in the woods' scenarios in my day. Of course, they all involved a sturdy woodsman and a chick who for some reason went hiking in a bikini, but I imagine there's something equivalent on the gay side."

"Indeed there is," James replied with a chuckle. "You have to admit that there is a certain symmetrical appeal to having them both be sturdy woodsmen. Mmm, all that plaid." He resumed mixing whatever was in the big yellow bowl while looking dreamily into the distance.

Oliver watched him, smiling. "You know, I see it now. It looks good on you."

James shook off his reverie. "What does?"

"Gay."

James looked at him blankly.

"When you started coming into the club, I figured you were one of the closet cases the guys told me to expect on Sundays. You were kind of... sad, I guess? But on the drive here, and seeing you now, I get it. It's like the closer you got to being free, the more you became yourself." He noticed James's concerned look. "Don't worry—I like you even more here."

"The things you say," James said with a wink. "You could turn a guy's head with talk like that."

"Tell me you have coffee, and I'll let you turn whatever you want."

"What's your pleasure, then, sir? I and my espresso maker are at your disposal."

"Latte with as many extra shots as you can stuff in there?"

"I'll start frothing. Why don't you step out onto the deck to enjoy the midmorning air, and I'll bring it out."

"Best abduction *ever*," Oliver muttered lightly as he walked past James on his way to the french doors that opened onto the deck.

The morning sun had warmed the deck, and the lakefront was alive with birds and other wildlife going about their daily scrabblings for sustenance. Oliver sat down on an extravagantly upholstered chair and leaned back to feel the heat and light on his face. James's footsteps were barely audible behind him a few minutes later.

"One latte, absolutely packed with extra caffeine," he said, handing Oliver the gleaming porcelain cup and saucer. He sat down in the chair next to Oliver's with his own mug of steaming coffee.

"To life on the run," Oliver said, holding his cup aloft.

James touched his to Oliver's and took a long sip. "I'd forgotten how much I loved this place." He sighed, looking out over the lake.

"It's beautiful," Oliver said. "So is this how you passed the time with your high school and college buds? Sipping lattes and appreciating the view?"

"Hardly," James said wryly. "They wanted to get drunk, watch porn, and talk about all of the women who wouldn't give them the time of day."

"That sounds like no fun at all," Oliver observed.

"Well, watching porn with them was fun," James said with a grin, which faded quickly. "In a blue-balls, look-but-don't-touch kind of way."

"Again, sounds like no fun at all." Oliver sipped his coffee. "It must have been really hard, growing up that way."

"I think everyone grows up that way, honestly," James replied. "Sexual frustration kind of goes with the territory at that age. I was no closer to getting busy with my buddies than they were to getting lucky with the ladies. Different sex, same sad story. It's a common bond of humanity." He looked at Oliver. "Though I imagine you had any lady you winked at."

Oliver laughed. "Sure, because there's nothing sexier than the valedictorian who chairs the Latin club. I had to fight them off, especially during review sessions for honors biochemistry. Hot, hot, hot." He sat up in his chair. "Actually, it is kind of hot right now." He took off the Dartmouth T-shirt and tossed it over another chair to his side.

"Fuck," James exhaled softly and turned his eyes back to the lake.

One of the benefits of his work at Burn was that Oliver no longer felt embarrassed by someone appreciating his body; it rolled over him like a comment on the weather. "Here's something I don't get," Oliver said, looking thoughtfully at James. "You are built. Like fucking *built*. You have the perfect body. Why do you want mine? I don't have anything you don't."

James seemed to ponder this for a moment. "You know how they say men have a one-track mind? Well, I don't think that's true. I think we have a two-track mind. Of course we're attracted to physical beauty, of which you are the possessor of an unparalleled example. But we're also attracted to smart, insightful, compassionate people who 'get' us, right? I think the stereotypical man checks that first box with the most gorgeous woman he can find, and then he has his buddies to talk to. Two tracks." James looked with open pleasure at Oliver's chest. "Lucky is the man who finds both in one person." He glanced up, caught Oliver's eye. "Yep, lucky me." He grinned, but a little sadly.

"Back where I come from, there isn't much in the way of a gay community," Oliver said matter-of-factly. "When I got to college, it was kind of a surprise to find people being so open about their sexuality. But they also seemed to be mostly focused on hooking up. It never occurred to me that real relationships were possible."

"College is mostly about hooking up, for everyone," James replied. "I think the only thing that's different is that a lot of gay guys from small towns have never had much of a dating pool to swim in, so they kind of go crazy when they get away from home. Kind of a candy-store phase."

"Did you have that when you went to college?"

James shook his head. "I was pretty messed up after my parents died. Part of me thought they died because of the impure thoughts I had about guys." He put up a hand. "I know, I know, but you can't underestimate how a conservative upbringing fucks with you. I really believed I had somehow doomed them by sneaking peeks at my roommate in the shower. So after they died, I just crammed all of that away and tried to be one hundred percent completely straight." He took a drink of coffee. "As that effort has resulted in my wife scheming to ruin my life while the most beautiful man I've ever met sits shirtless and unavailable next to me, I have to admit it was an abject failure. Time for a new plan."

"What's your new plan going to be?" Oliver asked. He realized in asking it that some small part of him was hoping he might have a part in whatever this new plan entailed. It was crazy, but he had to admit he would miss James were he to disappear into a new life somewhere far away.

"To make you the most amazing breakfast ever, then go for a run around the lake. How does that sound?" James got up. "The hash and scones should be ready to come out of the oven in a minute. Sit tight and prepare to be awestruck."

Oliver laughed and watched James go. Why did everything he did have to be so damn… sexy?

THEY SAT basking in the sun, now approaching its midday peak, digesting the breakfast that, true to James's word, was amazing.

"Ready for that run now?" Oliver asked. He usually worked out in the morning, and his body was letting him know he was ignoring his obligations.

"Absolutely. I have some running shorts and an extra pair of trail shoes, if you'd like to borrow them," James said. "I'm afraid, however, there are no shirts to be had in the entire county."

Oliver laughed at James's intentionally clumsy flirtation. "I may never wear a shirt again," he said.

"I have no objection whatsoever." James led the way into the cabin and soon presented Oliver with a neatly folded pair of running shorts and nearly new shoes that fit him as if they were his own.

They struck out onto a rough path that ran around the lake, sometimes right on the water's edge and other times venturing deep into the green. After about half an hour, James pulled off to the side of the trail and slowed to a walk. He strode to a stone pillar near the water's edge to which a small spigot was mounted. Crystalline water flowed from it, splashing gently onto rocks at the foot of the pillar.

"The lake is spring fed," James said, pointing to the water flowing from the tap. "My dad had this installed when he built the cabin. A little of the spring water flows through here, and the rest runs into the lake just over there." He nodded to an inlet about twenty feet away. He leaned down and took a drink from the tap. "Best water in the world—try it."

Oliver came to the tap and took a long drink. It was cold and tasted like nothing he'd ever known. "Wow, that's really good."

"I use it to water the good Scotch. I like to think it makes it even more authentic."

They each took another drink and then continued their run. As they rounded their full circuit of the lake, they approached a small sandy beach area and a pier with a boathouse next to it right on the surface of the water. Oliver hadn't seen this from the deck as it lay far below the commanding sightlines of the cabin. James walked onto the pier, near the end of which was a bench facing the water. He stood, breathing hard from the run, and gazed out over the lake. Oliver joined him there, and they shared a quiet moment of listening to the soft lap of the water on the pilings below the pier.

"Well, I'm going in for a swim," James announced. He grinned at Oliver as he heel-toed his trail shoes off. Then he slid his thumbs into the waistband of his running shorts and whipped them down. Before Oliver had time to even take in this bold move, James had launched himself in a long, perfect dive into the water. To his mortification, Oliver couldn't look away from the graceful arc of his powerful buttocks as they curved effortlessly into the water. *Shit.*

James surfaced a shocking distance from the pier, paddling idly. "Coming in?" he called.

Oliver kicked off his shoes and whipped off his shorts in short order and then executed a dive that, if it lacked James's practiced elegance, compensated with sheer vigor. He stroked easily out to where James was treading water, watching his every move.

"Good God, it's like being back in high school," James sighed with a grin. "Skinny-dipping with a boner."

"Did your friends ever know how you felt about them?" Oliver asked, bobbing in the cool water.

James shook his head. "I learned that lesson early on. One of the first times I brought a friend here, back in high school, I kind of read the signals wrong. We were up late talking shit and, as is normal for horny teenagers, the conversation turned to sex. He said he was determined to get a blowjob before freshman year was over. Well, I figured that was something I could help out with—I thought I was making his dream come true. It quickly became apparent he had a different view, and it turned into a very uncomfortable weekend."

"Yikes. But things got better at some point, right?"

"Hardly. My parents were conservative—not religious conservative as much as 'keep your filthy government hands off my money' conservative, but there's a lot of overlap—and I knew they wouldn't be happy about their only son being gay. High school guys were off limits, for obvious reasons previously established, and I couldn't wait to get to college. But then my parents died, and the guilt set in, and I never really had the chance to develop any relationships. My entire sexual experience is a couple of awkward hookups in a campus bathroom and my wife, the ice queen. I know this sounds pitiable, but I've never in my life just held someone and been held. I used to dream of having someone to cuddle with while watching television or just dozing, lolling about in bed for a day, and I've never had that. It makes me feel like an orphan or something, to want that at my age."

"What a waste." Oliver was deeply saddened by James's tale of loneliness.

"Tell me about it. Best years of my life, right?"

"Not that—you only count time as wasted if you haven't done anything to help someone else. You've probably helped a lot of people in your career. What I meant was what a waste of a body like that, not to share it with anyone."

James looked at Oliver, his face wearing an expression of pure bafflement. "Thanks, I guess? It's nice to hear, but hearing it from you is kind of like having a vegetarian compliment me on my filet mignon."

"Wait. There's filet involved?"

"Eight ouncers. Dry aged, caressed with a Moroccan spice rub that I brought back with me from a sister-city visit last year." James looked at Oliver's face and laughed. "Considering giving up your vegetarian ways?"

"For that I would consider a marriage proposal," Oliver said, and sent a jet of water shooting toward James.

They splashed and frolicked for a long while and then swam smoothly to shore. James took the opportunity to show off his butterfly, which was not only still competition-worthy, but also showed off his muscled ass to greatest advantage—or so Oliver tried not to think.

They drip-dried in the sun, sitting on the bench at the end of the pier, Whitmanesque in the purity of their nudity, unabashed.

"How about that nap you were talking about earlier?" James asked, once they were dry.

"Sounds great. But it's kind of warm to climb back in bed."

"I have just the thing," James said, standing. "Follow me."

Oliver did, though he would have preferred it if James had put his shorts back on before asking Oliver to follow him. Or at least Oliver thought he would have preferred that. Upon further reflection, he began to suspect he actually wasn't sure why he would have preferred that. James's buttocks were a model of masculine strength, and surely there was nothing wrong with Oliver giving them the objective viewing they seemed to deserve. Then he realized he was rationalizing watching another dude's naked ass, and he looked away. For a moment.

James led the way up the stairs from the lake frontage to the deck, and then into the house. He walked down the hall to the room at the end—his bedroom, Oliver knew—and then out a french door into a kind of sunroom.

"A sleeping porch," James said, holding out his arms. There were two ceiling fans that began to turn as they entered the room, and Oliver felt a cool breeze coming from the screened windows that made up the walls of the room. The only furniture in the room was a kind of daybed, and a Swedish modern recliner next to a table holding several books.

Oliver sat on the bed, relishing the cool breezes blowing over his body—his entire body, he hardly even noted to himself. "This is so nice," he said softly.

"I hope you'll be comfortable here," James said, smiling warmly. "I'll leave you to—"

"No, stay," Oliver said, in a voice he didn't recognize. He held out his hand to James.

"What?" James's voice was taut and yet plaintive.

"Stay here with me."

James, silent, appeared not to breathe. He blinked, swallowed. "Is that what you want?"

Oliver nodded. "Today has been amazing. You've helped me see there's a life outside of studying and working every minute. Now I want to help you. You've never just cuddled, and I'm pretty good at the cuddling, if I do say so myself."

James swallowed again, tried to catch his breath. "You don't have to—"

"I know. That's the best part. I don't have to do anything. I can do what I want. And what I want to do right now is this. Please, stay with me." He held out his hand again.

James walked slowly toward the bed, his face wearing an expression of disbelief. He took Oliver's hand, and Oliver pushed himself up onto the daybed, still holding James's hand. He stretched out and motioned for James to do the same. Once James's head was on the pillow, Oliver put his other arm around him, and held him tight.

"Thank you," Oliver said. "Thank you for changing my life."

James blinked, tears running freely down his cheek. He shook his head, unable to speak.

"It's okay," Oliver whispered. "It'll be okay."

They lay that way a long while, in wordless communion, until sleep took them.

CHAPTER NINE
ABSOLUTE BEGINNERS

THE SUN was low in the sky when Oliver awakened, long shadows striping the room. During their nap they had shifted position slightly as James's head now rested on Oliver's chest, Oliver's arm still draped protectively around him.

Oliver had long suspected that the course of one's life is determined not by months and years of conscious effort, but in moments of decision. The impulse, the instinct, the intuition that dictates a turn to the right rather than the left; these are moments that shape us.

Oliver lay cradled in one of those moments.

He looked at James, the sleeping man at peace for the first time since Oliver met him. *I did that. I gave him that.* Oliver smiled, watching the regular rise and fall of James's rib cage. Oliver knew the names of all the muscles and tendons laid out before him, but he had never appreciated their beauty. And he knew, and acknowledged he knew, that James was beautiful.

It was something Oliver had never imagined himself doing. Well, he had long hoped for someone he would be so comfortable with that he could simply slip away into slumber while holding them, not worrying about whether he was doing the right thing, or snoring, or making the other person's arm fall asleep. That part he had imagined. And lying in a posh daybed in a lakeside cabin that looked like something out of *Architectural Digest*, that part he may have dreamed of having much later in his career. So maybe there were parts of this he had imagined.

What he had not imagined was having someone he could talk to, and listen to, as an intellectual equal, whom he could then run several miles with and then rinse the sweat off with a skinny dip, then lay down with as if their bodies were meant to be next to each other. An unexpected unity of the intellectual, physical, and emotional. That he had never imagined. Had he found it? Was James what he was looking for, never knowing the truth of what he sought?

Somewhere, back in the depths of his mind, a voice scolded him, warned him, menaced him because it was a man next to whom he lay, around whom his arm was draped, with whom he was breathing in effortless unison. He listened to that creaky, angry voice just long enough to hear that it spoke of fear and loneliness and thoughtless adherence to a smaller life, a poorer life, one lived without love because sometimes when love comes, it doesn't look the way one expects. He heard that voice, and he closed his ear to it. It wheezed its final imprecation and faded from his consciousness.

James stirred, heaved a great breath, and jolted awake. He lifted his head from Oliver's chest and glanced about the room in a panic. Then he looked back to Oliver's face, though haltingly, as if reluctant—fearful?

Oliver smiled at him, a smile he hoped conveyed all of the sudden happiness he felt at finding the two of them intertwined. A shy smile appeared on James's face, and all was right with the world.

"So, this is cuddling," James said, his voice still thick with sleep.

"No," Oliver said. He brought his hand up to the back of James's neck and slowly grazed his fingertips along his hairline, down to his broad shoulders. He felt a riot of goose bumps rise in their wake. "This, my good man, is cuddling."

James's eyes had closed as Oliver's fingers tickled their way along the nape of his neck, and he shivered with obvious joy. "For a straight guy—"

"Shh," Oliver interrupted him. "Let's stop with the name-calling. How about from now on you just be James, and I'll just be Oliver, and whatever this is between us will have no name because holy fuck, who knew this kind of thing could happen?"

James beamed. "I never even let myself dream this could be."

"That makes two of us," Oliver said with a laugh.

They lay for a long while, just looking at each other, into each other.

"You're really okay with this?" James asked, softly, his voice astonished.

"Yes. This feels… right. Plus, I was told there'd be steak."

"For every meal if that's what it takes," James replied with a laugh.

"Well, let's get moving. All of this cuddling makes me hungry."

"Yes, sir," James said teasingly, then sat up and looked around the room. "That's what this place was missing all these years."

"What's that?" Oliver asked, still stretched out on the daybed.

"A naked go-go boy. You complete the decor."

"We go-go boys make the world better everywhere we go," Oliver said with fake modesty. He sat up as well and then looked out over the placid surface of the lake.

"Shall we?" James asked.

"We shall," Oliver replied, and they got up from the daybed.

Once again, James led the way. This time, Oliver allowed himself to enjoy the view. It was, after all, spectacular.

"You have to let me help this time," Oliver said when they reached the kitchen.

"All right," James agreed. "But I'll handle the meat."

"Promises, promises," tutted Oliver.

"I'm a politician. I keep my promises," James said in a radio-interview voice.

"If you don't, I'm going to hold it against you."

"Promises, promises," James repeated and went laughing out to the deck to start the grill.

Oliver found the bar cupboard and began working on a drink for them to share before dinner. He found, as he expected, that even James's bottom shelf was strictly top-shelf, and there were things on his top shelf that beggared imagination. Soon, though, Oliver had a concoction he was quite happy with, and he ventured out onto the deck to share his invention.

"What's this?" James asked as Oliver handed him a tall glass containing a pearlescent blue liquid.

"Something new. I call it the Limnal Epiphany. Let me know what you think."

"I think you're pretty handy with your Greek roots. Limnal for lake, and epiphany for sudden realization. So, this commemorates something that you realized here?"

Oliver nodded. "Indeed."

"And may I inquire as to the nature of this epiphanic event?"

Oliver shrugged and gave a coy smile. "I cuddled with a boy, and it was pretty awesome."

James blushed but beamed. He practically vibrated with happiness. "To limnal epiphanies," he said raising his glass. "May there be more to come."

"I have a feeling there will be," Oliver said with a laugh.

"Oh, this is good," James said, looking at the deep blues in his glass. "You going to start making this at Burn?"

Oliver shook his head. "You are the only one who will ever taste my cocktail," he said.

"Good God, you're sexy," growled James.

"Save it for tonight," Oliver said, turning to head back to the kitchen.

"Tonight?" James asked, his voice breaking a little as he spoke.

"If your meat proves worthy," Oliver said without turning around—he knew James would be enjoying the view too much to say anything more. Oliver was teasing, but some part of him was ready to bring truth to his words. He was quickly coming to like that part of him.

They ate dinner on the deck, watching the shadows of trees lengthen over the lake. Torches lined the railing, and stars were beginning to populate the sky.

"That was amazing," Oliver said, pushing his plate away. "What did you say you rubbed on your meat?"

"Astroglide," James replied.

Oliver burst out laughing. "Juvenile humor suits you. Would never have thought it from the stiff and stuffy act you were doing every Sunday at the club, but I love to see you laugh—really laugh."

"It wasn't an act at the club, you know," James said, a serious note coming into his voice. "I wasn't happy, and that probably came through pretty clearly. And I was trying to work a strategy—a stupid one, granted—and so falling in love with you really complicated things."

"Falling in love?" Oliver asked, his voice cracking.

James looked at him searchingly, then nodded. "I'm afraid so. I've never done it, so I might be wrong, but I think this is what falling in love feels like."

"Tell me what it feels like."

James looked at his hands, his brow knitted. "Like when I walked through the door of the club every Sunday, my heart would race because I feared I might not find you there. Or when I offered to buy you a drink, and I felt like I had thrown myself off a cliff, not knowing how far down the rocks were at the bottom. Or when I saw you dance, and I knew there had to be a way for us to reach each other." He took a breath and a stiff sip of port. "I knew I was in love with you when I realized I was hanging on every word you said and wishing I could put my hand on yours as you talked, put my hands on you everywhere. People would probably say I'm too quick to use a word like 'love,' but to those people I say, fuck off, because they clearly haven't met you."

Oliver gave a flattered laugh, but he knew if James's definition of "falling in love" was the way love actually worked, he might be guilty of it as well. Of course, eating a gourmet dinner on a deck overlooking a private lake, naked, might encourage objective observers to come to the same conclusion. The whole thing looked pretty intimate.

"Burn will be opening up soon," Oliver observed, glancing at the sky. "I hope they're not too worried about me. This morning I missed class for the first time ever, and tonight I'm missing work for the first time ever. It's a pretty big day."

"I imagine this happens with some regularity there—a member of the staff runs away with a generous and maybe not-terrible-to-look-at older patron and isn't seen for a few days. Plus, you texted Xander that I wasn't going to butcher you, so they probably just assume we're holed up somewhere until I collapse from exhaustion or break a hip or something. Then you'll go back to work and wait for the cycle to begin again."

"Sounds like great work, if you can get it," Oliver said sarcastically.

"Again, that's fine for the standard-issue go-go boy. What they'll make of your disappearance we have no way of knowing. If you're desperate, phone signal starts about five, ten miles that way." James pointed down the driveway.

"The old Oliver would have been desperate. I would have gladly walked ten miles to be able to send a text saying I would be absent from work and would make up the time later. But the new Oliver, the post-epiphany Oliver, figures that everyone deserves a little time away, and I'm just going to take the occasion of my abduction to get my first-ever serving of it." Oliver looked out over the lake and nodded. "Thank you for making me see what I needed."

"You are an amazing young man, Oliver," James said warmly.

"You're pretty amazing yourself," Oliver replied. He stood up from the table and walked over to the side of the deck where two loungers and a sofa were gathered. He sat on one side of the sofa, and looked expectantly at James to come join him.

James walked over and sat on one of the loungers.

"No," Oliver said. "Here." He patted the sofa next to him. "It's getting a little chilly."

"We could go in if you're cold," James said as he got to his feet.

"We could also put some clothes on, but what's the fun in that? It's so beautiful out here—just come cuddle for warmth." He loaded his smile with insinuation, which he was certain James recognized.

As James settled onto the couch, Oliver leaned toward him. He wrapped James's arm around his shoulders and then rested his head on James's strong clavicular deltoid. It felt so good to stop thinking about what he should be doing and just… do. He closed his eyes and breathed in the clean, masculine scent.

"Mmm, nice," he murmured into the night.

James placed his other hand in his lap, as if trying to hide something from Oliver. What he was hiding was no secret to either of them, but for the present they would simply turn a blind eye.

"Oliver?" James whispered.

"Mm-hmm?"

"Can I…?" James swallowed and took a sharp breath. "Can I kiss you?"

The question sent a shiver down Oliver's spine, though he had to admit when one has already whiled away an afternoon cuddling naked with a guy, kissing him probably isn't that big a deal. "I really wish you would," Oliver answered. He lifted his head off James's shoulder and looked into his eyes.

James's face was so happy, his brows peaked in joy, that Oliver knew at that moment and in that place he was right, right for the first time in his life. This is what he had been missing, this man. He smiled and nodded, and James leaned in.

The first contact was electric. Oliver felt a renewal of the shiver down his spine, this time radiating out across his entire body. Kissing James was so different and so familiar at the same time; he was coming home to a place he'd never been before. Their first kiss began with tentative, halting contact, and ended with a passion Oliver had never before known.

Oliver took a deep breath and looked into James's eyes once more. "Oh. So that's what that's supposed to feel like. I've been doing it wrong for years."

James gave him a look of utter bafflement.

"I've been kissing girls. No wonder it wasn't working." He smiled, thrilled with his discovery.

"Oliver, you have made me the happiest man on earth." James beamed and shook his head.

"I'm just getting started," Oliver said and kissed him again.

COOL DARKNESS settled around the deck, but with the torches flickering and the stars shining overhead Oliver felt warm and—for the first time he could remember—at peace. James's arms were around him, holding him in their strong embrace. He felt the great heart beating with its slow rhythm and he knew, not just hoped, but knew, that James was as happy as he was.

"How about we bring the dishes in and then get to bed?" Oliver asked, still looking up at the stars.

"It's kind of early," James replied. "Are you ready to go to sleep?"

"I said bed, not sleep," Oliver said, running a hand gently along James's leg.

"Oh, fuck," James exhaled. "I mean, yes, that is an eminently suitable suggestion."

They got up from the sofa and gathered up the plates and glasses, piling them rather quickly into the sink.

"I'll take care of them in the morning," James said. "Or I'll let the raccoons in and they can clean them up for us."

"I like the raccoon idea," Oliver said, as they padded down the hallway to James's bedroom. "Don't know why no one's thought of that before."

"People are so limited," James said pityingly.

He opened the door to his bedroom, then led Oliver over to the side opposite the one with the sleeping porch. He switched on the lights, revealing a marble bathroom that was almost the size of Oliver's apartment. It boasted a large tub set in a bay window overlooking the forest, and an enormous shower with more showerheads than the group shower at Oliver's gym.

"Get freshened up a bit?" James asked, touching a pad on the wall. Water exploded from all sides of the shower, and steam began to rise.

"Hell yeah," Oliver said.

James opened the heavy glass door, and waved Oliver in, then followed him and closed the door behind them.

"Temperature's over there, and water control is here," James explained, pointing out controls to the left and right.

"Everything I need's right here," Oliver said, putting his arms around James, bringing him close for a kiss. They kissed until the room filled with steam.

Finally James reached out and picked up a bottle of soap and a sponge. He soaped up the sponge and began to wash Oliver's chest, massaging him as he scrubbed.

"Oh, man, your hands are so strong," Oliver said. No woman had ever made him feel this way. "That feels amazing."

James smiled. "Turn around," he said, his voice low.

Oliver turned, and James scrubbed and massaged the muscles of his back for a long while. Finally he did what Oliver had been expecting him to do all along, and strayed down to his buttocks. His touch was tentative, as if uncertain Oliver would allow him to touch there.

"It's okay," Oliver said over his shoulder. "It feels amazing. You can touch whatever you want." He moaned as James did just that. "But I get to do the same." He laughed wickedly.

James stroked Oliver's taut ass with slippery strong hands. Oliver groaned as the tight muscles responded to James's firm attention. No woman had ever touched him there with such frank purpose; some had admired the round muscularity, but they had done so with a delicate touch rather than James's athletic kneading. He knew which he preferred.

James's husky voice was in his ear. "Sit," he said, tipping his head toward the bench built into the shower wall.

Oliver stepped over to the bench, turned and sat on the cool marble. James knelt, and smiled up at him. He lifted Oliver's right foot, and cradled it in his hands. He kissed Oliver's big toe delicately and then picked up the soapy sponge and starting scrubbing with strong, massaging strokes.

"Oh, fuck," Oliver moaned. He'd never experienced anything like this luxurious pleasure. That it was brought to him by a man—a naked, wet man—was such a huge departure from anything he had ever experienced, he could only marvel at how they had gotten here. As there was no rational way to explain or justify it, he simply let go of rationality and enjoyed the sensations of being loved so completely by the man with the amazing hands.

When James had finished massaging Oliver's feet, he rose, and Oliver joined him, grabbing the sponge out of his hands and beginning his own ablutions. As much as he had enjoyed being touched by James, now that it was his turn to do the touching, the strangeness and novelty of it struck him. Under his hands the unyielding muscle of James's chest responded to his touch with a multitude of twitchy, ecstatic movements that communicated James's pleasure directly through Oliver's fingertips. There was an immediacy to this joy that was entirely new, and he loved it.

He put his arms around James and swept his fingers down to the swimmer's ass that lay below. "Oh, I get it now," he said, feeling the strong, rounded muscle. "Asses are awesome."

James laughed and squirmed under Oliver's touch. "I love seeing you experience this for the first time."

"I think there's going to be a lot of firsts tonight," Oliver said. "How many people have you been with, anyway?"

James frowned thoughtfully. "Well, there was the awkward blowjob in high school, but I'm not sure I should count that one. Then in college, there were three different guys, but I only saw each of them once—that's the glamour of cruising bathrooms for guys so desperate they'll stick their dick in anything that won't bite it off. And then Stella, who basically froze shut once she said 'I do.' So, not many. How about you?"

"I was a complete dork in high school, so no love there. The girls in Latin club and on the debate team were not really into the whole dating thing, at least not with me. In college I got in better shape and women started flirting with me, but the kind of woman who flirts with a guy because he works out is not the kind of woman who can keep up a conversation over dinner. I dated a few of them, and the sex was… nice enough, but the pillow talk afterward made me want to sneak out and never come back—even if we were at my place. After the first couple of tries, I just sort of gave up and figured I was there to get my work done and get my degree, so I focused on that. Med school has been kind of overwhelming, especially since I'm working in addition to the classes, but I'm handling it. No time for dating, though, unless you count the workout my flexor carpi radialis gets every morning and night." He made a wanking motion with his right hand.

"So what we're saying is that the closeted politician and the hot go-go boy are, together, about as sexually experienced as the average high school chess club."

Oliver laughed and then looked into James's eyes with dramatic seriousness. "This ends now," he said in the manner of an action-movie hero. "Tonight, we make up for lost time."

James laughed delightedly in response and then set the shower control to the kind of power rinse one normally finds at the car wash. They were squeaky clean in a matter of seconds, and then the water abated completely. He snagged a pair of ridiculously fluffy towels off the high shelf in the corner of the shower and handed one to Oliver. They dried themselves, stepped out of the shower, and walked to the bedroom.

As they stood at the foot of James's bed, Oliver turned to him with a shrug. "This is going to sound strange coming from someone who has studied anatomy, but I have no idea what two guys do in bed."

"You're looking at me? I've never actually been in bed with a guy, remember? All of my sexy times were in bathroom stalls." He wrinkled up his nose. "That sounds exactly as awful as it was." But then he smiled again and wrapped his arms around Oliver. "Anything we do together will be the most amazing thing I've ever experienced— hell, the shower alone was the stuff of fantasy for me—so there's no way to do it wrong." He kissed Oliver sweetly, slowly. "You are my dream come true, Oliver. I have never, in my entire life never, been as happy as I am at this moment."

"How lucky am I," Oliver murmured, pressing his cheek to James's shoulder. "I never knew this is what I wanted until you showed up to offer it to me. You're a miracle."

James kissed his way down the side of Oliver's face until their lips met again. Then he led Oliver by the hand over to the side of the bed, where he pulled the covers open and invited Oliver in.

"Such a gentleman," Oliver said. He kissed James one more time and slid between the silky sheets.

James stood at the side of the bed, looking down at Oliver with a smile that was somewhere between elation and dismay. "I can't believe this is happening," he said with wonder in his voice.

Oliver held out his hand. "More is going to happen when you join me."

James's smile broadened into one of pure joy, and he laid himself next to Oliver. They kissed, more passionately now, grappling with each other in an attempt to bring more of their bodies into contact.

Oliver lifted himself over and straddled a surprised James, coming to rest on his lower hips. He cradled James's head with both hands, running his thumbs in the stubbly hollow under his cheekbones, and smiled. "You're beautiful," he whispered.

"And you're on top of me," James whispered back. He cleared his throat nervously. "There's no way to make this sound romantic, I'm afraid. I swear to God if you move back an inch I'm going to come all over you."

Oliver beamed. "That's absolutely the most romantic thing anyone's ever said to me." He leaned down and kissed James again. "But I have to see if that's true." With an aching slowness, he slid down an inch, no more; then he thrust his hips forward in a slow grind, their bodies caught in the heat of friction.

"Oh," James gasped softly, his brows peaked in surprised pleasure.

Oliver started the cycle again. This was a move he knew well from the dance floor, though performed in slow motion and with full-body contact it served an entirely different purpose; it didn't promise sex, it was sex itself. With every thrust he slid down a little farther, until finally their erect penises were in direct contact. Oliver slid his against James's, and from one or both, a slick of precum glazed them, easing the friction and intensifying the urgency of their motion. James's eyes rolled back in his head before he closed them completely.

"Look at me," Oliver whispered, cradling James's head in his hands once again.

James's eyes opened and looked into Oliver's. Oliver continued his grind, and they never lost eye contact as the heat and the pressure built. James was not far wrong; after only a dozen of Oliver's thrusts, he gasped several times, each time more urgently than the last, and finally he held his breath and began to shiver. But his eyes never left Oliver's.

"I love you," Oliver whispered in the second before his own orgasm took him.

James went stiff all over his body as his cock throbbed out his passion, filling the space between them with hot wetness, to which

Oliver added his own before James had stopped ejaculating. And still their eyes never left each other.

Oliver thrust until he felt the last spasm ebb from him, leaving just a feeling of warmth and completion and... love? *Oh shit. I told him I loved him.*

James kissed him softly. "I love you too," he whispered.

And in that moment, Oliver knew it to be true. He had found someone to love, and to love him.

"SO THIS must be the place," Donnelly said as they rounded the corner and saw the blue flames of Burn.

"Ya think?" Brandt asked. "Not terribly subtle, is it?"

"And the rough-hewn heavy oak beams and piles of dark leather in that cigar bar he sent us to were completely understated, right? I think it looked gayer than this place, actually."

"We'll see once we get inside. At least the cigar bar wasn't a glitter parade the way this one promises to be."

"Yeah, it was just a bunch of pumped-up guys sucking on long, thick, smoking hot things. Nothing gay about that."

Brandt laughed. "Okay, you're right. Maybe we'll find out all the worry about having two different venues is needless. The inside of Burn is probably tasteful and discreet."

"That's the spirit," Donnelly said cheerfully as he opened the door and they stepped inside.

"Or not," Brandt said as the intensity of Burn washed over him.

The troopers stood, stunned by the pounding beat, the wildly flashing blue lights, and the bouncing energy of the crowd on the dance floor.

"Yep, nothing gay about this," Brandt muttered.

"Oh, you're here, you're here!" called Bryce as he hustled over to meet them. "Isn't it just perfect?" He looked from Brandt to Donnelly and back again, clearly eager to see their reaction.

"It's... kind of overwhelming," Brandt said.

"I know, right?" hooted Bryce, clapping his hands. "Now, please follow me for the full tour." Bryce walked elegantly away, motioning for the officers to follow.

"Ready?" Donnelly asked.

Brandt simply shrugged. When Bryce was involved, it was always simpler to just go along. They followed.

Bryce made a quick circuit of the bar, passed by the dance floor (pointing out several of the grindier dancers and fanning himself), and threaded through the tables to a booth near the back of the club. Nestor was lounging there, talking with one of the waiters. He stood to greet the troopers with a kiss on each cheek.

"I like you to meet Hander," Nestor said, holding his hand out to Xander. "Hander, this is Officer Ethan, and this is Officer Gabriel."

"Pleased to meet you both. I'm Xander." He turned to Nestor. "I love your *pronunciación muy auténtico*, Nestor."

Nestor bowed his head in acknowledgment. "You bring joy to my tongue," he said quietly.

"Now, Xander, dear, where is that amazing hunk of man-waiter I ordered?" Bryce asked, craning his head around the club before turning to the troopers. "Just wait until you see him—you'll be shaken *and* stirred."

"Oh good lord," Brandt muttered, plopping himself next to Nestor on the banquette.

"Tut," Nestor said soothingly. "Bryce still love you more."

"Thanks, Nestor. That's exactly what I was worried about."

"Okay, here's the thing, Bryce," Xander said. "Oliver isn't… exactly… here right now."

"Oh, is he on a break? Or decanting something into a special patron?"

"No, actually, he's—"

"Xander, where the hell is he?" demanded a woman who had stalked up behind Xander.

Xander whipped around. "Millie, what a surprise! How are you?"

"Just about ready to strangle you if you don't tell me what's going on."

"All right, all right, in a minute," Xander said with his eyebrows up, tipping his head at the group behind him in the booth, who were watching this new drama with interest. He straightened and bowed to the group. "Oliver isn't here this evening, I'm afraid, but he assured me he was very interested in working your party, so I am certain he will be back before then."

"Back? Back from where?" Millie demanded.

"Now, I'd be happy to bring you a round of drinks—on the house. What'll you have, gents?"

"He took him, didn't he?" Millie plowed ahead, undaunted. "That bastard took Oliver."

Xander turned and fixed Millie with a look so fierce Brandt was startled to see it flash across his face. It faded quickly, replaced with the cheery, vacant smile of the service professional. He turned back to the table and asked again for their drink order.

"I'm going to the police if you don't tell me." Millie's voice was flat and certain. "There's no way Oliver went willingly with that guy. He's gotten mixed up in that asshole's ritual suicide, and I am going to get him out of it."

Xander closed his eyes and shook his head, taking several deep, calming breaths.

"Miss? Millie, is it?" Brandt said. "I'm Officer Brandt, and this is Officer Donnelly. Is there some problem we can help you with?"

"Oh thank God," Millie said in a voice that was equal parts exasperation and relief. She sat next to Brandt, and he scooted down, causing Nestor to slide over as well. "It's my friend Oliver Mitchell. He's a bartender here."

"He's your friend?" Bryce asked. When Millie nodded, he continued. "Lucky you." His voice conveyed his certainty that the luck was all on her side.

Millie smiled dismissively at Bryce and continued talking to Brandt. "He got tangled up with this slimeball closet-case politico, and I think he's been abducted."

"What makes you think he went against his will?" Donnelly asked, leaning across the table, his voice full of concern.

"Oliver is in med school. All he does is school, work, and exercise. He's never missed even a single day of any of them, and now he's missed all of them. No one's seen him—not his study group, not the people at the gym, and now he's not here either. He won't reply to any of my texts or calls, and his phone doesn't show up on my GPS. That's just not like him."

"When did you see him last?" Brandt asked.

"Monday. He came to my place after he got himself out of a hotel room that fucking slimeball tricked him into. We watched when he did his stupid press conference thing in the alley behind the hotel, and I knew right then the guy was trouble. Oliver knew it too."

"Wait, are you talking about… ugh, who was it?" Donnelly looked at Brandt for help. "He had a weird name… after a president or something. Grover Cleveland something?"

"James Buchanan Whitford," Millie said.

"That's the one," Donnelly cried, slapping his hand on the table. "There've been rumors about that guy. When I saw that alley-door thing on the news, I thought there was something brewing. Didn't I say that, Ethan? Remember Monday at breakfast?"

"I remember I was trying to read the sports section," he said with a shrug.

Donnelly dismissed him with a wave. "So what do you think happened, Millie?"

"Best-case scenario is that he threatened Oliver into going with him. Worst-case is that he straight-out abducted him."

"It wasn't either of those," Xander said in a low voice.

Millie turned to him, a shocked look on her face. "You know what happened?" She looked ready to leap up and thrash him right then and there.

He nodded and sat down next to Donnelly, causing him to scoot down. Bryce and Nestor now found themselves wedged together at the vertex of the parabolic booth.

"James came here last night. Told Oliver they had to get away quickly. I think Oliver was ready to call bullshit on him when some guys in serious suits came in, showing Oliver's picture around the bar. It was kind of blurry and telephoto, but you could tell it was him. No one gave him away, but it was only a matter of time. James had his car in the back, and I distracted the suits while they made a run for it."

"Where did they go?" Brandt asked.

"I don't know," Xander replied. "He didn't say where he was taking him."

"Well, if that's not enough to consider this a kidnapping, I don't know what is." Millie crossed her arms and looked expectantly at the troopers.

"It sounds as if he left willingly," Donnelly offered gently.

"I think Oliver got his wings," Xander said with a shrug.

"What the fuck does that mean?" Millie spat.

"It means he found a man who will take care of him." He turned to the officers. "It happens all the time here. That's why no one's really concerned. Well, except for Gavin, who had to find someone to take Oliver's side of the bar, but it's not like that's never happened before."

Brandt turned to Millie. "What do you think?"

"That's not Oliver. I've known him for five years, not a month like the guys here, and he would never do this. Plus, he's straight."

Brandt's eyebrows shot up in surprise. Both Bryce and Nestor sighed sadly at this latest outbreak of heterosexuality.

"Millie, when he left I told him I would text him in an hour, and if he didn't text me back with a secret sign, I would call the police myself. I texted him, and he sent the secret right back. I asked him to tell me the name of the special drink they made for him the first night you guys came to the club. There's no way James would know that."

"But what if James held a gun to his head and told him to text you back?" Millie demanded.

"Then he could have texted me a different drink name. James wouldn't know the difference, but I would call the police. They could trace his cell, and they'd have found him right away." Xander looked to the officers for confirmation.

"Well, there are a couple of steps you skipped over," Brandt confirmed, "but that's basically how it would work."

Millie huffed angrily and shook her head. "You people can't see what's right in front of you. My friend has been abducted, and you're not doing anything about it!" She was crying now, her face flushed with anger and grief.

Donnelly turned to Millie. "Tell us why you think this is an abduction, Millie," he said compassionately. "Help us understand."

"This guy Whitford is the classic closeted politician. He knows Oliver is going to be a liability to him, so he's getting him out of the way. The hatchet-faced Mrs. Whitford was on the news this afternoon telling people she has absolute faith in her husband, and the many rumors of his homosexuality are simply untrue. That's the clearest sign in the world that they are absolutely true, but about to be brutally erased. The douche bag himself was nowhere to be seen, by the way. Don't you think he would make it to his own photo op?"

"You've had a lot of time to think this through," Brandt observed.

"And your conclusions seem reasonable," Donnelly admitted. He looked at Brandt and shrugged.

Brandt pondered for a moment. "I guess it wouldn't hurt to have a chat with Mrs. Whitford. See if she knows where her husband has gotten to."

"Millie, we'll check it out. Can you write your number on a napkin? We'll call to follow up with you if we find anything."

"Thank you, thank you so much." Millie handed the napkin to Donnelly and got up. "Sorry to come unglued like that."

"You're a good friend. Oliver's lucky to have you."

Millie nodded and stepped away from the table.

Brandt looked at Xander. "Anything more you haven't told us? Anything at all?"

Xander hesitated, as if trying to decide whether to say anything. "Just that... well, I know Oliver says he's straight, and Millie insists he is, but... when he's with James, it's like... he's not."

"Do you mean he plays gay for tips?" Donnelly asked.

Xander shook his head. "No, it's more like... when they're together, they both just seem so happy. I know the guy's married and all, and Oliver says he's super straight, but... I don't know. There's something more going on there."

Brandt handed Xander a card. "Can you call us immediately if you hear anything from Oliver or Mr. Whitford? Anything at all."

He took the card and nodded.

"All right, then, partner, shall we get to the office and start making some calls?" Brandt got to his feet.

"It's a very nice place," Donnelly said to Xander as they stood. "I'm sure the party will be just great."

Xander smiled.

"I'd just like to point out," Bryce announced before everyone left, "that I'm still waiting for a Dirty Altar Boy."

"Do I want to know?" Brandt asked Donnelly as they walked to the door.

Donnelly shook his head.

CHAPTER TEN
SCANDAL

"MRS. WHITFORD? This is Officer Ethan Brandt from the state police."

"Good evening, Officer. I trust there is an emergency of some kind that required you to disturb me at this hour."

Brandt looked at Donnelly, who was listening on the line, with wide eyes. This Whitford woman was frightfully composed.

"Yes, I'm sorry for calling this late, Mrs. Whitford. We've received some information that has concerned us, and we would like very much to speak with your husband. Is he available?"

There was a brief silence on the line. "I'm sorry, Officer, but Mr. Whitford isn't available at the moment."

Brandt nodded. "Is he at home, then?"

Another pause. "He's not available, Officer."

"I see. Mrs. Whitford, I think perhaps I haven't conveyed the gravity of the issue to you, and for that I apologize. We need to speak with Mr. Whitford about a potentially serious allegation, and we will secure a subpoena if necessary."

A much longer silence ensued. "I must refer you to Mr. Whitford's attorney. His name is Charles Noble, and he will handle any questions you might have. Good night."

The line went dead.

"Well, isn't she a charmer?" Donnelly observed as he set his receiver down.

"I don't think she knows where he is," Brandt said.

"Why do you say that?"

"Don't know. Just a sense I got from her tone. She clearly didn't want to admit he wasn't at home."

"So we have a little chat with his lawyer tomorrow morning? It's kind of late to expect him to be in his office," Donnelly said with a glance at the clock, which indicated it was now ten thirty.

"Let's get an address for Mr. Noble, and we can start there in the morning."

Donnelly nodded. "Already have it." He waved his phone at Brandt. "So now we can either go back to Burn, or...."

"I will do anything you want at home if we don't go back to Burn tonight." He looked at Donnelly with a serious arch in his brow. "Anything."

"Home it is," Donnelly cried and lunged for the door, pausing only to straighten his pants. "Shake a leg, Officer." He disappeared down the hall.

Brandt chuckled to himself as he followed, switching off the lights. He was the luckiest straight guy in the world.

"WELL, THIS is new," Donnelly said.

"I just wanted it to be a surprise," Brandt said lightly as he guided his blindfolded partner into the bedroom.

"I didn't even know you had a blindfold."

"I may have done some shopping you don't know about," Brandt said slyly.

"Ethan, you're being mysterious and sexy. I thought we were clear that you were allowed to be either of those, but not both at the same time, because both at the same time will make me come in my pants. We had an agreement."

"That agreement has been suspended," Brandt whispered into Donnelly's ear.

"Oh, fucking fuck," Donnelly exhaled.

"Now, hold still," Brandt said. "This won't hurt a bit... unless you struggle."

"What are you...? Oh, that feels nice. Is that leather? Did you get me leather bracelets? I'm not really the bracelet kind of guy, but I could go for something new.... And anklets? Seriously? This is an interesting look you're going for. I can hardly wait to see how these look. Can I take off the—"

"Shh." Brandt pushed him backward onto the bed. "All will become clear in a moment." In a lightning-fast series of moves, Brandt's work was done. "There."

Donnelly was lying on his back, spread-eagled, his wrists and ankles attached by their leather cuffs to ropes at each respective corner of the bed. He would not be getting up. His head turned side to side, as if he might be able to see something that would give him a better sense of his predicament. He tugged each extremity in turn and found them all secure.

"Well, this *is* something new," he said slowly, his head turned toward where Brandt had previously been standing. "What exactly did you have in mind?"

"It's a surprise," Brandt whispered from the other side of the bed.

Donnelly jolted his head to that side, clearly disoriented by the blindfold and the restraints. But Brandt saw the flicker of a smile on his face and knew his partner was enjoying this new adventure.

"Do you know what it's like sharing a bed with a former wrestler?" Brandt asked. He didn't wait for an answer. "I never get to be completely in control. You can always flip me, or pin me, or simply take command and get what you want. Now, what you want is almost always the same as what I want, but tonight what I want is to be in control. Complete control. You will experience what I want you to experience, and you will come only when I decide to allow it. Of course, I may decide I want you to come twice, or maybe three times in a row, ready or not. You are mine tonight, Officer Donnelly, and I will do with you what I want."

Donnelly swallowed hard. "We'll see about that," he said, a little belligerently.

"Do I detect some attitude? Do you think it's a good idea to test me like that, given the position you're in?"

"I may be tied up, but I doubt you'll be able to make me do what you want if I don't want to. Plus, you forgot that I'm still wearing underwear. You're going to have to untie my legs to get those off."

"Oh, shoot," Brandt said, frustration in his voice. "What am I going to do now?" He reached over to the drawer by the bed and picked up the hunting knife Liam had given him for his high-school graduation. He never hunted with it, but it was a fearsome-looking blade. It had not been sharpened all the way to the tip, so the end was pointed but not sharp; this he ran down Donnelly's bare chest to his waist.

Donnelly sucked in a surprised breath, but he did not speak. Neither did he exhale.

Brandt slipped the knife over the top of Donnelly's boxer briefs and then up under the elastic at the leg opening nearest to him. He stopped, letting the blade warm against Donnelly's skin. He listened to his partner's shallow breathing as the suspense built. Then, without warning, he yanked the blade up and sliced cleanly through the fabric up to the waistband, which he left intact.

"Oh," he whispered. "I guess I won't have to untie you after all."

Donnelly licked his lips and swallowed. Brandt traced a line under his belly button and down his other leg. This time when he slid the blade under the fabric, he lifted it slightly and sliced slowly through the fabric. He put the knife down on the nightstand, and looked down at Donnelly, quite pleased with his work.

Donnelly's underwear was in ragged pieces, held together at the waist only. Brandt peeled back the fabric on his legs, leaving just his crotch covered. Brandt ran his fingers up this bulging package, bringing a groan to Donnelly's lips. He slid his fingers under the waistband and gripped the band of fabric in his fists. With a wrenching yank, he tore the fabric apart, and then flung the pieces away. Donnelly was completely exposed, and from the way he shivered, he felt it keenly.

"Now, aren't I the lucky one?" Brandt said conversationally. "I have the strapping Officer Donnelly laid out before me. How many people would love to have a go at this? I see the way people look at you—men and women both. That tight blue T-shirt you wore tonight shows every muscle in your arms, every ridge on your abs. That waiter at Burn—Xander?—he could hardly drag his eyes away from you. And yet here you are, naked and helpless, and you are mine." He ran a finger up Donnelly's rib cage. "All mine."

Donnelly jerked to the side in a ticklish, terrified squirm.

"Now, I've thought about what I would do with a tied up and helpless Gabriel Donnelly. I thought long"—he ran his fingers up Donnelly's cock—"and hard"—he gripped it, felt its growing heft—"about it. And here's what I came up with."

He went to the nightstand and pulled out a bottle of the special lube he'd purchased when he bought the wrist and ankle restraints. He returned to his favorite spot, the one between Donnelly's legs, popped the top off the bottle, and drizzled the gel all over his partner's steely erection. Setting the bottle aside, he smoothed the lube all over Donnelly's cock, slicking it up thoroughly.

"Mmm," Donnelly moaned.

"Feel it getting hot?" Brandt murmured.

"Mm-hmm."

"Do you like it when I do this?" Brandt asked, squeezing Donnelly's cock as his hand moved up and down in a spiral motion. It was the kind of move he knew Donnelly did on himself, and it would be the most effective for his purposes.

"Oh God, yes," Donnelly moaned. His powerful legs began to tense and twist as his erection grew even harder.

"You are so hot, I think I could come just by looking at you," Brandt whispered, urging Donnelly on. "Ah, your nipples are getting hard. It won't be long now. Give it to me, Gabriel, give it to me. I'm going to spray it all over you, and then I'm going to lick it all up."

Donnelly's moaning seemed to jump up an octave, and his writhing increased as he thrashed and pumped into Brandt's clasping hand.

"Your balls are coming home, love, pulling up tight and getting ready to unload on me. I'll bet you can feel it now, deep inside, can't you? Feel your load building, getting ready to soak me? Come on, give it to me," Brandt urged.

Donnelly's back arched and he sighed softly. He was ready, Brandt could see it, he knew all the signs, he knew everything this body was capable of. It was time.

He dropped Donnelly's cock.

Donnelly's pelvis continued its frenzied thrusting, but with no grip, no friction, it was pointless. His moan turned into a whine, and he thrashed against his bonds with renewed strength. The bed shook with his enraged need.

"You forgot the rules," Brandt purred tauntingly. "Tonight, I'm in control. You will come only when I allow it."

Donnelly stopped thrashing; Brandt knew he wasn't going to give him the satisfaction of displaying his unsatisfied lust. He lay still, trying to keep his frustrated breathing regular.

Brandt reached out and gave Donnelly's cock three quick strokes. Instantly the tortured flailing returned, as he was launched to the brink of orgasm by Brandt's sure touch.

Brandt dropped him again.

"Sorry," he said, his voice dripping with sweet sarcasm, "I keep getting distracted. You should see the color your balls have turned."

Brandt leaned close to them and planted a delicate kiss on each. "They're so hot and red. I know what will help." He reached back for the ice bucket he had brought in earlier in preparation for this moment. Grabbing a handful of ice cubes with one hand, he cinched his fingers of his other around Donnelly's scrotum and pulled the balls tight in the bottom of their sac. Then he brought the handful of ice up and pressed the cubes against the taut skin of Donnelly's scrotum, with perhaps more pressure than he had intended.

Donnelly's scream was piercing but short; he bit down and breathed through it, huffing out the shock.

"There, that should cool everything down," Brandt said with a satisfied smile.

"Fuck… you," growled Donnelly.

That was exactly what Brandt had been hoping to hear. It meant Donnelly was losing his composure—something Brandt had rarely seen him do.

"You know, I might just fuck *you*," Brandt mused. He tossed the handful of drippy ice back into the bucket. "But then again you might like that more than what I have planned for you. We'll see."

Donnelly was silent, refusing to give Brandt the satisfaction of another outburst.

Brandt wrapped his fist back around Donnelly's cock, which had softened a bit from the shock of the ice. He reapplied the heating liquid, smoothing it up and down in long, slow strokes. "There, nice and warm again," he soothed.

Donnelly lay stock still.

Brandt ramped up his grip and speed, working Donnelly's cock the way he knew Donnelly liked it. He couldn't hold out forever. Brandt leaned forward and kissed noisily at the tip. The lube had a delightful cinnamon flavor. "Mmm, that's nice," he moaned, then ran his tongue all around Donnelly's cockhead. "But I still like your taste the best." He ran his tongue up over the top of Donnelly's cock, and found the slit that he knew would be leaking precum like a faucet. He made a point at the tip of his tongue and drove it into Donnelly's penis, then sucked hard to urge out the liquid inside.

Donnelly, though he fought it, moaned.

Got you.

Brandt returned to his aggressive stroking, and Donnelly began to twist and thrust once more. Soon his nipples were hard again, and his breathing grew labored and shallow.

"That's it," Brandt urged. "Come for me, Gabriel, come for me." He pounded hard on Donnelly's cock, knowing exactly what would push him over.

Donnelly's back arched again, and his pelvis began to thrust.

Brandt froze. He kept hold of Donnelly's cock, but didn't move. Donnelly thrust, but Brandt kept his wrist loose and didn't allow his hand to provide any friction.

"Aaarrgh!" Donnelly growled angrily.

"Oh, sorry, were you working on something there? I can get the ice again—that seemed to help last time."

"Fuck. You," Donnelly said, more clearly this time.

"Again, I'm happy to take your suggestion under advisement, but you are really in no position to make demands." He let go of Donnelly's cock again and slid down farther between his legs. "And these poor boys keep getting ready to rumble and then have to stand down. They look like angry plums. I think I'll give them a little kiss." He again pulled them tight, causing Donnelly to squirm a little bit from the pressure that Brandt knew was just on the edge between pleasure and discomfort. He leaned in and kissed Donnelly's balls delicately, but then scraped his teeth against the smooth, tight skin, nibbling his way from top to bottom, feeling the resilient testicle underneath.

Donnelly groaned and clutched at the sheets in his torment. "Please," he moaned.

"Please... what?" Brandt asked, then returned to chewing on Donnelly's most sensitive anatomy.

"Please," Donnelly whined, "let me come."

"Are you sure that's what you want?" Brandt asked, keeping up his teasing massage on Donnelly's balls.

"More than anything," Donnelly whispered.

"You're lucky I'm feeling generous," Brandt replied. "You may be luckier than you want to be."

"Just please get me there, please," Donnelly begged.

Brandt said no more, but released Donnelly's balls and grabbed up his cock; he was rewarded with a relieved sigh. He dripped more lube, got back on his demanding rhythm, and had Donnelly arching and moaning in the space of a minute.

"Please… please… please…," Donnelly chanted.

"As you wish," Brandt said. He intensified his stroking as Donnelly thrashed for a third run-up to orgasm. "Come for me," he murmured.

Donnelly sucked in a great breath and froze, muscles quivering across his entire body. He grunted, then huffed out five or six desperate breaths before he stopped breathing altogether. Tiny pulses in his pelvis told the story: the surge was coming.

Brandt kept stroking and urging and giving the special spiral twist he knew Donnelly loved. The first spray splattered across Donnelly's belly, followed by eight or ten more that sent white streaks as far as his collarbone.

Donnelly panted and moaned as the orgasm ebbed and released its hold on him. He took a deep breath and sighed. "That was amazing," he whispered.

Brandt didn't stop.

Donnelly laughed and began to twitch and dodge, but Brandt didn't stop. He knew Donnelly's cock was exquisitely sensitive in the afterglow of his ejaculation, and he was going to exploit that mercilessly.

"Stop," Donnelly cried, thrashing desperately to get away from Brandt's insistent fisting of his cock. "Stop it!"

"You don't get to choose," Brandt said seriously. "I get to choose, remember? And I say you're not finished." He kept stroking, and every third stroke or so, he swept his fingers over the head of Donnelly's cock.

"Oh God, stop," Donnelly pleaded. "It's too sensitive!"

"Poor baby," Brandt tutted. "Let me kiss it better." He leaned down and ran his tongue over the head of Donnelly's penis, then wrapped his lips around it and sucked and kissed roughly.

Donnelly screamed, and laughed, and cried, and most of all tried to get his cock out of Brandt's grip. Brandt wasn't letting go. He stroked until Donnelly's thrashing slowed, and his breathing calmed.

"Well, that was a nice start," Brandt said happily. "But I was really hoping you would shoot a little farther. Let's try again." He dripped more of the heating lube onto Donnelly's still-red cock and began stroking again.

"No, I can't—"

"Oh, but I think you can. Don't worry, I'll stroke as hard as it takes to get you there."

"Shit," Donnelly expectorated and threw his head back on the pillow.

Brandt squeezed the semierect cock in his hand, stroked more, and squeezed again. "Well, that's coming along nicely."

Donnelly was keeping his thoughts to himself.

Brandt stroked with vigor, stopping every once in a while to kiss and nuzzle, but generally keeping up a strong drumbeat. It took nearly ten minutes of this before Donnelly began to moan and writhe again under Brandt's ministrations.

"That's it. Come for me," Brandt urged as he stroked. The crackle of the heating lube was the only sound in the room as Donnelly again began to arch and gasp. Brandt's fist was a blur, beating out a punishing rhythm.

"Oh," Donnelly growled, and his body stiffened. The first jet of semen arced gracefully through the air and, as commanded, landed on his chin. The rest of them splattered out over his belly, layering atop his previous load.

"Good boy, I knew you could do it," cheered Brandt. He squeezed the last drops out of Donnelly's exhausted cock.

But he didn't stop.

"No, no, no, no," moaned Donnelly, head thrashing side to side. "No, no, no. Stop."

"You don't get to choose," Brandt whispered, and he gripped Donnelly tighter.

Donnelly's moaning rose to a squeal of helpless overstimulation. He bucked even harder this time, and Brandt wasn't sure the bed frame could take his frenzied thrashing. It had stood up over the years to some aggressive pounding, but Donnelly was in the grip of a ferocious spasming desperation.

Still he didn't stop.

"You have another in you, I just know it," Brandt said teasingly. "What kind of lover would I be if I walked away and left that third orgasm on the table? Irresponsible, that's what I'd be. No, sir, we're going to make sure we get you completely cleaned out tonight."

More lube and a stronger grip slowly, slowly brought Donnelly back to full erection. Brandt felt the surge and smiled.

"I'll help you out, buddy." He reached for another bottle of lube—not the warming kind, not where this was going—and slicked up two fingers. These he introduced with vigorous impatience directly into Donnelly's ass. He planted his fingertips directly above Donnelly's prostate and slowly, surely, drew his fingers down, pressing upward as hard as he dared against that secret gland.

Donnelly jolted, and his moaning took on a more focused cadence. He grunted in time with every transit Brandt's fingertips made across the delicate and needy gland. Finally Brandt increased the pace and force of his "come hither" motions, and Donnelly's breathing accelerated accordingly. Brandt's stroking of his cock fell into rhythm as well, and the internal and external stimulation put Donnelly over for the third time.

Brandt milked aggressively, rubbing Donnelly's prostate all the while, and forced another orgasm onto, and out of, his partner. Donnelly's teeth were gritted as though this orgasm cost him greatly, and he hissed out his passion through a grimace of stout perseverance. This last ejaculation only laced three or four streaks of white up as far as his belly button. He groaned out a dry, exhausted rattle and fell back onto the pillows.

This time he didn't ask Brandt to stop—he had learned that lesson. He simply lay, open, in Brandt's control, panting like a racehorse.

That was the moment Brandt had been waiting for; had been working hard for. That moment when Donnelly surrendered, gave himself up entirely to Brandt, to be handled as Brandt desired. This was the moment.

Brandt leaned forward and kissed the purple head of Donnelly's cock, tasting the thin, exhausted semen that seeped from the tip. Then he kissed his way up Donnelly's torso, slipping his tongue through all three loads, taking up a sample of each as they mixed with the clean sweat of his exertions. Finally he reached Donnelly's lips, and he kissed them, delivering his samples for his lover's delectation.

He reached up and pulled off the blindfold. Donnelly blinked into the light.

"I love you," Brandt murmured as he kissed Donnelly again.

"That was... life-altering," Donnelly replied. "I think I actually passed out there for a moment when you started round three." He blinked and looked into Brandt's eyes more intently. "I had no idea you had that in you."

"I had no idea you had three of those in you. How awesome was that?"

Donnelly laughed, though he was clearly exhausted. "Pretty fucking awesome. We'll have to do that again sometime. But, you know, the other way around."

"You mean with you tied face down?" Brandt asked with a smile. "Hmm, I can think of a few things to do with you in that position...."

"Kiss me," Donnelly asked. "Tell me you love me, and you can do anything you want to me."

"I love you," Brandt said, with a low and serious voice.

"And I love you, you bastard," Donnelly said with an elated smile. "Now, can you unchain me? I need to pee."

"Well...," Brandt replied, eyeing him up and down.

"Oh hell no," Donnelly said. "We've done enough new stuff for one night."

"Just trying to find ways to keep it fresh," Brandt said with a laugh as he unbuckled Donnelly's wrists.

"One step at a time, cowboy," Donnelly replied, rubbing his wrists and grinning happily.

CHARLES NOBLE'S office was in one of the steel-and-glass high-rise office buildings that ringed the state capitol. Donnelly had called every fifteen minutes from seven in the morning until the receptionist at the law firm finally picked up at half past eight. The request for a meeting with the state police had gotten the secretary's immediate attention.

"Ready?" Brandt asked as he shut off the engine. The parking garage under the building was nearly empty at this early hour; it was not quite nine.

"A little dehydrated, but good to go," Donnelly replied with a laugh. "You were really on your game last night."

Brandt blushed and grinned. "But now we have work to do," he said, opening the car door and stepping out.

They were shown into the waiting room outside Noble's office; it had commanding views of the state capitol and the park surrounding it.

"Nice place," Donnelly mused, looking around at the expensive furnishings.

"I find that the more expensive the couch, the less chance the attorney will actually give us information we can use," Brandt replied.

"Let's hope Mr. Noble is more forthcoming than this amazing leather would imply. I mean, seriously, did you feel this?" Donnelly stroked the upholstery with the palm of his hand.

"Stop shopping, Officer," Brandt scolded.

"Mr. Noble will see you now," the secretary standing in the doorway said in crisp British tones. She held the door for them to enter, then closed it behind them. Brandt and Donnelly approached the desk while she waited by the door.

"Officers, pleased to meet you," the man behind the desk said, rising and extending his hand. He shook hands with both, then motioned for them to sit in the leather chairs in front of his desk. "How can I help you today?"

"We're here about James Whitford," Brandt said.

Noble nodded, his face showing no trace of emotion.

"Were you aware, Mr. Noble, that Mr. Whitford has recently become a regular patron at a club downtown with a certain… reputation?" Brandt knew himself to be singularly inept at insinuation, but he felt he had to approach the subject carefully.

Mr. Noble looked up. "Amanda, will you excuse us?"

His secretary silently left the room, closing the door behind her. Noble turned his gaze on the officers. "What kind of club are we talking about here?"

"The club is called Burn, and it attracts a clientele of—"

"Party boys and men with more money than sense," Noble interrupted. "Officer, I'm an attorney representing a number of people with powerful positions in our state's government. I think a moment's reflection will make clear to you that I would be familiar with such an establishment. I was not, however, aware that James had become a regular. Can you fill in some details on that aspect, please?"

"From what we gathered last night, he began coming to the club on Sunday nights about a month ago and struck up an acquaintance with a young man who works there, a bartender. Then on Wednesday night—two days ago—he showed up unexpectedly and convinced this bartender that they needed to leave immediately. As far as we know, neither has been seen since. The bartender's best friend—a Ms. Millie Flynn—is certain he's been abducted."

Noble closed his eyes and rubbed his brow with his hand. "Would this happen to be the same party boy who may have accompanied Mr. Whitford to a downtown hotel on Sunday night, resulting in what I consider to be the worst press conference ever given by a local political figure?"

"That would be the one," Donnelly replied. "But he's not a party boy, at least in the usual sense. He's a med student and very serious about his studies, apparently. Working at Burn is how he pays the bills while he's a student."

Noble was quiet for a moment. "Have you talked to Stella?"

"Do you mean Mrs. Whitford?" Brandt asked.

Noble nodded.

"Yes, we had the pleasure of her conversation last night. She said he was unavailable to come to the phone."

Noble chuckled. "She's a peach, isn't she? Just between you and me, I tried for months to talk Jimmy out of getting hitched to that star."

"Stella…. Stella for star," Donnelly said. "Funny."

"Thank you. Good to know someone's still reading *A Streetcar Named Desire*." Noble smiled. "Let's be frank, gentlemen. Are you considering any kind of charge against Mr. Whitford in connection with these events at Burn?"

Brandt shook his head. "We don't have compelling evidence that Mr. Whitford abducted anyone. However, the bartender's friend is adamant that he would never have done something like this willingly, so we felt we should investigate it. But right now, as far as we're concerned, it's just a case of marital infidelity."

Noble's eyes widened, as if he'd just had a bad shock. "Marital infidelity," he said slowly. He repeated the phrase, making no sound. He pounded the desk with a fist. "That bitch."

"Excuse me?" Brandt said, leaning closer.

Noble looked up. "I know where he is."

"You… what?" Donnelly asked.

"I know where he went."

"Would you be willing to take us to him?" Brandt asked, astonished at the turn this conversation was taking.

"Look, we're on the same team here. If I take you to him, will you hear him out on this deal with the party boy and not go flying off the handle and make a big media spectacle? It's going to be hard enough on him when this all breaks." He looked at the officers. "I don't expect you to have much sympathy for a guy who's trying to get his shit together in the spotlight like this, but Jimmy's going to need some space to come to grips with having run off with a party boy."

"Actually, we do have some sympathy with that," Donnelly said.

"You're looking at the state task force on Section 28 enforcement," Brandt explained.

"No shit? Wait, you're the guys who handled Peter Laurence's wedding?"

Brandt and Donnelly nodded.

"Pete was a good guy. Went up against him once in court, and he took me to school. Damn shame what happened." Noble looked at the ceiling for a moment, as if trying to decide something. He looked back down at the officers. "I'm going to tell you something, and I hope we can keep it just between us."

Brandt tensed. "Mr. Noble, you know we can't guarantee—"

"It's nothing criminal, Officer. It's just that Jimmy and I go way back. Like all the way back. From elementary school. He's good people, and I love him like a brother. But he doesn't always make great decisions. This may look like he's gotten himself wrapped up in something messy, but I think what he's actually doing is unwrapping the last mess. There is no way in hell Jimmy abducted anybody. If he felt he had to run, then he had a good reason. And I think I know what it is."

"Care to share your theory?" Brandt asked.

Noble shook his head. "Jimmy's my friend *and* my client. I need to see him first." He stood abruptly. "Shall we go?"

"How far are we going, approximately?" Donnelly asked.

"It's about two hours out of the city. Why? Does that require different paperwork?" Noble asked with a snicker.

"No, I just need my fourth cup of coffee, and I'm trying to plan."

Noble laughed. "I like this guy," he said to Brandt. "You should hang on to him."

"I plan to," Brandt said with a smile.

After a stop at the cafe in the lobby of the building, they walked through the parking garage to the troopers' cruiser.

"You know," Donnelly said, "it occurs to me we might want to see if Millie Flynn would be able to come with us. Not that I think

Oliver is being held against his will, but however this works out, it could be nice for him to have a friend there."

"Seems reasonable," Brandt said. "Any objections?" He turned to Noble.

The attorney nodded. "Makes sense to me."

Donnelly took his phone out of his pocket and dialed. He stopped for a moment, allowing the others to walk ahead. Brandt heard him talking, a brief conversation, and then he jogged to catch up.

"She's coming. We just need to swing by her work—it's on the east side of town. Is that on the way?"

"Actually, that's exactly where we're heading," Noble replied.

They arrived at the cruiser, and Donnelly opened the passenger door. "Mr. Noble, why don't you ride shotgun so you can navigate."

"Thanks, and please, call me Charlie."

"Charlie it is. I'm Gabriel, and your driver today is Ethan."

"Nice," Brandt muttered as he got behind the wheel. He threaded the car through the tight passages of the parking structure and then rolled out onto the boulevard, heading for the east side.

CHAPTER ELEVEN
A DAY IN THE COUNTRY

OLIVER AWOKE just as the approaching dawn was beginning to erase the stars from the sky. A riot of birds began their overlapping cacophonies of welcome to the sun, and he turned his head to take in the peaceful slumber of James on the pillow next to him.

He ran through a list of things that had changed for him since James had appeared unexpectedly at the club, and it was staggering. He had absconded from work, he had skipped his classes, he had been out of contact with Millie for longer than he had since they'd met in the dorms during his freshman year. He smiled as he realized the things he listed last—having sex with a man, kissing a man, telling a man he loved him—were the ones that, to an outside observer, would probably have seemed the most drastic departures.

Not to Oliver. His identity as a scholar, his work ethic (even as a jock/slut bartender), his devotion to his best friend: these were the qualities that defined him, not the sex of the person next to him in bed. It was not a conclusion he would have come to on his own, though. He was lucky, so lucky, that James had appeared in his life to make him realize it.

As the room lightened, he lifted himself up on his elbow to look at the man who had changed his life. Out here, in his native element, he had been transformed from the sad, exhausted man who frequented Burn into an energetic, vibrant presence who looked years younger. The wrinkles of care and worry around his eyes were gone now, and the silver flecks in his hair—even at thirty there were a few—added gravitas rather than age.

Oliver was happy.

He slid out of bed and padded naked down the hallway. He sought what he knew must lurk here somewhere: an exercise room. There was a staircase behind the kitchen that led to a lower level housing several smaller bedrooms and, at the end of the hall, a small but expensively equipped workout room. Oliver had never worked out naked, but that was just one more first to add to the growing list. He let himself imagine more firsts that might arise today, but then realized that lifting weights with an erection is awkward, so he closed his eyes and thought of baseball for a while. He did an upper-body workout that got the blood pumping to other places than his cock and felt his body start to wake up.

After his dumbbell set, he put a moderately challenging weight on a long bar and began his squats. He was in the middle of his second set when he heard the voice behind him.

"Now there's a view I could get used to."

At the bottom of each rep, Oliver's knees were bent and his ass splayed wide open; the view was certainly obscene. But James's appreciation of it thrilled rather than embarrassed him. He grinned into the mirror and finished his set, even more slowly, watching James's reaction as he did so.

"Need a spot?" James asked.

"Thought you'd never ask," he replied.

James walked over, his erection bouncing before him. Oliver glanced at it in the mirror, then back up at James's face.

"Did you just wake up?" he asked with a grin.

James shook his head. "It's merely saluting your dedication to fitness."

Oliver took up the bar again, and James stood right behind him, leaning close, following his motions with his hand near the bar in case he was needed to bring it back up. The contact between their bodies was extensive. Oliver took this set even more slowly, pushing his ass back, reveling in the feeling of James's heavy cock dragging along his lower back. His own penis responded in kind, and by the time he had finished his set, he was fully boned.

He set the bar back on the rack and turned around to embrace his spotter. He put his arms around James and held him tight, then kissed him hard, sliding his tongue in to find its mate.

"Sorry I'm all sweaty," he murmured.

"No, fuck…," James whispered in response. "It's intoxicating. I want to lick you all over."

"Unh…" was the only reply Oliver could manage.

"Do you mind if I suggest a change to your routine?"

"Does it involve cardio, resistance, and stretching?" Oliver asked with a sly grin.

"Two out of three ain't bad," James replied. "I'm afraid I will offer no resistance."

"Good man."

James took Oliver's hand and led him over to the weight bench. "Here," he said simply.

Oliver sat on the bench and lay back, stretching himself up to where the weight bar would normally rest—it was still on the squat rack. He placed his feet on either side on the bench, just as he would if he were going to do a press set. But all he could do was watch James as he knelt at the end of the bench.

"God, you're beautiful," James whispered as he ran his hands up Oliver's legs from his knees to his hips. He wrapped his hands around the base of Oliver's fully erect cock. "And you... you're a work of art." He leaned forward and kissed the tip.

Oliver groaned and tipped his head back. James's kiss was a simple gesture, but it contained more love and passion than he had ever experienced. He knew how much James wanted it, and how long he had deferred the dream of having a man to love. That Oliver was that man, the focus of all of those years of denied want, made his head light. He was what James had been waiting for, and James was what he never knew he needed.

James licked a drop of precum from Oliver's tip. "You even taste amazing," he breathed. He kissed and kissed again.

Then Oliver felt James's mouth close over the head of his cock. Such heat, such wet grasping pressure, he had never known. His pelvis thrust unbidden, greedy. His chest pounded.

James's throat rumbled with his pleasure, and he worked more of Oliver's cock into his mouth, slicking its passage with saliva that dripped down the shaft. He gripped the base with a fist, squeezing and massaging until Oliver could feel the mechanisms of orgasm swing into action, a throb somewhere deep inside that meant inevitability.

"Oh," he moaned, which was the only way he knew to let James know what was coming, and coming soon, and coming, ready or not. His back arched without him arching it; his hips thrust in time to music he couldn't hear. He was nearly out of his body, transported by what James was doing between his legs.

Then he was brought crashing back into his body, helpless in the steely grip of this orgasm. He could hardly draw breath as the spasms racked through him. Pleasure displaced consciousness, and he was elated to feel it slip away.

James grunted as Oliver filled his mouth with semen, jet after jet. The overflow ran down his shaft, trickled over his balls. He had never come so much, so hard, so completely.

James was still swallowing, creating a gentle suction, and Oliver looked down to see an expression of complete bliss on James's face. He smiled—a neat trick with his mouth full of dick, but his eyes crinkled joyfully—and then with a great show of reluctance, let the head of Oliver's cock slide out from between his lips. He immediately began lapping up every drop of cum he had missed. Oliver leaned back to enjoy the feeling of James's tongue slipping along the shaft of his penis, and he laughed when it reached the ticklish skin of his scrotum. James slurped in Oliver's balls one by one, which set him groaning again.

James licked and kissed and suckled in a transit of devotion, from the secret skin under Oliver's balls all the way up to the top of his trimmed pubic hair, where some of the semen had flecked during his spasms. Then he kissed his way up Oliver's torso, pausing to nibble with delicate insistence at his nipples, until finally he reached Oliver's lips, which, with a slow tenderness, he kissed again and again.

"That was amazing," Oliver sighed.

"I agree," James said with a grin. "It was more than I had even dared hope for."

"You are a miracle," Oliver said, not for the first time and probably not for the last. "Where did you come from, and how did you find me?"

"I figure we each had an empty spot only the other can fill. It was just a matter of time before the pieces fell into place."

"I know my piece was glad to fall into your place," Oliver said with a wicked smile. "Now it's my turn. Spot me?"

"You want to lift more? Shit, I don't know if I can keep up with you young guys."

Oliver reached his hands up to James's neck and held him close. "One guy. One." His voice was low and serious.

"One and one only," James said with a nod and sealed his vow with a kiss.

"Now, up to spotter's position, mister," Oliver ordered with a smile.

James got up and stepped around to the weight rack at the head of the bench. "Do you want me to get the bar for you?"

"Hell no," Oliver said. "Just scoot forward a little."

James shuffled his feet forward, which brought his legs to either side of the bench, straddling it—and Oliver's head.

"Perfect," Oliver said. "Now bend your knees."

James looked at him quizzically, but then seemed to come to the conclusion that if you're standing naked with a willing guy between your legs, and he wants you to bend your knees, you should just bend your knees. So he did.

"More," Oliver ordered.

James complied, bending until his balls were almost resting on Oliver's forehead.

"Perfect," Oliver whispered, and he tipped his head back and slid up a little. He reached his arms up and gripped James around his hips, holding him in place as he brought his lips up to James's balls. He kissed the loose skin gently, then nibbled at the warm folds, tugging playfully.

"Oh my God," James moaned.

"I'm just getting started," Oliver said. He opened his mouth and craned up, capturing both of James's balls in his mouth at once. He was rewarded with a litany of grunted swearing, which pleased him greatly—it was high praise for his first adventure between another man's legs.

He kissed and suckled and tugged, delighting in feeling the twitch in James's strong legs every time he made a new move. He pursed his lips and pulled back, letting each ball slip out, and James cried out in pleasure. Oliver brought his hands around, feeling along James's pelvis until he reached the base of the erection that stood nearly vertically from James's body. He felt along its length until he reached the tip, which was glossed with a thick coat of precum. Oliver growled around the balls he still held in his mouth and began to slide his hand along James's cock, spreading the slick and using both hands in unison to stroke the entire erection with each circuit.

"Oh fuck, Oliver," James moaned as the quivering in his legs intensified. Oliver hoped James was gripping the weight stand for support because there was no way he was stopping. He gripped tighter and sucked harder, and drove James on toward the orgasm Oliver so badly wanted to give him, to let him know how much he loved him.

James drew in a breath and froze. Oliver kept stroking. He jolted and shook. Oliver kept stroking. Finally Oliver felt a rain of hot droplets shower over his chest and belly, and even some on his legs. Still he stroked.

Finally James straightened up, pausing only when Oliver refused to let his balls go. But then Oliver relinquished them, kissing them as they left him. James took a step back and then bent down over Oliver and kissed him upside down. It was disorienting and wonderful, and Oliver kissed him back and was delighted to find his tongue rough on the wrong side. Like everything in his life over the last couple of days, it was completely different from what he was used to. He loved that.

"I kind of made a mess," James murmured, looking at Oliver's splattered body, covered with his ejaculate. Then he looked back into Oliver's eyes. "You are amazing. I had no idea it could feel that way."

Oliver looked up at him. "Can we just stay here forever and figure out all the ways we fit together? Can we say 'fuck real life' and just be together here?"

James grinned broadly. "That sounds like the best idea ever. There's nothing outside of this place that I need anymore." He leaned down and kissed Oliver again. "Now, let's get you cleaned up," he said, walking around to the foot of the bench and holding out his hand to Oliver. He helped him to his feet, and they walked together back up to the bedroom.

IN TEN minutes they arrived at the veterinary office where Millie worked as a technician while she was in vet school.

"Thanks for coming on such short notice," Donnelly said as she slid into the backseat next to him.

"I'm just really glad you're doing something about this," she replied. "If that Whitford asshole has hurt him, I swear to God."

"Millie Flynn, I'd like you to meet Charles Noble," Donnelly said. "Charlie is that Whitford asshole's attorney."

"Oh." Millie looked at him critically.

"Charlie volunteered to help us find Whitford," Brandt said, trying to placate her. "We wouldn't have any idea where to look for them if he hadn't offered."

"Hmm." Millie squinted at him. "What's your angle, lawyer?"

Charlie looked at Brandt, an eyebrow raised in amusement. "I'm trying to help Jimmy get this sorted out. And for the record," he said, turning to look Millie in the eye, "I grew up with that Whitford asshole, and he wouldn't hurt a hair on your bestie's head. Or anywhere else on him, for that matter."

Millie, from the look on her face, was reserving judgment.

On the outskirts of the city, the freeway narrowed down to two lanes each way, and the traffic lightened. As they drove past a large truck stop, Brandt noticed Donnelly in the backseat looking out the back window.

"Something up, Gabriel?" he asked.

"This is going to sound strange, but I think we're being followed."

"Seriously?"

"Yeah, I think so. Try a double back at the next exit?"

"Why would someone be following us?" Brandt asked.

"Not going to tell you how to do your job," Noble said, "but I'd listen to your partner. Jimmy's getting a higher profile across the state, and there are people who'd be interested in sniffing out the scandal."

"Or maybe he has hired muscle to keep us from rescuing Oliver," Millie suggested darkly.

"How would anyone even know we're looking for him?" Brandt asked, trying to understand how his traveling companions had suddenly come down with the conspiracy flu.

Shrugs all around.

Brandt sighed. "Okay, we'll do a double back and then my partner can reflect on whether he's reading too many spy novels."

"Not going to take reading advice from the guy who considers falling asleep over *Sports Illustrated* every night to be a literary enterprise."

Noble looked from Donnelly to Brandt and burst out laughing. "You guys are the real deal, aren't you? That's awesome."

"We normally try to keep a professional demeanor while on the job," Brandt said by way of scolding Donnelly. "But apparently that's out the window today."

"I love it. This is the kind of relationship I always imagined Jimmy in. I hope when he's done with his party boy, he'll be able to find one."

"Excuse me?" Millie growled. "That 'party boy' is the smartest person I know, and he's absolutely killing med school, if you'll pardon the expression."

"I'm sure he's a very nice boy. But Jimmy's going to be on a hell of a rebound coming out of whatever shitstorm of a divorce Stella will put him through."

"Have you known for a while that he's gay? Or bisexual?" Donnelly asked.

"Yeah, since freshman year of high school. We had a little misunderstanding that resulted in something regrettable falling from his lips."

"What was that?"

"My dick," Noble said and burst out laughing.

"Ugh, men," groaned Millie.

"So, are you...?" Donnelly asked with eyebrows raised in insinuation.

"Unfortunately, I'm as straight as they come. I was just horny, like every other high school kid, and he thought he'd help a brother out. It wasn't exactly what I was looking for."

"That's the kind of thing that can end friendships," Donnelly said, "especially in high school."

"Ah, but you don't know Jimmy," Noble said. "He's the best friend I've ever had. He's a great guy, and I knew that even then. We just kind of sidestepped the surprise blowjob thing, and we've never even mentioned it since."

"So that's why you tried to talk him out of getting married?" Brandt asked.

"That and the fact that Stella could give bitch lessons to Marie Antoinette. If he was going to marry a beard, he could at least have chosen one who wouldn't bust his balls every single minute. I tell ya, that bachelor party was like a wake—or a prisoner's last meal before execution."

Brandt pulled smoothly off the freeway. "Here we go, Gabriel. Enjoy your spycraft."

Donnelly watched the car that had been behind them since they pulled out of the parking garage. It exited as well. "They're still with us."

Brandt turned across the overpass and then turned to merge back onto the freeway, heading back into the city.

"They're confused, but they're… yep, here they come."

In the rearview Brandt saw the car come up to speed behind them. "Hmm."

"Okay, so they may be following us," Noble said, "but now we're heading the wrong direction."

"Second the objection," Millie called. "Why are we driving back to the city? Aren't we trying to rescue my friend?"

"We'll double back at the next exit," Donnelly explained. "The first U-turn could be coincidence, but the second one pretty much proves it."

"So here's a hypothetical," Brandt said as they drove back toward the exit with the truck stop.

"Ooh, lawyers love those," Noble said.

"Let's say that Whitford and this party boy decide to tie the knot and go-go dance into the their happily ever after—"

"Hey, now," objected Millie.

"I agree with the lady," Noble said. "Please can we hypothesize him with a nice surgeon or a lawyer or something? Someone his age, who maybe has distinguished salt-and-pepper hair and just a little gut that he's trying to get rid of by going to that spin class on Thursdays?"

"So stipulated," Brandt deadpanned.

"Thank you."

Donnelly tried to stifle his laughter in the backseat.

"Okay," Brandt continued. "Let's say that he and his surgeon want to get married, and they ask you to throw the bachelor party. But they have a lot of straight friends—"

"Like you claim to be," Donnelly cracked.

"And these straight friends will also be at the bachelor party. So where do you go, and what do you do?"

Noble pursed his lips. "That's actually a really good question." He tipped his head thoughtfully and looked out the window for a moment. "I guess you start with what they have in common. That would be booze, and food in small enough portions that the gays can justify eating just a couple to sample them all, and the straights can load up their plates. Late night, the bachelors kick off the dancing with a super sweet spotlight dance, and everyone's drunk enough to join in and dance with whoever's handy, regardless of sex. Done and done." He looked at the troopers with eyebrows up, as if this should have been obvious all along.

"Wow," Donnelly said.

"I'd go to that," Millie opined. "Not that I'd be invited or anything, but it sounds like a good time."

"Indeed," Brandt agreed. "Hang on for the double back." He pulled off the freeway at the truck stop and turned onto the overpass.

"They're still with us," Donnelly reported. "We got ourselves a tail."

"Can you get a tag?"

Donnelly turned back to get a better look. "Any way to get them closer?"

"I'll try," Brandt answered. He slowed, and came to a long stop at the intersection by the truck stop. He watched, and the tail pulled over to the shoulder rather than get any closer.

"There's no front plate," Donnelly reported.

Brandt turned and merged back onto the freeway, but the tail car stayed much farther back now. "They know we've made them."

"Now what?" Noble asked.

Brandt picked up the radio. He gave their position and asked for another cruiser to come up behind them to get an ID on the car following. "We should have an answer in a few minutes."

About fifteen minutes later, the display on the console between the front seats updated with the information about the car behind.

"Registered to a private detective. Looks like you might be right, Charlie. Someone may be expecting us to lead them to Whitford."

"We'll just have to get there first," Noble said with a grim smile.

"SIT," OLIVER said, pointing to a stool at the kitchen island. "I'm making breakfast."

They had just come from the shower, where James had diligently scrubbed off the mess he'd made on Oliver's torso, and then scrubbed a few other things for good measure. They'd spent nearly an hour. After their shower, they had made one concession to formality: both wore sweatpants.

"The supper club was started by my mom's family in the fifties," Oliver said as he rummaged in the fridge. "She wanted to expand the business, so she opened it as a cafe in the mornings. I got to spend several months helping her experiment with recipes before she opened it, so breakfast is now one of my core competencies."

"Can I at least make some coffee?" James said, an adorable pout in his voice.

"I would love some coffee," Oliver said. Then, as James rounded the corner of the counter, Oliver caught him in a clumsy, energetic hug. "And I fucking *love* you."

James kissed him, holding him tightly. "I love you, Oliver Mitchell. You unbroke my heart and made my life complete."

Suddenly both men had tears in their eyes as they kissed again.

"Best. Abduction. Ever." Oliver laughed and swatted James's ass as he walked toward the espresso maker built into the wall on the other side of the oven.

Oliver looked back at the counter and took inventory of his finds. "Frittata," he announced, then started dicing and mixing.

"I can hardly wait," James said as he handed Oliver his cup of coffee. He returned to his stool and watched as Oliver worked with sure, deft motions.

They were finishing breakfast on the deck, drinking down the last of the mimosas, when James tipped his head to the side. "Do you hear that?" he asked.

Oliver turned his head from one side to the other and didn't hear anything. But James jumped to his feet and ran into the house. Oliver followed.

James went to the front door and peeked through one of its small square windows, set in a craftsman-style row at about eye level. "Someone's here," he said, his voice ominous.

"Is it your guy who takes care of the place?" Oliver asked hopefully.

"No, he drives an old beater truck. This is a sedan—looks like a fleet car of some kind. Maybe unmarked police."

Oliver peered through one of the windows. The car came to a stop at the bottom of the stone steps, just where James had parked when they arrived here before he pulled the car into the garage around the side of the cabin. The passenger door opened, and out stepped a man in an expensive suit.

"Oh, shit. It's Charlie," said James.

"Someone you know, then?" Oliver asked.

"It's my lawyer, Charlie Noble."

The other doors of the car opened, and more people stepped out. "And he's brought some company." James looked away from the window. "Stay inside, okay?"

"What are you going to do?"

"I need to go see why they're here. If you stay out of sight, then you won't get caught up in whatever mess this is. And believe me, Charlie would only be here if there was some kind of mess. Some big kind of mess."

Oliver took his hand. "I'm going with you. I don't care what happens or what people say. I won't let you go alone."

"If we step out there together, there'd be no taking it back. Everyone would know about us."

Oliver smiled. "I want them to know. And anyone who doesn't like us being together can go fuck themselves."

James smiled and kissed Oliver. "Let me go see what's up. Stay here, out of sight, okay? I want to be sure it's safe for you."

Oliver nodded reluctantly.

James kissed him one more time, and opened the door.

THE FRONT door opened, and the man Brandt recognized from Donnelly's research the night before stepped out onto the porch. James Whitford was wearing gray sweatpants and a smile. The troopers, as they had been trained to do, turned their searching gaze out into the surrounding woods and down the driveway, looking for threats and private detectives.

"Charlie, good to see you," James said.

"Jimmy, you're looking well."

"Who are your friends?" James asked, his voice carefully calm.

Brandt and Donnelly turned back to James, faces impassive.

"James Whitford, I'd like you to meet—"

"Officers Brandt and Donnelly of the Section 28 task force," James said, finishing Noble's sentence for him. "I'm very familiar with your work, gentlemen."

Brandt, startled in spite of himself, exchanged a quick glance with Donnelly.

Noble continued. "They came to me this morning with a somewhat disturbing story about you and a go-go boy from Burn. I thought it would just be easier if we came directly here to settle this whole thing before it blows up. Sound good?"

James sighed, visibly relieved. "Pleased to meet you, officers. I'm sorry you had to come all this way for what is really—"

He stopped and looked over the heads of the men standing next to the sedan. Another car was making its way up the long driveway.

Donnelly turned, following James's gaze. "It's them," he said.

"Charlie, did you bring anyone else?" James asked.

"We may have been followed," Charlie said apologetically.

The tail car pulled up behind the trooper's cruiser, and its engine shut off. The driver's door opened, and a husky man in a tight but clearly expensive suit stepped out. "Mr. Noble," he said, nodding to Charlie. "Officers Brandt and Donnelly."

"I don't believe we've had the pleasure," Brandt said, advancing toward the man with his hand extended.

"Richard Knox," the man said, gripping Brandt's hand with a huge, doughy fist. "And this is my client." He stepped back and opened the back door of the sedan.

Out of the backseat stepped Stella Whitford.

"Oh, shit," Charlie and James said in unison.

Stella's high heels dug into the graveled driveway, and she stepped with as much elegance as she could muster around the front of the car. "Good morning, darling. What a charming place you have here. So… rustic."

"Stella, delightful to see you," James said, his voice devoid of emotion.

"I'm sorry, Jimmy," Charlie said under his breath.

"No, no, Mr. Noble," Stella simpered gaily. "I think you've done James a great service. Your bringing me here will save a great deal of time and costly discovery once my legal team begins to dismantle you."

James looked morosely at Charlie.

"The trust that holds title to this property, as you will shortly discover," Noble said to Stella, "was structured separately from your prenuptial agreement, and as such will not in any way be affected by the divorce proceedings, which, if there is any justice in the world, will be commencing shortly."

"You are correct, of course," she replied with a treacly sweet smile. "That's not the provision of the agreement that is the most germane to our present situation."

Charlie's eyes widened with dread recognition.

"I think we're forgetting the reason we're here," Millie cried as she flung open her car door and stepped out.

"Millie, I asked you to stay in the car until we'd sorted everything out," Brandt said.

"But you weren't sorting anything out. Where's Oliver? He's probably tied up somewhere—"

"I'm sure that James has no idea whom you're talking about, does he?" Charlie glared at James, clearly trying to convey more than his words implied.

James took a confused breath, and looked back toward the house. He was about to say something when Charlie held up his legal pad. As he was closest to James, neither Brandt nor anyone else could see what was written upon it. James's eyes widened, and he looked at Stella, aghast. It was clear from his face that all of the pieces were coming together in his head. He turned back to the house again, then faced forward, his jaw set.

"Stella, why did you come here today?" James asked, his voice taut.

"Because I missed you, darling. You had me so worried." She smiled sweetly at him.

"If you'll excuse my bluntness, *darling*, that's a crock of shit, and you know it. You're here because you figured you finally had a chance to catch me with someone else. It just now occurred to me why, when you managed my campaigns, you always hired the most attractive women to work as my personal assistants. You kept throwing bimbo after bimbo at me, hoping I would nail one of them and give you what you wanted. But I never took the bait. So you came up with this quite frankly ridiculous plan to have me caught with a go-go boy under the delusion that it would help advance my career. You intended no such thing, of course. Your goal was always the same, and it had nothing to do with getting me elected."

"Is anyone else lost?" Millie asked Brandt and Donnelly under her breath.

They shrugged.

Noble turned to her. "Stella had her own plan all along, and I think you're about to find out what it was."

"All you wanted was to catch me in violation of our prenup," James continued. "Now it has suddenly become clear to me why you insisted on a marital infidelity clause. You weren't going to be happy with half of the estate. You wanted it all. And if you caught me having an affair, you would get it."

Stella narrowed her eyes. "I'm the victim here, asshole. You're the one holed up in your secret mountain getaway having a fling with your boyslut."

James drew himself up to full height. "That's where you're wrong."

"Wait, so Oliver *isn't* here?" Millie asked, her voice angry.

"I'm not having a fling, and he's not a boyslut." James turned back to the front door and held out his hand. "Oliver, come out here?"

The front door opened slowly, and Oliver stepped out onto the porch. He took James's hand and then turned and kissed him.

"Oh!" Millie cried, her face beaming. "Oh, oh, oh!"

"This is not a fling. Oliver and I are in love, which is something that you would have no idea about," James said to Stella, his voice taking on a dignity that had been previously absent. "And this is not marital infidelity, because our marriage was something you used for your own ends from the very beginning. It was never a partnership; it was a con. You're an elegant grifter, Stella dear. But you know what? I don't care anymore. Go ahead and claim marital infidelity and exercise your rights under the prenup. I won't contest it. You can take it all. I have enough in the prior trust to live on, and I have this place, and I have this man to share them with." He fixed her with a withering stare, somehow imperious and humble at the same time. "More than that I will never need."

Stella fumbled a bit, having gotten all of what she came for without the satisfaction of watching him grovel and beg for her not to take it.

"Now get the hell out of here, or I will ask the good officers to escort you off the property."

Stella turned a stunned face to the rest of the assembled group. She seemed about to say something, but then closed her crimson lips, needlessly primped at her helmet of impervious blonde hair, and tottered back and stepped into the car as gracefully as her tight skirt would allow. Her detective shrugged and got in as well. They drove away.

Millie dashed up the stone steps to Oliver, and they embraced joyously. Then she took a step back, held him by the shoulders, spoke to him in the voice she likely used for recalcitrant cats.

"Don't you *ever* do that again," she snarled at him. "You had me worried to death."

"I'm so sorry," Oliver replied. "There was just no time to let you know what was going on, and then once we got here, I couldn't reach you. Forgive me?" He batted his eyelashes and pouted a bit.

"You have to tell me first that this is really okay. Are you and this Whitford guy for real?"

Oliver nodded. "I love him, Millie. I really do. I know it seems sudden, but it's real."

"So I was right all along. You were just waiting for the right guy to come along."

"If you're saying I was gay all along, I have to tell you I don't think that's true. But then again, maybe it is. I don't know, and I don't care anymore. I'm whatever I need to be to fall in love with him," he said as he tipped his head toward James. "That's what I am." He led her toward the front door. "Come on in, you've got to see this place."

They walked in, leaving the four men on the porch.

"Jimmy," Noble said, pulling James into a bro hug.

"Thanks for coming," James said. "It kind of forced the whole situation, and now it's done."

"I don't think she's really done with you yet," Noble replied, warning in his voice.

James shrugged. "She has everything she wants. I'm not going to fight her."

Brandt stood, puzzled. "You don't have to tell me anything more about it if you don't want to, but I don't understand how the whole thing went down."

James smiled at him. "First let me thank you and your partner for all you've done to secure equal rights for the people of this state."

Brandt looked at him quizzically but nodded. "Thank you, sir."

"I had been hoping to be appointed the state's first commissioner of human rights, who will oversee Section 28 enforcement, as well as other aspects of the equality effort, but once this whole thing breaks, I'm not so sure."

"I think you still have a shot," Noble replied bracingly. He turned to the officers. "The prenup I did for Jimmy and the monster stipulated, at the monster's insistence, that any proven marital infidelity will result in immediate divorce at the option of the wronged party, and at the fault of the one who had the affair. That means Stella gets everything they held in common." He held up the legal pad, on which he had scrawled "MARITAL INFIDELITY PRENUP" in block letters. He turned back to James. "A fact I tried to warn you about, but then you went ahead and introduced your go-go boy anyway." He shook his head at his friend, but then laughed. "On the subject of whom, by the way…." He extended a fist for James to bump. "He's hot, buddy."

They bumped and laughed.

"When you held up that sign," James said, "it occurred to me if I just gave her what she wanted, she would go away and we could keep living the happy life that we've been enjoying here the last couple of days. Honest to God, Charlie, when I'm with him I feel like I am actually myself for the first time in my entire life. I don't give a crap about anything else."

"Good for you, buddy. Good for you." Noble embraced his friend again. "I'm really happy for you."

"Well, we should get back," Brandt said. "It's going to take us a while to figure out how to write all of this up."

"Thank you, officers. I really appreciate all you've done." James smiled and shook their hands. "Charlie, want to stay for a bit? I'd like for you to get to know Oliver. We can take you and Oliver's friend back later."

Noble nodded. "Sounds great." He turned to Brandt and Donnelly. "Oh, hang on." He leaned through the doorway. "Miss Flynn, would you like to enjoy the hospitality of the Whitford-Mitchell household for a while? The troopers need to get back to the city."

"I'm not letting this guy out of my sight, so I'm sticking tight," she called back. "Thanks, officers!"

"You're welcome, Millie," Donnelly called back. He smiled and shook his head at Brandt as he got back into the car.

CHAPTER TWELVE
FOUND WEEKEND

JAMES AND Noble stepped into the cabin and shut the door behind them as the troopers' car pulled away. "Oliver, I'd like you to meet my best friend and attorney, Charlie Noble."

"Charlie, nice to meet you," Oliver said, extending his hand.

Noble beamed. "I have been waiting many, many years to meet you," he said, pulling Oliver into a hug.

"Ever since you were a freshman in high school?" Millie asked, a light teasing in her voice.

James's eyes widened. "How did you—"

"We had some time to talk on the way up here," Charlie replied with a shrug.

"And that's what you chose to talk about?" James cried.

"James," Oliver said, "he's the guy you… in high school?"

"I was his first," Charlie answered for him. "So I'm here to be sure you treat him right." He looked at James. "He ruined me for other men."

James burst out laughing. "You leapt out of that bed like a snake had bitten you."

"It *was* a bit of a shock," Charlie said with an attempt at dignity.

"Not so much of a shock that you didn't finish first," James shot back.

"I was young! The whole thing lasted all of thirty seconds. There wasn't time to tell you to stop."

James smiled and wrapped his arm around his friend's shoulders. "I am so glad you stayed my friend all these years, even after I blew you against your will."

Charlie smiled. "You were better at fourteen than most of the women I've been with since," he said.

"Just to be clear," Millie said, "you're supposed to be the straight one?"

Charlie nodded. "Not that my buddy here didn't make me think hard about playing for the other side. But as much as I wanted to, I just couldn't get over the fact that women do it for me."

"Not that many women, given how much time you've spent building your practice," James said with an old friend's gentle scolding. "When was the last time you dated, Charlie?"

Charlie shook his head at his friend but then shrugged as if giving in. "It was Valentine's Day," he answered, then sighed. "Two years ago."

"Hmm," Millie said, looking at Noble with her head tipped to the side.

"I know that look," Oliver whispered into her ear.

"You already landed your dream guy," she whispered back. "Don't ruin it for the rest of us."

Oliver laughed. "At the risk of becoming a cliché, can I make everyone a drink? It's past noon, and it's been kind of a stressful day already."

The consensus of the group ran along the lines of "hell yeah," and Oliver got to mixing. He brought the drinks out to the deck overlooking the lake, where the other three were gathered.

"Here you go," Oliver said, handing glasses around. He ended by sitting next to James on a love seat by the deck railing. They kissed.

"Aww," Millie and Noble said in unison, which surprised them both. They laughed and raised their glasses to each other.

"So how long have you two known each other?" James asked Millie.

"I met Oliver when he was a nerdy freshman on my dorm floor," Millie said.

"And I met Millie when she was a nerdy freshman on *my* dorm floor," Oliver rejoined with a laugh.

"He was my token straight-guy friend," Millie lamented. "I guess I'll need to find a new one now."

"So let me be sure I understand," Noble said, in a jury-summation kind of voice. "Oliver, you were straight before this whole adventure began?"

Oliver shrugged. "I guess so. Doesn't really seem to matter much now, though." He put his arm around James and rested his head on James's shoulder.

"So it worked on him, but not on me," Noble said with a chuckle. "Damn."

"Hmm, a straight guy with a no-homo guarantee," Millie mused, looking at the lawyer. "Sounds like a pretty good deal."

"Unless I miss my guess," James said conspiratorially to Oliver, "your friend has taken a bit of shine to my friend."

Oliver grinned. "I guess whatever happened to us is contagious."

"If we could bottle that stuff, what a world it would be."

The four friends whiled away an hour on the deck, drinking Oliver's concoctions and talking.

"Oliver," Millie said, "want to show me around the lake, stretch our legs a bit?"

"Sure," he replied, getting to his feet. "You guys okay for drinks?"

"I think we'll do fine without our bartender for a little while," James said. "But I'll need a kiss before you go."

Oliver was happy to oblige, and found what James needed was not only a kiss but a squeeze of Oliver's butt cheek as well. This, too, he was more than happy to indulge.

He and Millie walked down the long flight of steps to the water's edge, then out along the trail he and James had gone running on the day before.

"Leave it to you," Millie said as the forest closed over them and the cabin disappeared behind, "to run away with a guy who turns out to be Prince Charming with a castle in the woods. You're like the gay Cinderella. This is all amazing."

"I'm glad you like it," Oliver said. "I feel like I'm a completely different person than I was when I got here."

"Yeah, about that," Millie said, her voice taking on a more serious tone. "I'm going to ask you something, and I don't want you to get offended, okay?"

He squinted at her skeptically. Millie could offend the devil himself without breaking a sweat; that she would warn him about the possibility made him a little uneasy. "Uh, sure?"

"Are you really here of your own free will? Is this thing with Whitford all kosher?"

Oliver smiled. "Yes, and more than yes. He's amazing. I can't believe it's all turned out this way."

"And you two have…?"

He laughed. "We have. Not everything, but enough for me to know that it's right."

"Thank you for sparing me the details." She paused for a moment. "Well, if you wanted to offer a couple of small details...."

"Like does he still have his swimmer's body?"

"Oh, sure, anything along that line. Whatever you're comfortable with." Then she suddenly grabbed his hand. "So? Does he? Does he? Give, girl!"

Oliver burst out laughing, unable to keep his composure in the face of Millie's frantic insistence. Finally he was able to catch his breath. "There is not an ounce of fat on that man. And I checked. I checked *everywhere*."

"Wow. Thanks for being, uh... thorough." She punched him on the arm. "Bastard. I've spent my entire adult life looking for smart and muscular and rich and you bag one your first try. I hate you." She laughed and hugged him. "I'm so happy for you." She kissed him on the cheek.

"You are a strange woman," he said, very much enjoying basking in the glow of her excitement about his good fortune in love.

"So, what was it like, the first time? How does it feel to throw heterosexuality out the window and make giddy love to that hunk of man?"

Oliver looked at her with an eyebrow up. "You make it sound like I meant to do this. I didn't. When I left the club with him, I really thought we were just trying to contain the damage. It wasn't until we got here, and I got to see what he's like in real life... it just suddenly felt like the right thing to do, to fall in love with him."

"There's love, and then there's this, dear. I mean, I love you, but I don't ever intend to have your dick in my mouth."

"I am so relieved to hear that," Oliver replied with a laugh. "I know this is going to sound all gooey, but once I realized what a great guy he is, all the physical stuff just seemed to fall into place. The first time, all we did was cuddle."

Millie turned a skeptical eye on him. "Cuddle?"

"Yep. I know it sounds dorky, but because of the way he grew up, he'd never gotten to cuddle with another man. It was like I could suddenly give him this amazing gift, so I did it. And it was fucking awesome, by the way."

Millie nodded. "I can see, from a certain objective viewpoint, that the two of you cuddling might be a pleasant sight... wait, you weren't naked, were you?"

"Hell yeah, we were naked."

"Okay, that's like thermonuclear hot. Dude." She held out her fist, and they bumped.

"It was pretty hot. And it kind of led to other things, which were, in some senses, even hotter." He winked at her.

She fanned herself and rolled her eyes, but then snapped back to her serious self. "But Ollie, dear, have you really thought all of this through? What are the good people of your hometown going to do when their great hope for the future, their pride and joy, their local boy makes good, turns out to be a local boy who makes out—with another boy? From what you've told me, it seems like a pretty conservative little place."

"What are you suggesting?" Oliver asked, more angrily than he intended. Millie's question had inflamed something that had been buzzing around the back of his head but that he had been doing his best to ignore. "That I pretend to be straight so they don't get offended? That I marry someone out of concern for appearances, like James did? We know how well that works out."

Millie put a soothing hand on his arm. "All I'm asking is if you've thought about all of the ripples this glorious escape into the mountains—into the arms of your loving James—is going to send out across your entire life. I don't think Stella's going to go softly into that good night, no matter what James says. If I know my bitches, and you know I do, she's going to trumpet this affair from the mountaintops. Every time she tells the story of how her lying sack of shit husband ran off, she's going to include the bit about his whoring go-go boy home wrecker, and I'd bet anything she's going to call you by name just to make it sting. The people of your hometown are going to find out about this as soon as the estranged Mrs. Whitford gets hold of a microphone. Which, unless I miss my guess, is going to be"—she consulted her watch—"right about now."

"Shit." Oliver stopped dead on the trail. "Shit, shit, shit."

"Indeed. So what you need to ask yourself, my dear, is the question every woman has to ask herself whenever she starts dating a new man: is he worth the damage he's going to do?"

"Seriously, women ask themselves that?"

"Every damn time, if they know what's good for them. There's no such thing as a man who doesn't break things. That's why I'm only friends with the gays. Y'all at least know how to clean up after yourselves."

"I've been gay for like a day. I think it's too early to tell what kind I'll be."

"I hope you'll be one who makes good decisions. Now, the decision before you is this: is he worth the epic swamp of tabloid shit you're going to have to slog through to be with him? Because if you aren't sure, then you should get yourself the hell out of Dodge until the whole thing blows over. At this point all they have is a blurry snapshot of you, and that's going to get tiresome on the news every night. If you make yourself scarce for longer than their attention span, you might come out of this intact."

"And if I stand by him?"

Millie smiled. "The way you ask that tells me you've already made up your mind."

"I can't leave him, Millie. He changed me, and I think I changed him. We just found each other—I won't lose him, not because some people back home might not understand."

She nudged him with her shoulder as they walked. "Good for you."

They walked along in silence for a while, listening to the birds and the breeze in the trees.

"It's not going to be easy, you know," she ventured.

He nodded. "I know. I think the only way to keep it from blowing up completely is by heading it off."

"How are you going to do that?"

"I'm going to come out to my parents."

She stopped dead in her tracks. "All the ways to commit suicide, and that's the one you pick?"

"I don't want them to find out on the news. And I can't just show up out of the blue and tell them that the son they always thought was straight has now discovered he's gay, because that's not the truth. I'm only gay because James is a guy. If he were a woman, I'd be straight."

"If he were a woman he wouldn't have been stuffing fifties down the jockstrap of a go-go boy bartender."

"He never stuffed anything down my jockstrap," Oliver sniffed with all the dignity he could muster. "And he always gave me hundreds."

She rolled her eyes. "The denomination is not the issue at hand. The big question is why you want to tell your parents you've fallen for a guy you've been with for less time than it takes to work the Sunday crossword puzzle. That sounds like a recipe for freaking everybody out, including the new love of your life."

"You must be terrible at crossword puzzles."

"I am. And you are terrible at humans."

"That's mean."

"Tough love, baby. Do you really think James is going to be thrilled with this coming-out idea?"

"He was willing to give up everything for me. He gave up all that money—hell, his whole political career—for me. What I'm giving up is the goodwill of my entire town, all those people who trusted me and put their savings into my education. If I can at least salvage a relationship with my parents, then I hope he would try to help me do that."

She frowned and nodded. "All right. If he's as amazing as you keep saying, then maybe it will all work out fine." They walked along a little farther. "Now I have just one more question for you."

"Promise it's the last one for a while?" Oliver said with a chuckle.

"Promise. Do you think I might have a shot with this lawyer guy?"

"I thought you were kind of down on straight guys. They break things, remember?"

"Yeah, yeah. But this girl hasn't been broken for a while, and I'm starting to think I've forgotten how. He seems like a nice guy, and I could do worse than finding a nice lawyer."

"Well, if he's James's best friend, that says a lot about him. And I saw the way he was looking at you. I think you would definitely have a shot. Want to hang out for a little while and see where it goes?"

"Hell yeah. You shouldn't be the only one to come out of this with a boyfriend."

"All that cynicism and you still just want to be loved. It's so sweet." He pinched her cheeks as if she were a big happy baby.

"You make me believe in love again," she said in an emotionless monotone, then the fire snapped back into her eyes. "Now get your mitts off me or you'll pull back a stump."

He dropped his hands to his side and kept walking, looking straight ahead, unable to keep from laughing at Millie's theatrics. They strolled back to the cabin and rejoined James and Charlie on the deck for another round.

"Well," James said some time later, as the afternoon shadows grew longer. "We should probably get you folks back to the city."

"Do you have to go?" Oliver asked. "It's really nice having you here."

Millie held her hands up, indicating surrender to Oliver's suggestion. "I figured I'd be spending the entire weekend doing post-traumatic intervention, helping you overcome your abduction. I've got nowhere to be."

Noble held up his hands in an imitation of Millie. "I cleared my calendar as well."

"Excellent!" James cried, and he leapt to his feet. "Oliver, shall we?"

Oliver jumped up as well. "We shall. And then we'll make dinner."

James laughed delightedly and they kissed before heading into the cabin.

"Just as long as there's food when you guys finally exhaust yourselves," Charlie called after them.

"We're going to waste away out here while you're busy sexing each other!" added Millie with a laugh.

"Those two," groaned James as they stepped back into the cabin. "Already thick as thieves."

"They'll be thicker than that soon if Millie has her way."

"Did she say something about him on your walk?" James asked as he started to root through the refrigerator.

"She did," Oliver replied. "Nothing serious, but she thinks he's nice."

"Well, this old cabin is sure working its magic. Charlie said basically the same thing about her while you were gone. Perhaps we can fan the spark of romance."

"Speaking of which," Oliver said carefully, "I have something I need to ask you."

James set down the package of steak he was holding and turned to give his full attention to Oliver. "Anything. Anything at all."

Oliver smiled. "You don't even know what it is yet."

"I don't need to. If you ask me, I will say yes. To anything."

Oliver kissed him on the nose. "You are amazing. But you should probably hear what it is first."

"If it makes you feel better," James replied.

"I'm kind of worried about how this whole thing with Stella is going to play out. If she goes after you, she's going to be going after me too, and I don't know the effect that's going to have on the people back home."

"You're worried the townsfolk are going to be angry the guy they've been putting through school isn't the kind of man they thought he was?" James took Oliver's hand. "You don't have to worry about money."

Oliver shook his head. "Thanks, but I'm mostly worried about my parents. I don't want them to find out about... us... from the news. They're good people, but they're kind of conservative."

James pulled him close. "Are you asking me to go home with you and meet your parents?"

Oliver looked down, suddenly feeling very silly for asking this. "Yes," he said softly.

"I would love to," James cried, kissing Oliver excitedly.

Oliver laughed. "Are you sure you're ready? It seems like a big step."

James put his hands on either side of Oliver's face and held him close. "I tried to protect you, to keep you out of this mess with me and Stella, but I couldn't do it. The least I can do is help you smooth things over at home. And," he smiled slyly, "I would be honored to meet your parents. They made you, so I have some thanks to deliver."

"I love you, you know," Oliver murmured, putting his arms around James's waist.

"I know. And I love you more."

THE FOURSOME sat in the twilight, the wreckage of dinner strewn across the table on the deck.

"This has to be the best-catered abduction in history," Millie observed.

"Seriously. What do you rub on your meat?" Charlie asked.

"Oliver," James and Millie answered in unison.

There was much laughter around the table.

"So, are we taking you two back to the city tonight, or can I have another of Oliver's amazing cocktails?" James asked.

"I'd love to stay the night," Charlie said. Then he looked at Millie, while clearly trying to not look like he was looking at Millie.

"Do you have room? And a spare toothbrush?" Millie asked.

"Of course," James replied. "We'd be delighted to have you stay, wouldn't we, Oliver?"

Oliver smiled. "Of course. As long as you promise to ignore any sounds that might come from the bedroom. We think there's a rabid badger in the wall, and he sometimes makes this moaning noise like he's having an orgasm. It can be kind of distracting."

"Oliver, honey, we're all grown-ups here," Millie scolded. "If you and James are going to be making the beast with two dicks, we're happy for you. Aren't we, Chuck?"

Charlie's eyebrows shot up to hear his name chopped this way, but he laughed raucously and patted Millie on the knee. "We may simply have to make some noise of our own," he said slyly.

Millie offered no objection, Oliver noted. Good for her.

They all pitched in to wash the dishes, and James got Millie and Charlie settled into the two guest rooms on the lower level of the cabin, where the rabid badger would not be quite so bothersome. They all said their respective good nights, and then James and Oliver retired to the master bedroom.

"Well, that looks promising," James said as he stripped off his clothes.

"I'll say," Oliver replied, doing the same. "I wouldn't be surprised if we find another rabid badger, this one in a wall downstairs."

"Let's hope so. The world could use a few more rabid badgers." He pulled the now-naked Oliver to him. "Now, how are we going to celebrate our two-day anniversary?"

"I'm trying to recall what the gift is for two days," Oliver said, scratching his head. "Oh, I remember now. It's semen. Luckily I'm all stocked up."

"I'm going to enjoy unwrapping that," James said with a wink. He reached down directly to the source and began supply chain operations.

"First I need to know something," Oliver murmured.

"What would that be?" James asked, kissing his way along Oliver's neck.

"What your dick tastes like," Oliver quipped lightly.

James laughed and pressed Oliver to him tightly. "Can I tell you a secret?"

"You can tell me all of them."

"Let's start with just one." James took a deep breath. "No one has ever tasted it."

Oliver startled back. "What?"

James shook his head. "Charlie certainly wasn't going to reciprocate, and those guys in the dorm bathroom were only looking to get off, not to date. And Stella… well, the only thing that goes in there is caviar and the blood of the innocent. So yeah. You'd be the first."

Oliver smiled. "You'd be my first too. Never thought I'd say this—ever—but lie back, mister. I'm going to suck your dick." He pushed James back onto the bed and pounced atop him. "Good God you're solid." He grabbed two large handfuls of James's heavy pectorals and squeezed as hard as he could; the muscle barely yielded to his grip.

James tipped his head back and moaned, as if being handled by a man's strong hands was a dream come true. "All those lonely nights, I dreamed of this without even knowing what it would feel like. But having you here, on top of me, it's like I'm finally home—my body and my emotions are finally in the same place. Underneath your strong thighs, feeling the heat of your naughty bits on my belly button. Nowhere in the world I'd rather be."

Olive leaned down and kissed him. "You are such a romantic, which I love. But right now I'm out-of-my-mind horny, so I'm gonna stick a pin in the romance and we'll come back to it later, okay? I'm just going to give you the best fucking blowjob ever, even though I have no idea what I'm doing. But I have a mouth and you have a dick and I'm going to make sure they get properly introduced." He grinned at James, ecstatic at the possibilities before him.

James laughed. "Sucking first, romance after. Got it. But if you keep up that sexy talk, I may get there before you really have a chance to start."

Oliver grinned and launched himself eagerly into the space between James's legs. Looking up along the muscular expanse of his torso, Oliver was struck again by the beauty of the male form. How had he not noticed this before? Or was it James alone who could inspire this reaction in him? He shook his head—plenty of time later to work out the identity politics—and focused on the parts of James that were immediately at hand. And mouth. Oliver leaned forward and studied them closely. He hadn't yet gotten to the clinical part of his schooling, which would require him to handle actual patients, so this was the first time he had looked directly at another man's penis. Sure, he had glanced occasionally in the locker room over the years, and he had certainly looked at James's over the last couple of days, but there's a difference between a cock at a distance and a cock three inches from one's nose. Plus, all of the penises he had seen on a casual basis were flaccid, whereas James's looked hard enough to cut glass. It rose up his belly, straight and true, and tapered elegantly from base to tip. It bobbed in time with James's pulse, tapping his navel with each dip and then rising again.

Oliver reached out his hand and grasped it, barely able to touch his fingers together around it. It was hot and solid, and he immediately compared it to the sensation of holding his own, which was very different. James's had a pronounced corpus spongiosum, which stood out from the rest of his penis like the big fuel tank on the space shuttle. The thing was built like a battering ram, and Oliver had a flash of panic when he considered the penetrative use that might be made of an instrument so thick. That was a conversation they would have another day. He leaned in close and licked James's erection from the base where the soft folds of his scrotum gathered all the way to the tip.

James gasped and then exhaled as if the key to all secrets of the universe had been revealed to him. His thighs twitched restlessly against Oliver's shoulders. He seemed about to come undone by the simple contact of Oliver's tongue on his cock.

Oliver knew he would need to work quickly to stay ahead of James's twitchy ecstasy. He lifted himself up on his elbows, pulled James's cock away from his belly, and kissed the tip. This brought another gasp from James's throat, and his legs writhed wildly anew. Oliver leaned forward and wrapped his lips around the head of James's cock.

It tasted… male. It was an almost disturbingly familiar taste to Oliver; it was reminiscent of locker rooms and soap, of fabric softener and clean sweat. It was masculine and strong and salty, and Oliver shocked himself by delighting in it. This was the most perverse thing he could have imagined doing, and yet it was so fucking right. He closed his eyes, licked around James's cockhead to make it slippery, and then pushed himself down on it, welcoming it into him. He was aware of his legs being battered by James's as they flailed, but he held strong. James sat up, as if to keep him from continuing, but there was no way Oliver was going to stop. He wrapped his left fist around the base of James's cock, placed his right hand in the middle of his chest, and pushed him back down, letting him know exactly who was in charge here. Once James had settled, Oliver pinched one nipple and then the other with the fingers of his right hand, bringing moans from James, who clutched the sheets in his frenzy.

Suddenly James's entire body went rigid, and he called out softly, "No...," as if mournful about crossing this boundary, as if having someone love him physically was so foreign he was afraid of how it would change him. Oliver somehow sensed how critical this boundary was to James, and he was determined to help him the only way he knew how.

He sucked harder. He gripped harder. He pinched harder.

James stopped breathing, his body quivering. Oliver felt a spasming transmitted through James's steel-hard cock, revealing the inner workings, the contractions of deep muscles whose only job was this: bringing to the surface the liquid manifestation of passion. Of desire. Of love.

Oliver's mouth was suddenly full. A connoisseur of potables, he found little to love in his first taste of semen. But he looked up and saw what it meant to James that he had received it. He read in the torque and tension of his body how deeply he felt this. And Oliver was glad to have received the gift that was in his mouth, and the taste and texture of it faded away, and all he felt was humbled—in James's thirty years he had never before experienced this.

Oliver swallowed and lapped and nibbled, and finally slid his body up James's, kissing his way along the muscled form until they were again eye to eye.

James swallowed and licked his lips as if he'd just crossed a desert and reached an oasis. "That was...."

"Beautiful, is what that was," Oliver sighed. "Thank you for sharing that with me."

James smiled and looked at the ceiling as if trying to divine how he had gotten so lucky. "You give me my first blowjob ever, and it's perfect, and you're thanking me for allowing you to give it to me? How the hell did I end up here? Where did you come from?"

Oliver smiled slyly. "Doesn't matter where I came from. You found me, and you brought me here. And here I'm going to stay."

"I hope so," James replied. "I have some favors to return."

Oliver stretched out on his back next to James. "The favors return desk is now open for business." He winked. "So get busy, mister."

"With pleasure, sir. With pleasure."

JAMES AND Oliver, trying to be good hosts, were in the kitchen Saturday morning making breakfast for their guests, from whom they had heard not a peep since the night before. Oliver was working on eggs while James sliced up fruit.

"Have you heard any movement from down there?" James asked as he handed Oliver another cup of coffee.

"Nope. Millie's not the sleep-late kind, though, so we should see her soon."

"I'm not sure Charlie ever sleeps, actually," James added. "As far as I've ever been able to tell, he spends every moment of his life in the office." He glanced at the clock on the wall. "This is a real change for him."

At that moment Millie appeared, climbing the staircase from the lower level.

"There she is," cried Oliver. He walked over to her to bestow a good-morning hug. "Nice look, by the way."

Millie was wearing a pair of James's athletic shorts, tightly cinched around the waist, and a dress shirt.

"Well, wasn't Charlie chivalrous, giving you the shirt off his back," James said.

Millie looked down and smoothed the placket as best she could. "I may have taken it off him myself, actually," she replied, with a surprising amount of dignity in her voice.

"Lucky man," James said. "Now, how do you take your coffee, my dear?"

"Like I take my men… straight," she said with a smile. "No offense."

"None taken," James replied with a laugh. "I guess, statistically speaking, it stands to reason that out of the three of us one would have to be straight."

"No need for statistics, my good man. I have firsthand knowledge of Chuck's straightness."

Oliver wrinkled his nose. "Feel free to keep the details to yourself," he said.

"Well, that was fast," Millie said. "From ostensibly straight to passionately gay in two days—and now you're so far gone you can't even hear about men and women together."

"Millie, I love you like a sister," Oliver replied. "And though I don't have an actual sister, if I did, I don't think I'd want to hear about her having sex."

"You're just jealous that you're the only one here who hasn't blown Chuck."

"I'm trying to think of a grosser way for you to say that, and I can't come up with one."

"Thank you," Millie said with a courtly bow. "And thank you." She took a steaming cup of black coffee from James, which she sipped with a sigh. "Now, since we're in a dead zone here in terms of phone service, we have no idea whether the dragon lady has alerted the media about yesterday's little kerfuffle. What's the strategy, gents?"

James and Oliver exchanged a look. "We're going home," Oliver said.

"Well, I assumed that. I mean, we all have jobs."

"No, I mean after we drop you two off at home, we're going to Crystal Lake."

Millie's mouth dropped open. "You're… what now?"

Oliver put his arm around James's waist. "I'm taking James home to meet my parents."

She shook her head as if clearing it of Oliver's nonsense. "No offense, and I hope you know I mean this in the kindest and most loving way possible, but are you fucking crazy?"

"Not last time I checked," Oliver said in a gruff monotone.

"Then what are you thinking?"

"I'm thinking that even if Stella hasn't started her jilted-Madonna tour, she's going to shortly, and my parents are going to find out soon enough. So I'd rather beat her to it, and tell them my way."

"And he's roped you into this crazy scheme?" she asked James.

"I would go anywhere he asked me to, and do whatever he wanted me to do when we got there." He ruffled Oliver's hair. "In fact, I'm really looking forward to meeting his parents."

Millie shook her head pityingly. "I know you wanted to come out to your parents, and I was with you on that. But if you think that Ronnie and Jasper are going to welcome their suddenly gay son and his recently outed, disgraced-politician boyfriend, whom he met on the job as a slutty bartender, then I suggest you check yourselves in for rehab because whatever you're smoking is just too damn strong."

"Ouch," James said, but his hint of a smile showed he wasn't offended.

"Millie tends to shoot from the hip," Oliver offered consolingly. "With an elephant gun."

"Ollie, love, I've met your parents. Every time I went home with you during college they treated me like the future Mrs. Oliver Mitchell. They looked at my finger like they were measuring it for an heirloom engagement ring. Your mother twice used the phrase 'child-bearing hips' in my presence. They are going to be devastated when you come out to them; to have James there as well is just too damn much for them to handle all at once."

"You forget they're going to see all of it on the news soon anyway. Wouldn't it be better for them to hear it from us?"

"Given that what you're telling them is that they can kiss good-bye all their cherished visions of a wedding and grandchildren and the acceptance of your backward little town, I'd have to say it would be better to see them safely into their graves without ever having this conversation at all."

Oliver walked over to Millie and clasped her shoulders. "You know there's no reason why they can't still have all of those things. It's probably too early for us to be talking about kids," he glanced at James, whose face was a comic mask of panic, "but there's no reason why all of that can't still happen."

"You know that, and I know that, but you have to remember when you come out to your parents, you aren't just sharing something about yourself. You're telling them something about themselves, and the future they imagined—not just for you, but for them. They won't immediately think how lucky it is that marriage equality has finally come to this benighted state of ours right when their only son has need of it because he's decided to forgo the usual white picket fence and love of a good woman in favor of having his butter churned by an old man."

James took a step back.

"Sorry," she blurted, putting out her hand to him. "I'm just worst-casing this for you. I think you're wonderful, and I can't think of anyone in the world I'd rather see Ollie with, but you have to understand parents are always going to see things differently. They're going to look at you as the malevolent force of darkness that seduced their only son into a bleak hellscape of buttsex. The fact that you are hotter than hot is only going to make things worse."

"Wow, when she gets wound up, she just goes like hell, doesn't she?" James asked Oliver.

Oliver nodded and rolled his eyes, then turned back to his friend. "Millie, I love you, but I think you're selling my parents short. It may take them some time, but they love me enough to accept who I am and to accept James as a part of my life."

James took Oliver's hand and pulled him close. They kissed.

"Whatever happens," he said softly, "we'll get through it together."

"I'll be rooting for you," Millie said with sudden cheer. "Or helping you root through the wreckage," she added in a mutter.

"Well, aren't we just farting out rainbows this morning," Charlie cracked as he came up the stairs. He walked up behind Millie and put his arms around her, nuzzling up to her neck. "This shirt looks much better on you than me."

"That's because I have an amazing rack," Millie replied, nuzzling him back. "But these shorts would definitely benefit from that bubble butt of yours. Fucking people up in court must build some serious muscle."

"You talk like a sailor. A sexy, sexy sailor." He kissed her passionately, and they grappled for a long moment.

"Well, this is a side of Charlie I haven't seen," James observed. He sipped his coffee while his best friend made out with Oliver's. "I think she looks good on him."

"One thing you should know about Millie because it's not obvious from her current behavior," Oliver said. "She's actually really picky about guys. She hardly dates because it's hard for her to find the one percent of guys she can stand. And of those, only a small fraction are able to put up with her, so it's kind of a big deal when things work out this way."

"One thing you should know about Charlie," James answered back. "He has always told me he's straight, but this is honest to God the only time I have ever seen him with his arms around a woman. Up until now it's been purely theoretical. She's really something special."

"She's eighty-five percent something special and fifteen percent raging bitch on wheels. That's the part that called you old," Oliver said, kissing James on the cheek. "She didn't really mean that."

"But she did mean the 'hotter than hot' part, right?"

"Of course she did," Oliver replied in the tone of voice one would use when one's dog is such a good boy, yes he is.

James looked back over at Charlie and Millie in their clinch. "Let's get these people some breakfast. They're going to burn through a lot of calories the way they're going at it."

Oliver and James finished making breakfast, which they served on the deck in the bright morning sun.

"So, you're really going to do it?" Millie asked as they finished.

Oliver nodded. "It's the right thing to do. They deserve to hear the truth from me. The whole truth."

"I think that's the right way to do it," Charlie said, reaching over and clapping Oliver on the back. "Let it sink in a little bit before it all hits the news." He glanced over at James. "Because we all know Stella's going to go full-bitch mode on this, and anyone in her way is going to feel her wrath."

"That's very comforting, buddy, thanks," James said with a fatalistic grin.

"You know I'm not one to beat around the bush," Charlie replied. "And you were the one who decided to forfeit all of your bargaining chips before the game even started. You didn't leave me a lot of maneuvering room, did you? Attorneys like options—you've got very few here."

"I really hope Stella will take her complete financial victory and slink off to gloat somewhere out of sight." He sighed and looked out over the lake. "Though I fully expect she will find a way to make things worse along the way."

"I will be by your side the entire time, Jimmy. We'll get through this."

"Thanks, man. I'm really glad I chose you for my first blowjob."

"Yeah, that's what made us friends for life. Nothing like a little oral sex between friends." Charlie turned to Millie. He mouthed to her, "You were better."

She laughed and slapped him on the shoulder.

"Well, if we're going to hit the festival of homophobia in Crystal Lake, we should probably get going," James said to Oliver. "And get these two back to their respective homes."

Charlie and Millie exchanged a look.

"How about you just drop us at my office, and I'll take Millie home," Charlie said. "That way you can get on your way more quickly."

"You would do that for us?" James asked, batting his eyes with mock appreciation.

"Just one more in a long line of sacrifices I've made for you, starting with enduring your first awkward blowjob. It's an honor to serve."

"Honestly, the way you two flirt," Millie scolded. "I'm going to take a shower." She rose from the table and walked into the house. Then she reappeared. "Aren't you coming?"

"I will be shortly," Charlie said with a laugh as he followed her into the house.

"Straight people are always so obsessed with sex," Oliver complained loudly as the two disappeared down the stairs.

"Feel like you might need a shower?" James asked with a wink.

"Thought you'd never ask," Oliver said as he gathered up the dishes. "Start lathering, and I'll be there to scrub the dirty bits."

The drive back to the city was raucous and full of laughter, as the foursome did their best to avoid mentioning the possibility that Stella had laid a network of public-relations land mines in their path. A quick search of the local news sources revealed nothing of concern, but it was early on a Saturday, and she had perhaps not had a chance to get fully locked and loaded. Oliver texted an extravagantly apologetic message to Gavin, who replied immediately with relief that Oliver was safe, and assurances that he should take the rest of the week off and get his personal business together.

"I guess he's used to this kind of thing," Oliver said as he read Gavin's message.

"I expect most of the guys there eventually have this happen. What did Xander call it?"

"Getting their wings," Oliver said with a roll of his eyes. Then he looked at James and realized it had kind of happened to him. Life could be like that sometimes.

James dropped Charlie and Millie at Charlie's office, where he had left his car, and after swinging by Oliver's apartment to pack a weekend bag, they headed back out of the city toward Oliver's hometown.

CHAPTER THIRTEEN
HOMETOWN BOY

THE DRIVE to Oliver's hometown took about four hours along the back roads James preferred to drive. He slalomed the sleek black sedan along the winding roads that ventured into the foothills.

"It's pretty up here," he remarked to Oliver as they neared their destination.

"That's what keeps people coming back year after year," Oliver replied. "All of this natural beauty is good for business."

"So the entire economy is based on tourism?"

"Pretty much. There used to be a logging industry, but sometime in the 1950s, the locals realized they could make more money renting cabins in the woods than cutting down the trees. Turns out city folks are the real renewable resource."

"Were your parents locals, or did they come on vacation and decide to stay?"

"Mom grew up here, and Dad came with his family on vacations. He came back after college and fell in love—with her and with the place. The supper club was her parents' pride and joy, but things were slower back then. The season was only in the summer, and the town kind of hibernated in the winter. But then the ski resorts opened up nearby, and it became a year-round vacation spot. Good for business, but it also means there's never a slow season; people come for the lake, they come for the fall colors, they come to ski and ice fish, they come for the spring wildflowers. Mom and Dad work nonstop, serving the locals breakfast in the morning, brunch to the tourists, sandwiches during the day, and then dinner every night. It's a grind, but they still say they love it."

"How have they been getting by without you while you're in med school?"

"They seem to be doing okay. I stopped even coming home for summers after my freshman year in college, actually. I started doing internships rather than coming back to work at the club, so I haven't actually been behind the bar there for a few years. It'll be kind of fun to see it again. The end of spring is a nice time, since things don't really get crazy until the kids are out of school and families start coming up for weeks at a time."

James reached over and put his hand on Oliver's knee. "You sure you're ready to do this?"

Oliver took a deep breath and nodded. "It's not the timing I would choose—I mean, I'm still getting used to the idea of… us. But I think giving them the honest truth before they hear whatever they're going to hear on the news about us will help. In the long run. In the short run, it's going to suck pretty hard."

"Nothing we can't handle," James said and turned his eyes back to the road.

Oliver looked at him as he drove: one hand on the wheel, eyes sharply focused on the curves ahead. Oliver knew he could be a control freak—pretty much every doctor he'd ever met was guilty of that—but with James, he could be different. He could give up control, surrender himself to the strength and experience that James brought to their relationship. Though he would never have imagined himself feeling this way, it was really nice to be taken care of sometimes. And his current situation might well turn out to be one of those times. He thought about what might happen when he talked with his parents. The closer they drew to town, the quieter Oliver grew.

"Whatcha thinking?" James asked as Oliver stared blankly out the window.

Oliver shrugged. "How much I've changed since the last time I was here. How much I've changed since this time last week."

"Is this still where you want to be when you've finished your degree? Being a small-town doc?"

"It's what I said I would do," Oliver replied. "And it's what I've always imagined for myself."

"You have other options now, you know," James suggested.

Oliver looked at him, surprised by his implication. "What does that mean, exactly?"

James shrugged. "Just that you agreed to come back up here because the town was paying for your schooling. You are probably earning enough at Burn now that you can pay for it yourself."

"Oh. I thought you were suggesting that you would—"

"Pay for your med school?" James darted a sidelong glance at Oliver. "I would do that in a heartbeat. Even if you come to your senses tomorrow and decide I'm too old and boring for you to spend another minute with. I would do it because you came into my life right when I needed you, and you accomplished in a couple of days what I've struggled to do for a couple of decades." He looked over at Oliver, really looked at him. "I'm not a sugar daddy, or whatever they call such people these days. I freely admit I'm being overly romantic because everything I can imagine about my life in the future assumes you being right where you are, next to me. It's just that you are the answer to every dream I've ever had, every prayer I've ever said, and I cannot for the life of me believe you are really real. I would do anything to see you happy, and if you are happy with me, then my life is complete. If you decide to go be happy somewhere else, with someone else, then I will find a way to survive. Won't like it, not one bit, but I will do it. Not because I'm strong, and not because I don't really love you, but because you believed in me, even when I lost faith in myself. I would carry on because you proved to me I could. So yes, I would pay for med school. I would do anything, give you anything, because no matter what I give you, it cannot come close to what you have given me."

Oliver realized his mouth was hanging open, and he managed to shut it before he drooled. "Wow. That was… wow." He reached out and took James's hand, lacing their fingers together. "Next to you is where you will find me, for as long as you want me here."

James beamed and squeezed Oliver's hand.

At Oliver's instruction, James pulled off the winding highway and navigated an even smaller, windier road for the last ten miles into Crystal Lake. As they entered the tiny center of town, he braked to just under the posted twenty-five miles per hour. They drove slowly past antique shops and jewelry stores, boutiques and cafés.

"This is really charming," James said as the sedan idled along the main street. "And judging from the cars parked along the road, it's a pretty wealthy bunch who spend their vacations here."

"I'm kind of surprised to see that," Oliver said, taking notice of the expensive European vehicles that lined the street. "It seems like a much higher-brow sort than when I was growing up."

"I'd call that a good sign," James said hopefully. "You know, more money usually means better education and more liberal social attitudes."

"Fingers crossed," Oliver said with a grim chuckle.

Oliver directed James to the supper club, which lay at the end of the main street, just where it ran smack into the pristine body of water that was Crystal Lake's claim to fame and fortune. About a block along the shore, the not-very-imaginatively named Crystal Lake Supper Club stood with banks of windows overlooking the water. There was a pier out front, allowing vacationing captains to dock their recreational craft just feet from the entrance to the restaurant. James pulled the car into the small lot behind the club, which, at this early afternoon hour, was less than a quarter full.

They sat for a moment in the hushed interior of the car, Oliver taking deep, calming breaths, and James looking at him with peaked eyebrows.

"Take as long as you need," James said softly. "Would you like me to wait out here while you go in?"

Despite his anxiety, Oliver couldn't keep from smiling. "I can't tell this story without you. Of course you have to come with me." He looked over at the entrance to the supper club and took one last deep breath, steeling his resolve. "Let's go."

"Kiss for luck?"

Oliver leaned over the center armrest and kissed James with a bracing quickness.

They nodded to each other—just in case this was the last positive affirmation they received today—and got out of the car.

James took a deep breath and looked around at the trees. "Smell that mountain air," he cried. "This is beautiful."

"I'm glad you think so," Oliver said. "This place is pretty important to me."

"Then it's important to me too," James said with a smile.

They walked to the door, and Oliver pulled it open. At the hostess station was his mom, with her trademark upswept silver hair and wide smile. When she saw who had entered, she dropped the menus she was holding and rushed around from behind the podium. Giving a squeal of delight and surprise she ran toward Oliver, arms spread wide.

"Oh, my baby has come home," she cried, pulling him into a bouncing embrace. She kissed him six or seven times, and then held him at arm's length to observe him more carefully. "Every time you look stronger and healthier and"—she leaned close, studying him—"happier. Oh, Oliver, it's such a treat to have you here!"

"Hi, Mom," Oliver said in a voice he recognized from his youth. Something about being home always made him sound like a twelve-year-old.

They hugged again.

"Mom, I'd like you to meet James," Oliver said, holding out a hand.

"Welcome, James, welcome," she said, and then flung her arms around the surprised man before he had a chance to say anything. "I'm delighted to meet you."

"Thank you, Mrs. Mitchell," James managed to eke out from her enthusiastic embrace.

"Please, call me Mom. All of Oliver's friends call me Mom."

James swallowed hard and looked at Oliver with panic in his eyes, but he complied. "All right…. Mom."

"Now come on and let's surprise your father. He's been under that griddle all day trying to get that twitchy burner to stay lit—he's too cheap to just replace the damn thing. Assuming he hasn't succumbed to a gas leak, he'll be thrilled to take a break, and what better occasion than Ollie coming home?"

They walked through the club, in which about one table in five was occupied with either late lunchers or early diners, and then past the bar, which was about half-full, and on to the kitchen in the back.

Oliver's father was two legs sticking out from under an enormous griddle that seemed to be of the same vintage as the mountains outside. A clanging echoed out from somewhere deep inside the steel behemoth, and with each impact the legs flailed as if he was using all his strength to beat on some recalcitrant part. A steady stream of garbled invective issued from under the range between clangs.

James looked at Oliver, clearly conveying with his eyes that he had little desire to confront the man who wielded such fearsome tools and swear words. Oliver just shook his head and smiled as he knew his father to be one part bluster and nine parts teddy bear.

"Jasper, dear," Oliver's mom leaned down and called under the appliance, "there's someone here to see you."

Jasper's response was a flurry of crashing impacts under the range, followed by a whoosh of gas igniting. He slid out from under and beamed up at his wife. "There, good as new," he chirped.

"That thing was new during the first Roosevelt administration, and you know it." But she smiled lovingly at her prone and grinning husband. "Now, look who's come to see you." She jerked her head in Oliver's direction.

"Ollie!" Jasper shouted and leapt to his feet with an impressive agility. He embraced his son as energetically as his wife had and kissed him about as many times as well. "What a surprise! Why didn't you tell us you were coming?"

"It was kind of a spur-of-the-moment thing," Oliver said, once his father had released his hold and Oliver could draw another breath. "Dad, I'd like you to meet James."

Jasper extended his hand. "Good to meet you, James. Welcome to Crystal Lake."

"Thank you, sir," James said, smiling and shaking Jasper's hand.

"Let's sit and have a chat before the dinner rush starts," Ronnie suggested. "Ollie, grab us some beer?" She smiled as if she knew her son would be eager to get back behind the bar he had tended in his youth.

"Sure, Mom," Oliver said, and the group left the kitchen in the care of the other staff and walked out to the dining room. Oliver ducked behind the bar and poured four pints, while James stood awkwardly at the end of the bar, waiting. Oliver put the glasses on a tray and hurried over to him. "Well, what do you think?"

James shrugged. "They seem great. Of course, they don't know why we're here yet." James glanced quickly over at the table in the corner by the window, where Ronnie and Jasper had seated themselves, away from other guests. "I'm glad your mom suggested beer. I could use something right about now."

Oliver nodded. "Well, let's go do this thing," he said. He led the way over to the table and set out the beer glasses. He took the seat next to his dad, and James sat next to Ronnie.

"So, what brings you here out of the blue?" Ronnie asked, eyes bright with expectation. "Classes going well, job working out?"

"All that's fine, Mom," Oliver replied, then took a couple of healthy swallows of beer. "I came here to tell you something important."

Ronnie's face grew serious, but she simply nodded and waited. Jasper took a drink and looked out the window, his expression stoic.

"Mom, Dad," Oliver began, but his voice faltered.

Ronnie reached out a hand and took Jasper's, and their eyes met. It was how his parents had always faced uncertainty—hand in hand, strong in each other. Ronnie turned to Oliver. "You know you can tell us anything, Ollie. Out with it." Her voice was upbeat but with an undertone of quiet strength.

"It's just that…." Oliver began again, then lost the thread—or his nerve.

Ronnie turned to James next to her. "Do you know what it is?" she asked. "I assume he brought you along for moral support." She looked knowingly at him.

James gave half a nod but then looked down at the table.

"Well, since my darling son has come all this way to sit here tongue-tied and flustered, perhaps you would do us the favor of ending this suspense and just tell us what's going on?"

James looked helplessly at Oliver, who met his gaze with a look just as helpless. Then James smiled slyly at Oliver, as if their secret were a treasure they shared rather than a hand grenade they were about to toss at Oliver's parents. A momentary shiver of relief worked its way through him.

"Ah," Ronnie said, glancing from Oliver to James as if watching a frantic rally in a Wimbledon tiebreaker. "I see it now."

Oliver's mouth went arid, and he looked at his mother with a wild, panicked expression. She stretched out her other hand to him (the one not still clasping her husband's) and he reached out cautiously and took it.

"It's okay," she said softly to him, nodding. "Go ahead and say it."

"James is…." He coughed. "My boyfriend," he whispered.

Next to him, Oliver sensed Jasper slump forward, shaking his head. Oliver turned to look at him, terrified.

"Good God, Son," he muttered. "You had me thinking the worst things. I thought you'd come down with cancer or something." Jasper reached up a hand and slapped Oliver on the back of the head. "Don't ever do that again," he scolded with a chuckle.

"Oliver, you should see your face," Ronnie said with a laugh. "You look like you're about to be thrown in a volcano."

Oliver felt tears run down his cheeks. He wiped them and saw that James was similarly afflicted.

"What, did you think we would smack you with a shovel, throw you in the lake, and start work on making a replacement child?" Ronnie asked. "Honestly, I'm a little hurt." She smiled to show that any hurt was purely for rhetorical effect.

"I just never imagined you would be so...." Oliver began to cry again.

"Well, I'm not too happy about it," Jasper said. "How long have you been hiding this from us, letting us go on and on about whether you have a girlfriend? I feel a little foolish about all of that now."

"Here's the funny thing," Oliver said, taking a deep breath before launching into what would likely be an involved story. "I was straight until... when was it, James? Wednesday?"

"Probably Thursday," James offered, then laughed.

"Right, Thursday." Oliver looked back to his parents. "It's kind of a recent thing."

Ronnie frowned, her eyebrows up in surprise. "Well, I don't know that I've ever heard of it sneaking up on someone like that, but...." She looked at James. "You must be some kind of guy."

"Oh, he is," Oliver agreed, smiling at James.

"And were *you* gay before Thursday?" Jasper asked.

James shrugged. "Sort of, I guess. It was a little complicated."

Ronnie nodded. "These things sometimes are."

"I'm really kind of surprised at you guys," Oliver said. "I kind of figured you would have some trouble with this."

Ronnie laughed. "A few years ago we might have," she said. "But over the last few years, things have changed, even way up here."

"You remember that camp across the lake?" Jasper asked.

"The church place?" Oliver replied.

Jasper nodded. "Back about ten years ago, one of those horrible ex-gay groups started using it for their 'therapy.' Those poor people." He shook his head, looking across the lake. "Anyway, they finally came to their senses and closed the place down. Sold it to some of the local folks. Then about... what was it, Ronnie? Four years ago?"

"Almost five now."

"That's right, almost five. A group of survivors of the church camp rented the place for a reunion of sorts. They thought they'd get a couple dozen people, tops. Well, nearly a hundred showed up and turned the entire lake into a weeklong celebration like you've never seen. The crowning event was a kind of pride parade on the water, and let me tell you everyone in town came to see that. No one had ever seen such a thing—it was dinghies and drag queens as far as the eye could see." Jasper shook his head and chuckled at the memory.

"So it became an annual event," Ronnie continued the story. "One of the survivors is a drag celebrity out west, and has a big following. She really packs them in, I tell you what. For one week every July, all of Crystal Lake goes into a rainbow frenzy, and it all leads up to the water parade—they call it 'Dame Camilla deMillion's Flotilla Cotillion.' Everyone dresses up either as a drag queen or a sailor, and it's like fleet week in Sodom." Ronnie dissolved into giggles. "It's so much fun! We convinced them to hold the awards ceremony here afterward, and so the entire parade ends up at our dock. I swear to God, I'm still vacuuming up glitter at Thanksgiving!"

Oliver's mouth hung open. "I had no idea you guys would be okay with the whole gay thing," he finally managed.

"Well, it was a little out there at first," Ronnie replied. "They came here after the first parade, and we were a bit overwhelmed. But we have always run the restaurant with the idea that all customers deserve our best service and are entitled to our respect, regardless of who they are, and so we welcomed them in. And it turns out they are just the nicest people! Now, there are some folks in town who don't much like the entire place turning into the Castro or the West Village for one week every summer, but given the kind of money that it brings in, most people have found it in their hearts—or their wallets—to be tolerant."

"The Castro or the West Village?" James asked, looking agog at Ronnie. "You are amazing."

"You act like you expected it to be 1950 here," Ronnie said scoldingly. "I think you'll find we're a pretty modern bunch." She turned to Oliver. "Now, Ollie, dear, tell us about how you and James met."

"Well, I got a new job to try to earn money so I can take a service internship in the summer. I found a club where I could bartend and earn several hundred dollars more a night than I'd been bringing in at the steakhouse, so I started there about a month ago. James was one of the regulars on Sunday night, and we kind of got to know each other."

"Oh, that's just so sweet," Ronnie exclaimed.

"I'm afraid Oliver's leaving out some of the details," James said, cocking an eyebrow across the table.

Oliver sighed. "You're right. The job is at a gay club, and part of the requirement is that I wear... well, as little as possible."

Ronnie leaned over the table. "You're a stripper?" she asked, without judgment in her voice.

Oliver laughed. "No, no, nothing like that. I just wear clothes like I would to work out. Shorts and a cut-off shirt, that kind of thing."

"Well, why the hell not?" Jasper grunted. "You work damn hard to stay in shape, you might as well let people appreciate it."

Oliver turned his head and goggled at his dad.

"What?" Jasper protested. "I'm just saying you're looking pretty buff these days, is all. You'd take the wind right out of most of these boy-sailors we get during the cotillion. I mean, they're hot enough as twinks go, but you've filled out your chest to the point that I think you might be in otter territory. Isn't that right, Ronnie?"

Oliver's mom nodded. "But you could pull off twink if you wanted to. You'd just have to be sure to shave your chest. Are you shaving your chest, dear?"

Oliver looked helplessly at James. "Oh my God, we are *not* having this conversation."

James burst out laughing. "I love your parents." He raised his glass to them and they shared in his toast. "But there's another aspect to our relationship that we should probably tell them about," he prodded gently.

"James is a politician."

"We'll try not to hold that against you, son," Jasper said with a hint of a smile. Ronnie slapped at his arm from across the table.

"I'm a county executive—nothing too high-level," James said modestly.

"But he was—is—also married."

Ronnie and Jasper suddenly grew very serious.

"Oh," Ronnie said, her voice low.

"I'm afraid I made a grave mistake, and chose as my wife a woman whose ambitions extended only as far as the money in our joint accounts," James explained. "She engineered a scandal that has recently resulted in our marriage ending, rather abruptly in fact. My primary concern is that Oliver not be dragged into a messy public dispute; to that end I have surrendered completely to her demands and will not contest her claim on all of our assets. However, it is still likely that she will sell an exaggerated version of her story to the media in an attempt to further embarrass me— embarrass us." He looked at Oliver, clearly struggling with how to condense a bizarrely complex few days into a brief synopsis. "I know this must sound crazy. But I want to assure you that Oliver and I only began our relationship once I saw that my marriage was beyond repair."

"And how did you determine that?" Jasper asked, his eyes narrowed skeptically.

"When she hired some goons to hunt Oliver down in an attempt to use him as leverage to make me do what she wanted, I figured it was probably just best to call it quits."

"Up until that point, we were only friends," Oliver added. "And I was still straight." He shrugged. "It's been quite a week."

Ronnie looked intensely at her son. "You might want to just take some time to think through all that's happened," she said. But then she sat back, squinted at him, then nodded knowingly. "Nope, you're done thinking, I can see it on your face. Well, then"—she looked at Jasper and winked—"we're happy for you."

Jasper put an arm around his son and ruffled his hair.

"So," Ronnie said to James, "do county executives make a good living?"

"A terrible one, in fact," he replied with a smile. "But I was left a considerable sum by my parents, and enough of it was outside the community property agreement with my soon-to-be ex-wife that I don't really need a salary."

"So you're not expecting my son the doctor to support you?" she asked with a hint of a smile.

"Furthest thing from my mind," James said, hands raised in front of him. "He's so smart and handsome and charming that the sacks of cash he will no doubt earn as a world-famous physician hadn't even come up."

A more serious look came over Jasper's face. "Would you still come back here, Ollie?" he asked.

"Do you think they'd still want me?" Oliver asked quietly. He looked from his dad to his mom, trying to read on their faces how the town might view him now. "Does Crystal Lake want a gay doctor?"

"Honey," Ronnie replied, "what the people here need is a doctor. Some of them might not be crazy about the idea of having a gay doctor, but you know how this town is. Folks here are practical. They made a deal with you to put you through school so you could come back here and be their doctor. They'll keep up their end, I'm sure of it."

"The question is, will you keep up yours," Jasper added. "I know Crystal Lake is a poky little town in the middle of the forest, but—"

"But it's my home," Oliver replied. "The people here have been so great supporting my schooling. I wouldn't go back on that for anything."

James smiled at him. "I'm so glad to hear you say that," he said softly. "You are such a good man."

Oliver beamed. "What would you think about living in a place like this?"

"Anywhere you go, I would go with you." He looked out the window at the lake. "I think it's beautiful here."

Oliver's parents beamed at the two men as if their dreams for their son had instantly morphed to accommodate this new reality.

"Dinner rush is starting," Jasper said, looking toward the door. "Oliver, would you like to take the bar tonight? For old time's sake?"

"I'd love to, Dad." Oliver turned to James. "Be my back?"

"If you are willing to overlook my complete lack of knowledge behind the bar, I will be happy to serve." James saluted smartly.

"It's a weekend for trying new things," Oliver replied with a wink.

"You'll stay with us?" Ronnie asked. "I keep your room ready… you know, just in case you think to surprise us with an unannounced visit."

"Thanks, Mom. That would be great." He turned to James. "Ready?"

"I've got your back," James said suavely, and all four stood. There was work to be done.

CHAPTER FOURTEEN
SUNDAY MORNING

"JAMES," OLIVER whispered.

"Wha…?"

"I'm going to help out with breakfast. You can sleep in if you want to."

James rolled over, blinking the hangover out of his eyes. "I can't believe you're up already. What time is it?"

"Nearly seven," Oliver replied. "I kind of slept in." He leaned over and kissed James softly on the lips. "God, I hate getting out of bed when you're in it. Especially the bed I used to sleep in as a kid. Having you here kind of makes it dirty. And fun."

"It was nice of your parents to let us use it," James said as he ran his fingers down Oliver's chest. "Want to use it again?"

"I'd love to, but I've got to get up. Duty calls." He took hold of James's hand, brought it to his lips for a kiss. "But later we can pick up where we left off."

James smiled broadly. "Then please convey my best regards to Sunday morning, and maybe I'll see the afternoon for myself."

Oliver leaned down for one more kiss. "I'll see you soon."

"Love you," James murmured and turned over.

"Love you too," Oliver said, smiling.

Oliver dressed and brushed his teeth quickly, then headed across the parking lot that separated the Mitchells' home from the supper club. There were already some cars in the lot, though breakfast service had only begun a few minutes before. He opened the door and walked smack into the olfactory wall—bacon, potatoes, waffles—that he hadn't experienced in far too long.

"There he is, the sleepyhead," called his mom at her hostess station.

He walked up and planted a kiss on her cheek.

"Morning, Mom."

"Your Prince Charming still down for the count?"

"It's been a rough few days for him, so I let him sleep."

She beamed at him. "I am so happy for you. To see you in love, it just… well, it just warms a mother's heart."

"I can't tell you what it means to me, to us, that you and Dad are being so great about this."

His mom smiled. "All any parent wants is to see their child happy. Plus, he is just about the nicest guy I've ever met." She leaned in close. "Don't tell your father I said this, but he is a hottie to boot." She stepped back and laughed joyfully at her son's shocked reaction.

"Mom…."

"Oh, don't be such a fuddy-duddy," she scolded, whacking him with one of the long laminated menus in her hand. "Now go see if your dad needs help in the kitchen." She giggled raucously as he walked into the restaurant.

Oliver shook his head and walked toward the kitchen, passing by a few occupied tables as he went. The place was about a quarter full, but he knew it would be packed within an hour.

"Morning, Dad," he called as he pushed through the swinging door to the kitchen.

"Hey, Son," his dad cried, turning from the griddle to embrace Oliver. The griddle seemed better behaved today, which was fortunate given the expanse of breakfast foods sizzling away on it.

"I came to see if I can help."

"Actually, it's perfect that you're here." Jasper pointed to a plate of food that sat on the pass. "Can you run this out to table fifteen? It's the one next to the fireplace, by the window."

"I know where fifteen is, Dad," Oliver replied, picking up a towel and grabbing the hot plate by its rim.

"Glad to see that some things haven't changed."

Oliver stopped, and turned back to his dad. "What?"

"Just glad to see you still remember us out here in the sticks now that you're a big-time city slicker with your fancy job and your rich boyfriend." Jasper took a step closer. "Don't tell your mom I said this, but James is pretty damn hot."

Oliver burst out laughing. "Dad, you're a piece of work." He left the kitchen with the plate, bound for table fifteen. As he rounded the corner of the bar, he froze as he caught a glimpse of the customer sitting there: it was Dr. Allen, the long-serving physician who had organized the town's support of Oliver's studies. Now in his early sixties, he was holding on to his small downtown office until he could hand it over to Oliver as the final, and most valuable, manifestation of the town's interest in him.

Oliver swallowed hard, took a deep breath, and continued his progress to table fifteen.

"Dr. Allen?" he said in greeting as he neared the table.

Dr. Allen looked up in surprise and smiled broadly. "Oliver," he cried, his voice still morning rough. "What a wonderful surprise."

"It's good to see you, sir."

"And it is a joy to see you looking so strong and healthy. Please," he said, motioning to the empty seat across from him, "please sit for a moment and tell me how school is progressing."

Oliver set the plate of food in front of the doctor and tried desperately to figure out what to do. "There's one thing I need to do in the kitchen. Why don't you enjoy your breakfast, and I'll come back in a few, and we can have a chat over coffee?"

"You are a gentleman and a scholar, sir," the doctor replied, tucking his napkin into the collar of his neatly pressed dress shirt.

With a smile, Oliver turned and walked back to the kitchen.

"Dad?" he said, coming up behind his father at the griddle.

"Yes, Son?" Jasper replied, not turning around.

"You sent me to fifteen on purpose."

The back of his dad's head tipped to the side, but he didn't turn around. "The food was ready," he replied with a shrug.

"And that it was Dr. Allen's food never entered your mind?"

Jasper turned around finally and looked at his son with a sly smile. "It all just kind of worked out that way."

Oliver opened his mouth to complain further, but his father stopped him.

"Now, Ollie, listen to me for a second. You came here to tell us something really important, and we're glad you did. But if you left without talking to him"—he jerked his head in the direction of the dining room—"you would spend the next who knows how many months worrying that although your parents love and accept you for who you are, the people who sent you to school and want you to come back as their doctor may not. I know you, Ollie. You're just like me that way. You'd be thinking about this every single minute of the day, building it up until it made you crazy. You don't need that."

Oliver tried to think of some way to protest but gave up with a shrug.

"Now, take a minute to walk around out back, get some fresh air, and come back in when you're ready to go talk to him. You will feel better once you've done that, I promise."

Oliver looked at the wise man his father had become—and probably always was, if Oliver had paused to think about it—and hugged him before turning and walking out the back door.

A light morning breeze whistled through the tall pines that rose on all sides of the supper club, bringing a bracing mountain air with which he gratefully filled his lungs. He looked out at the lake and felt the tug of home he'd forgotten during his time in the city. Suddenly the question of whether this is really what he wanted seemed answerable only one way. He pulled his phone out of his pocket.

It was on the fifth ring that the call connected.

"Mmmmello?" James's sleepy voice came on the line.

That voice. It sent a warm chill down his spine to hear it, to know the man who made it was in his bed.

"Hey, sorry to bother you."

"No one I'd rather be bothered by, though for future reference, I prefer to be bothered in person."

"Noted. I plan on bothering you several times later today, in fact."

"Then all is forgiven. What's up? I figured it must be important if you called the Batphone."

Oliver chuckled, having forgotten how ridiculous the phone in his room was. "Just a little freak-out here. The doctor who arranged the whole scholarship deal is here having breakfast, and I'm going to talk with him in a few minutes."

"Wow. Doing the full tour, aren't you?"

"I guess I am." Oliver puffed a breath out through his cheeks and looked up at the sky.

"You okay? I can get dressed and come over," James said, and Oliver could hear him getting out of bed.

"Are you still naked?" Oliver asked.

James paused, then chuckled. "Yes, yes I am."

"So what you're telling me is that there's a tall, gorgeous, naked man in my bedroom waiting for me, and all I have to do is come out to the town doctor and I'll be able to get back in bed with him?"

"That about sums it up."

"Well, gotta go. You stay naked, okay?"

"Consider it done," James replied with a laugh.

"Love you."

"Love you too. Good luck with the doc."

"Thanks. Be ready to drive getaway if it goes badly."

"Wait, I'm supposed to be naked *and* ready to drive? Hmmm, okay."

"I'll see you in a few."

Oliver pocketed his phone as he walked back into the kitchen.

"You called him, didn't you?" his dad asked.

Oliver nodded, feeling his cheeks heat as he did.

"That's just what I would have done. If I'm facing something difficult, I just want to hear your mom's voice, and I'm good to go. So if you're wondering whether this thing with James is real, think about who you turned to when you needed to feel like you can face the world."

Oliver's mouth dropped open. This was more relationship advice than his father had offered over his entire lifetime. "Thanks, Dad."

Jasper shrugged modestly. "Now go talk with the doc. And don't be afraid to be who you are."

Oliver hugged his father, then smiled gamely and made his way out of the kitchen and back to table fifteen, stopping by the coffee station to pick up two mugs and fill them. Dr. Allen was just finishing his breakfast of an egg-white omelet and dry wheat toast as Oliver walked up. The doctor motioned for him to sit, and Oliver set the coffees on the table and lowered himself into the chair.

"So, how go the studies? Second-year preclinicals are where most people wash out, in my experience."

"Classes and labs are going really well, I think. My grades are still good."

Dr. Allen smiled. "As I can see from the transcript you send me every semester. You don't really need to do that, Oliver. I trust you are making satisfactory progress without your having to prove it."

"I just want you to know I take really seriously the commitment you and the others made to supporting me."

Dr. Allen sat back in his chair.

"So studies are going well, and yet there is something else that you have not told me. What might that be?"

Oliver tried to stifle a gasp.

Dr. Allen chuckled and held up a hand. "I have no mystical foreknowledge, Oliver. As you will understand when you take up the practice, being able to read people quickly is the most important part of the job. There are often things a patient desperately needs to tell you so you can address his real issue, and not just the ones he feels comfortable talking about. But he suspects you are going to judge him, or lecture him, and so he hesitates. The key is to find a way to encourage him to talk about what frightens him. So, Oliver. What frightens you?"

"I'm gay."

"All right, then." Dr. Allen's expression did not change.

"Um," Oliver stumbled, "I guess that's it."

"As your doctor I must first ask, are you being safe?"

"Of course," Oliver blurted. "Even before my epidemiology course, I knew to be safe."

Dr. Allen nodded. "Any concerns about physical, mental, or emotional impacts?"

Oliver shook his head.

"Is there anything you would like to ask?"

Oliver took a deep breath. "Just... I guess I need to know whether you want to continue supporting my studies."

Dr. Allen tipped his head thoughtfully. "Are you asking me because you wish to be released from our agreement or because you are concerned that I may so wish?"

"The latter," Oliver replied, looking into his coffee mug because he could not possibly look at Dr. Allen's face.

"I see." Dr. Allen took a meditative sip of his coffee and looked out the window at the lake for a moment. "Oliver, I have known you since before you were born. As a friend of the family, and—I hope—as your friend, I want you to know that your orientation will not alter my affection for you one bit. But please understand I have a second interest. I must ensure this town has a general practitioner to see to its medical needs in the future. With the new hospital down in Junction, there's little chance we'll see any doctors set up shop here, not when they could be an hour away and have access to that facility. We need a doctor, Oliver, and I was hoping that doctor would be you."

"I was too, sir," Oliver replied with miserable dignity.

"If we are still in agreement, then is there a problem?"

Oliver started. He looked at Dr. Allen's face and saw the same crinkled smile he always wore when bucking up his patients. "You're really okay with this?"

Dr. Allen nodded. "Of course. Now, tell me you have taken up smoking, and you and I will go have a little conversation behind the parking lot, just you and me and a switch I will break off the tree."

Oliver laughed.

"Oliver, one of the things you will learn when you begin clinicals and working with patients is that the best thing you can do for people is focus on what will matter to their health and well-being and leave the rest of it by the wayside. Now, just between you and me, I think you'd be surprised at the number of people in this town with whom I have had a similar conversation. You are not alone, and you should never feel alone. Even here."

"So you think the town would be okay having a gay doctor?"

Dr. Allen paused, and looked out the window again. "There are some problems you can solve by changing people's minds, and some problems you have to solve actuarially. Intolerance to other people's sexual practices will die the day we bury the last intolerant person." He looked back to Oliver. "There will be a few people who will drive an hour to Junction to see someone else, but the vast majority are going to be just fine with having a gay doctor. Most of them won't even think about it, particularly when you come to their house at two in the morning to comfort their colicky baby. I predict that the worst you will suffer is the occasional off-color remark on the golf course about prostate exams. I think you can handle that. Am I right?"

"Thank you, sir," Oliver said, his voice a little thick.

"Never be afraid to be who you are, Oliver," the doctor replied. "Hiding something like this will only lead to trouble. You would not want to end up like that poor politician from across the state." He pointed to the newspaper that lay neatly folded on the table at his elbow.

Oliver's heart skipped a beat. "What was that?" he asked, his voice barely audible.

The doctor picked up the paper and folded it back, then handed it to Oliver. "This poor man tried to hide who he is, and look how it worked out for him." He shook his head empathetically.

What Oliver held in his hands was James's nightmare. A picture of Stella before microphones, looking carefully coiffed and groomed, wiping a tear from her expertly lined and shaded eye. An inset photo showed James in an awkward moment, as if he was emerging from late-night budget negotiations that were not going well. He looked harried and frantic, which was clearly Stella's intention. And the paper had delivered him up on a platter.

"There's one more thing I haven't mentioned," Oliver said, looking up from the paper.

OLIVER OPENED the door to his bedroom as quietly as he could.

"You're back," James's sleepy voice drifted over to him from under the covers. "What time is it?"

"It's not quite nine," Oliver replied. He set on the desk the newspaper Dr. Allen had been happy to give him—he had proven sympathetic indeed to James's plight, and only the more so once he knew of Oliver's entanglement in it—and stripped off his clothes. He pulled back the covers and slid in next to James.

"Mmm." James's hands roamed over Oliver's body, and then he simply wrapped Oliver in a full-body embrace and held tightly to him. "Missed you."

Oliver kissed him. "Missed you too." He ran his fingers through James's sexily rumpled hair and considered whether he shouldn't wait a bit to deliver the bad news.

"How'd it go?"

"Really well," Oliver replied. "He was great about it—about everything."

James pulled back from kissing along Oliver's clavicle and smiled. "That's terrific. Good for you."

"Yeah, it's really good." He took a breath. "There is one thing, though."

James's eyebrows shot up, but his smile stayed in place.

"There was something in the Sunday paper."

The light left James's eyes, and his entire being seemed to sag. He took a deep breath, and nodded. "So let's see it," he said, in a grim-yet-determined tone.

Oliver reached over to the desk and grabbed the paper. He handed it to James and watched him as he read. An entire catalog of emotions flashed across his face, from surprise to anger to sadness to something at the end that looked like resolve. His jaw was set, his eyes bright, his breathing even. If this is how James faces down adversity, Oliver reflected, adversity had better start packing.

"Pretty much what I'd expected," James said. He reached over and picked his phone up off the nightstand. He switched it on, and it pinged for nearly a full minute as messages poured in. James looked up at Oliver with an ironic smile. "People have seen it."

"Let me guess. The first twenty messages are from Charlie."

James looked back down at the phone. "He's up to thirty-two as of an hour ago. There are still some coming in." James looked up at him. "I am so sorry about this."

"No. Don't be sorry," Oliver replied, putting his hand on James's arm. "And don't worry about me. I have you, and I have amazing parents, and I have a town that still wants me as their doctor. Nothing Stella can do will change any of that. I will be by your side, no matter what. She can't hurt me, and I'll be damned if I'm going to let her hurt you."

Tears were instantly in James's eyes. "Oliver, I...."

"Shh." Oliver took James's phone and dropped it into the top drawer of his nightstand. "We have all day to figure out what to do. Let's just take an hour and remind ourselves why we're in this mess in the first place, okay?"

James beamed. "You are a miracle. How did I get so lucky?"

"I could tell from the moment I saw you that you were different. You were a good person among a room full of fakes and phonies. I'm the lucky one, because the best guy chose me."

They kissed, and they passed an hour in which neither of them even thought about Stella. Not once.

Chapter Fifteen
Going Public

"YOU REALLY have to go so soon?" Ronnie asked as Oliver and James packed up the car.

"Honey, you read the paper," Jasper said, wiping his hands on his splattered apron. The after-church rush was well underway as it was now nearly eleven. "She called our son a 'gold-digging go-go boy.' Nobody should be able to do that and get away with it."

"At least the article didn't name you, dear," she said to Oliver. "And you, sir,"—she turned to James—"you stay strong. This will all blow over, and soon you'll be looking back on it and laughing. You'll have a great story to tell us all at the flotilla cotillion."

"I hope so," James said with a brave smile. "It's been so nice meeting both of you. Oliver is the most amazing person, and it's easy to see why, now that I've seen where he comes from."

"Oh, come here you," cried Ronnie, pulling James close. Jasper piled on from the other side, and then Oliver joined from the rear.

When they stepped back from the Mitchell family tackle hug, James stood with tears running down his cheeks. He looked somewhat helplessly from face to kind face, overwhelmed. He took a deep breath and swallowed hard. "My parents…," he said, before his voice broke.

Oliver took his hand, then pulled him close and put an arm around his shoulder.

James cleared his throat. "My parents… they died before we could ever have a real relationship. They didn't have time for me when I was growing up, and I don't know whether we could ever have had the kind of bond that you all have. It's something I had given up on ever experiencing." He looked at Ronnie and at Jasper in turn. "Thank you. Thank you for being such good parents, and for welcoming me. It means more to me than you can possibly imagine."

"You take care of our boy, okay?" Ronnie said warmly as Jasper put his arm around her, nodding.

"I fully expect he will be taking care of me, at least at first," James said, smiling at Oliver. "But I promise to be the best boyfriend he's ever had."

Oliver burst out laughing. "Not much competition for that title."

"You two," Jasper said, joining in their laughter. "Drive safely back to the city, okay?"

Oliver held up the key. "He said I could drive it," he said excitedly.

James held up his phone, mirroring Oliver. "I have a few messages to return."

"Good luck, dear," Ronnie said. "Let us know if there's any way we can help."

"You've done so much already," James replied. "Thank you."

Oliver kissed both his parents again, and then they stood in the parking lot waving until Oliver pulled the car out onto the road. He guided the car cautiously through the main street of town, filled as it was with Sunday drivers, and then gradually sped up as the town fell away behind them.

"Guess I should get to this," James said, looking at his phone as if it were a coiled cobra.

"Who's been texting you?"

James flicked down the list. "Charlie, Charlie, Charlie, Charlie, Charlie, Charlie...." He looked up. "The first three screens are from Charlie." He looked back down. "Then, let's see... ah, here's one from Millie asking me why I'm ignoring Charlie and telling me to text him back right away because she wants him to stop texting me and come back to bed."

Oliver laughed. "You'll have to excuse Millie—she's been in kind of a drought."

"I fully appreciate her position," James said. "I just feel bad that she sent this message four times over three hours and I'm only now looking at it."

"If I know Millie, she's already whipped a pillowcase over his head, whacked him with a vase, and dragged him back to bed. She's not one to let a problem like this go unsolved for long."

James laughed and dialed.

"So you didn't throw yourself off a cliff," Charlie said over the car's stereo. "I was thinking we would have to drag the lake so I could bring you to a press conference, *Weekend at Bernie's* style."

"Nothing so drastic, Charlie."

"Good to hear."

"And please extend my deepest apologies to Millie, who suffered far more than I did this morning."

Charlie said something with his hand over the phone, then came back on the line. "She sends her gracious forgiveness." There was a loud clunk on the line, as if something heavy had been thrown at Charlie, and he hadn't dodged quite quickly enough. "Or something like that."

Oliver laughed. "Tell Millie I'll bring some of the stuff from the place and make it all okay." He leaned over to James and whispered, "Mint chip gelato from the place on Alta Avenue—it's simply mind-blowing."

"Millie says she may forgive you in the fullness of time. Now, to our current clusterfuck. James, what do you want to do?"

"I want the whole thing to go away."

"Yeah, I'm starting to think that's not going to happen. Did you catch the performance live?"

"No, Oliver found it in the paper."

"Oh, you should see the whole thing. She put it on YouTube herself."

"Why would I want to watch that, Charlie?"

"Because she pretty much fucks herself sideways in it."

James cast a confused glance at Oliver, then turned back to interrogate the dashboard. "How'd she do that?"

"Well, she started out like she'd been coached very carefully. You know, like she was sticking to a script but not really understanding it. Think Sarah Palin trying to answer a question on Kashmir. So she says you two are splitting, and that it was because one of you violated the marriage contract. Pretty clear who she's blaming for that. Anyway, then this reporter asked her if there was another woman, and she blinks and then, as they used to say about Sarah, she went rogue. That's when she dropped the 'gold-digging go-go boy' line. Sorry about that, Oliver."

"No worries. I asked James to call me that when we were drowning our sorrows in sex this morning, so it only has positive associations now."

Charlie grunted. "God, gay guys are so lucky. Sex fixes everything." Another clunking sound, this one followed by a sort of awkward cough, as if something had knocked the wind out of poor Charlie. "Anyway, that's where she fucked herself. The prenup has an adverse publicity clause, specifically related to the marital infidelity clause. It's fine for her to announce that you two are splitting, and it's fine for her to make veiled implications as to fault. But when she made a specific allegation about marital infidelity, she crossed the line."

"So what does that mean?" James asked.

"It means the marital infidelity clause is rendered inoperative, and the divorce reverts to no-fault. She gave your half of the estate back, buddy."

"I don't want it back," James replied immediately.

"What?"

"I don't want it. Once she realizes she's lost it, she's going to make our lives miserable. This press conference will seem like high tea at the Ritz compared to the throwdown we're going to see once she gears up."

"Well, there's not much we can do about that."

"Yes, there is," James said. He reached out and took Oliver's hand. "Get on the phone with her lawyer and offer her the previous terms if she shuts up now. I'll let her keep everything if she doesn't have another press conference. Ever."

The line was silent for a long moment. "You really love him, don't you?"

James looked at Oliver. "I do."

"Do you think Stella will take the deal?"

"Stella loves money the way humans love oxygen. She'll take the deal."

"I'll give her lawyer a call. Can I reach you at this number when I have an answer?"

"Yes. And I'll actually pick up this time, so tell Miss Millie she can have you back."

"Miss Millie and I thank you kindly, sir. Talk soon." The line clicked off.

"Why did you do that?" Oliver asked.

"Because this is the only way I can think of for us to be free of her. My career probably sleeps with the Titanic now, but yours is still ahead of you, and this is our best shot at getting a chance to live our lives."

"That's… a huge sacrifice you're making," Oliver said.

"The only thing I care about is right here with me, and there's no way she can take you away. But if we can get her to shut up, things will be a lot easier."

They drove in silence for a while.

"You know, you may not have to give up your career," Oliver said after a few minutes.

"I don't know how anyone rebounds from the tearful-wife press conference, Oliver. That's sunk more political careers than all the showgirls in Vegas."

"I think there might be a way." Oliver described his plan to James.

A few minutes later, the phone rang.

"She took it," Charlie said. "I talked to her lawyer, and I could tell she was trying to do damage control with her client—Stella was right there in the office. I could hear her snacking on woodland creatures in the background. Anyway, I offered her the way out, and it took her about four seconds to sell it to Stella. Agreement should be on my desk within the hour."

"That's great, Charlie. Thank you."

"All in a day's work. Actually, a Sunday's work, for which the billables are going to make your eyes pop out of your head like a cartoon character."

"I would expect no less from you, buddy. Now, I need your help with one more thing."

"Meter's running, bro. What do you need?"

"I need you to set up a press conference for me this afternoon at your office."

"Why do you want to do that? You know the adverse publicity clause cuts both ways, right? You can't get up there and trash Stella, as redundant, yet satisfying, as that would be."

"I'm not going to trash Stella. Oliver came up with a great plan, and I'm going to make an announcement. We're about two hours from the city now, so plan on a two o'clock appearance?"

"I'll get Amanda on it now. Her time is billable too, by the way."

"Sounds like it's time for you to buy that boat, Charlie. I have just the lake for you to put it in."

"Keep laughing, buddy. I hope you know what you're doing."

"For the first time, I think I do."

"TAKE THE next exit."

"We're pretty close now. Can't you hold it till we get there?" Oliver asked. They were nearing the city, and James's press conference was less than an hour away.

"I brought a suit, just in case. I need to show up at the press conference looking cool and composed, so I need to change and freshen up."

"But the next exit is the interchange with the truck stop. You want to stop there?"

James shrugged. "What better place? It's like the intersection of our old separate lives—the place where our paths met before we even knew the other was out there. I'll always think of it as our truck stop."

Oliver laughed and signaled to exit. He guided the sedan smoothly around the off-ramp, then pulled into the same parking place James had used on their previous visit. They hopped out of the car and walked around to the trunk, from which James pulled his suitcase, and then walked into the truck stop trying to keep from laughing out loud.

A quick stop at the service counter secured the key to shower number six.

"Yes, I know which one it is," Oliver solemnly told the desk attendant as he took the key card.

They walked down the hall to the door. Oliver swiped the key in the lock, and the familiar (familiar—how his life had changed!) shower room lay before them. James set his suitcase down on the wooden bench as Oliver shut the door.

"Now *strip*," Oliver growled as he turned back to James.

James's face showed his surprise and delight, and he slowly unbuttoned his shirt.

"Faster! Get on it," Oliver ordered.

James threw the shirt aside, and got to work on his pants. Kicking his shoes off and to the side, he stood in his boxer briefs and socks, rocking back and forth in a very realistic portrayal of nervousness.

"All of it," Oliver said menacingly. He stepped forward and stood imperiously before James.

James nodded and slipped off his socks, then slid his underwear down and off.

"Turn around," Oliver commanded.

James turned to face the back wall.

"Just going to check for contraband," Oliver said, in the matter-of-fact voice the uniformed police officers on television always used when fingerprinting someone. He ran his hands down James's muscular back to the powerful globes of his ass, tickling his fingers in the space between.

James gasped in surprise.

Oliver's hands roamed around James's hips to the front, and he wrapped them around the base of James's fully erect cock. "Found something."

James spun around and kissed Oliver with such vigor that he had to take a step back under the onslaught.

"Wow, truck stop shower rooms really do it for you," Oliver said, trying to catch his breath.

"This one does," James murmured.

"But we need to get going," Oliver said. "You don't want to be late for your own press conference."

James sighed but nodded. He looked down at his jutting erection. "I don't think I have underwear big enough," he said with a comic sadness.

"I'm on it, chief," Oliver said. He took hold of James's cock and began a gentle stroking. Then, leaning down, he spat heartily into his hand and stroked more aggressively.

Soon James was moaning, head tipped back, knees threatening to buckle.

Oliver knelt down and kissed the leaky tip of James's cock, which drove his moaning into a higher register. Oliver didn't miss a stroke, and within a minute, James's breathing was short and quick, his moans urgent. Oliver looked up at him, this man he loved, and their eyes met. Neither blinked or wavered as James's orgasm tore through his body. Oliver took it all in, urged it with his suction, prodded it with his tongue—he wanted it all.

Finally James fell abruptly to his knees. Before Oliver could even swallow, James was on him, kissing him, and their tongues thrashed in the warm wetness of what James had created and Oliver had received. They both swallowed and sat back, panting.

"Dude," Oliver exhaled. "That was amazing."

James nodded and wiped his brow. "*You* are amazing."

"Now we gotta get you dressed," Oliver said, rising.

James opened his suitcase and pulled out the expensively tailored suit he had tucked neatly in a zippered compartment clearly made for such use.

"You brought a suit like that? Did you think maybe we would be running into the Queen of England?"

James laughed. "Funny you should say that. She actually is the reason I brought it."

Oliver looked at James, trying to determine whether getting a truck-stop blowjob had completely deranged his boyfriend.

"Back before she was the queen, Princess Elizabeth went on a trip to Australia. Her father, the king, was ill, and had been for a while, so she was representing him on the trip. He died when she had only gotten as far as Kenya, and she had to return immediately to start doing queenly things. But she had no mourning clothes with her, and she had to return to London wearing just regular—but, you know, impossibly expensive—clothes. From that time on, she has always traveled with mourning clothes, just in case someone kicks it while she's on the road. Because the worst thing in the world when someone dies is to have the queen wearing the wrong color. Anyway, I always travel with a suit, because you never know."

"That was really complicated but completely charming," Oliver said and kissed James on the nose. "Now get suited up, your majesty. The court awaits."

Oliver noticed there seemed to be more in that compartment of the suitcase than just the one suit. He cast a glance at James, who shrugged a little guiltily.

"I thought since we wear close to the same size, I'd bring some stuff for you too."

"You are not seriously proposing that I be there when you do this… are you?"

"My life in politics has been short," James said as he pulled on his pants, "but it has taught me to be prepared for anything. Even the stuff you never think will happen. So, no, you don't have to be there. But I would love it if you were, just in case."

"Just in case someone needs a Dirty Altar Boy?" Oliver said, smiling in spite of the enormity of what they were about to undertake.

James smiled. "I understand if you want to stay away from this spectacle. But I would never be ashamed to have you by my side."

"By your side is where I would like most to be," Oliver replied. Then he looked into the suitcase. "So what'd you bring me?"

James handed him a pair of light gray summer trousers and a brilliant lapis dress shirt that doubtless cost well into three figures.

"These are beautiful," Oliver said, feeling the expensive fabric of the pants.

"They will be when you get into them," James replied.

"I always suspected truck-stop showers were romantic, but I had no idea it would affect you this way," Oliver replied, grinning.

"Anywhere you are is romantic," James said. "Now let's get ready to meet our public." He pulled out his shaving kit and began to lather up, making room at the sink for Oliver to join him.

In a few minutes, they walked out of the shower room far more elegantly than they had gone into it; even the attendant at the service desk raised his tired eyebrows at the change. They swept through the truck-stop store and out to the car.

"I should probably drive in case they're waiting in the parking garage," James said as they approached the sedan.

Oliver tossed him the key fob. "Do you really think they're going to swarm you like that?"

"I don't know. The kind of stuff Stella lobbed at us during her little event yesterday has probably got some of them on the hunt, especially because this domestic stuff makes for good weekend viewing. Remember, these are the folks who hunted me down in an alley last week."

"God, has it really only been a week?" Oliver sighed as he sat in the passenger seat.

"Sometimes life can change in a week." James started the car and looked over at Oliver. "Ready?"

Oliver nodded. "Let's light this candle," he said, with astronaut bravado.

HALF AN hour later, they pulled into the parking garage under Charlie's office and into a space marked for his visitors' use. As they stepped from the car, Oliver could hear the echo of shutters firing rapidly. The parking garage was mostly empty on a Sunday afternoon, and the sound seemed to come from everywhere at once.

"Just keep your head up and pretend you don't notice it," James said through a pleasant smile, as if the distant sound of paparazzi was an everyday part of life.

Oliver pasted his Burn smile on, the one that was not perturbed even by Ulysses rubbing against his ass as he walked behind, and fell into step next to James for the walk to the elevator. Once inside, James turned and cradled Oliver's face in his hands.

"I love you so much," he whispered. "You are the man I was waiting for and never thought I'd find." He kissed Oliver softly as the elevator rose.

Oliver was overwhelmed by the whole thing. He would never have imagined himself here, even a week ago. He was in love—with a man. He was on his way to a press conference occasioned by charges of marital infidelity after coming out to his parents and basically the whole of his hometown, and there was a fair chance he would be on the news tonight. The talking heads might even remind everyone that he had been called a "gold-digging go-go boy," just in case anyone had forgotten to connect those dots. But despite all of that, there was nowhere he would rather be.

"When this is over, can we do something normal?"

"Like, for instance?"

"I don't know, like maybe go have dinner without photographers buzzing around? We could even talk about something other than politics and intrigue."

"Sounds awesome. It's a date."

They kissed again, breaking off just as the elevator doors opened. James led the way to Charlie's office, where he was waiting for them to arrive with Millie standing next to his desk.

"James, you're looking well," Charlie said in an exaggerated British gentleman's club voice.

"Thank you, my good man," James replied in kind.

"Oliver, you're looking like you've sucked a lot of dick," Millie said in the same clenched, upper-crust accent.

"Thank you my dear," Oliver replied. "That means a lot coming from such a whore as yourself."

All four laughed, releasing the tension in the room.

"Okay," Charlie said, in a "let's get down to business" voice. "Amanda's gathering them in the large conference room downstairs. I'll let her know we'll be there in ten?" He looked to James for confirmation.

James nodded. "Good to go," he said heartily.

Charlie dialed the phone and turned toward the windows to talk.

"So, you're going to get up there and just own that gold-digging go-go boy thing, aren't you?" Millie asked.

"I honestly don't know what's going to happen," Oliver replied. "James has some stuff prepared, and I'm just going to stand off to the side, I think." He looked at James. "Unless he needs me."

"All I need is to know you're there," James replied with a smile. He took Oliver's hand.

"You know, I liked the gays better when you were all about sex, all the time. This romantic stuff that's sprung up since marriage equality is making me a bit queasy." She winked at them. "And jealous."

Charlie hung up the phone. "Amanda says it's a pretty good group down there. Anything you want to go over?"

James shook his head. Oliver was struck by how calm he looked. He was preparing to face a room full of journalist sharks who smelled chum in the water, and he was resolutely placid. Oliver felt himself loving that man a little more, something he hadn't thought possible a moment ago.

"All right, then," Charlie said. "Let's head down and get this circus underway."

"Ready?" James asked Oliver.

By way of answer, Oliver simply took James's hand and squeezed it. They walked back to the elevator together, and all four got in. They rearranged themselves on the way down; James and Charlie stepped to the front, while Oliver and Millie stood together at the rear. When the doors opened, Charlie stepped out, followed by James. Oliver and Millie followed about ten feet behind them.

The conference room was dominated by tall windows overlooking the capitol, which was brilliantly illuminated by the afternoon sun. Charlie walked up to the sleek wood-and-glass podium before the windows, and James stood near him, behind and to the side. Millie and Oliver slipped into the back of the room and stood along the rear wall.

Charlie motioned for silence. It was a while in coming, but eventually the rowdy group settled down.

"Thank you for coming on such short notice," Charlie began. "I'm Charles Noble, and I represent James Whitford. Mr. Whitford will come to the podium in a moment to address issues relating to his wife's statements of yesterday afternoon. You have all widely reported on Mrs. Whitford's remarks, and in the interest of balance, I hope you will give Mr. Whitford your attention. He has prepared a brief statement; please hold your questions until he has completed it." He turned to James. "Mr. Whitford?"

James stepped up to the podium. "Thank you, Charlie. And thank you to everyone for coming today. I stand before you for the purpose of responding publicly to remarks my wife made yesterday afternoon."

Oliver winced to hear Stella referred to as James's wife. He had already gotten so used to thinking of her as his ex-wife—or that horrible harpy—that being reminded of James's married state was uncomfortable.

"It will surprise no one, I think, to hear that our marriage is over. The reasons for that are and will remain private, something between the soon-to-be former Mrs. Whitford and myself. I will make no comment on her conduct or mine that may have led to our deciding to divorce, nor will I make such comment in the future. What I want to talk to you about today is how I got here."

James took a deep breath before continuing. "Growing up, I knew I was different from other boys, but I had no way to articulate my difference. And as our state was so slow to extend equal rights to its LGBT citizens, I never admitted even the possibility that I might be able to live a full life as a gay man. So I did what generations of gay men have done in the face of a repressive society: I married a woman whom I could never fully love. It was unfair to both of us, and it was the greatest sadness of my life. I have come to realize, quite recently, that I can no longer live half a life. And I am grateful that the laws of this state have evolved as I have evolved, and today I can say, without fear of discrimination and without giving up any of my rights, that I am a gay man, and from this day I will live openly as my conscience—as my soul—dictates. I am proud to live in a state where these rights are guaranteed. To my constituents, I offer my heartfelt apology. I never intended to mislead you—I was too busy misleading myself. I will continue to execute the responsibilities of my position to the best of my ability, and I hope you will give me the chance to do so. And one final note, to Ethan Brandt and Gabriel Donnelly, members of the state's Section 28 task force, I say thank you for your fine work. I am heartened to see that the equal treatment of our citizens is in such capable hands. Thank you."

Hands shot up all around the room.

"Mr. Whitford, how do you respond to your wife's accusation that you are having an affair with, and I quote here, a 'gold-digging go-go boy'?"

James smiled robotically. "I will not respond to that accusation. As I said, I won't comment on the conduct on the part of either of us that led to the divorce."

"Do you deny, then, that you have been seen in the company of a dancer from the gay club Burn?"

James's smile flickered for a second, but then came back full strength. "I have been to the club several times over the past month. And one of the bartenders there—not a dancer—has become a very dear friend. But he is in no way a gold digger; in fact, he is a hardworking man who is paying his way through medical school by working at the club."

Another reporter raised a hand. "So, Mr. Whitford, just to confirm, you are not romantically involved with one Oliver Mitchell?"

"I didn't say that," James replied smoothly. If the mention of Oliver's name shocked him, he gave no sign. "Mr. Mitchell and I have been friends for some time and have recently begun a romantic relationship. For the record, the decision to divorce had already been made by the time that romantic relationship began."

"So you *are* involved with the dancer from Burn," the reporter rather brutally summarized.

"Mr. Mitchell is not a dancer; he's a bartender. And yes, we are involved. I am not ashamed of that fact."

"If you aren't ashamed of it," called another voice from the middle of the room, "why isn't he here with you? What are you hiding, Mr. Whitford?"

James paused and chuckled. "For the first time in my life, I'm not hiding anything." He looked to the back of the room, eyebrows up.

Oliver nodded.

"Mr. Mitchell, would you care to join me at the podium?"

Oliver shot a quick glance at Millie, who smiling bracingly, and then he walked to the front of the room. He stepped up to the podium and stood next to James.

"This is Oliver Mitchell."

There was a buzz in the room, and many photos taken. Oliver was keenly aware that part of the effect James was going for in introducing him was to prove he looked nothing like a "gold-digging go-go boy." And in his crisp linen trousers and button-down shirt, he certainly achieved that.

"Oliver," called one of the reporters.

Oliver noticed that James was referred to by his last name, while he himself was not. It rankled a bit, but he simply smiled and looked attentively at the reporter.

"Are you with Mr. Whitford," the reporter continued, "because he is one of the wealthiest people in the state?"

Oliver looked surprised by this because he was genuinely surprised by this. He leaned forward, closer to the microphones. "I was not aware of that. So I guess the answer would be no." There was an oppressive silence in the room, so Oliver nervously continued. "I'm with James because he is smart and funny and charming and one of the best people I've ever met." Still silence. "Plus, if you google him, you'll see what he looked like in college, and he still looks like that." Oliver stepped back from the microphones before he could ramble any further.

At the back of the room Millie held her face in her hands. But James, standing next to Oliver at the podium, simply looked at him and beamed.

"What are your plans for the future?" a reporter asked, seeming to include both of them.

James stepped back to the microphones. "We have some legalities to sort out in terms of the divorce, but I'm sure Charlie will be able to handle all of that smoothly. I will go back to running my county government, and Oliver will go back to medical school, and my fervent wish is never again to have the opportunity to address a room full of reporters on a Sunday afternoon."

He stepped back, put his arm around Oliver, and smiled broadly to the room. Oliver followed his lead and did the same. Shutters clicked madly, and Oliver hoped this would be the picture people would see: him and his boyfriend, standing strong, together.

They were going to make it.

CHAPTER SIXTEEN
BLOWBACK

"WELL, THAT snowballed quickly," Brandt said, closing his laptop and setting it on the coffee table. "She lashes out yesterday, but today he's cool and collected. Now all of a sudden she's got nothing to say."

"I hope it works," Donnelly said, getting up from the couch and heading for the kitchen. "Though I can't imagine what he could have done to make the problem go away so quickly. You saw her, though—there were a dozen reporters around her, ready to catch whatever hand grenade she wanted to toss in the wake of his press conference. But she just said the divorce was private and she had no comment."

"Makes me wonder if there wasn't a big ol' skeleton in Stella's closet somewhere."

"Speaking of closets, Oliver and James looked really happy at the end, didn't they? It was kind of a bold move, standing up there together, but it looks like it's going to work out for them."

"We'll see. You know how quickly these things can spin on you. Today he may have shaken off the go-go boy rap, but tomorrow something else may come along to screw with them. On that note, I'm not sure I'm thrilled with being name-checked in his remarks either. Seems like that's just asking for trouble."

"Oh, I don't know," Donnelly replied, bringing fresh cups of coffee from the kitchen. "If people watching the press conference find out there is such a thing as a Section 28 task force, then we're probably ahead. I often think people don't even realize what we do."

"Laboring in obscurity is its own reward," Brandt said, raising his cup to his partner.

"As toasts go, that one's kind of Puritan," Donnelly replied, sticking out his tongue.

"BRYCE MY man! How's it hangin', bro?" Liam was clearly taking the offensive this time around.

"My goodness," Bryce replied, startled. "I'm going to be shaking the testosterone out of my phone for the next week. But how lovely to hear your manly voice again, Liam."

"Likewise, Bryce, likewise. Are we all set for the big night?"

"Well, I should hope so. Both of the venues are booked—Burn and that cigar-is-just-a-cigar bar, where apparently the menfolk will be safe. The cigar chomping will begin at eight, and we'll move to the actual fun by around ten thirty. The walk is only two blocks, but I've arranged for the limo to wait outside in case the weather doesn't cooperate."

"Wow, that's excellent. Thank you."

"Don't mention it. Until the best man's toast, at which point you may freely expand on my virtues as your hosting partner."

"I shall. You've done a terrific job. Can't tell you how much I appreciate it."

"It was my pleasure, Big Brother Brandt."

"I guess I'll see you on Saturday, then."

"You shall. I'll be the one surrounded by all the soon-to-be-formerly-straight boys."

"That I can hardly wait to see."

SINCE THEIR last visit to Burn ended with a suspected abduction and a pursuit into the woods, Brandt and Donnelly decided to give Burn another try before the bachelor party. So a week before the event, they went and got themselves a table in Xander's section of the club.

"Is that Wendell over at the bar?" Donnelly asked.

Brandt glanced over through the maze of intersecting bodies. "Yeah, it is. And look who's with him."

Standing next to their wedding planner was Charles Noble, and seated next to them was Millie Flynn.

"Should we go say hi?" Brandt asked.

"Let's," Donnelly answered. "It'll be nice to talk to him about something other than wedding plans. I've been wondering how everything turned out after that press conference. Maybe Charlie can give us an update."

The couple walked across the club to the bar. Brandt put a hand on Wendell's shoulder.

"No way," Wendell cried. "Ethan, Gabriel, good to see you." He shook hands with both men. "I'd like you guys to meet—"

"Charlie and Millie," Donnelly interrupted. "How are you?"

"Things just aren't as exciting without the abductions and hot pursuits you guys bring to the party," Millie cracked. "But it's good to see you again."

"You too," Donnelly said, smiling.

Wendell looked wide-eyed at the foursome, surprised that they all seemed not only to know each other, but to have some kind of history involving crimes unknown.

"Charlie, how's James doing?" Brandt asked. "We saw the press conference. Pretty exciting stuff."

"You can ask him yourself," Charlie said, nodding behind Brandt.

James was making his way across the club from the direction of the bathroom. His face lit up as he recognized the troopers.

"Ethan! Gabriel! Great to see you," he called as he neared the group. He shook their hands and smiled broadly. "Actually, it's really lucky we ran into each other."

"Why's that?" Brandt asked.

Wendell interrupted. "I was waiting to get in touch with them until I had all the arrangements made," he said to James. He turned to Brandt and Donnelly. "I've got some good news and some bad news."

"Oh," the troopers said in unison.

"This isn't about our wedding, is it?" Donnelly asked, in a low but not dismal voice.

"Don't worry," Wendell said consolingly. "We have it all under control."

"Well, as the bad news is entirely my fault, I'll start," James said. "Did Charlie tell you that my soon-to-be ex-father-in-law is a judge?"

Brandt and Donnelly shook their heads.

"Well, he's an asshole. But a useful asshole, since it was his draconian ruling that was overturned by the state supreme court, making gay marriage legal. Anyway, in this case he's just an asshole. He's currently the commodore of the yacht club."

"The one where we're having our wedding reception?" Donnelly asked, color draining from his face. "In two months?"

"That's the one," Wendell replied.

"Well," James resumed, "Stella told him about the little drama in the woods, and the part you guys played in it. So he finds out you've booked a room at the yacht club for your reception, and he pulls rank and cancels it."

"What?" Donnelly's voice was hollow.

Wendell put his arm around Donnelly's shoulders. "It'll be fine, you'll see."

"So, what now?" Brandt asked, anger edging into his voice. "Do we get a court order? Charlie, think we can make them uncancel?"

Charlie took a breath and grimaced. "There really isn't anything we can do, I'm afraid."

"But they can't cancel just because it's a gay wedding reception," Donnelly cried. "We're pretty clear on that, right? I mean, that's what we've spent the last year going around the state telling people."

Wendell spoke in soothing tones. "They're not canceling because it's a gay wedding reception. Any member of the governing board of the yacht club can veto the use of any club facility by a nonmember, for any reason. That's part of their bylaws, and it's perfectly legal. Now, they've done it badly in the past, where every Jewish wedding or bar mitzvah was refused, and they got sued and lost. But they hold gay wedding receptions there all the time now. I've had three there in the past year."

"He's not doing it because you're gay," James added. "He's doing it because he's an asshole, and you were just collateral damage in his effort to hurt me."

"How does ruining our wedding hurt you?" Donnelly asked. Tears were welling in his eyes, but he kept his voice steady.

"Well, that's the other news. After our press conference, the governor's office got in touch with me. He wants to wait another week or two for things to settle down, but he's going to appoint me to be the state's first commissioner of human rights. And he's going to formally reassign you two to the new, expanded task force for LGBT equality."

Brandt blinked. "Wow. That's a lot to take in," he said slowly.

"For my part, I'm thrilled to be working with you two. You have a sterling reputation among everyone I've talked to. Unfortunately,

Stella's vengeful father has some connections in the governor's office, and they let slip to him what was happening. So canceling your reception was just one of the many and varied ways he's going to be trying to even the score with me. I'm really sorry my domestic mess has spilled over onto your plans. You two deserve a really great wedding, and it's just not fair."

Donnelly heaved a great sigh and looked at Brandt with a pained expression of loss. He shook his head slowly.

"Now, now," Wendell broke in. "Don't worry. As soon as I got the call this morning from the yacht club, I started working on plan B. Which by the time I'd finished with it, was plan A-plus. You're going to love it."

"Seriously, love it?" Brandt asked, looking again at the devastated expression on Donnelly's face. "How can you possibly fix this?"

"Okay, I understand you're skeptical. But hear me out. Now, first, it's only two months away, so everything in the city is pretty much booked solid. So we need to think on a bigger scale. I have two words for you," Wendell said mysteriously, stepping back as if to make room for this big new idea. "Destination wedding."

Brandt didn't think it possible for Donnelly's face to fall any further, but it did. He looked at Wendell with an expression normally reserved for dogs that poop on one's lawn.

"The wedding is two months away, Wend," Brandt huffed. "How can we possibly—"

"We can possibly, because I'm going to take care of it for you," James said calmly.

"How are you going to do that?" Brandt asked, more astonished than upset.

"It's my fault that you are in this spot, so I'm going to fix it. Years ago my dad got this idea to see the town in England that we're named after, so next time he went to Europe on business, he stopped in. Whitford is kind of in the middle of nowhere, but it's pretty in that English pastoral sort of way. Not much excitement, though. Anyway, as he was driving back to the closest airport, he saw a castle off in the distance, and he pulled off the highway to take a look. It was an ancient old pile, but still habitable, and he stopped in to see if he could take a little tour since he had an hour to kill before his flight. The owner, who Dad said looked about as old as the castle, showed him the place, and mentioned he would probably need to be selling it soon as he was too old to take care of it anymore. Dad said it was probably the American accent that made the guy offer to sell, because there clearly wasn't a lot of money in the area. So right then and there, Dad bought it and still made his flight to Brussels."

"Get to the part where this helps out Ethan and Gabriel," Wendell murmured, looking at the stony expressions on the faces of the troopers.

"Right. So my dad wasn't one to spend money on sentiment. He got a crew in there to refurb the place, and then hired a manager and staff to take care of it. He opened it up as a wedding venue, and most weekends the ultrasmart set from London make their way to little Whitford in Devon and have blowout wedding extravaganzas. Just so happens that the weekend of your wedding, the place isn't booked. Some emir with sacks of oil money had rented it, but apparently some of his other wives didn't take to the new one, so he had to call it off. The place is yours for the whole week."

Donnelly just shook his head, clearly bewildered at the turns this conversation had taken.

"We've already spent so much on the wedding here," Brandt said. "It would cost an arm and a leg to get everyone to England on such short notice."

"It would be my wedding present to you," James said simply. "The castle is yours. I will take care of getting everyone there, your entire guest list. I know you have a relationship with your cake and flowers guys, and I will get them there as well. It will all be taken care of. And, at the risk of sounding proud, it will be the most gorgeous wedding anyone has ever experienced."

"You can see why I was trying to get everything nailed down before talking to you," Wendell said apologetically. "I know it's a lot to take in."

"Why would you take on that expense?" Donnelly asked, finally shaking off his shock.

"Because it's my fault your reception got cancelled. Plus, since the governor hasn't made the appointment yet, I can spend the money without going through a ton of disclosure stuff. Please let me do this for you, please? It would mean a lot to me to be able to fix this for you."

"Look at it this way," Wendell added, "if we find another place locally for you, there's a chance that Commodore Asshat will find a way to pull shenanigans again. In fact, that could happen pretty much anywhere in the state—you guys are getting quite a public profile. Getting completely out of his range would be the only way to be sure he can't do anything to mess this up."

"But all the way to England? There's got to be a simpler way to deal with this."

"There may be," James said. "But I'm telling you, this place is amazing. Here—" He pulled his phone from his pocket. "—let me show you the place. I have pictures here from the last time I was there." He swiped and poked, and then handed his phone over to Brandt. "Take a look."

Brandt took the phone, while Donnelly looked over his shoulder. The pictures showed a grand cathedral-like setting with ceilings so high they were outside the frame. The grounds were lush and green, and the castle itself was a masterpiece of stonework. A majestic drive through parkland, the castle shrouded in mist, was the final picture. "Wow," Brandt said.

"That's nothing compared to what it looks like in person. And everyone can stay right in the castle, so no running around to hotels trying to keep things organized. Rehearsal dinner Friday night, ceremony Saturday, reception Saturday night. Simple! June is gorgeous there, and it's near the sea if a drive along the coast appeals." He looked from Brandt to Donnelly and back again, eyebrows up in hopeful excitement. "Please let me do this for you?"

Donnelly shrugged and looked at Brandt. "Unless we want to just go to the courthouse, this is probably our only shot."

Brandt nodded. "This is outrageously generous, James. We really appreciate it."

"Excellent," James cried. "Let's have some champagne to celebrate. First thing Monday morning I'll have my travel agent get on setting up everyone's trip—Wend, you can get me the guest list, right?—and I'll have the events director at the castle call you to make sure all the arrangements get made."

"Thank you," Donnelly said. His face showed that his native optimism was successfully fighting off the shock of being told his wedding had been cancelled. He turned to Brandt. "Do you ever get the feeling nothing we do will ever turn out the way we think it will?"

Brandt nodded. "We do seem to collect extraordinary circumstances the way other people gather pocket change. But we may as well just learn to roll with it. How about from now on, whatever plan we make we'll call Plan B, and then when the utter chaos finishes crashing down on us, we can just dust ourselves off and call whatever we're left with Plan A?"

"With one exception," Donnelly replied. "You'll always be my Plan A. Okay?"

"You got yourself a deal," Brandt said with a smile.

Chapter Seventeen
Bachelors Party

"Gabriel! Liam and Noah are here. Get your ass up, mister!"

"My ass was up last night. That's why I'm having trouble getting it back up this morning," Donnelly grumbled from the bedroom. "Put it in park. I'll be there in a minute."

Brandt went to the front door to meet his brothers as they came up the walk from the street where they'd parked.

"There he is, Bachelor number one!" Liam cried, grabbing Brandt into a hug.

"Good to see you guys," Brandt managed to get out from under the pressure of Liam's boisterous affection.

Liam released him, and Noah took over crushing his little brother.

"It's been way too long," Brandt said to Noah. "How are the little guys?"

"They're doing great. Wearing me out on a daily basis, but that's what you expect with twins."

"Don't know how you do it, man," Brandt said, shaking his head as he welcomed his brothers into the house and shut the front door behind them.

"You guys ready to hit the links?" Liam asked, looking around as if he might find Gabriel lurking somewhere.

"Almost. My fiancé is allergic to morning, so he's being kind of poky." Brandt turned toward the bedroom door. "Gabriel, let's go!"

The bedroom door opened and Donnelly walked out. The bathroom, in the hall between the bedrooms, was visible from the living room where the Brandt brothers stood. Donnelly shuffled toward the bathroom fully naked. "Stand down, Officer. I'll be along in a sec." He walked into the bathroom and shut the door behind him.

"Oh my God," Liam whispered.

"I know, right?" Noah whispered back.

"Sorry about that, guys. Normally he doesn't walk around naked in front of guests."

"They're family, Ethan, lighten up," Donnelly called from the bathroom. The running of the shower precluded any further conversation.

"Ethan, I have just one question for you," Liam remarked casually.

"Shoot, bro."

"You don't actually... take... that thing, do you?" Liam asked, wincing a bit.

"Because Gabriel is a fuckin' horse," Noah added gratuitously.

Brandt pressed both hands to his face, mortified. He tried a breathing exercise Donnelly had recommended to him for stress relief, but it didn't help. "I don't really want to talk about that with you guys, okay?"

"That means he takes it," Noah murmured to Liam, who nodded.

"More power to ya, man. That's like superhero shit, right there," Liam added.

"Can we please not—"

"It probably gets even bigger when he's, you know...," Noah continued.

"Oh shit, I hadn't even—" Liam gasped.

"Stop! Can we just stop talking about this, please?"

The water shut off in the bathroom, and Donnelly reemerged, wet and wrapped in a towel. "I'll just be a moment, gents. Sorry for the delay. I set the coffeemaker to have a pot ready. Did Ethan offer you some?" He strode purposefully into the bedroom and shut the door behind him.

At that moment there was a chime in the kitchen, indicating the coffee was ready.

"Guys want some coffee?" Brandt asked, glad to have the distraction from the previous topic of discussion.

"I could do with a long, thick cup," Noah said with a wink.

"Yeah, do you have a mug that takes two hands to really get a grip on?" Liam piled on.

"Fuck. You. Both." Brandt turned on his heel and walked to the kitchen to pour.

A little while later, the foursome was on the golf course. Golfing was a favorite pastime of Liam's, as it had been for all three Brandt brothers growing up.

"Can't remember the last time I played a round," Noah said as they walked to the first tee.

"You used to play every week," Brandt said, surprised his brother had given up the game when he quit his job to take care of the twins.

"Yeah, I did. But I was lucky—when people are going to buy machines that size, they want to have a personal relationship with the sales guy. I was out on the course with clients a couple of times a month, and the company paid for it all. It was pretty sweet."

"Dads can play golf you know, right?" Brandt teased.

"Beth keeps pushing me to. But I just don't feel like I can leave the kids for that long just to play golf. Plus, I'd only be able to do it on the weekend, when the course is full of yahoos drinking and shooting the shit instead of playing the damn game."

"Like us, you mean?" Donnelly asked, smiling.

"Precisely. It's fun and all, but if you come to play golf, you want to play golf. Now, who brought a flask?"

Liam reached into a pocket on his golf bag and pulled out a large metal vessel. "Gotcha covered. I assume bourbon is appropriate for the morning?"

"Appropriate any damn time," Noah said, taking the flask from his older brother. He took a shot and handed it back. "Damn, you lawyers can afford the good stuff."

"Nothing's too good for my little bro and his fiancé," Liam said, taking a quick swig from the flask and holding it out to Brandt and Donnelly.

Donnelly took the flask and sipped quickly, then passed it to Brandt, who shot his partner a warning glance and then did the same. Brandt's goal was to arrive at the bachelor party still upright.

"Let's get this show on the road," Liam cried and set his tee.

"Sure you have the right club?" Noah teased. "Perhaps Ethan knows where you can get your hands on something with a longer shaft."

Liam looked at his middle brother and rolled his eyes. "You're just jealous that Ethan's clearly better at sex than you are."

Donnelly looked at Brandt, confused.

Brandt sighed. "Noah and Liam were... impressed by you this morning during your little stroll to the shower."

Donnelly burst out laughing. "They were? I figured the Brandt boys wouldn't be impressed by little ol' me."

Noah and Liam looked at each other and shrugged.

This made Donnelly laugh even harder. "You mean to tell me Ethan got all the dick in the family? I figured it must be in the Brandt genes, but I guess it's only in Ethan's jeans. Lucky me, finding a man who's bigger than I am." He kissed Brandt and gave him a quick pat on the ass before turning back to Noah and Liam. "I'm sorry for your shortcomings," he said in a somber tone before bursting out laughing again.

"Did he say 'bigger'?" Noah asked Liam.

Liam just nodded and looked at his brother with an expression Brandt couldn't really read. Envy, perhaps? Pride?

"Can we just get this thing rolling, please?" Brandt said with a sigh.

"Absolutely," Liam said, approaching the tee again. He turned back. "I can hardly wait to see you swing."

"Fuck off," Brandt said, reaching for Liam's flask. It was going to be a long round.

The day was beautiful, though, and the foursome enjoyed their good-natured ribbing all along the way. They retired to the clubhouse for lunch afterward, and over good food and a great wine, they discussed Brandt and Donnelly's plans for their honeymoon; first, however, the troopers had to tell the story of their spring break.

"So, after all of that drama, you're going to head right back to the Villa Hermes for your honeymoon?" Noah asked.

"I know it sounds like it was completely crazy," Donnelly said, "but Winnie and Vic are really great people. Plus, it'll be so nice to just have a quiet couple of weeks in the sun."

"Plus the clothing-optional pool," Noah said, with something like envy in his voice.

"Now, little bro, no one wants to see your little bro floppin' around by the pool," Liam scolded, trying to sound serious despite the chuckles he couldn't completely suppress.

"What, we gonna whip 'em out right here and make it official that you're the smallest?" Noah challenged with a smirk.

"Guys, I was expecting we might get thrown out of a club tonight, but I wasn't expecting it to be the country club. And right in the middle of my tuna salad croissant," Brandt groused. "Can we please all just keep it in our pants?"

"At least until we get to the club tonight," Donnelly said. "I hear Burn can get pretty hot, so who knows what'll happen once Ethan gets some tequila in his system. During our spring break trip, he was dancing on a bar, and someone dared him to—"

"That'll do!" blurted Brandt. "It's a charming story, and you tell it well, but can you please leave me with one last shred of dignity?"

Donnelly nodded seriously, but out of the side of his mouth, he murmured something to Noah that sounded a lot like "tell ya later." His face, however, remained the very picture of innocent virtue.

"Thanks," Brandt deadpanned. He turned to his brothers. "So what's the plan for the afternoon?"

Liam's face lit up. "You are going to love this," he said. He looked at his watch. "It's two o'clock now, and we have reservations at this great spa downtown at three. It's a place one of the senior partners in my firm took the guys who made partner last year. We're going to get massages and then a haircut and an old-fashioned shave—with a straight razor and everything. Finally we'll have dinner in this incredible steakhouse in the same building. That'll get us to the cigar bar just in time for the party to begin. Huh? Huh?" Liam looked from Brandt to Donnelly and back again, clearly dying to have them say how excited they were about his plan.

"Sounds amazing," Donnelly said, beaming.

"Perfect," Brandt agreed. He could feel the tension of the day already starting to ebb. He had been so tense about how this party would go that his shoulders ached. Though he'd never had one, a massage sounded like just what he needed.

"So bottoms-up on the vino, and let's get moving," Liam cheered.

Liam drove into the heart of the city, where tall glass buildings dominated the skyline. Tucked in among them, however, was a classic old pile of elegant brick and wrought iron, surrounded by trees. He guided the car around the curving front drive and pulled to a stop under gilded letters engraved in the limestone porte cochere that read "City Club." They hopped out of the car, and Liam took a slip from the valet.

A beautiful woman in her twenties wearing a stylish lab coat stood waiting for them at the building's entrance, clipboard in hand. "Brandt party?" she inquired, in a tone of voice that indicated she knew the answer before asking.

"Yes," Liam answered.

She nodded in recognition and turned to lead them into the building. The lobby soared over them, replete with intricately carved dark wood on a scale that was truly astonishing. To the right was a room full of overstuffed leather club chairs, each occupied by an overstuffed club member. To the left a lounge served discreet drinks in heavy crystal glasses. Aside from their guide, there were no women to be seen.

The group was escorted to an ancient elevator, around which a grand staircase wrapped. The woman opened the glittering brass cage and waved them in, then joined them and pulled the door shut. The elevator car ascended smoothly, no sign of its antiquity in its movement. They rose four floors and emerged in a very different environment.

She opened the door and welcomed them to the spa floor.

"It looks like a hospital," Brandt murmured to Donnelly. "A really expensive one. In the 1940s."

Donnelly nodded. The entire place was blindingly clean and smelled of luxurious disinfectant. There was still ancient carved wood around the edges, but everything else was white marble and gleaming white tile.

"I guess a happy ending is out of the question," Noah whispered to them.

Brandt responded with a jab of his elbow.

"Oof," Noah grunted.

She led them through a series of doors, until finally they stood in a smallish anteroom. "Please change into robes you will find through there," she said with a delicate British accent, pointing to one of the heavy wooden doors, "and your massage therapists will collect you here." She pointed to a gunmetal-gray banquette against one wall. "Any questions, gentlemen?"

"No, thank you," Liam replied.

"I have a question," Noah said.

"Yes, sir?" she asked, smiling in a stately way.

"Under these robes, do we wear…?"

"You may disrobe to your own level of comfort," she replied. "If there's nothing else?"

"Thanks again," Liam said, finality in his voice.

She took her leave.

Liam opened the door she had indicated and found on the other side a dressing room appointed in an orgy of wood and brass. There were three separate dressing areas, with louvered doors on each, and a sink and mirror off to the side.

"Looks like a Brandt in each, and I'll work myself in somewhere," Donnelly quipped.

Liam and Noah immediately put their fingers on their noses.

"No offense, Gabriel, but we all know there's only one place you could possibly work yourself into," Noah said.

"If you weren't my brothers…," Brandt grumbled as he opened the door to the first dressing nook. He turned back to Donnelly. "Coming?"

"Once all you Brandt boys are naked, I may very well be," he replied as he followed Brandt in.

"Ugh," Brandt sighed, rolling his eyes but smiling at his partner's saucy wit. He swung the door shut.

Soon all four men were back in the anteroom, wrapped in the luxurious spa robes that had been hanging in the dressing areas, waiting to be summoned for their massages.

"So," Noah said, breaking the silence, "who's going commando?" He held his own hand up and looked side to side.

Donnelly put his hand up, followed by Brandt who raised his more reluctantly. Noah turned to Liam, eyebrows up.

Liam rolled his eyes and put his own hand up even more slowly than had his youngest brother. "When I was here before, the senior partner was the only one who did that, and it completely grossed me out. Guy must weigh three hundred pounds." Liam shivered.

The door on the opposite side of the room from the one that led to the dressing area opened, and four people entered. Two were petite but strong-looking women, and two were men whose tight T-shirts bulged with muscle. Each looked down at the slip of paper in their hands.

"Mister Liam?" the first woman said.

Liam got to his feet and stepped toward her, and she led him through the doorway.

"Mister Noah?" the second woman read off her card. Noah stepped up, and they walked through the doorway.

The remaining two therapists looked at each other. "Ethan and Gabriel?" the first one said.

"Yes?" Brandt replied as they both stood.

"If you'll excuse me for saying, sir, we've never done a couple's massage before. It's something quite new, as I'm sure you understand. But we have prepared an experience we hope you will both enjoy. Please, come this way." He motioned for them to follow.

Brandt and Donnelly walked behind the men down a gleaming white hallway. As they passed two rooms on the right side of the hall, they saw Noah and then Liam lying facedown on a massage table in their respective rooms as their therapists closed the doors. Brandt and Donnelly were led through a door on the left side of the hall.

They walked into a large room that held two massage tables and a large tub bubbling with steaming water. Exotic herbs perfumed the air, and a soft soundtrack, heavy on wood chimes and ethereal harmonies, lulled in the background.

"We will give you a moment to take off your robes and lie on the tables," the therapist said. "Simply pull the towel over you and make yourself comfortable." With that, they stepped out into the hall and closed the door.

"How awesome is this?" Donnelly said, pulling off his robe and hanging it on the hook by the door.

"What the hell—massage guy gave you a semi already, before he even touched you?" Brandt asked, looking down at Donnelly's jutting penis.

"You have to admit he's kinda hot," Donnelly said with a sly smile. "But I still choose you every time." He blew Brandt a kiss.

Brandt shook his head as he hung his own robe on the hook next to Donnelly's. "Very comforting, thanks."

They lay down and covered themselves with the towels that were folded at the foot of each table.

"I hope this isn't uncomfortable for you," Brandt said, looking over at Donnelly.

"Why would it be—"

"You know, lying on your boner and all." Brandt smiled wickedly at him.

"Don't you go getting all sexy on me now, or I'll never be able to lie flat."

There was a quiet knock on the door, and the massage therapists slipped back into the room. Each stepped to the side of one of the tables and drew down the towel to expose them to the waist.

"Mr. Brandt, I'm Tag, and I'll be providing your massage services. How do you feel today, sir?"

"I'm fine, thanks," Brandt replied.

"Excellent. Have you had a massage before, sir?"

"No, I haven't." He glanced over at Donnelly, who smirked at him. He had tried several times over the years to get Brandt to agree to a massage, but he had always refused. The reason was, of course, rooted in the same anxiety he harbored about the bachelor party: he would have felt weird about having a woman massage him, but having another man's hands all over him wasn't what he wanted either. Liam, in setting up this appointment, had simply sidestepped his reluctance.

"Normally when it's the client's first massage, I tend to go lightly," Tag murmured, his soothing voice just over the level of the ambient music. "But with someone of your... musculature, if I go lightly you won't even feel it. Would you like me to be a bit more aggressive?"

"That would be fine," Brandt said, shrugging off the fact that he was asking another man to be aggressive in handling his body. He desperately hoped someday he would be over all of this angst.

"Very good, sir."

Brandt heard him rubbing his hands with lotion and then felt the application of those hands to his shoulders, and the anxiety left him. He was not aware of conscious thought for the next hour and a half.

The massage therapists, finished with their labors, retreated from the room, leaving the two troopers relaxed and nearly dozing in the aftermath of their bodywork.

"Ready to get into the tub?" Donnelly asked dreamily.

"Shh, in a minute," Brandt replied, hearing his own sleepy voice as if it had come from someone else.

"I've never seen you like this," Donnelly said. "You're completely loopy. It's like for once in your life you can't deny you are actually in that amazing body of yours."

"I can think of one other time I've felt this way," Brandt said, closing his eyes to the ceiling.

"When was that?"

"After the live show we did with Nick."

"Seriously? I thought that freaked you out. I know it did me."

"I've never really been able to admit this before, but Tag's hands kind of demolished my resistance. Right after Nick shut off the camera—like, right in that instant—I felt… complete. Like I had finally shared with someone my most secret side, the parts I'd never let anyone see. I wasn't able to deal with it then because Nick was there, and I was worried about what you were going through, but for just a moment all I had was clarity." He turned his head to the side and looked searchingly at Donnelly. "I knew at that moment. I knew."

"What did you know?" Donnelly whispered.

"That we would get here. This feeling, right now, of being completely relaxed and at peace and alone with only the two of us in the world—this is what I got just a glimpse of in that moment. It only lasted a second, but I recognize it now. This is what it feels like when you get remade into something… better."

"That's beautiful," Donnelly replied.

"I am so glad… so completely amazingly wonderfully blissfully glad… that we are going to be together forever. Marrying you will be the best thing I've ever done, or will ever do. You are the best part of my life, and you will be the best part of me for the rest of my life. I love you, Gabriel. Never doubt that. I am sure of nothing in this world if I'm not sure of that."

Donnelly reached out his hand and took Brandt's. "Say that as your vow on our wedding day, and I will cry all over you," he said, his voice thick.

"Sounds like a great time," Brandt said with a smile. "Now, about that whirlpool…."

An hour later, freshly shaved and still basking in the relaxation of their massages, they walked into the lobby of the grand building. They found the elder Brandts enjoying a predinner drink in the heavily paneled lounge.

"We thought you'd decided to spend the night up there," Noah said as they sat.

Brandt looked at Liam. "That was the most amazing experience. I don't know how to thank you." The brothers hugged.

"Is there a waiter around?" Donnelly asked. "Because I'm gonna need a to-go container for that guy with the magic hands. He turned my gruff fiancé into a big ol' teddy bear."

"You're okay with another man having his hands all over your Ethan?" Noah asked with a grin.

"Hell yeah. As long as I still get to go home with him, I'd be happy to have Tag get him warmed up for me any day."

"Let's get you guys a drink," Liam said. "Our table will be ready in a few."

They drank, then they ate and drank, and then they had a drink. As the clock drew closer to eight, Liam settled up and guided the group out to the front of the building, where instead of his car, the limo Bryce had chosen was waiting for the group.

"Really?" Liam grunted as he stood on the steps looking at what Bryce had arranged. "This looks like the airport shuttle Satan uses."

The vehicle was completely black, with black-tinted windows, but through the open door the interior was visible, glittering with a million tiny purple lights. The black leather seats, which ran down both sides of the van, surrounded the stripper pole that was mounted dead center. Their chauffeur, a stunning young man wearing the tightest imaginable black leather pants and a form-fitting tuxedo shirt with bow tie, held the door open for them and smiled sexily.

"Welcome aboard, gents. The department of motor vehicles requires me to inform you that pole dancing is prohibited while the vehicle is in motion." He winked saucily. "And I must inform you that I cannot see into the passenger cabin while the vehicle is in motion."

"Thanks," Noah said excitedly as he stepped aboard, as if taking a turn on the pole was his most fervent wish.

They settled into the seats, and the van started out the sweeping driveway of the club.

"Are you honestly looking for a seat belt?" Liam asked his youngest brother, smacking him on the shoulder.

Brandt looked up sheepishly and stopped digging in the seat cushion.

"Just let it go, Ethan," Donnelly said. "Think what a glamorous end it would be, crashing and exploding in a stripper van. There would be so much purple glitter at the scene the entire city would be talking about it. We'd live in legend."

"Yes, among the tribe of Bryce. Forgive me if I hope for no explosions."

"As you wish," Donnelly sighed and then kissed him on the nose.

The ride to the cigar bar was under a quarter hour, and they arrived right on time to find their party already getting the party underway. More than a dozen of their friends, including Bryce and Nestor, were gathered around several tables in the corner of the club, eagerly awaiting the arrival of the guests of honor. Brandt and Donnelly made their way around the tables, greeting all and spending a few minutes chatting with people they hadn't seen for some time—friends of Donnelly's from college and a few people Brandt had known since grade school. Finally they made their way around to where Bryce and Nestor sat observing the group like aliens from a more fabulous planet. Bryce rose and kissed the men on both cheeks, to Donnelly's delight and Brandt's mortification.

"Lovely to see you, darlings," Bryce twittered. "I trust you've spent a relaxing day? And did the chauffeur delight you? Don't tell him I said so, but you simply *must* implore him to show you what he can do on the pole—you've seen him drive, now take him out for a spin!"

"Thanks, Bryce," Donnelly replied. "We'll take it under advisement."

"That's all I ask, dear. Now, I'm lucky enough to be able to slip a Cuban between my lips any time I want," Bryce said, patting Nestor's knee, "but when do the rest of these boys start sucking? We've been waiting for the show to start!"

"I think Ethan's brother made all of the arrangements, so you should ask him," Donnelly said, pointing out Liam.

"Oh, there he is, in the flesh. We've had phone relations several times, but this is the first I've been able to lay eyes on him. Now to lay hands on...." Bryce shot to his feet and hustled over to make Liam's acquaintance.

Two of the bar staff appeared to take drink orders and to present the selection of cigars Liam had chosen for the event. The crowd was soon puffing and sipping.

"This is what I always imagined it would be like," Liam said to Brandt as they enjoyed their drinks and cigars. "Can't believe this is the last bachelor party for the Brandt boys."

"But, for what it's worth," Noah added, "I think you landed a keeper, Ethan. If I can be sappy for a minute, I think he brings out the best in you. I've never see you this calm and... what's the word?"

"Un-butt-clenched," Liam offered with a laugh.

"That's the word I was looking for," cried Noah. "He's really good for you, bro. Congratulations."

"Of course, with Gabriel around, clenching would be damn near impossible," Liam observed, then burst out laughing as he and Noah bumped fists.

"Yep, that will always be funny," Brandt grumbled. "My fiancé has a huge dick. Ha ha ha." But then the ridiculousness of the whole thing got to him, and he joined them in their laughter.

The evening passed smokily, and then it was time for the group to make their way to Burn for the second half of the party. The limo was large enough to take them all—though it was only two blocks to the club—and there were calls during the short drive for Brandt or Donnelly or both to bust out some moves on the pole. They politely declined.

The limo pulled up in front of Burn, and Bryce leapt out to ensure proper welcome for the party. He had a quick word with the bouncers and then returned to the van to ask all but the fiancés to disembark. Then, a moment later, he popped his head back in. "Gents, please come this way," he said excitedly.

Brandt and Donnelly stepped from the limo to find the rest of their party formed into two lines and holding blue sparklers, providing a glittering pathway for the bachelors to tread. They walked up to the club, bathed in the sparkling light.

"You ready for this?" Donnelly murmured to Brandt.

"As I'll ever be," Brandt replied and took a deep breath when they reached the door. How bad could it be?

Burn on a Saturday night was already the stuff of legend among the fabulous set across the city, and the closeted set across the entire state. As the bachelor party swept into the club, however, all eyes in the place turned toward them.

Xander and Oliver were standing by the door, waiting to greet the group.

"Welcome, gentlemen," Xander said, then turned to lead the way to the back corner of the club, where private parties were held.

"Didn't think we'd see you here, after all of the excitement of the press conference," Brandt said to Oliver.

Oliver smiled. "Yeah, I may not be able to keep it up for long, especially once James starts his new job. Sounds like it's going to be pretty high profile. But for now, I'm still having fun, and I really wanted to be here for your big night."

"I like the outfit," Donnelly said, looking Oliver up and down.

Oliver had chosen a navy blue T-shirt that read POLICE ACADEMY in bold yellow letters across the front. In his usual manner, he'd torn off the sleeves and collar, and it rode up his hard abdomen about at the level of his navel. Tight blue shorts completed the look, along with the strap of a black jock that protruded above the level of the waistband.

"Picked it out just for you," Oliver replied with a wink.

The entourage made their way into the club behind the bachelors, and every head turned to watch them as they settled into the dark and glittering back corner. Black-and-blue leather couches formed an intimate U-shape around a low table with several blue-flame votives flickering along the center.

"Welcome to Burn, everyone! I'm Xander, and I'll be your server this evening. With me is Oliver, who will be your bartender. We're going to start you off with a drink Oliver has created just for this occasion. Oliver?"

"I wanted to make a special drink for the bachelors. Something to pay tribute to their upcoming wedding, but also to the fact that they are still completely hot. So I present to you, for the first time anywhere, the Frat House Trooper."

Xander picked up two trays of drinks in red plastic cups and passed them out to the guests, all of whom laughed delightedly at Oliver's choice of vessel, a throwback to the college parties with which all in attendance were familiar.

"To Ethan and Gabriel!" called Liam.

"To Gabriel and Ethan!" cried Noah.

"Kiss! Kiss! Kiss!" chanted Bryce and Nestor.

Brandt and Donnelly blushed and kissed and everyone held their cups high and then drank their Troopers down.

"Damn, that's good," Donnelly said, looking somewhat sadly into his now-empty cup.

"Is that tequila?" Brandt said, smacking his lips deliberatively.

"You know, I think it is," Donnelly said with a smirk. "Another round!"

"Coming right up," Oliver said, and hurried off to the bar with Xander.

"This is awesome," Noah said, looking about the club. "So much better than that stodgy cigar bar. And the music is amazing."

"Going to become a regular?" Liam asked.

"Hey, you spend six months getting barfed and peed on twenty-four/seven and see how much you appreciate a night out."

"You should get out there and dance," Liam said with a grin.

"Another couple of these drinks, and I just might." Noah knocked back his drink.

A second round of Frat House Troopers arrived, followed shortly by a third. The group was lively, even the straight guys seeming to enjoy themselves, and after an hour of conversation and even more rounds of drinks, Bryce and Nestor decided it was time to get the party started. They each took the hand of a bachelor and led him to the dance floor. Nestor and Donnelly leapt into the thick of it, but Brandt hesitated, preferring to stay at the edge of the fray.

Bryce, feeling resistance, turned to face Brandt, moving to the beat. "Darling, dancing is like sex. It's better if you do it where everyone can watch." He tugged Brandt's hand, leading him into the middle of the floor.

Brandt could easily have hauled Bryce out of the melee—lifting him over his head with one hand, if needed—but decided to play along since the party was going so well. They danced, near Donnelly and Nestor, through several seamless changes of beats. Then they were joined by Oliver and Xander, who had just delivered another round of drinks to the group and apparently decided to join the dancing on their way back to the bar.

Brandt and Donnelly moved closer together, while Bryce and Nestor faded into the crowd, clearly shopping for someone to bring home for a late-night snack.

Xander leaned over to Oliver. "I'd better go check and see if they need anything." He departed the dance floor.

Donnelly reached over and tapped Oliver on the shoulder. "I'm going to sit one out. Stay here and dance with Ethan, okay?"

Oliver nodded and faced Brandt with a grin.

Abandoned, Brandt had a choice to make. He could follow Donnelly off the dance floor, as he would normally do since dancing wasn't really his thing. But tonight seemed like a time for not doing the thing he would normally do. Plus, it would be rude to Oliver. Oliver, who was clearly enjoying himself.

Oliver, who was actually kind of… hot.

Brandt studied him in motion for a long moment, watching not just the way his muscles moved but how his muscles' movement clearly brought him joy. His face was elated, his body tight but fluid. Just being next to him, Brandt could feel the heat and the energy radiate from him, and for once in his life, he let it come. The tequila joined with the adrenaline, and Brandt let himself go. Brandt and Oliver danced as if no one was looking.

Everyone was looking.

Brandt hardly noticed when Donnelly came back out onto the floor, bringing with him a new dance partner: Noah.

Noah?

Brandt cast a look at Donnelly, who grinned and blew him a kiss. And then he and Noah started to dance. They gave the professional go-go boys a run for their money. Brandt was shocked at the flexibility his older brother had apparently maintained in his pelvis, which was in constant, thrusting, frankly sexual motion. The look on his face was the pure bliss of release. Brandt laughed, enjoying watching his brother let loose.

It was when Noah whipped off his shirt that Brandt grew a little concerned. Not that dancing shirtless was an unusual occurrence of a Saturday night at Burn; but among straight guys, dancing half naked in a gay club might be viewed as going a bit too far. Donnelly, though, always knowing the right thing to do, threw off his own shirt as well, and the two of them danced together, admiring eyes all around. Donnelly was, of course, a specimen of muscular form, but Noah must have been getting away from the twins on a regular basis to his basement gym. His chest and arms were solid, and his abs showed in glistening relief as he breathed athletically.

Suddenly the music shifted to a downtempo rhythm, and the frenetic motion of the dance floor slowed as bodies drifted closer together. Brandt and Donnelly nodded to their respective dance partners and embraced each other in a slow, sensual movement. Brandt looked into Donnelly's eyes, those brilliant green pools he loved so much, and felt the wave of elated certainty wash over him. He chose. And he had chosen the right man. They kissed.

Donnelly smiled when their kiss ended, then his eyes darted to the side with an alarmed expression. Brandt turned and saw Noah hadn't left the dance floor when the music slowed; he had simply switched places with Donnelly and was now dancing with Oliver. Actually, Brandt reflected, a more accurate description was that he was now dancing around Oliver. Like, all around him. His arms were around Oliver, and their entire torsos were in writhing contact. Upright, they were dancing; horizontally, they'd be doing what Bryce had suggested earlier.

"Seems like Noah really needed a night out," Donnelly observed.

"I guess so," Brandt agreed. "Think we should tell him that Oliver has a boyfriend?"

"Then we'd have to tell Oliver that Noah is married, and there goes everyone's fun evening." Donnelly shook his head. "Bachelor parties are supposed to be where everyone does something they wouldn't normally do, and then they forget they've done it the next morning. Let's give Noah that chance."

"Gabriel Donnelly, you are the finest, and the sexiest, man I've ever met. Everyone is better around you, and I'm the luckiest man in the world."

"Wear a kilt to our wedding and I'll be the luckiest," Donnelly growled, a suggestive eyebrow cocked up.

"We shall see, laddie, we shall see."

The music rose once again to its fevered tempo, and Oliver disentangled himself from Noah, who looked bereft until the rest of the bachelor party swarmed the floor and everyone danced with everyone. It was exactly the kind of party Brandt didn't know he wanted until it happened.

THE LIMO/party bus was the scene of a boisterous after party. Brandt and Donnelly sat together at the rear of the van while it made the rounds of neighborhoods across the city, dropping partygoers safely at home or hotel. Last to be dropped off were Liam and Noah at their hotel near the City Club.

"I don't know how to thank you guys for tonight," Brandt said.

"It was our pleasure, little brother," Liam replied.

"Getting my shirt back would be thanks enough," Noah said, sobriety starting to reveal to him just how wild a night he'd had.

"I don't think the guy who caught it wanted to let it go," Donnelly said, laughing. "You only tuck things into your pants you intend to keep."

Noah sighed. "I'm going to regret some things in the morning, aren't I?"

"No," Brandt said emphatically. "No regrets. You've been a full-time dad of twins for six months, and you finally got a night out. You had fun. You drank. You gave a guy a lap dance. No harm, no foul, and that guy tipped you a fifty. It was awesome. Now you can go back to your family and tell Beth the party was a boring cigar thing, and no one but us will ever have to know. And you'll be a better husband and father because you got to live a little."

"Just make sure you get the blue glitter out of your hair," Donnelly suggested.

"You make it sound like no big deal," Noah said.

"It wasn't, Noah," Brandt said. "People do crazy stuff at bachelor parties all the time."

"But not with other guys," Noah muttered.

"So what? If this had been any other bachelor party, and you danced with a stripper, would you go home and tell Beth your marriage was over? And you were going to adopt a lap-dancing lifestyle from now on?"

"No, of course not."

"This is no different. You haven't become a different person just because you danced with a guy."

"Or two," Donnelly said.

"I thought it was four, or maybe five," Liam added. "My count may be off because people kept dropping clothes."

"But there were only two that he did body shots off of, I'm sure of that," Donnelly said.

"Yeah, I don't think I was really watching anymore by that point."

"Fuck," Noah groaned and buried his head in his hands.

Brandt got up and knelt at Noah's knee. "Look. You're with Beth because out of all the women on the planet you might have had a relationship with, you chose her. You *chose* her. And it was a good choice—she's terrific for you. Now, tonight showed you that maybe you could have chosen from either gender and been happy, and that's great. But you chose, and you've got a family, and they will be happy to see you when you come home. And if once in a while you come visit and go dancing with us, we'll just call that boys' night out, and it'll be our deal, no one else's. Okay?"

Noah nodded and smiled at his younger brother. "Thanks," he said. "You're a good brother. And a great friend."

They hugged.

"And your fiancé is a pretty hot dancer."

"I know, bro, I know."

The van pulled up before Liam and Noah's hotel just as the rising sun was starting to pink the sky. The four hugged and laughed and teased, and then it was just Brandt and Donnelly in the van for the ride home.

"Take a turn on the pole?" Donnelly asked with a wink.

"Don't let me stop you," Brandt replied, laughing.

"This was a pretty great party." Donnelly lay against Brandt in the wide backseat of the limo.

"It really was. Thank you for making me do it."

"I think Liam and Noah had fun."

Brandt laughed. "We'll see how much fun Noah thinks he had in the morning. He really surprised me tonight."

"I think he surprised himself. But maybe he's more like you than he is like Liam."

"What do you mean?"

"Maybe he could be with either a woman or a man. He chose a woman, and you chose a man. For which I am prepared to be grateful my entire life."

"You're really okay with marrying a kinda straight guy?"

"Life wouldn't be nearly as exciting if we were exactly the same, love."

"I don't think our lives are ever going to be anything but exciting. Monday we have to start planning for our all-of-a-sudden destination wedding in a castle."

"In kilts," Donnelly added under his breath.

Brandt scowled good-naturedly at him. "Let's just try to get there in one piece, okay?"

Donnelly grinned. "What could possibly go wrong?"

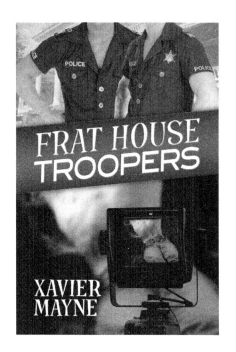

Wrestling Demons

Brandt and Donnelly Capers:
Case File Two

By Xavier Mayne

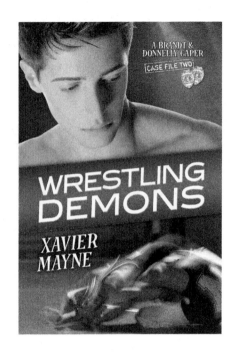

Jonah Fischer's high school wrestling career has been stellar, but now he's the unwilling star of a series of videos that have hit the web. The whole world may have seen the evidence that his best friend turns him on. Jonah's conservative family wants him cured, and his conventional town and school want him normal. The only person who still wants him just the way he is is Casey Melville, the same best friend who turned him on for all the world to see. Meanwhile, Casey begins to wonder if there's more to his feelings for Jonah than he thought.

Officers Brandt and Donnelly—lovers as well as partners on the job—have been assigned to find the culprit who posted the video. While investigating the case, they also help Jonah and Casey find their way through their feelings, and steer them toward refuge when Jonah's family turns against him. But the mystery remains: who wants to hurt Jonah badly enough to post those videos, and why? Thank goodness Jonah and Casey have found friends—they're going to need all the help and support they can get.

http://www.dreamspinnerpress.com

A Wedding to Die For

Brandt and Donnelly Capers:
Case File Three

By Xavier Mayne

When a high-profile gay celebrity couple asks two of the city's most established vendors to provide cake and flowers for their wedding and they refuse, a resulting boycott threatens to shut them down. It's up to the next generation in the family-owned businesses to save them from ruin. Justin Capella, baker's son, and Roman Montgomery, floral scion, work together to plan the gay wedding of the year.

Justin and Roman haven't seen each other since that fateful day in third grade when a single kiss shocked Justin and sent Roman to boarding school. As fate would have it, Justin and Roman rediscover love while working on the wedding. But disaster might pry them apart again.

Troopers Brandt and Donnelly are working with a statewide task force for the rights of LGBT citizens—all while searching for a killer wedding planner. As guests at the "wedding of the year," they are the first responders when all hell breaks loose. In investigating, the troopers are led to a shadowy figure they believe seduced Roman into doing his bidding. But the real murderer will cover his tracks at all costs, including Roman and Justin's lives.

Spring Break at the Villa Hermes

Brandt and Donnelly Capers:
Case File Four

By Xavier Mayne

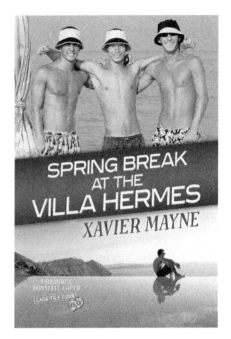

Troopers Ethan Brandt and Gabriel Donnelly celebrate the one-year anniversary of their engagement by flying south for a week of calm relaxation at the Villa Hermes, a gay boutique hotel on the beach. But when the rest of the guests turn out to be college guys on spring break (unwittingly booked into a gay hotel by a passive-aggressive travel agent), their week turns out to be anything but calm.

Ted, one of the spring breakers, has harbored a crush on his roommate and best friend, Bark, since they met freshman year. Now, on their fourth and final spring break, Ted knows they must soon say good-bye. A lacrosse star and ladies' man, Bark has no idea Ted has fallen for him—until a storm forces the entire group underground for twenty-four hours of stress and truth-telling. Bark doesn't want to say good-bye to Ted at graduation either. He just didn't know how to put his feelings into words or if he could face the consequences of speaking them. Brandt and Donnelly help the college guys through their crisis by showing them what love between best friends can grow into.

But Ted and Bark aren't the only spring-breakers with secrets.

http://www.dreamspinnerpress.com

XAVIER MAYNE is the pen name of a professor of English who works at a university in the Midwest United States. Versed in academic theories of sexual identity, he is passionate about writing stories in which men experience a love that pushes them beyond the boundaries they thought defined their sexuality. He believes that romance can be hot, funny, and sweet in equal measure.

The name Xavier Mayne is a tribute to the pioneering gay author Edward Prime-Stevenson, who also used it as a pen name. He wrote the first openly gay novel by an American, 1906's *Imre: A Memorandum*, which depicts two masculine men falling in love despite social pressures that attempt to keep them apart.

Website: http://www.xaviermayne.com

Husband Material

By Xavier Mayne

Husband Material is a long-running reality show, where eighteen lucky guys compete for the hand of one lucky lady. Meet contestant number one, Riley. Since being left at the altar, he's hit the gym to get into the best shape of his life. Now he's in it to win it. Contestant number two, Asher, doesn't really want the bachelorette; he needs the prize money for his sister's cancer treatment. Asher's upbeat personality brings Riley out of the funk he's been in since his breakup. They make a formidable team, with one complication: Asher's falling for Riley.

Producer Kaitlyn has her hands full when two bachelors are found in the shower soaping up inappropriately, then another live-tweets the entire debacle. If another scandal erupts, the network will cancel the show.

The two bachelors are on a collision course under the watchful eye of a producer torn between wanting them to find true love and trying to keep her show going. In the end, Riley must choose the bachelorette or the bachelor.

http://www.dreamspinnerpress.com

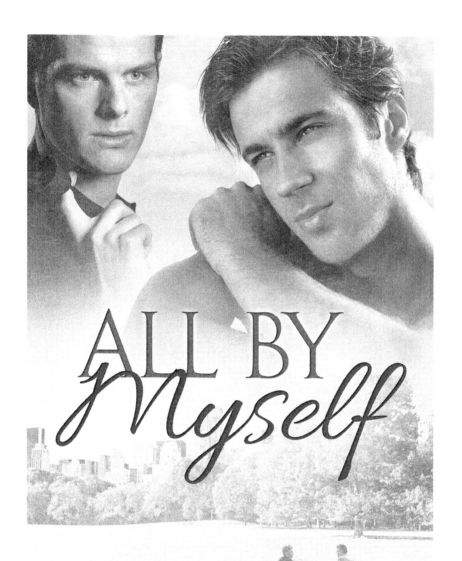

ALL BY Myself

KEN BACHTOLD

http://www.dreamspinnerpress.com

http://www.dreamspinnerpress.com

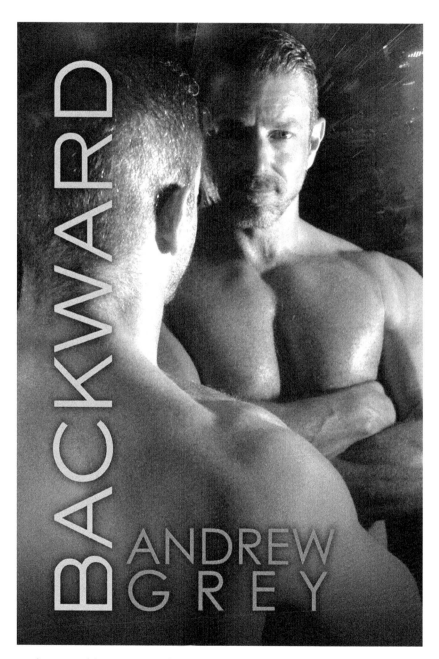

http://www.dreamspinnerpress.com

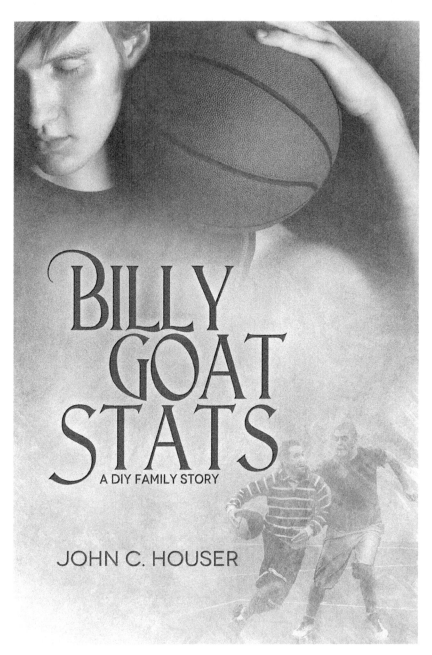

BILLY GOAT STATS
A DIY FAMILY STORY

JOHN C. HOUSER

http://www.dreamspinnerpress.com

BLACK JOHN
AMY LANE

http://www.dreamspinnerpress.com

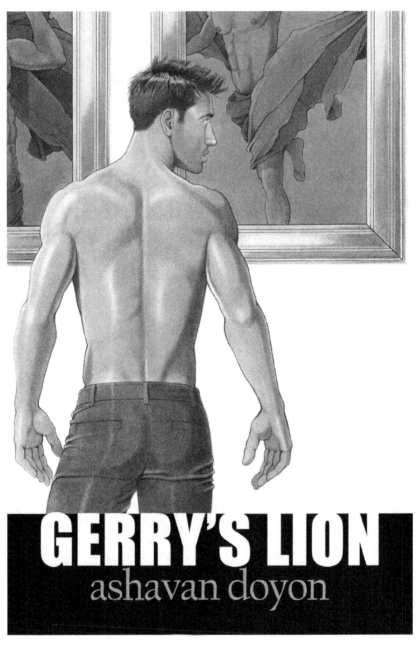

GERRY'S LION
ashavan doyon

http://www.dreamspinnerpress.com

SEX,
LIES
&
WEDDING
BELLS

EM Lynley

http://www.dreamspinnerpress.com

CPSIA information can be obtained at www.ICGtesting.com
Printed in the USA
LVOW04s0808020615

440485LV00021B/64/P